A Fall From Grace

The Delamere Files

Book Two

A Fall From Grace

The Delamere Files Book Two

First published in Great Britain in 2023

Copyright © Jackson Marsh 2023

The right of Jackson Marsh to be identified as the Author of the Work has been asserted by him in accordance with the Copyright, Designs and Patents Act 1988.

All rights reserved. No part of this publication may be reproduced, stored in a retrieval system, or transmitted, in any form or by any means without the prior written permission of the publisher, nor be otherwise circulated in any form of binding or cover other than that in which it is published and without a similar condition being imposed on the subsequent purchaser.

All characters in this publication are fictitious and any resemblance to real persons, living or dead, is purely coincidental.

Proofread by Ann Attwood

Cover Design by Andjela V

Illustration by DazzlingDezigns

Formatting by Other Worlds Ink

Printed by Amazon.com

ISBN: 9798864341926

Imprint: Independently published

Available from Amazon.com and other retail outlets.

Available on Kindle and other devices.

ALSO BY JACKSON MARSH

Other People's Dreams

The Blake Inheritance

The Stoker Connection

Curious Moonlight

The Mentor of Wildhill Farm

The Mentor of Barrenmoor Ridge

The Students of Barrenmoor Ridge

The Mentor of Lonemarsh House

The Mentor of Lostwood Hall

The Clearwater Mysteries

Banyak & Fecks (A prequel)

Deviant Desire

Twisted Tracks

Unspeakable Acts

Fallen Splendour

Bitter Bloodline

Artful Deception

Home From Nowhere

One Of A Pair

Negative Exposure

The Clearwater Inheritance

The Larkspur Mysteries

Guardians of the Poor

Keepers of the Past

Agents of the Truth

Seeing Through Shadows

Speaking in Silence

Starting with Secrets

The Larkspur Legacy

The Delamere Files

Finding a Way

www.jacksonmarsh.com

www.facebook.com/jacksonmarshauthor

A Fall From Grace

The Delamere Files

Book Two

CONTENTS

ONE	1
TWO	3
THREE	15
FOUR	31
FIVE	44
SIX	54
SEVEN	62
EIGHT	75
NINE	84
TEN	97
ELEVEN	108
TWELVE	119
THIRTEEN	130
FOURTEEN	144
FIFTEEN	154
SIXTEEN	168
SEVENTEEN	180
EIGHTEEN	194
NINETEEN	204
TWENTY	218
TWENTY-ONE	228
TWENTY-TWO	240
TWENTY-THREE	252
TWENTY-FOUR	262
TWENTY-FIVE	272
TWENTY-SIX	284
TWENTY-SEVEN	294
TWENTY-EIGHT	306
Author Notes	317

ONE

Summer, 1880

Jaques Verdier hit the rockery at some time between midnight and two o'clock in the morning of the thirty-first of July, eighteen eighty. A few seconds earlier, he had been a living, breathing man of eighteen, but the moment his head came into contact with the lavender and creeping thyme, his time on earth ended.

At the inquest, the headmaster of Sinford's School for Boys described Verdier as a quiet, determined student with many friends, who, once he had completed his years at university, was expected to follow his father into the diplomatic service.

The evidence pointed to Verdier leaving his study sometime after ten-thirty, and taking himself to the roof of Grace Tower to smoke a pipe, a privilege enjoyed by young men in their last year at the school.

It was likely, the inquest heard, that he sat on the battlements to smoke, and at some point forgetting where he was, reclined, and toppled over. It was a calm, starlit night, with no wind. There was no trace of a suicide note, no reason for him to take his own life, and no suggestion of foul play. Nor were there any witnesses to the tragedy.

After taking evidence from staff, students and the officials who attended the scene the following day, the coroner returned a verdict of accidental death.

His friends and the school had failed Jacques Verdier, and so had the inquest, because the coroner was wrong.

TWO

London

Twelve Years Later
July 1892

Jack lay between silk sheets looking at the ceiling and thought about his life two weeks ago.

Poverty among boatyards and barge-builders, chandlers, wharfingers, and makers of everything needed for the river trades. Anchor-smiths, blacksmiths, whitesmiths and nail makers. Carpenters, greasers and labourers. Factories, refineries, and warehouses, offices and timberyards. The smell of fish hanging in the lanes, and the stink of tanners' vats catching in the throat. The nonstop clunk and clank, creak and hammer of long workdays and too-short nights. Shouts of harbourmasters and whores, of penny-a-lace sellers and newsboys. The constant churning of engines, and grinding of chains. Tumbledown pubs with ladders to the foreshore. Societies and boxing halls, warring neighbours, and cash-starved madness. All of it seething and pushing through life like a mudlarker wading through years of rot and waste, and for one purpose: To survive in Limehouse.

Jack lived like that for twenty-five years, but would not live like that again.

A large bed in a huge room in a massive house where rugs softened every floorboard, and framed paintings hung on every papered wall. Where food was hot and plentiful, and the company welcoming. The conveniences were inside, and never far from a stuffed armchair or a padded couch, a leather-topped desk or an oak bookcase. Days began late and ended at a billiard table, or a pub that didn't stink of grimy sailors and opium, and where the ale had nothing swimming in it and didn't taste of piss water. No need to save pennies in jars, or plug the windows with rags. Fear of the rent collector was a thing of the past, as were mouldy walls, shared hallways, and insecurity.

Delamere House was so far removed from his previous life it had taken him the two weeks since moving in to adjust, but waking on his first morning there, with the window open and the sounds of the park floating in on sunbeams, he'd made a decision. To pull up the cab of his old life and park it safe and ready if needed, while he climbed down and set his mind to his new job, his new life and good fortune.

His brother, of course, adjusted to it all as if he'd been brought up in Knightsbridge and expected to live in nothing but luxury. The other men in the house took to Will quicker than they took to Jack, but then Jack Merrit was a different barrel of salting to his brother, who impressed them with his knowledge of books. The only knowledge Jack had was that of the cabbie; routes and reins, horses and highways, working day and night, storm or shine.

That, though, was before, and the change from past to present was complete. During the time since Mr Wright had made his offer, he'd retrieved Shadow from the livery and stabled her alongside Emma and Shanks. Jimmy, as Jack had come to call him, said they were Lord Clearwater's beasts, and were shared between the two houses, and Jack's interest lay in keeping all three fit and well. In the last fortnight, he'd learnt to drive the carriage and trap, which required a different technique to the hansom cabs and carts of his past, and his teacher and the way he taught had provided more surprises. Joe was deaf, as Jack had assumed the first time they met, but knew his animals and vehicles, and despite the lack of language, taught well by example.

As did Jimmy, who had taken Jack on as his assistant, and had called him in that morning to begin work on his first case as a private investigator.

'All you have to do is sit there and listen,' Jimmy said from behind his desk. 'The client will be here soon. Max will answer the door and show him in. I'll introduce you as my assistant, and if the client asks you anything, and you're not sure what to say, just look at me, and I'll take over. I doubt he will, but he may be uncertain at first.'

'Of what?'

'Of you, me, and telling his story.' Jimmy waved an envelope. 'Very often, a client is reticent to tell the full tale, and needs prompting. I have two theories on why this happens. One is, that by coming to a private investigator, the client believes they have done something wrong. That's never the case, though. I'd see through it in the way a police officer would see through a criminal reporting their own crime. My second theory is that people don't like to admit they need help. For those reasons, a new client takes time to let us into their private lives, especially in a case like this.'

Jack was already lost in the words. Theories were things for Will to talk about, and 'criminals' reminded him of the Flay family. 'Private investigator', however, stirred his excitement, because that was what he now was.

An assistant to one, at least.

Grabbing the end of Jimmy's sentence, and keen to show he wasn't stupid, he said, 'A case like what? Do you know about it already?'

'All I know is this...' Jimmy took a letter from the envelope. 'The client is the son of Viscount Beresford, and, as a gentleman, we must refer to him the Honourable Marcus Havegood, and call him Sir. A socialite, well-known and respected, and at thirty, the youngest ever vice-chairman of the Board of Trade. He's come to us via Lord Clearwater. The two know each other from a charity committee. Havegood isn't titled yet, but will succeed his father one day, and possibly his father's role as Leader of the House of Lords. The man is already noteworthy, and is set to become somebody even more significant. More importantly for us, he has contacts in the upper strata of society. Therefore, it will go well for us if it goes well for him.'

Jack's apprehension increased. His first case, his first real day at his new job, and already he was up against lords, strata and things having to go well.

'You look concerned.'

'What? No, not really, only... Never mind.'

'Remember the promise you made in Hackney? It remains valid. What's on your mind?'

Honesty was the first rule of the house. It was one of the first things Jimmy had made clear when he was still Mr Wright.

'I can talk plain?'

'Of course.'

'I'm a bit nervous about a mate of a lord coming to me with a problem he expects me to sort out. I'm just a driver.'

'As I have said before, you are much more than that. It's in you to be a good investigator, Jack. Don't ask me how I know, I just know. Anyway, it's natural to be nervous at the start of a new case, but you'll soon be swinging along.'

'Yeah, but, I don't know how.'

Jimmy glanced at the letter, and ran a knuckle along his moustache, before clicking his fingers.

'Think of it like this,' he said. 'The client's a fare who wants you to drive him from Chelsea to Charlton. You don't know him, and he doesn't know you, yet by accepting the fare, you've entered into a contract. You drive, he arrives, and as long as you drove well, he'll use you again and tell his friends to look out for your cab number. Meanwhile, you've made two shillings.'

It was ten miles from Chelsea to Charlton, a five-bob fare, at least, but Jimmy made some sense.

'Yeah, alright.'

'You shouldn't need to do any talking, but if you have a question, tip me the wink and I'll invite you to join the discussion. As for the honourable gentleman's problem, here's what his letter says.'

Dear Mr Wright,
 I have been referred to you by Earl Clearwater who says you are a man

who will be able to assist me in a very delicate matter. His Lordship has assured me of your discretion, and tells me that of all private investigators in the city, you are the only one who will understand my particular needs.

A great friend of mine is missing, and it is imperative he is found before the thirtieth of this month.

If it is convenient, I will call on the...

'Blah blah, and so on. What does that tell you?'

Not much, was what Jack wanted to say, but he guessed at, 'He wants you to find someone who's missing.'

'Wants *us*, Jack. You're a Clearwater detective now.'

Jack had never heard such an unlikely statement. If anyone should have been a detective it was Will with his memory, intelligence and meticulous ways. The words, though, had something about them that caused a twinge of pride.

'Assistant investigator,' he said, and changed the subject with, 'How do we find someone who's gone missing?' The question would, he hoped, quell what his father would have called stage fright.

'Depends on what he tells us. First, we have to understand what kind of client he is.'

'Er, a rich one?'

Jimmy sniggered. 'Yeah, there's that, but there's more in this letter. Listen.' Referring to the paper, he reread, '*Very delicate matter, discretion, particular needs, a great friend.* Suggest anything to you?'

Will always said it was better to remain silent and let people think you're an idiot than to open your mouth and prove them right. Jack shrugged.

'It suggests to me that this man is as we are, and his friend is more than a friend. They are both one of us.'

That was a phrase Jimmy had used when Jack was imprisoned in Dalston Lane police station. Since coming to Delamere, he'd learnt there were more who were 'one of us' than just him. Dalston and Joe, for a start, others Jimmy knew in Cornwall and elsewhere, and even Jimmy himself. Realising he was not alone was a comforting thought.

'This, obviously, is not something we question him about,' Jimmy said, putting the letter to one side. 'It's important to remember that our agency specialises in working with men who are, by birth, as criminal as we are.'

'You what?'

'I mean the way we are.' Even though they were alone, Jimmy lowered his voice. 'Thanks to the laws of this country and its oppressive government, men like us are criminals even before we have done anything wrong. Our agency doesn't make it public, but it's known among men who love men that we exist to help them, being men of similar hearts ourselves.'

Jack had never thought of himself as a criminal, but he understood Jimmy's point.

'So, we're like the honest thieves in a den of burglars, is it?'

Jimmy flicked his eyebrows knowingly. 'We're criminals assisting criminals,' he smirked. 'Which is why prudence is my middle name.'

'I thought it was Joseph... Oh, right, yeah. Got it.'

'Good.' Jimmy changed his tone as he returned to the case. 'That said, I have spoken with Clearwater and have some information about the Honourable Marcus Havegood.'

'Like how he got such a daft name?' Jack grinned, but the humour was not returned.

'Parents. Can't choose them and you can't choose your name. Clearwater tells me Havegood is or was a sportsman. Went to a public school where he excelled at football, rugby, rowing, tennis... An athlete, a big man, as in, muscles and strength, rather than height. He's thirty years old, went to Cambridge University, and is highly thought of at the Board of Trade. Beyond that, and what we could look up in the peerage directories, it's up to us to learn more if we need to. Any questions so far?'

Jack arranged the information in his head, said he had nothing more to ask, and sat in silence while Jimmy prepared a new casebook.

As he waited, he imagined his first client as a broad man, well-spoken, well-groomed, and well-educated. He could have been describing the only person Jack knew who'd gone to a posh school; Larkin Chase. The thought stabbed him with regret for the opportunity he'd let escape, and he wondered what Larkin was doing at that moment. If he was missing Jack, why hadn't he written? Larkin knew where he was, so he could have called. Then, he remembered how he'd returned their clothes, told Jack he was welcome at any time, but had written his note in such a way for it to sound polite, not sincere. On his first day at Delamere, Jack had decided that, sadly, that journey was over. Although he'd picked Larkin up as a fare, and driven him on a long and arduous route involving kissing, crooks and court, the job was done, the fare was gone, and he'd left no tip.

'Here's a casebook if you want to make notes.' Jimmy had stood, and dropped a notebook in Jack's lap as he passed. Standing at the window, he peeked from behind the nets and said, 'Any moment now, if he's a punctual chap,' and returned to his chair to drum his fingers and shuffle papers.

Jimmy's desk stood before the window, so the sunlight poured over his shoulder onto its leather, where the files and documents allowed, and the gold rim of his inkwell glinted in the morning beams. The house, he'd told Jack, belonged to his patron, Lord Clearwater, and much in it had been left by a friend of his, Lady Marshall. That accounted for the ornate furniture, but it didn't account for the cabinets and effects Jimmy had collected in his office. It was a good job it was a large room, what with the busts, books, magnifiers, satchels hanging where pictures should have been, ship's instruments Jack recognised from the chandlers of Limehouse, the maps pinned to the walls, chalkboards, medical equipment and sporting trophies. Jack was imagining how Will would love to rearrange it all, when Max slid into the doorway in his guise as the butler.

'Your man be 'ere,' he said, before clearing his throat and trying again. 'Your client, Mr Wright, is downstairs.'

'Downstairs?'

'He came via the back yard. Don't ask me why. Want me to show him up?'

'It would help, Max,' Jimmy replied dryly.

'It's Pascoe, Sir, and sarcasm be the butler's privilege.'

Max made his exit like an undertaker, leaving Jimmy chuckling. Banter, they called it in the Limehouse Boys' Boxing Club, where you could insult your best mate with no fear of retribution. If the backchat went too far and someone took offence, the pair bashed it out in the ring until one drew blood, and then, with swollen eyes and misshapen noses, they went together to steal a bottle of ginger beer from behind The Grapes, and all was well. There was no need for that at Delamare, but there was the same air of friendship, and no-one was a servant. Not even Max, or Jack, the driver.

Driver and assistant detective, he reminded himself, and as such, pulled himself up, concentrated, and waited for his client to appear. This was his first opportunity to prove to Jimmy, to Will, and more importantly to himself, that he was more than a cabman from the docks, and he was determined to do well.

'The Honourable Marcus Havegood.'

The man Max announced and showed in was nothing like Larkin Chase and not what Jack had pictured.

Witheringly thin and pale, Mr Havegood walked with a cane. His eyes hung in his face as two dark circles above prominent cheekbones, themselves overhangs of hollow cheeks. Jimmy had said he was Larkin's age, but he looked twenty years older, had stubble on his chin, and his lips were almost non-existent. The only thing that suggested his thirty years was his hair, cut in a younger man's fashion and thick, the temples, however, showed streaks of grey against the black. He held a briefcase beneath one arm, and his expression suggested it was heavier than his own bodyweight.

Unmoved by the man's appearance, Jimmy greeted him with a handshake. 'Can I offer you anything, Sir?'

'Just a seat,' Havegood croaked, and tottered to a chair.

'Nothing, thank you, Pascoe,' Jimmy said, and Jack caught a shared look of concern before Max left.

'You are James Wright?'

'I am, Sir, and this is my assistant, Mr Merrit.'

Jack was sitting in shock at the sight of the apparition, but leapt to his feet when Jimmy glared. His offered hand received a scornful grimace, and he waited until Jimmy was at his desk before he retook his seat, there to do as he'd been told; observe, listen and learn.

'Are you sure I can't get you something?' Jimmy said. 'Some water, perhaps?'

Havegood leant his cane against the desk, and pulled off his gloves to reveal fingers like sticks, all the while eying Jimmy with narrow, yellow eyes.

'Of late, I have grown accustomed to the reaction you display,' he said, his voice clearer now he'd caught his breath. 'Have no fear, Mr Wright. I am suffering no disease or disability, and nothing is amiss with me. I am, however, gravely concerned for…' There, he paused, and although his head hung, he turned it to Jack, who half expected to hear his neck snap.

'You have our full confidence, Sir,' Jimmy said. 'Nothing spoken in this room is repeated outside of it. Discretion is assured, else Lord Clearwater would not have suggested us.'

'Hm,' Havegood grunted. 'He said I could trust you, and as I have no choice… Very well. I am concerned for an old friend. I have come to you because I cannot think of what else I can do to find him, and I have little time left.'

It was on the tip of Jack's tongue to ask if that was because he had a fatal illness, but he remained silent, thankful that Will wasn't in the room. That was exactly the kind of blunt question he would have asked.

Jimmy was more subtle. 'Little time left in which to find him? You mentioned the thirtieth.'

'Indeed.'

'And this friend, I would suggest, is a very dear friend.'

The client held Jimmy with his stare, and neither man moved. Havegood must have been wondering how far he could trust the detective who was, after all, a stranger.

After an age, he said, 'Why do you say that?'

'Excuse the forwardness, but it is my job,' Jimmy replied. 'I suggest you have not eaten or slept well for two or three weeks at least. I am no doctor, Sir, but the description His Lordship gave of you bears little resemblance to what I see.'

Another pause, and the client's glare faded.

'Continue,' Havegood said, apparently more interested than affronted.

'Again, forgive my boldness,' Jimmy continued. 'As you say you are physically fit and well, I have to conclude you are suffering from nervous exhaustion. You suggest a problem with a friend, but this person must mean more to you than the average chum, else why worry yourself to starvation? The fact that you are running out of time suggests you have already invested much in trying to locate this person, and the fact you sought a recommendation through His Lordship suggests you fear others knowing your purpose and concern. Thus, your friend is a man whom you care for beyond the norm. I also have a dear friend, and if he were to go missing, I would be as worried as you clearly are.'

Havegood again turned his weary expression on Jack, who shivered.

'You are his assistant?'

'I am, Sir.'

'What is your impression of your employer?'

Jimmy raised his eyebrows, but there was no need for him to worry.

'A fine man, Sir,' Jack said, trying his hardest to impersonate Larkin while remembering the stories Will had researched when they moved to Delamere. 'And a fine detective. You might have heard how he solved the case of the poisoned parakeet. Or how he saved an opera singer from being killed during a performance. Mr Wright was also responsible for rescuing the son of a famous author, and has exposed exhaustion and other crimes. Not long back, he brought members of an East End gang to justice at the Old Bailey.'

'Exhaustion?'

'Extortion,' Mr Wright said. 'I'm sure that's what I heard. Thank you for the résumé, Merrit,' he added. 'Mr Havegood, I assume you took a reference from Lord Clearwater.'

'I did, Wright, and I wouldn't be here were I not reassured of your abilities and discretion.' As if to state his satisfaction, he put his gloves on the desk, undid his jacket, and rested back in his chair with his briefcase in his lap. 'Very well, gentlemen,' he sighed. 'I will entrust to you the history and facts, but before I give you my story, I wonder if I might, after all, accept the offer and ask for tea? Already I feel less agitated, and with the relief comes a welcome longing for refreshment.'

Jimmy rang, and while the detective and the client exchanged pleasantries about the weather and Lord Clearwater, Max came, went and returned with a tray. Will came with him, but said nothing, and acted as a professional as he carried in plates and fancies, set them out in matching groups and placed them before each of the men. When he put Jack's on the table beside him, he gave him a wink and whispered, 'Good luck,' before leaving him to pay attention to the client.

'Shall we begin?' Jimmy brought the room to order, and Jack prepared his notebook and pen. 'What is it you wish us to do, Mr Havegood?'

The client had been nibbling the corner of a biscuit, but grimacing, he set it aside, and said, 'Simon Stape, who I have known since school, is the man who is missing, and I am gravely concerned for his welfare. I need to know where he is, so I may prevent him from a drastic course of action.'

'I see,' Jimmy said. 'Why do you think he is missing?'

'We used to meet regularly once a year for reasons which will become apparent. This year, he cancelled our meeting, and that was so out of character, I knew something was very wrong. I wrote to Diggs immediately but received no reply. I...'

'Excuse me, Diggs?'

'Ah. A pet name that dates back to our years at Sinford's,' Havegood said, with a slight glistening in his eye. 'Simon Diggory Stape, was... is known affectionately as Diggs.'

'I see. Go on.'

'I called at his house to find it abandoned, and I called at his workplace, to be told he had resigned. I also wrote to his mother and telegrammed his brother, but neither was able to help. Diggs has vanished, Mr Wright, and no amount of investigation on my part these past three weeks has produced a result, not even the advertisements I have placed in the newspapers. With no more threads at which to pull, I come to you in desperation, and in the hope that you will be able to reunite me with my friend before the end of the month.'

Jimmy had still not shown signs of emotion, but Jack had a lump in his throat and felt nothing but sadness for his first client.

Client. He reminded himself to be professional, and imagined Havegood was a passenger in his hansom. No matter what the fare wanted, or where he wanted to go, no matter the weather, or if the driver was tired, and his horse exhausted, if a fare wanted to travel from Wimbledon to Wembley, that's what the driver did, and he did it with good cheer.

'Why the hurry?'

'I knew you would ask,' Havegood said. 'That's why I brought this. It arrived three weeks ago, and I have not eaten since.' The client passed Jimmy a piece of paper. 'Read that, gentlemen, and I will happily answer all your questions.'

'I will,' Jimmy said, 'but I must do something first. Excuse me one moment.'

The detective swung around to a low table on which sat a contraption. There, he turned a dial and tapped keys, waited, and repeated the actions. When he finished, he apologised again, and came to sit beside Jack, who had no idea what he had just done.

Havegood had watched with concern etched on his feeble face.

'You have your own telegraph, and you know Morse?' The client sounded impressed, and Jack wondered if that was what Jimmy had intended. 'I trust you were not contacting anyone about this case?'

'Not at all,' Jimmy said. 'I was arranging dinner. Now, to your evidence, Sir, and then, to solve this mystery.'

'The mystery is a simple one,' Havegood said, and drew a deep breath. 'I firmly believe my friend intends to kill himself. Please, Sir, you must help me stop him.'

THREE

With Jimmy pressed beside him on the settee, it was easy for Jack to read Havegood's letter. What wasn't so easy was understanding the language.

Dear Marcus

Perhaps, as a man grows older, it is natural for him to feel nostalgic for his youth and recall all of it in the tiniest detail. I have been doing much of that these past days, and my mental wanderings have led me down a path I never expected to take. A change has come upon me since my wife and child left this earth to join dear Jacques.

How fondly I remember our schooldays, the summers at the wicket with you, my greatest supporter, in the other crease. The winters by the fireside in our study where you read to me the classics, and I the great scientists to you. Verdier and Hunter scuttling in and out, merrily disrupting our peace with their effulgence, bringing teacakes and house news. Our year of rule as prefects in gold and champion sportsmen in whites. I even enjoyed the square bashing in greens, the nights at that hide in the forest we called 'HQ' while we sought the other team's pennant, and the manoeuvres on the Downs.

The time for our annual meeting fast approaches, but this year, I shall not be attending. I shall, instead, be answering the vengeance of a greater power, if He will listen to me after the evil deeds of my life.

I apologise for the blunt statements, but there is no point being other than honest. I always enjoyed our reunions, and the memory of them stays fondly in my heart to this day, and will do so until my last. Other memories and knowledge, however, do not lodge so tenderly, and of late, have pressed heavily on my heart and in my head where they cloud my path.

Wifeless and childless with no-one to share the loss, there is nowhere to turn. You will cry, 'Me!' but my troubled mind will not, cannot, bring itself to burden you as it burdens me.

Their deaths were God's retribution for my past, and have made me re-evaluate my life and reflect on my inactions, which, in their turn, led me to consider my options. History judges us not by what we do, but what we fail to do, and I have failed the world since my devotion of that time. The years have increased the weight of the burden that pushes me to these suffocating depths, and there is only one direction I can now take.

Marcus, you must consider me nothing but wasted paper in the basket, the kindling of our old study that flamed for a moment, and then became ash. I shall not meet you again. I shall see no-one, and far later than I should, I will face the truth and accept the consequences. Only then can I be forgiven.

Goodbye, old friend.

Yours in eternity,

Diggs

'I see,' Jimmy said, as he made more notes in his casebook.

Jack didn't see anything apart from a man letting another know he was desperately sad after losing his family. What had started out as an exciting opportunity to work with a detective, was turning into a depressing afternoon of long words. He'd not admitted it at the time, but when he'd rescued Will from the Flays and appeared in court to be a witness, he'd found the whole thing more exciting than galloping Shadow along The Mall at full speed. When Jimmy suggested he come to work for him, he thought he'd be in for more of the same. However, this detecting lark seemed to be nothing more than conversations and complicated words. Even the element of illegality, helping men who admitted to loving men, wasn't as thrilling as he'd expected.

Still, it was eighty pounds a year and a place to live, Will was happier than he'd ever been, his housemates were good people, and who knew what Jimmy was going to ask him to do? Maybe more thrilling times lay ahead.

Jimmy put the letter to one side, and said, 'I have to tell you, that in my experience, when a man vanishes, it is for one of three reasons.'

'Oh?'

'Usually, and obviously, it is because he doesn't want to be found. Sometimes, it is because he is being held captive, but in those cases, someone connected to him would have learnt of a ransom demand, but you have not mentioned one. Ultimately, though, and don't panic at this, it is because he is dead.'

'Dead?' Havegood's cheeks paled further.

'Whatever information you can provide will help us decide. You have given us only a week, Mr Havegood, and there are many more facts to learn and questions to be asked. If you can tell me...'

Jimmy asked Mr Havegood where Mr Stape worked, who he had spoken to there, if he had talked to any of the neighbours in Clapham, and for the address of the missing man's mother. There was no father, apparently. He had been killed a while ago serving in the army somewhere, and Mr Stape's only brother lived in America and had been there for several years.

Jack did his best to note all the facts as the detective interviewed the client, asking for details and repeating questions, until Mr Havegood gave an uncontrolled yawn.

'I do apologise, gentlemen,' he said. 'As well as being unable to eat, I am unable to sleep until exhaustion drives me to it.'

'Quite understand, Sir,' Jimmy said, and was about to ask something else, when his telegraph machine hummed and clattered into life, and he excused himself to deal with the strip of paper spewing from one side.

'It is a marvellous way of communicating,' Havegood said. 'And to have one in your very office. Imagine!'

Jimmy tapped on his machine before taking his seat at the desk, where he scribbled a note. 'Lord Clearwater has one next door, and two at Larkspur Hall, one of which converts the Morse to words. It's very clever. One of his academy men designed it last year... Anyway, for now, I need to ask more questions, Mr Havegood. If you are up to it?'

'I came prepared for a lengthy interrogation.'

'I will take your case, employ utmost discretion, and do all I can to find Mr Stape. Mr Merrit here will assist me, as will his brother. Although I have a range of experts at my disposal, such as the scientist who built the telegraph translator, I don't think we will need extra staff for this assignment, therefore, if Merrit agrees...'

Jimmy passed him the paper on which was written the fee to be charged, and on seeing it, Jack swallowed. Wide-eyed and forcing himself not to swear aloud, he nodded.

'Which he does, then this will be my fee, plus mundane expenses. Half payment in advance as a deposit, fifty per cent of which is refundable if I fail to find your friend, which I will not. My first question is, do you agree to the fee?'

Havegood glanced, and waved away the cost. 'I will pay twice that if you find him for me on my terms.'

'Which are?'

'To tell me where he is, and only that,' the client said. 'I do not want you to charge in and rescue him from his intended suicide, for clearly, that is what his letter points to. All I require is that you inform me of his proven whereabouts before the evening of the thirtieth of this month, so I may go to him alone, and dissuade him from his action.'

'I see.' Jimmy made another note. 'Very well. We'll undertake to find him by then and to inform you where he is. You will be at your home address?'

'Yes.'

'Good. And next, our contract.' Jimmy passed him two other pieces of paper he had been scribbling on as though he was working as a clerk in an office. 'Standard, of course, but I have added your conditions, and you will see, we here are bound to absolute confidentiality. Knowing that, I hope, will encourage you to be frank.'

'I thought I had been.'

'More frank, Sir, because I feel there are details you have so far been reticent to tell us.'

Havegood held the papers and stared at Jimmy, judging him for a moment, before flicking his eyes over the contract. He turned his thoughtful gaze to Jack, and finally back to the writing.

'Very well,' he mumbled, reaching into his jacket. 'As I trust in Clearwater, so I trust in you.' After giving the contract another brief read, he signed both copies, kept one and put the other on the desk. 'Particularly as I now have the right to sue you should any of what I am about to share be made public.'

Jimmy ignored the threat. 'Have you had any other contact from Mr Stape in, say, the last year?'

'Yes, but such mementoes are dangerous for men in our position,' Havegood replied. 'If our affectionate notes were to be read by a servant, or left where a caller might see... These letters spoke of unnatural feelings, the love of the ancients, one might say, and although I no longer have qualms admitting my condition to a man such as yourself, I do not want my private life made public, nor Diggs' feelings towards me.'

'So you ain't got them?' Jack asked, cutting through the romantic ramble. Jimmy gave a sly smile at his bluntness.

'No,' was Havegood's equally sharp reply. 'I burnt them as soon as I read them.'

'Then why is finding this man so important to you?'

If it was possible for a ghost to blush, then that was what Havegood did. The reddening of his cheeks came with a mild gasp of shock, which he exhaled as one of resignation.

'I was also prepared to explain why I must find him,' he said, fishing in his briefcase. 'To save me what has become the arduous task of talking for long periods of time, I have spent time writing about our background. It is important for you to understand how we became close and just how close we were, and what effect our schooldays had on our friendship. The full tale involves other characters.' Havegood pulled a sheaf of papers from his case, but hesitated in handing them over. 'Must you?'

'You wouldn't have written it had you not thought it important.'

'Maybe I wrote it to exorcise the past,' Havegood whispered, and surrendered.

Jimmy brought the writing over and sat close beside Jack. 'You rest yourself, Sir,' he said. 'While Merritt and I read this.'

This, Jack thought, was where the real work started, and he cleared his throat as if it would help him clear his mind.

The private memories of the Hon. Marcus Havegood.

**Sinford's School for Boys, Kent.
1875 to 1880**

Sinford's School is now abandoned, but when I was sent there in 1875 at the age of thirteen, it was a rambling place full of terror, noise and prospects. I suffered an immediate longing to be back again in the orchard of my youth with Sandy, our family dog, with my playthings, and in the safe company of Nanny when the time came for bed. However, I was not to complain, for complaining was the same as running in the corridors or talking after the lamps were extinguished; it was against the rules.

Quid Faciendum Est. To do what must be done. The Sinford's school moto.

The institution was expected to turn out a fine gentleman who could not only recite his Latin verbs, complete mathematical conundrums, and talk fluently about the ancients, but also a man who knew how to play games like a gentleman. Like the school, my parents expected of me absolute adherence to discipline, and in return for their payment, they expected their child to be cared for, fed and raised in their absence by paternal tutors and motherly matrons.

None of which could have been further from the reality.

Like the world we live in today, Sinford's was a hierarchy, a Jacob's Ladder with new boys facing a seemingly impossible climb to reach the gods at the top. The 'Gods' in other private schools, was the name given to the men in their last year, the adults of the school, the prefects and heads of year, captains of house, sport and intellect.

At Sinford's, they were called 'Golds.' When one began the school life, one was nothing more than a grain in the gritty earth. The first-year boys were known as Leads because the ladder rose in stages of metallurgy. Beyond lead came copper, bronze, silver and ultimately gold. Some boys left at the age of sixteen after their copper year, but most, well-polished and gleaming, forged themselves into shining, silvery examples of all Sinford's stood for. Fewer still, the gentlemen of university fodder, achieved the ultimate position of becoming a gold.

My career began as a heavy, leaden object of no consequence to any but the occasional classmate with whom I formed a vague bond of friendship. We were housed, fourteen of us, in one dormitory known by the sanitised name of E-one. There were also E-two and E-three, and in the second year, D-one and two, and so on, counting down to the ultimate; the A dorms, the home of the golds. The boys called the dormitories 'Snugs' as if hoping to make the rooms sound homely, but there was nothing on the walls but a cross and a faded painting of Christ. Life was Spartan in the extreme.

I don't mean to paint a picture of Dotheboys Hall from Nicholas Nickleby, although Sinford's was not too far from the fiction, and conditions improved as one progressed from E-dorms in Courage House to the D-dorms of Humility, and from there, to the C-dorms of Chastity House.

As one progressed, life became more bearable and this, I came to realise, happened because of bonds. Not between masters and students, a relationship that remained static from the very first day, but because of the bonds of friendship forged through adversity. Through shared suffering and competition, the need to confide and survive, and through the enforced proximity of boys of the same age on the same rungs to the top of the ladder. As one climbed, one saw one's friends fall, taken away by military parents to be schooled abroad, or waved farewell to at the end of one term never to be seen again because of collapsed fortunes or lost investments, financial errors, family tragedies, illness, or simply because the boy made such a fuss about conditions and hardships, the parents found a quieter life by having their offspring taught elsewhere. Such boys were replaced, because for all its austerity, the school held a reputation akin to Westminster or Harrow. It had to, to justify its prices.

You may find in this scene setting an air of displeasure with the establishment, but the truth is, we knew nothing else. We were educated well, we were moulded into well-behaved young men who, although it was instilled by force on occasion, understood that to respect our elders and betters was the same as respecting God and the clergy. Or, in Sinford's terms, respecting the masters and golds.

Part of learning that respect was to fag; to act as an unpaid servant to a senior man. For some, it was an honour to be chosen to fag for a silver or gold, while others resented it for the servitude it was. Some Sinford's boys climbed to the top of the Jacob's Ladder using fear as their ice axe, and to fag for them was not an honour, it was a way of escaping the bullies. Fags were generally chosen from the leads, the new boys of that year's intake who knew no better, and the golds, of course, had first pick.

When I started at Sinford's, I was a handsome young man with good manners, a quick mind and a healthy body. To say I had angelic features would have been to quote from my grandmother, and I would never have said it of myself. My hair was short and dark, cut in the regimental style the school demanded, my face was always ruddy red and shining from soap, and my round eyes were made wider by the awe of the older men of the school; the dashing, self-assured icons I wanted to become. They were not fellow students to me, but aspirations. To be a top-floor gold was an ambition rather than an expectation, but to achieve such ambition, I had to begin as all others, with a tentative foot on the lowest rung. How I knew this, I know not, but I knew it from the moment I turned from my departing parents and faced the wide staircase on the landing of which stood a silver. (The man wore a silver waistcoat, they all did).

The deity was posed like the Colossus of Rhodes, and was looking nowhere but at me. Perhaps the stairs were a metaphor, for I knew what one was, and I understood that to reach his fantastic heights, I had to climb. This man—for all silvers and golds were men to us new boys—had singled me out from the other snivelling and abandoned wretches and raised an arm, pointed a finger, and beckoned. On reaching the first step, my cap in hand, he said, 'Stop,' and every movement in the entrance hall and on the staircase came to a halt.

'Name?'

'Marcus Havegood, Sir.' My stammered reply included the 'Sir,' but omitted the 'Honourable.' If I took nothing else from my preparatory school, I took a sense of caution.

'Come.'

That was the only experience I have ever shared with a condemned man being led to the gallows. How I climbed the stairs without my legs deserting me, I know not, but I had achieved all but the top two when he again ordered me to a halt. Then, he looked up to what I later discovered was a gallery, and said, 'May I, Mr Gold, or would you rather?'

I assumed Mr Gold was the name of a master standing above me, but I came to learn it was how all silvers addressed all golds. Most confusing, but confusion of all matters was rife at Sinford's.

'Your last year's average?' another low, loud voice echoed down the stillness of the cavern in which I trembled.

My silver recited some numbers and other sporting terms that I understood at the time to be impressive but have since forgotten, and the voice from above declared the silver could take me.

Take me for what, was a question soon answered, because having thanked the voice from on high, my silver made an announcement.

'Havegood is mine,' he declared to the hall. 'Let it be known. Carry on.'

The hubbub of conversation, the squeaking of shoes on tiles, and the clatter of trunks and tuck boxes being wheeled in, resumed. My silver clicked his fingers and pointed to the space beside him. Standing there, I looked up into his face some several inches above my own not knowing what I had done wrong, or possibly right, and not knowing what to say.

'Your snug is E-one,' he said. 'I will show you where that is, and after that, I will do nothing else for you, but you will do anything I require. Do so without complaint and do it well, and you shall be protected. Havegood, you have the potential to do two things at this place, either champion its regime and rise to become a gold, or fall by the wayside and be relegated to the pits of anonymity. Come with me.'

Thus began my career as a lead, a Sinford's scholar and, most importantly, the servant to one of the kindest men in the place. I was, to say the least, lucky.

'Luc Verdier,' my silver said as he marched me up, along, this way and that, and finally to a cold room with two lines of identical beds. 'You will call me Sir as though I were a master.'

The room was alive with boys of my age, silently transferring clothes from beds to wardrobes, but when they saw a silver at the door, they snapped to attention and stood like stalagmites in a cave.

'Men, this is Havegood,' my silver said. 'He is mine. Anyone who shows disrespect to my boy can expect a lashing at the horse. Verdier Sec?'

A blond boy stood by the window, sunlight turning his hair to the yellow of flame, and on hearing the name, hurried to stand before us.

'Sir?'

'He will have the pit beside yours. You will guide each other. You're fagging for Cassock, are you not?'

'I am, Sir.'

'Good, he's also in Temperance, so you two can come up together. You know our expectations?'

'Yes, Sir.'

'Then there we are.' To me, he said. 'My brother will see you put no foot wrong. I have told him who to beware and who may be trusted, but if you have any trouble, you speak to me, not the masters. Am I clear on this?'

Still trembling, I replied with a meek affirmative.

'Good.' With a flick of his head so fast I hardly saw it, and with a voice so loud it could crack a window, my silver yelled, 'You! Report. Shirt not pressed,' and with that, he turned on his heels and was gone.

The room gave such a sigh I was certain even the walls breathed with relief. The previous activity resumed, and my enforced acquaintance took me to my pit.

'Are you a pri?' he said.

'A what?'

'Pri, sec or ter?'

'Oh, none, I suppose. I have no brothers.'

This was something else I had been primed to expect from Sinford's. When there was more than one boy from the same family, the oldest was 'pri', from primis, the Latin for first. Secundo and tertius followed, but no-one had ever been able to explain what happened in the case of twins.

'Lucky you,' the blond boy huffed, and as with his brother, I detected a mild French accent. 'What can I call you? It's meant to be surnames only, but I am of the opinion that fellows of the same class may be more personal when alone. You are of the same class, are you not?'

'I don't know what classes I am in,' I said. 'I assume the same as you.'

Verdier smiled so infectiously, I was compelled to copy.

'What?' I questioned.

'Are you of the same class?' he emphasised, and then gave a massive slump of his shoulders as if already tiring of dealing with an idiot. 'Our father is the French Ambassador. Who's yours?'

'Oh, he's in business. We do very well, thank you.'

'You're not one of these New Rich, I hope. Not that we are landed, but the family descends from the Normans and parts of it have been here ever since we invaded. Papa is from Rouen, where we have a chateau. Here, we have Dashwood in Hampshire. Where are you?'

'London.' Thinking that too vague, I clarified. 'Hampstead.'

'Papa hates London. So, what can I call you? You can call me Jacques, if you like, but only when we are alone.'

'Marcus,' I told him. 'After Marcus Aurelius, apparently. He was a Caesar.'

As if already bored with that conversation, Jacques said, 'Luc has given me a full tutorial, so I know what's what at Sinford's. We have insider information, and will put it to our advantage, because you, Marcus Aurelius, are to be my new best friend.'

Jacques was a prophet, for, from that moment, we did indeed become the best of friends. The best of brothers in arms supporting each other through seas of troubles and oceans of learning, and through storms of adversity and suffering blown by gascon house captains and overbearing matrons, violent masters, and the boarding-school regime. Together, we overcame homesickness. As a pair we took the classroom bench together, and supported each other through the rigours of the first person indicative active, we declined verbs to the nth degree, and wrestled with the minutia of Gildersleeve's Latin grammar. It was Jacques who led me through the forest of calculus and kept me on the path during geometry. For my part, I assisted him with the classics and his reading, because where he was beyond fluent in numbers, he was not so imaginative with his use of the English language, despite his lust for the arts. Not that I was very much better, but as the friendship grew, so did my need to offer him something in return.

You may ask, in return for what? I shall tell you.

There was a mutual method of support that existed without debate or discussion; it was simply there as it should be with any strong friendship. There was something else, however, which, although not discussed, was also apparent. It is hard if not impossible to talk about when one is fourteen, as I was when these feelings emerged, and so there was no debate or discussion about this matter, but what Jacques gave me was, I would now say, more profound than friendship. It was something unexplainable, and it persisted.

In our second year, we moved up to Humility House and were awarded copper status. Two men of fourteen, he turning fifteen a month or so before me, and both with leads to look down on, as the coppers had looked down on us. Maybe that was why they called the house 'Humility'; an attempt to keep us in check so we didn't bully first years in the manner of the older boys of the first fifteen. There was another house, for each year had two. Where our first year had seen us in Courage House, its companion was Faith. Where we were in Humility, its identical set of snugs and bathrooms was Patience. Above us loomed Chastity and Honesty, and beyond them, the Temperance and Moderation of our silver years. The ultimate, as I have mentioned, was gold, where, if we made it, we would be in Grace Tower or Justice Lodge. No houses for the golds, they were men, and as such, lived independently in the lodge, or in the massive tower that stood central to Sinford's wide, workhouse-like edifice.

The tower stood proud over the grounds, and a border of rockeries and pedestals holding stone vases and eagles. At the front, it dominated the drive and the entrance, as if everyone entering the quad had to walk between its mighty stone legs as a sign of deference to the golds who peered down from on high.

I am running ahead of myself. The story of the tower and its mysteries is for later.

Jacques and I entered our second year together. The snugs were no less snug and no less unpleasant, and we still had our pits beside each other. Jacques' brother, Luc, became a prefect. He had never mistreated me, or beaten me at the horse, because I had never given him cause, nor had he taken advantage of me in other ways.

As Jacques said, 'Certainly not in *that* way, because my brother, my family, is not like that.'

We were taking one of our rare hours of freedom on the edge of the cricket pitch and enjoying an early spring. The second eleven were playing, and we watched vaguely from the edge of the wood. The wood, we called *beyond the boundary* because it was where only silvers and golds could wander without supervision, but the edge of it was a safe place, because the second eleven could never hit a six there. I, by then, was on the cusp of joining the first, and was capable of sixing the ball into the trees, because my enjoyment of physical exercise had turned me from a snivelling lead into a burgeoning copper with skills on the field and muscles to match. Jacques was more interested in the arts, sang in the choir, took extra music lessons and was a fair dab with a paintbrush. With him being blond, me dark, and the two of us inseparable, we earnt pet names and gossip too numerous and tedious to recount, but the opposites of our characters were what held us together. They, and what we discussed that afternoon on the edge of the boundary.

'When you say taken advantage of in *that* way, with such emphasis, what do you mean?' I asked.

With no hesitation, Jacques put his fist around the middle finger of his left hand and moved it up and down.

'What's that?' I laughed, because he looked ridiculous.

When he repeated the action in his lap, however, I understood. To say my blood ran cold would be a lie. It ran hot, as I wondered how one man could do that to another. More than wondered; I wanted, instantly, to know.

'That happens?'

'It does,' Jacques said, and picked at the grass. 'I've never had to do it for my man, but Hunter did it for his.' With a look of accusation, he said, 'Have you had to?'

'No,' I protested, or feigned protestation, because as he spoke, I imagined doing it to him.

'Diggs says he enjoys it.'

'Diggs?'

That was a revelation. Simon Stape, Diggs as we called him, was the other of our three. Although not as close as Jacques and me, Diggs was often with us, shared the same snug with a pit on my other side, and was becoming a firm friend.

Jacques changed his position and lay on his front with his chin in his hands, watching the cricket. I did the same, and we lay side by side, shoulders touching, and I was glad of it. The more I thought of what was happening between Diggs and his man in Grace, the more I became aroused, to the extent that I would not have been able to conceal my arousal had I been in any other position. I remember asking myself if Jacques had taken that position for the same reason.

'You mustn't tell Diggs I told you this,' he whispered, although we were quite alone. 'But he came to me not three nights ago as we were at the washstand, and came right out with it. "I know I can tell you this with no fear, but I have been giving my man the pleasure," he said, and I knew what he meant, because Luc had warned me about the practise. I told him I wasn't interested to hear, but that didn't stop him. It had, apparently, been going on for some time, and had been reciprocated. "It was good," he said. "I didn't mind one bit."'

'Diggs admitted that?'

'He did, but you must not repeat it.'

'I shan't. What did you say?'

'I told him he should not be speaking about such things, and he said he knew, but it had been so fascinating, he wanted to keep doing it. I told him not to be so vulgar, and do you want to know what he said?'

'Yes, please.'

'He asked if I would like him to do it to me.'

Again, Jacques made the gesture with his finger and fist, and what I imagined only increased the press of myself against the grass. Had I moved, I think I would have spent there and then. It was the curiosity of a boy of fifteen. It was the summer heat on my back, Jacques' shoulder against mine, the intimacy of the conversation which was about us and yet not about us, and it was the moment I knew exactly what Jacques could offer me that was beyond a usual friendship.

'And did you do it?'

'No,' he said. 'I didn't, but I thought about it.'

That gave me hope and courage that strengthened in the tension between us, as collared doves cooed, and the upper trees rustled in a high breeze for I don't know how long. The dull click of leather on willow was followed by distant applause, as if the far-away spectators were willing me on.

Trying to appear nonchalant, I said, 'I'd do it for you if you want. I don't mind.'

Jacques continued to stare at the match with his light lashes fluttering, and his usually pale cheeks the colour of autumn apples. Silent, and with the offer and all it suggested hanging between us, we remained like that until the end of the next over, when Jacques pushed himself to his feet, and said, 'They're going in for tea.'

I watched him walk away taking with him neither yes nor no, agreement or denial, and leaving behind the possibility of everything I wanted. Him. Not only as my friend, but my more-than-a-friend. The one with whom I could be intimate. The one with whom I could lie on the grass through endless summer days listening to the sounds of the season with no need to speak, because we loved each other without condition. We understood each other, cared for and protected each other as a pair who would stand against the injustices of the world until that world saw what we were. Lovers.

That was when it began, the strengthening of the bond between Jacques and me, and between us and Diggs.

It is about Diggs that I must now write, because without him in the story, the tragedy that would occur three years later would not have happened.

FOUR

The private memories of the Hon. Marcus Havegood. (Continued.)

**Sinford's
1879**

Not long after I made my offer beyond the boundary, I tried again, more brazenly, and again, Jacques refused my advances in silence. There, I left it, unrequited perhaps, but content to be his best of friends, and looked to satisfy my growing and undeniable flaw elsewhere.

The bronze year between copper and gold saw little change in the fast friendship Jacques and I enjoyed, but much changed between myself and Diggs. Jacques made it clear that he was neither interested in mutual pleasure with Diggs, who pined for him worse than me, nor with me, who did the same, but whose pining lessened as I matured. It was, I can now see, being the spurned hopefuls that brought Diggs and me together. A union as inevitable as it was, at first, unimaginable, but a union that finally happened during our silver year, because neither of us could have what we desired. Jacques Verdier.

It is difficult to recount the emotions of the bronze time, for there were so many. One day I would wake to watch Jacques dress and wash, and the next, we would ready for sports with no stirring desires while we undressed together. We would swim naked in the lake, as did all the boys, and I had no thought of examining him with intimacy, because I knew he was beyond my reach in that way, and I was unwilling to do anything to sully our friendship. At other times, I would watch as Diggs spent time with him and suffered no jealousy, because I knew that for all his seduction and effort, Diggs would find the same refusal.

The seniors above us left Grace Tower to make their way into the world as men forged by the callous pounding of the Sinford's hammer on the anvil of tradition that flattened any crease of individuality or creativity. Men were smelted from base material in the crucible of the public-school system, and once tempered, poured into moulds vacated by their fathers and theirs before them. Those who opposed were caught in the clamps and chiselled, worked, and drawn out until, free of all impurities, they became Old Sinfordians, free to set foot upon the green and pleasant land of Blake's imagination. There they forged their own progeny in their own image among the dark satanic mills of adulthood.

Our Bronze year was one of rebellion against the system, and acts of dissent that never escaped punishment. Central to the rebellion was inventing nicknames. I have said that we called Simon 'Diggs' because of his middle name; Diggory, a name he detested. Often, a nickname would come about simply because the boy didn't care for it. For others, we invented names appropriate to their failings. Thus, Judd became 'D-minus' because he once spectacularly failed in a simple French examination. Simpkins became 'Box' because he refused to wear one on the cricket field and received an off break to his testicles which caused him great pain and even greater embarrassment in Matron's surgery. Some came from surnames, so Arnold Vane became 'Weather', Bernard Rhoades became 'Street', and John Taylor was known as 'Stitch.' Such pet names were frowned upon by the masters as being too informal, but the rebellious Bronze boys took no notice. Many enjoyed ribbing the masters by using these names in class, earning them detentions where they would scribble off the lines or copy out the lengthy poem in minutes, and spend the rest of the time drawing images of Scroat, a boy with unusually large testes, Humpty, the fattest boy in the school, and Skinny, so named not because of his build, but because of his excess of foreskin. Bronze boys were horrid, vile to each other because the school wanted us not to be, irritable and evil, taking the rise out of a man's acne only to suffer from it later and object to being ridiculed in the same way. Although we were not unruly, we were certainly as difficult as we could get away with without receiving a black mark or a beating.

That was, until we learnt that we would be elevated to silvers only if lines were toed and expectations accepted. Military training, first fifteen, first eleven, and athletics for the dry bobs such as myself, swimming, diving and rowing for the wets like Jacques—the most magnificent of all competitors in his bathing suit. Study, prep, examinations, debates and rhetoric, performances of obscure revengers' tragedies and Greek comedy, recitations of Chaucer in the original, Voltaire and Balzac dissected, Johnson and Pope learnt by heart, the hours of nib dipping and ink blotting lasting for whole mornings, and afternoons for whole days that crawled into weeks that stretched ahead for months, until, exhausted, the year was over, and we were triumphant in its ending.

As triumphant as we were as we entered Temperance House as silvers. Not yet quite the untouchable gods of gold, but university fodder nonetheless, and with the greatest of rewards; two-man study rooms. No longer the fourteen-togetherness of the snugs, but privacy and a lessening of strictures, to a certain degree. Silvers still needed training so, in a year's time, we could be trusted as the doyen of Sinford's and become the unreachable. It was a long year, and I was glad of its length, because it allowed time for my attentions to turn from Jacques Verdier to Simon 'Diggs' Stape. Diggs had been under my nose this whole time, and yet, it took me until I had squared my circle with Jacques to see that what I craved was available in Diggs, and what he had always wanted was available in me.

It was to Jacques that I first declared my affection for Diggs. Jacques was my mentor, my confidant, my other self, and I was the same to him. Thus, the words came easily.

We were in our study, for the powers that were had seen there was no danger in our proximity and more in trying to separate us because we were students who supported each other. The study, housed in the more ancient wing of the main building, had arched windows set deep into the stone, giving enough room for two men to sit in comfort. With no thought of anything carnal, I sat against the stone with Jacques leaning against me reading, and me gazing down on the croquet lawn where Diggs was wielding his authority over the first years who had been tasked with weeding the borders. Jacques was in my arms, and I felt only platonic love for the man, for we were men, silvers and half-trusted.

'Has Diggs been pestering you of late?' I asked as if it were a nothing, and not an overture to a long-held confession.

'Pestering?'

I made the same gesture with fist and fingers he had made beyond the boundary, and he laughed.

'Christ, yes,' he said. 'Every bloody day, it feels like. Why?'

'I assume you have not given in to the temptation?'

'No, I have not, because there is no temptation. Once, when he had me cornered, he made his request in the name of science, would you believe? Science? I scoffed. How could bringing a man to that end be considered science? Well, we both know Diggs is the man when it comes to all things scientific, and he came up with a reasonably plausible reply. It had something to do with the number of strokes divided by time it took to ejaculate, leading to the formula that would produce the greatest... combustion, I suppose.'

I laughed at that too, because no-one but Diggs would have said such a thing, yet behind my laughter, was a very real desire to carry out the same experiment.

'What did you say?'

'That time, I tried laughing it off with, "Get thee behind me, Satan," but it didn't work.'

'Didn't work?'

'No. He said, "If I got behind you, I'd want to bugger you, for what man wouldn't?"'

'Me,' I said, because I was beyond those feeling for Jacques.

'So, yes, Diggs continues to dig away at my metaphorical garden, while I continue to throw back in the earth and refill his hole of hope.'

I guffawed at that, and when Jacques moved away and turned to stare at me, it didn't take him long to realise what he'd said.

'You're filthy,' he snorted, and resumed his intimate yet not suggestive position against my chest.

'I am also rather enamoured with your gardener,' I said.

'What?'

'With Diggs.'

I don't know what I expected from the statement, but Jacques scurried to the other side of the casement, and at first, I thought it was to be as far away from me, the abomination, as he could be. Intrigued, he flung aside his book with a flapping of pages.

'I knew it,' he beamed. 'Oh, Christ, I'd be so happy for you if it came about.'

'Good Lord. You mean it?'

'Oh, come now, Caesar, it's been bloody obvious since you tried it on with me out by the woods.'

'It has? Oh dear.'

'Don't worry, only I would see it. To everyone else, you are as manly as an ape and have no fear of anyone suspecting your... Whatever one would call it. You and Diggs? What's he said?'

'Nothing, because I've not told him.'

'Do you want to swap rooms?'

'Pardon?'

'So you can be together? I don't mind sharing with Hunter.'

'No,' I protested. 'You and I together, always. We swore.'

'Yes, but when love rears its throbbing, purple head...'

'Now who's being filthy?'

'Hell, Caesar, it would get him off my back.'

He'd called me Caesar because of my name, Marcus, and because I took the part in Shakespeare. By the same reckoning, I should have called him Calphurnia, but for all his angelic looks, lithe body, and sensitive charms, Jacques was always a man without a nickname.

A man who, caring for his friend's happiness and still harbouring a seam of bronze rebellion, engineered our pairing. Two nights later,

Diggs and I became clandestine partners in the crime of falling into bed, and very soon after, falling into love, joined both by physical pleasure and by the heart. Jacques remained my best friend, of course, but the three of us became closer. With his acceptance of Diggs and me, and with even Hunter in on it, we four took an oath of secrecy and loyalty. We kept the same study rooms, because to have requested a change mid-year would have aroused suspicion, but twice after the house captain had made his rounds, we swapped rooms for the night, and our friends let us celebrate our seventeenth birthdays in the same bed.

1879

Jacques, Diggs, I, and to a lesser degree, the swat, Hunter, became something of the Four Horsemen of the Apogee; the climax to our five years at Sinford's. We became golds, reached the apex of our time, moved to Grace Tower, and were not only awarded that ultimate bounty, but were given the top floor. Even Baston, who became Head Boy, was put on a lower floor, although it must be admitted, that was so he could have a private sitting room and his own lavatory. We, however, had the view, the ultimate privacy, the top perch, and respect of all those who cowered below. We also had the longest climb to reach the floor beneath the battlements, and we had a distinct lack of hot water, but, after Baston, at least we had first choice of the fags.

We employed distant younger cousins and the children of our parents' friends among first years to serve us, but, before doing so, swore to be compassionate employers, to teach the younger men humility through words, not beatings, and to teach them that to be in service needn't be a chore. This we somehow managed without being called weak. In fact, several masters complimented us on our diplomacy and fairness, and Hunter, surprisingly, was once singled out in chapel for his kind treatment of his 'helper.'

We were, I see now, full of our own self-worth while aiming to be the best of humanity, and, to be fair to us, and compared to the rest of the school, we were. Much of this was driven by Jacques and his father's history of calm diplomacy, and from that, we took the lesson that 'cruel to be kind' did not work. Cruelty led to rebellion, and the putting down of rebellion only led to more hatred.

Our fags knew nothing of our arrangements on the top floor, where, on Jacques' insistence, Diggs and I shared study A-one, while Jacques and Hunter lived in A-two next door. The four of us shared the bath, but not at the same time, and the fags still had to carry buckets up the stone staircases. The ironing room was in the basement, and we had to take on prefect duties in the main house, but none of that diminished our happiness. Nor did it diminish our resolve to work hard, excel on the playing fields as expected, and toe the line of Sinford's expectations.

We did, and it was a cover for the nightly union of Diggs and me, and the nightly debates among three friends. (The fourth, Hunter, was studying for a scholarship which he never achieved, and kept himself much to himself). We three talked of our hopes for the future, and vowed we would, at the very least, meet once each year until we were old men rotting away in leathery chairs. Before then, however, we had our university years to navigate, and it wasn't by chance that the four of us had places at the same institution, although not the same colleges. It was with that in mind that we settled into long hours of study, not knowing, then, that only two of the Triumvirate would live to take our place in the world.

1880

We returned for the last summer term of school to discover everything had changed. Not with the school, for that had not altered for over a hundred years, nor with our living arrangements, lessons, masters, teams, duties, fags, or any of the cogs that make a public school grind in timeless order. Something had changed within us. This was our last term. After this, there was to be no more childhood.

I remember feeling that I had wasted the last five years. When a lead, the years ahead stretched endlessly, but suddenly, without warning, there was no time left, and everything that had gone before had happened in a blink. What opportunities had we missed? What more larks could we have fitted in between the ceremonies and sports, and how many more friends could we have gathered between the loving cup of Michaelmas and the final breakfast gong of summer? Finding answers to these unasked questions was pointless because there was nothing to be done. We had done it, and whether we had made the most of our five years or not, there was nothing we could do to change them.

This realisation brought about in me an initial melancholy, which passed quickly because ahead was university where more adventures awaited for sure. Diggs simply carried on without a word, stoic as he was and bullish, but after the first few weeks of term, it became clear Jacques, like many senior boys, was not himself.

We put it down to the examinations looming ahead like the *Symplegades*, the clashing rocks of Greek mythology through which we had to pass to achieve our places at university. The men of wealthier families had already secured theirs with donations and patronage, while others, such as the Triumvirate, wanted to access places on academic merit. The last term was one of revision, seriousness, final achievements, and harder work than we had known. Assuming this was what was weighing on Jacques, Diggs spent time with him on science, while I spent time on the classics, and Hunter, when he could be prised from his books, worked with him on other texts. We assisted each other because we shared the same pressures, but as time passed, it became clear that something else was amiss. Jacques' brother, Luc, was, by then, enlisted, and had been sent to the Baloch tribal belt to again fight the Marri, but he served directly beneath Macgregor, and the troops were encountering little resistance. That was not Jacques' problem.

No end of cajoling and questioning could produce a satisfactory answer, other than he was worried about the future, and, to give him his credit, whatever troubled him, he mainly put aside as we put all our efforts into revision. However, as the examinations closed in on us, he reverted to being his usual self, and our initial concerns were laid to rest.

Sinford's might have been unique in the way it offered its university candidates what it called Praemisit, a not-quite accurate use of the Latin verb for 'looking ahead.' The sportsmen of the school called it extra time, and the bookworms called it the appendices.

Summer term ended in mid-July, but the golds had the option of Praemisit. Where those destined for the army or navy left for Sandhurst or Dartmouth, those of us coming up as university men could remain and spend the rest of the month in tutoring. Masters would donate a couple of weeks of their time to tutor us in the set texts we could expect, and the ways of our various universities. We discussed what we would encounter, were instructed on how to make our money last, what to avoid, and, to our great humour, the wiles and ways of loose women. This extra time, we didn't see as an extra chore, because we had the school to ourselves. After five years of being figures of authority, the masters were ordinary men who simply enjoyed passing on knowledge to a younger generation. Those who wanted could use the sports fields and equipment, and golds played cricket against masters (even the headmaster came to keep score), and others could take the boats on the lake, or wander the extensive forest discussing Homer or Euclid, Plato or Locke.

Diggs had taken an interest in cartography, and set himself the project of mapping the school grounds; the illegal cut throughs as well as the accepted paths. Jacques spent much time swimming, and we other three would take our novels there to read and watch, laughing on the way back as we melded the stories together, and came up with ridiculous titles. 'Wuthering Expectations', was my invention, while Diggs came up with 'Great Heights.' It was a relaxed time, and time well spent in preparation for life. Jacques, Diggs and I were free and joyous, and, particularly for Diggs and me, uninterrupted, unobserved and able to live at the top of the tower as we imagined we would at university, as two men sharing more than living quarters.

Even Praemisit had to end, but before it did, we made the most of our tower, and spent long nights on the roof, staring at the stars, naming them, discussing their mythologies, and talking about all manner of nonsense. Jacques had, by then, taken to a pipe which he smoked sitting with his back to the chimney stack because heights made him sick, while Diggs leant on the thick crenelations tending to his moustache, which we said made him look like a statesman. If one of us had been into the village and returned with a flask of brandy, we would sip and share, mapping our futures and making our promises, until dawn lit the eastern woods beyond the boundary, and with stinging eyes, we retired below to sleep late, knowing another Sinford's day had come and gone, and we, like hundreds before us, would soon pass under the tower for the last time, never to return. Never to know again days that had been both difficult and easy, painful and joyous, filled with fear and wonder, innocence and experience.

Somewhere along the way, we had passed from childhood to manhood, and it was as men that we took to our rooms on the thirtieth of July 1880, knowing that it would be our last ever night at Sinford's, but not knowing it would be Jacques' last on this earth.

* * *

Jack was glad when the reading was over. It was the first time he'd read anything so long and difficult. The story left him with images of rich men sleeping with each other, being far too romantic, and a headache, and he had to blink several times to moisten his eyes. That done, and thinking Jimmy was still reading, he glanced again at the last page, wondering what happened next.

Jimmy nudged him, and nodded across the room, and when Jack looked, his heart gave a bound. Havegood was slumped in his chair with his eyes closed, and his mouth open. Had his chest not been rising and falling, Jack would have thought him dead.

'What do you make of all that?' Jimmy whispered.

'Too many words?'

'To me, it reads like a man trying to impress upon us his strength of feeling for another. If this fell into the wrong hands, his career as the future respectable Lord Beresford would be over before it began.'

'Yeah, but it don't tell us nothing about where this missing man is.'

'But we can see why he is keen to find him. The date is interesting.

He wants to find Stape before the end of the month, the day they left their school. Why?'

Their whispering roused Havegood from his slumber, and after a glance to remind himself where he was, he struggled upright, and cleared his throat.

'So sorry, Mr Wright. A warm afternoon, a comfortable chair...'

'No need to apologise, Sir,' Jimmy said, and took the papers back to his desk. 'An interesting read, and I thank you for your candour. Not many men would commit such to paper.'

'Paper which must be destroyed,' Havegood said, and held out his hand.

'If you would let me, I'd like to keep it a while longer.' Jimmy pointed to his safe. 'I will keep it in there. Only I know the combination. It'll be secured, and I won't show it to anyone, but I might need to refer back to it.'

'Why?'

'For a better understanding.'

'But, Mr Wright, I have already opened my soul to you, admitted how I was then, and I have entrusted to you evidence which could damn me.'

'I am hardly likely to damn a client for his honesty,' Jimmy said, and Jack thought that was a good answer. 'You want our help? Then I must keep this. According to our contract, it will go no further, I assure you.'

Havegood cast wary eyes to Jack, who, taking Jimmy's lead, put on a serious expression, and nodded thoughtfully.

'I would only deny it, and my father would ruin you, so... Very well,' the client sighed, and watched as Jimmy slid the papers into the safe and spun the dial.

'I understand why this man is important to you,' he said, retaking his seat and reaching for his pen and casebook. 'The background you have given is very useful in establishing your motive for finding Mr Stape. What is missing, however, is what happened next. You refer to your last night at Sinford's being Mr Verdier's last night on earth. Is that important or a metaphorical reference to something?'

'I wish it were.'

'And what has what we have read to do with the disappearance of your friend?'

Havegood lifted his teacup to find it empty, and Jimmy rang for Max. 'I think there is more for you to tell us, Sir.'

'There is, Mr Wright.' Havegood took another paper from his case. 'I have written what I can, because it has more bearing on the disappearance. There is more to tell you after you have read it, but I will need fortification to help me through the memories.'

'More tea won't be long.'

Jack might have had trouble filtering Havegood's language to find its meaning, but when anyone suggested they needed fortification, he knew exactly what they meant. Without thinking, he said, 'Something stronger?' and realising he'd spoken out of turn, expected Jimmy to say something.

What he said was, 'A good idea, Merrit. Would you?' and pointed to a row of three glass bottles on a tray.

A sniff, and he located brandy, poured the client a glass and handed it over. Jimmy refused, and Jack had never liked the stuff, so he sat and waited while Havegood sipped. In a repeat of the earlier ceremony, Max appeared, and Jimmy asked him for more tea. He also asked him to send Will, and while Max took away one tray and shortly returned with another, Will appeared, hurriedly buttoning his jacket as if he had been caught relaxing when he should have been working.

'William Merrit,' Jimmy introduced him to the client. 'Our researcher. Will, could you look through the library index and see if we have anything on Sinford's School for Boys? It is in Kent.'

'Case twelve, rows two and three hold the volumes on educational establishments, Sir,' Will said. 'I'll start there.'

Had it been anyone else, Jack would have thought the information was made up to impress, but since moving into Delamere, Will had spent most of his time in the massive room of books Jimmy called Will's library, and with his memory for detail, he'd already know what he was talking about. Will at work was a warming sight to see.

'Anything you can find,' Jimmy said. 'Particularly about why it closed.'

Before he left, and sheltered by the open door, Will raised his eyes at Jack and pulled a smile of comic excitement which once would have made Jack laugh. Instead, he frowned a warning, because if Will overexerted himself, his enthusiasm could easily become anxiety.

'The school closed not long after I left,' Havegood said, bringing Jack back to business. 'It was something to do with regulations. Why do you need to know?'

'Background and interest,' Jimmy smiled.

Jack hadn't known him long, but he was sure the detective had another motive than curiosity. Not being in a position to ask, he said nothing but took the paper Mr Havegood offered, while Jimmy came and joined him on the settee. Again, despite the warm afternoon, they sat close with their legs touching.

'Enjoy your tea,' Jimmy said, and like Jack, turned his attention to the neat handwriting.

FIVE

**The private memories of the Hon. Marcus Havegood.
(Continued.)**

July 30th, 1880

Our last full day at Sinford's.
There was no end-of-it-all celebration, because that had taken place when the rest of school left for the summer holidays. In Grace Tower, our trunks had been packed and collected, our tuckboxes too, and all we were left with were our travelling clothes. We had duties the next morning, but only light ones; stripping our beds, turning back the mattresses, tidying the rooms, and we had tickets on the late morning train. The last evening of our school years, therefore, was spent taking an informal dinner with the remaining masters, swapping stories of when we were young students, and making jokes with them if not as equals, then as survivors of the same regime. There were final words of advice, words of wisdom and best wishes to exchange, and that done, we, the departing, retired to our rooms. Or, in the case of the Triumvirate, to the roof, where we shared our last flask, and where,

eventually, conversation ran dry because our thoughts were on the future, and none of us wanted to dwell further on our now-passed schooldays.

Diggs and I were alone by ten thirty, and Jacques was next door in A-two. I passed his room on my way back from the bath to find the door open, and looking in, found Hunter alone and fast asleep. I was not surprised, as he liked his sleep, was often in bed first, and rarely stayed awake past ten. Jacques, I discovered, was in my room, talking to Diggs, and when I walked in, I heard him say, 'I will.'

'Will what?' I asked, throwing my towel over the chair where it would dry.

'Write during the summer,' Jacques said. 'Which reminds me, I must complete my journal. I'll say goodnight, and we'll breakfast together, yes?'

We always did, so no-one replied, and Jacques left us, probably to do as he always did, to write up the events of the day in his diary. Needless to say, Diggs and I made the most of our last night alone, and although we dallied long in his bed, we were asleep in it before the chapel clock struck midnight.

July 31st

I was woken by bells. Not the usual sound of the house captain or one of his appointees rattling the old brass clapper, but shorter bursts, further away and higher in pitch. The sound came closer, and with it came voices. Again, not the gruff mumbles of eighteen-year-olds greeting each other outside the door on their way to cold ablutions, but more distant, urgent voices.

'What's the fuss?' Diggs complained, and wrapped himself tighter in his blanket.

Having no idea, I rose from my bed and knelt in the deep window recess to peer over the back lawns. I could see nothing wrong at first, but then the bells clattered again, and two horses appeared from the side of School House dragging an ambulance.

'Someone's had an accident,' I yawned. 'Probably, one of the masters had too much to drink last night and stumbled.'

The headmaster came running across the croquet lawn, and I remember thinking he should receive a black mark for that, but stranger, he was in his dressing gown and slippers, and when I opened the window and leant out to look down, directly below me, I saw Matron and two gardeners standing over a sheet.

Realisation can come like a slow, winter dawn, or it can crash home with all the speed of a bullet. For me, it took its time, because the sights were so alien, and had someone told me exactly what I was witnessing, I still would not have believed them. It wasn't until Diggs dragged himself from his bed, and knelt with me, that he said the words which froze my body to the stonework as though we were one entity.

'That's a person,' he said.

That's a person. His words stabbed because to see someone dead, even when hidden by a sheet, causes the blood to pound in shock, and the mind to race to the worst. In my case, it was as if I instinctively knew who it was four storeys down and dead, and without thought, I ran from the window, and barged into the next study.

Jacques' bed was empty, and Hunter was still asleep. As usual, it took me a while to rouse him, for he was always a heavy sleeper and fond of his oblivious time, but when I had him sitting up and halfway alert, I asked him where Jacques had gone.

'Gone?' Hunter glanced to the second bed. 'No idea, go back to bed.'

Hunter was to be no help, so I left him and returned to my room where Diggs and I dressed and flew downstairs. Jacques was not in the bathrooms, the refectory, library nor anywhere to be found, but we did meet one of the masters on his way to seek us out.

'Boys, you must stay in your rooms,' he said, and turned us in the other direction.

We were boys again whereas the night before we had been men; clearly a signal that something was very wrong. Diggs protested, but one master was joined by another, and then Matron who marched us back to the tower as though we were leads or coppers, and left us there with strict instructions to remain.

We watched from the window as the body, still covered, was taken away, and even Hunter joined us, for we were all concerned. Concerned is too gentle a word. We paced, glanced below, paced some more, looked into the corridor, impatient and afraid. Being Sinford's men, we did not panic or abandon our decorum to wild keening and histrionics, but little was said during that waiting time, and I am sure that had I spoken, one of the others would have charged at me. Diggs later admitted to feeling the same. Not knowing is the worst of all punishments.

Our fears were well-founded. An hour after the ambulance left, Mr Hogg, the housemaster, came and told us to gather in the common room. There, we joined the few others who had remained for Praemisit, and it was there, on battered sofas lit by dust-filled beams of morning sunlight, we were told that Jacques Verdier was dead.

* * *

This was a more interesting story than the last one, Jack thought, as he broke off reading to watch Havegood swill his glass and swig his brandy. The man had tears in his eyes, and Jack was not surprised. The same had happened to him when he watched Grandad Reggie die and later, Grandma Ida.

Jimmy, though, maintained a disinterested expression, and flipped the page to see there was nothing on the other side. 'I assume there was an inquest?'

'There was. We had to stay at Sinford's a few more days to give evidence, although it was no longer a place any of us wanted to be. From my notes, you will have gathered that Diggs and I felt very strongly for our friend, and to have him taken from us for no reason...' Breaking off, he pinched his eyes, and exhaled, loudly. 'I believe all of us, masters and matrons included, remained shocked for the days between the accident and the inquest, and beyond.'

'There is always a reason for death,' Jimmy said, and Jack thought it unkind. 'You wrote about him feeling low at the start of that term. Was it suicide?'

'No. At first, it was considered a suicide, but the inquest concluded it was an accident.' Havegood sniffed and searched for a handkerchief. Having dabbed his eyes, he said, 'We who lived in Grace Tower that year were asked a hundred questions about the night and the weeks leading up to it. Diggs and I could only say that Jacques had begun the term with melancholy, but ended it as happy as he'd always been. I was quizzed beyond belief, as were my friends, and Hunter in particular as the study mate, and all evidence was taken, written down and presented. We were in the courtroom for the inquest, but were not called to speak. Our statements sufficed. A terrible time, Mr Wright.'

'I'm sure. But the verdict was accidental death?'

'It was. There was nothing to suggest suicide. The investigating officers measured the height and depth of the crenellations, and decided it would be possible to fall by accident had one been sitting on them and leaning backwards. Diggs and I were able to say that Jacques always sat against the chimney to smoke his pipe, or lay on the stone to see the stars as we all did. Of course, I said nothing about the depth of our friendship, only that it was long-standing and firm, and neither Diggs nor I mentioned our relationship. It was an irrelevance. In fact, friendships never entered the minds of the police who were more interested in what we had seen and heard on the evening before Jacques...' Another sniff and another swig of brandy. 'We were not able to tell them anything other than the time we parted and went to our studies and beds.'

'I assume you have told us all of this because the anniversary of this man's death is approaching, and you think...'

'That Diggs intends to kill himself on the thirty-first. The anniversary of the tragedy.' Havegood swallowed. 'Yes. And you will ask me why.'

'I was about to.'

'I have two thoughts. One might assume that Diggs had something to do with the tragedy and has lived with guilt for all this time, but I find that highly unlikely.'

'Why?'

'I have no evidence to suggest he was involved, Mr Wright, but if that was the case, he has hidden his guilt from me for the last twelve years.'

'Perhaps he feels he could have prevented the fall, and the guilt caused by that has caught up with him,' Jimmy said, scribbling.

'I think his disappearance has more to do with circumstances of late,' Havegood said, and drained his glass. 'I have written of our schooldays to provide an understanding of how much we, as a group, cared for each other. I apologise that they were somewhat self-indulgent. My ramblings, however, are sincere. I bring the tragedy into them because I believe his recent bereavements have rekindled his memory, and the combination of now and then is what has led Diggs to want to end his life. As he hints in the letter, he may believe that his wife and child's deaths were God's revenge for his past. I refer to his infliction of loving men, myself in particular.'

'Who knows what it takes for a man to decide to bring about his own end,' Jimmy said. 'I'm sure you have no part to play in it, and my advice would be not to allow your thoughts to travel on that road.'

'They already have.' Havegood drew his hands down his wasted body, making it clear he was suffering guilt as much as his missing friend. 'I have one more piece of writing which explains more recent and relevant events,' he went on. 'This may help you appreciate the unfortunate state of Diggs' mind a little more. I am sorry to do it this way, but…'

'I understand.' Jimmy took the page. 'I expect I will have plenty to ask you shortly. You save your strength.'

July 1880 to July 1892

When we left Sinford's, it was as hurriedly as possible, and I was grateful. All of us were keen to be away from the place and the scene of the tragedy. That summer, Diggs and I had intended to take a tour to see Italy and Greece, but this, we delayed. It was wrong to continue as if nothing had happened, and I spent the summer at home, gradually accepting that Jacques had left us, and trying to fathom the reason. Diggs wrote often, and I replied, and we met once or twice before going up to Cambridge.

There, we spoke little of what had happened. I could see that it upset Diggs as much as it upset me, and I avoided the subject whenever possible. Other undergrads, having heard of the tragedy, were prone to ask questions, but these were quickly put down, and most men respected our desire for silence on the subject.

The months passed, Diggs and I remained as strong as ever, which gave me hope for a future with him, though how we could achieve it was another matter. We debated long into the night about the injustices of our society, as undergrads do, discussed the works of the philosophers and particularly the early Greeks and the Sacred Band of Thebes, how some civilisations accepted men could love men, and how others found it abhorrent. We pulled apart sapphic poetry, for which I cared not one iota, and delved into the reasoning of everyone from Dee to Marx. At no point could we see how the two of us might live as we wanted to, as a household, as, I suppose, a couple. Not without incurring the wrath of the church, the shackles of the law and the scorn of our peers. Naturally, we remained quiet on this matter, though there were others in our colleges and quads who were of the same inclination. There was even an underground society to which we briefly belonged, but word reached the Dean, and he sent us hurrying back to 'acceptable' behaviour on the threat of being sent down.

It was inevitable, then, that Diggs and I as a pair came adrift, and it was also inevitable that this should be a mutual decision. Expectations drew us apart as he, on his family's instruction, began to attend the London season to search for a wife, and I, on my family's insistence, spent my vacations in similar, though more aristocratic circles. Diggs' family was on the edge of society, and his mother, a widow, was keen to fully enter it. Without a title, however, that was a hard task, and, so far, she has not succeeded.

We remained in touch with letters, and we kept a promise we made after our education was done with; we would meet at least once each year. This date we set to be the last day of July. The day Jacques Verdier's life ended and ours changed. No matter where in the world, we would move heaven and earth to meet on that date, to raise a glass to our dear friend, to appreciate what we had in our lives, and to experience once again, the kind of intimate friendship we had once enjoyed.

We would laugh when we met and remembered how Jacques was the only pupil at Sinford's never to have a nickname and never to have slept with another student. (I am sure he was *not* the only one; it was a youthful jest.) These discussions happened after we had thrown our inhibitions to the wind and drunk too much wine at the hotel, for it was always a hotel and always a different one. Although, booking separate bedrooms, one of us would have to return to his room early the next morning and make it appear as if it had been used.

These two-handed reunions were a joy. Always, and for both of us. Until last year.

1891

Last year's reunion was the first to bring any change. We met at a hotel in town, and had dinner during which we exchanged news. I was able to tell Diggs of my new role at the Board of Trade, having worked up from a junior position to one of authority, and he was congratulatory and happy for me. For my part, however, I could sense that something was amiss with him, and had I paid more attention to his correspondence, I might have seen the clues. Where his letters had been addressed from his family home in Buckinghamshire, since March of that year, they had come from a London address. Maybe I had seen this and simply thought he had moved to be nearer to his work, but he told me that he had a new home for a very important reason.

Simon Diggory Stape had married.

On hearing the news, I was immediately struck down with a sense of betrayal; someone else had enjoyed intimacy with my special friend, and he and I would no longer know the pleasures of our youth. Then, having laid on him false congratulations and sentiments of joy, I realised that those sentiments were, in fact, genuine. As before, inevitability was the watch word, and I found it surprisingly easy to accept that Diggs was now a husband. I wasn't even upset that I had not been invited to the ceremony, not when he told me he had kept it a secret because his mother did not approve of the woman he had fallen in love with.

'To fall in love with a woman is different than falling in love with a man,' he said, over our cigars in a private corner of the hotel's smoking room. 'There is no challenge, as there was with you. There is no thrill of clandestineness, no sharing of the confidences needed to exist in secret. To be accepted in society is altogether too prosaic. Don't think that, because I pretend to love this woman, I no longer harbour greater feelings of love for you. We shall continue to meet once a year at least. This, I vow to Caesar.'

My nickname had persisted even into the first years of our third decade.

'I am happy for you,' I said, and I meant it. 'But *will* we be able to meet?'

'I am not letting a woman prevent me from being with my friend,' he said. 'The hours I spend with you are the most precious, and not only because of the...' A waiter was passing, and Diggs pointed to the ceiling and our rooms above. 'What happens upstairs is the icing on the cake, as the newspapers are now writing. We vowed we would remain together through life, and our lives are far from over.'

He had imparted his message, my initial shock was doused by the waters of his sincerity, and I knew we would continue as we always had, only, there would be a Mrs Stape, and she, the poor thing, would unknowingly be a cover for her husband's true self.

Despite the change in Diggs' situation, last year's meeting was one of the best, the most passionate and loving, and that, I think, was because he wanted to show me how even a marriage of expectation could not keep us apart.

We did part, of course. The next day, we went our ridiculous ways. Ridiculous because he worked not five miles from where I worked, and lived no more than ten from where I live, and yet, we would not see each other again for another year. Not unless some society event brought us together, in which case we would be alumni of Sinford's reminiscing about the old days, taking brandy, and guffawing at the world with the other men, all the while desperate to be alone together.

I heard from Diggs again in February this year, when he wrote to tell me he was to be a father, and the child was expected in July. *How wonderful it would be if it is a boy and born on that date,* he wrote. *If fortune rewards me, and that happens, he will, of course, be named Jacques Marcus. Or should I call him Caesar?*

That news imparted, I heard nothing about him until one day earlier this month, while idly browsing the newspaper at my desk, I read an obituary of Mrs Daphne Stape, nee Arrowsmith, of Clapham Park. Diggs' wife died in premature childbirth, and tragically, so did the child, a boy.

SIX

'You now know why I am certain Diggs intends to kill himself, and you have all the reasons and details,' Havegood said, when Jack and Jimmy finished reading. 'I have told you what I have done to find him, and you know when he intends to carry out his act.'

'We do,' Jimmy said, rubbing his eyes. 'What we don't know is where he is, or where he will be in seven days' time.'

'Which is why I came to you.'

'Quite. Just two more questions for you, Mr Havegood, if I may. Unless Merrit has anything to ask?'

A clock chimed somewhere, but Jack didn't count the number. He was too occupied trying to make up something useful to say, but came up with nothing, and said, 'Not right now,' because it sounded better than a flat no.

'In which case, Sir, I would like to ask you to make a list of as many contacts for Mr Stape as you can, with addresses if possible, but I understand if you don't know too much detail.'

'Of course,' Havegood said. 'Although my resources are exhausted.'

'No harm in us having another go,' Jimmy smiled. 'As for the second question, would you be available to stay for dinner?'

If Jack was surprised at the question, so was Havegood.

'You invite me to dine, Sir?' he said. 'Is this because you think I need feeding or because you believe I can actually eat?'

'Both,' Jimmy said. 'But mostly so we can discuss your case in more detail. A friend is joining me, so with the Merrit brothers, we will be five. My friend is a doctor, and as well as being a gifted physician and surgeon, he is also a man who studies the mind. He will be invaluable in helping us understand Mr Stape's mental state. That is, if you are willing to discuss the case in front of him. As he is a doctor, you can be assured of confidentiality.'

It was hard to tell if Havegood was considering the offer or suffering pain, his expression could have signalled either.

'I asked the housekeeper from next door to provide for us,' Jimmy said, indicating his machine. 'She has agreed, so we can expect a fine meal, which you don't have to eat if you can't face it. The purpose is to give us the opportunity to consider facts and possibilities in a less formal environment than my office.'

'It is very kind of you, Mr Wright, but I am not dressed.'

'An informal evening. Just men. No need to dress.'

'But I fear I shan't be good company.'

'Are you concerned about the doctor being there?'

'No, it sounds like a very good idea, but fatigue, you see...'

'Ah, in that case, you are welcome to use a spare room until then. Refresh yourself, sleep, whatever you need. When you have Delamere detectives on your side, you have every comfort, kindness and expertise included in the fee.'

So he should at that price, Jack thought, wondering what Jimmy was playing at.

'You mean, we delay the interrogation until this evening?'

'I do, Mr Havegood, though it will be more of a chat than an interrogation.' Jimmy was writing again, though this time, not in his casebook. 'To wait will give you respite from this matter for a few hours of comfort, followed by a fine meal during which we can discuss whatever you are comfortable discussing, and after which, Pascoe will find you a cab to drive you home.'

Knightsbridge to Hampstead; five shillings, was Jack's first thought, immediately replaced by, why the invitation?

Havegood gave a brief huff of laughter, the first sign of good humour he had shown since he arrived. 'You drive a tempting bargain, Mr Wright,' he said. 'I like you. I also like the stoic silence of your assistant, a man whose features would have stood him in good stead at Sinford's.'

Unsure if that was an insult, a compliment, or if the withered man was flirting, Jack made a mental note to ask Will what stoic meant.

'I accept,' Havegood said, and reached for his cane as Jack reached for the bell pull. 'If you have no objections, I will retire, and see if I can doze. I already feel the first signs of hope, Mr Wright, and that is thanks to you. At this rate, I shall be eating and sleeping properly within a few days.'

'Let's hope so. You'll find writing materials in your room. Please think of anywhere we might make enquiries.'

'Of course. I only hope we are not too late.'

'It's highly unlikely Mr Stape will have yet done anything drastic,' Jimmy said, his smile still apparent. 'He has set himself a poignant anniversary, and the date has meaning for him. To take his own life on any other would be pointless. Ah, here's Pascoe. Let's make you comfortable, and we will resume this at dinner. Shall we say seven?'

'What did you make of all that?' Jimmy asked when Max had taken the client away.

'Sounds like the poor man's desperate to find his old mate, and the other bloke wants to top himself because he's ashamed of what they did at school. Mind you, I didn't get half the words.'

'Don't worry about that. Our job is to find this Mr Stape, and to do that, we need a plan. Your first lesson, Jack, is to listen, make notes, and then think how to proceed. We'll learn more at dinner, but for now, we need to decide the way ahead.'

'Do you always ask your clients to stay and eat?'

'No, but I want to spend more time with Mr Havegood in a less formal setting. I think he may speak more.'

'And the doctor? Is that because you want to make sure he's not barmy?'

Jimmy looked up from where he'd been writing, his mouth in a crooked grin.

'Barmy?' he chuckled. 'No, I don't think he's barmy, but he might not yet feel able to tell us everything.'

'You think he's lying? Why should a man lie about having feelings for another man? If anything, he should lie about *not* having them.'

Jimmy must have seen Jack's confusion, because he pointed to the chair beside the desk and invited him to move closer.

'Not lying,' he said. 'Havegood is probably telling us the truth, but we can't always take what a client says at face value. Very often, there is more to a case than the client has thought of. That's your second lesson, Jack. Don't trust anyone, not even your client.'

'That don't sound very nice.'

Jimmy rested back in his chair, idly swinging it left and right, with his pen held between the middle fingers of each hand, and his lips pursed in thought.

'You're a trusting man, aren't you?' he said, and Jack shrugged. 'That's a good quality, usually, but if you're to be an investigator, you have to be more cynical.'

'I'll ask Will to look it up.'

'Put it this way, why do you think Mr Havegood looks like a skeleton and no longer a captain of sports?'

'Like he said, because he's worried. I don't feel like eating when I get worried. When Grandad Reggie was dying, and my wages from the docks weren't enough to keep us all, I didn't sleep through worrying. Anyways, perhaps he gave up sports. Twelve years is a long time ago.'

'Possibly, but I think you're right. He is worried.'

'There you go then.'

'But is he worried enough about a man he has only seen off and on for those twelve years? How worried would you be if someone from your past disappeared and sent a letter suggesting he intends to commit suicide? What would you do?'

Jack scratched behind his ear where the clammy afternoon had dampened his skin, and pondered the question.

'Twelve years ago, I would have been thirteen and working at East India Dock. The only people I knew was family and them in my street, and they was coming and going all the time. The Jewish families who brought their friends over from wherever they came from... We'd meet them, Ida would invite them in for tea, they'd get to know us, and then they'd be off to some other part of town, and we'd never see them no more. Then, there was the tars who'd come in off the ships, take rooms at the pub down the road, and play ball in the street with me and Will and the other lads. We'd get on alright with them, then they'd bugger off back on the ship. So, I can't tell you, Jimmy. I ain't never had a friend like the one our client's talking about. Come to that, I ain't had many letters of any sort neither.'

'Yeah, but what do you think you would do if you got a letter like this one? Who would you tell?'

'Will.'

'Mr Havegood doesn't have any brothers or sisters.'

'Then, maybe if I were a God botherer, I'd tell the vicar.'

'Good. Anyone else?'

Jack didn't feel comfortable being questioned like he was back in court, and was about to tell Jimmy so when he reminded himself he was there to learn, and assumed this was Jimmy's way of testing him.

'Police?'

'Worth a try, but no crime has been committed.'

'I don't know, Jimmy. You tell me.'

'How about Mr Stape's family? I know the brother is abroad, but he hasn't always been. Then there's the mother. Surely she would appreciate a note warning her that her son is in need?'

'Didn't he say the mother doesn't like him or something? He contacted her,

but she didn't sound interested.'

Jimmy stopped playing with his pen, and sat forward. 'Excellent,' he beamed. 'You see? You have the makings of a good investigator. You were listening.'

'That's what you told me to do.'

'And having listened, your job is to think and ask why, but it is also to stay in the middle.'

'Of what?'

'Of the case. Don't feel sympathy for Mr Havegood, nor for Mr Stape. Don't feel revulsion at their past. Nor must you say, "Good for them for being in love," because our job is to remain impartial. To examine facts, while being suspicious of everyone and every word. That is why I invited the doctor.'

'Oh? So you hadn't already arranged that?'

'No, I messaged him while we were talking. Markland will be here later, and I'll brief him before the meal. Before then, though, I need to draw a plan.'

'Dalston's your one for drawing plans and stuff,' Jack said. 'Shall I go find him?'

'Not that kind of plan. I'll write up a strategy of action for us both. Logical order is key. For background, I want to know more about the school in case there was anyone there who might be able to help us. There were other students. Where are they? That's a job for Will. While he's doing that, we'll visit Stape's last known address, see if we can get in, speak to the neighbours, and find out when Stape was last seen. We need to write to his workplace and his mother, telegraph his brother in America, whatever we can think of. At the same time, I want a professional opinion on Havegood's state of mind as much as Mr Stape's. Now then. I expect, you want to make sure your horses are alright.'

Was that a brushoff or was Jimmy thinking aloud? Thinking aloud, Jack decided, because he'd just given him a job that had nothing to do with horses.

'So, you want Will to find out what we can about Sinford's?'

'Yes. We need to know why it closed, what it is now, and where it is, so we can visit. Lesson number three. It's always useful to visit the scene of a crime, even years later.'

'What crime? Oh, you mean two blokes fucking?'

Jimmy spluttered, but when he recovered, he grinned.

'Do you think that's a crime?' he said with his blond eyebrows arched.

'Yeah... Well, no. I mean, it is, we all know that, but it shouldn't be. It would have been at his school same as it is anywhere. He said they had to keep it all secret. But you want us to go and take a look at the place, see where these two blokes... did their stuff, and then what?'

'Not exactly what I was getting at,' Jimmy said, and his grin became something more serious. 'I want to get a feel for the past, and seeing the school will help. Also, there may still be people in the area who remember the old pupils. Every scrap of detail may produce a lead. But...' he leant forward, '...do you see two men being together in that way as wrong?'

'Obviously I don't, not inside this house. You've all made it clear we're in the same club when it comes to that. Except Will, of course. And Max. Possibly. Who knows?'

'And, like them, you aren't offended by the way we are?'

'No.'

'Because you are the same.'

'Yeah.'

'Only, less experienced.'

Jack's experience consisted of giving one man two minutes of manual pleasure, and a far more rewarding half hour with Larkin Chase in a locked bedroom. The flash of memory brought longing, as it always did, but Jimmy's office wasn't the place to talk about that time. They might be overheard, and he wasn't sure where Jimmy was leading. The conversation had nothing to do with the case and was becoming embarrassing.

'I suppose I'd like to get more experience one day,' he whispered.

'What you getting at?'

'To understand a client, you have to think like a client,' Jimmy said. 'We'll come back to this as we go along. I know I was right to employ you, Jack. We're going to work well together both on and off the case, and I'm looking forward to spending more time with you. It'll be good to share my experience and show you how I do things. I can give you some tips and tricks. You have big potential, and will do well, if you're willing to put yourself in my hands.'

There was something in the way Jimmy spoke that convinced Jack he was hiding another meaning beneath his words, and needing time to think about what he might have been suggesting, he said, 'Alright,' as he stood to leave. 'I better go and see to the horses.'

His skin was hot, and his mind was misbehaving, leaping from Jimmy's undeniably handsome face to salacious thoughts of them in bed together, and the only way to distract himself, was to think of Shadow and how her mane was regrowing. The sudden image of him, Jimmy and a bedroom had no place in his day, and with half of him confused about the case, and the other half excited about it, he left to tend to the stables.

SEVEN

The sun was heading towards setting, and the garden doors of the book room were open, letting in birdsong and the fragrant smell of the garden. Delicate white curtains drifted in a breeze, and the light poured down from above them in blue streams through the coloured glass of the upper windows and fell on tables and cases, carpets and cabinets.

Jack leant on the doorjamb with his arms folded and, concerned how Will was coping with his new job, watched him working. His brother wandered among the shelves, returning to a central table to point at an open ledger before collecting another book or folder from a case and placing it beside those he'd already collected.

Will was, as always, precise, but the sheer number of books and their variety was overwhelming for Jack, let alone someone who had problems accepting that not everything could be the same height and thickness. Concerned that Will wouldn't be able to cope with accepting the amount of information he had to examine, remember where it was and how he might sort through it, Jack was determined to keep a close eye. Staying at Delamere depended on their working well, and whereas Jack already felt more confident within himself, he was less sure about Will.

A FALL FROM GRACE

This was not a sight he had ever expected to see. It was so far removed from their two rooms in Limehouse, where Will's precious reading had to be kept on the floor and avoided as the family moved around the piles as though they were a priceless collection in a museum. There was no racket from warring neighbours or the strange woman upstairs, no call of children playing in the street, or the claxons of steamers and the bells of clippers in the docks. There were no shadows cast by tall chimneys and unforgiving brick warehouses, and no stink of refineries or factories. Just peace and lavish beauty a man from Limehouse could only read about in pamphlets, assuming that man had been taught to read, and could afford to buy a pamphlet.

'Are you spying or detecting?' Will said without looking up from his work. His voice was nearly lost in the vast chamber.

'Just seeing how you're doing.' Jack sauntered closer. 'Everything alright?'

'No, not everything is alright. I doubt the situation in The House of Commons is particularly *alright*, as Lord Salisbury fights for his seat, with Mr Gladstone straining at his leash. If you meant the situation in Africa being any more settled between the Congo Free State and...'

'You know what I mean.'

'Yes, Jack. I am alright. Whoever organised this library before me made an almost good job of it.' Will glanced up, gave Jack a once over, and looked down again. 'Meant to say, nice suit. We must make sure we repay Mr Chase as soon as we receive our first wages.'

The name wasn't out of place in such a magnificent room, and Jack imagined Larkin alongside Will, poring over the volumes, enjoying the smell of leather and paper, and muttering about authors. Larkin wouldn't be so engrossed in his work, though, he'd have eyes on Jack, and Jack would be studying him, knowing what he was thinking and thinking the same thing. Larkin would excuse himself from the task, and passing Jack, whisper, 'The room opposite mine, Mr Merrit?' Jack would follow, and as soon as they were alone...

'Hello? Are you in there?'

Will was waving in his face.

'What?'

'I said, what do you want? Have you finished your interview?'

63

'If you can call it that. Yeah. The client's gone up to get some rest, and he's staying for dinner. There's a doctor coming, and you've got to be there as well.'

Will gave him another up and down and shook his head. 'Look at you,' he said. 'Clients, dinners with doctors? I hope our new-found good luck won't spoil the Jack Merrit I know.'

'Or be too much for the Will Merrit I have to put up with.'

Will closed his eyes, gave a gentle shake of the head, and hissed as though he'd just sucked on a lemon.

'Your assisting has come to an end,' he said, resuming his work. 'Having delivered your message, you are off to see to your horses.'

'How do you know?'

'It's obvious. What time is dinner, and where?'

'Seven, in the posh dining room, I suppose, but I've got to be there early to meet the doctor. Jimmy needs to talk to him before Havegood comes down.'

'Then away to your stable, Jack, and leave me in peace. I have found some information about the school, but there should be more. However, what exists appears to be buried within other works, and there is no single book.'

Will set off to the far end of the room, and Jack left him to it, happy, that for the time being, he was managing. Reggie and Ida would have been pleased with them both, and Will had been right. They had stumbled on good fortune, but it wouldn't have come about had it not been for Larkin Chase. The mention of his name had set his imagination running, and it kept pace as he left the library through the garden doors and crossed the terrace.

Who'd ever have thought Jack Merrit would have a garden to walk in, let alone a terrace to cross? Come to that, who'd have thought he would be paid to care for three horses, to drive expensive wagons, and sit with a detective before investigating a missing person? Life had often dealt him unexpected turns, but usually unhappy ones; his mother abandoning them when he was too young to remember; his father doing the same later, to take up a career on the music-hall stage and appear with the likes of Marie Lloyd and Lottie Collins, only to drop dead during a performance; learning the cabbie's knowledge in one year, only to find himself wanted by East End criminals. This current turn on the map of his life was as welcome as it was unexpected, but even though he was happy to embrace it, it was still hard to believe his luck, or his fate, or whatever it was that brought him to a stable yard on the edge of Hyde Park on a summer afternoon with a dinner to look forward to and a case to solve.

'How on earth, eh, Shadow?' he mused after an hour of brushing her.

The regrowth of her mane was going to be slow, the animal doctor had said when Jack collected her from the livery stable. 'Expect one inch per month with this breed, and there's nothing you can do to hurry it. Be patient,' had been the man's advice. The expert's payment had come from Larkin Chase, as had the payment for Shadow's own stall, better feed, and extra exercise. More favours that Jack would one day repay. Thanks to him, Shadow was healthy, but also thanks to him, Jack was lost.

'Well, not lost as such,' he told his horse, as the curry comb glided over her shoulder. 'More like, not knowing where I'm going.'

Shadow snorted, as if she was laughing.

'Yeah, you're right. A cabbie who don't know where he's going. What use is that? No, I meant me and Larkin was getting on alright, weren't we? Yeah, we're not the kind of pair you'd think would hitch up easy like a hansom to a horse, but I thought it were going that way. I won't tell you what we done, because you're not old enough, but we done it, and he asked me to stay. Said he'd like to have me there. Then, after the court thing, one letter and nothing else.'

Shadow shuffled her feet, either to ask for the brushing to continue, or because Jack wasn't being honest.

'Sorry. Yeah, you're right,' he said, attending to her flank. 'It's my fault. He said he'd be there if I wanted to go back, but then all this happened. I got a job, a decent one, and an exciting one. Yeah, I miss the driving, but I still get to do some, and Joe's teaching me to ride.'

Another snort and a shuffle.

'Not you, old girl, don't worry, but your new mates, Shanks and Emma. They've been trained to take a saddle.'

On hearing their names, the pair in the next stall pricked up their ears.

'Oi, she's as good as you two,' he told them, and lowered his voice to Shadow. 'Purse-proud beasts, them two. Take no notice. To be honest with you, girl, it ain't that I don't want to see Larkin again and find out where all that might lead, it's... and you got to keep this to yourself... it's because of Jimmy. I know Dalston said he's got a friend in Cornwall, and they've been together nearly four years, but he also said they don't see each other a lot, and they ain't getting on too well. Then, see, Jimmy was talking earlier like he was hinting at something. Talking about giving me tips and tricks and me putting myself in his hands. Reminded me of when Larkin said he was going to thrust his insistence on me, like he was telling me a dirty message. Only, I didn't mind it being dirty. Rather hoped it was.'

Shadow turned her head to throw him a look of disapproval, and stepped up to her water.

'Sorry, I'll keep me mouth shut if it upsets you, but if it's there, wouldn't you take it? Jimmy's a good-looking fella, and he's really easy to get on with. Seems to like me, too, so, I reckon... Anyways, if they're both on offer, who do I choose?'

'If two things are equally offered, you choose whichever you want.'

For a second, Jack imagined Shadow had a voice, but it was Will, leaning on the lower stable door.

'I know you're safe here, Jack, but you should still take care with your words. I could have been anyone.'

Annoyed with himself for being caught talking soft, Jack brushed harder, and Shadow snorted her approval.

'What you come for?'

'To tell you it's time to get ready for dinner. Mr Wright's doctor friend has arrived, and Max asked me to come and fetch you. Wash your hands, and be in the parlour in fifteen minutes.'

'They call it a drawing room, Will.'

'And I say the breakfast room is the drawing room because that is the room where Mr Blaze draws. There is a small army of women downstairs with a nice lady from next door putting things in the oven. Your client is expected to come down soon, and Mr Wright wants you.'

Jack finished his brushing and threw a blanket over Shadow. All three horses had feed and water, and with nothing else needing to be done, he hung his cap and apron. He was crossing the yard when Will said something that lifted his pensive mood and reset his mind.

'Whatever you decide to do will be the right choice, and I will stand by you,' he said as he held the back door for Jack to pass through. 'For now, though, may I suggest you concentrate on your case, and try not to worry too much about your feelings for Mr Chase, or your desires for Mr Wright? These matters will resolve themselves in time, but you must make a good impression tonight. I am here when you need an ear, and you will get more sensible replies from me than you will from a horse. Wipe your feet.'

Feet wiped, hands washed, hair and tie straightened, and all checked by his brother, Jack made his way upstairs to the hall, where Will left to help Max in the dining room. The drawing room was another unnecessarily large place decorated with ornaments and paintings, and another place it had taken Jack the last two weeks to accept. Without Jimmy's help and Max's tutoring, he'd never have known how to behave and talk in such a magnificent house, but he had been practicing, and when he entered to find Jimmy and another gentleman talking, he thought it would be an easy job to fit in.

Just because a man thought something would be straightforward didn't mean it would be; a lesson Jack had learnt years ago at the West India docks. The owner wanted this, but the foreman expected that, and the other workmen had their ways of doing it which didn't match any instructions. Jimmy had said his friend was a doctor, there to assess Mr Havegood's physical and mental state, and Jack expected to listen to the learned man talk about ailments and disorders.

After Jimmy introduced them, however, the first words the doctor said were, 'You look like you could anchor a long one at the crease. I doubt you'd ever be castled by a yorker.'

There was a long pause of expectation before Jimmy said, 'The doctor is a keen cricketer.'

Not knowing how to reply, Jack could only offer a dull, 'Oh.'

'I've briefed him on Havegood's story,' Jimmy went on. 'And I have drawn my plan, which you and I will discuss tomorrow. All you have to do tonight is remember what Havegood says, and hold in your mind anything you think we need to talk about later.'

'Alright.'

'Jack will make a fine investigator,' Jimmy told the doctor who was fishing something from his wine glass with a finger. 'Recently tracked down a gang of thieves I was commissioned to catch. Did my job for me. Fine man.'

A heavy slap on Jack's back caused him no pain, only embarrassment. It had been Will and Larkin who had found the Flay gang, all Jack did was run to the police and identify the criminals. It didn't seem appropriate to say so, and the doctor didn't look interested, he was examining whatever he had pulled from his drink using a pair of spectacles attached to his ears by a cord. Like Larkin, he had a well-kept moustache, but it was thicker and darker, and twitched more as he contemplated his find.

'Liquid in the lungs,' the doctor said. 'Simple case of accidental drowning.' Looking at Jack with surprise, he said, 'Hello. Philip Markland. You are?'

'Er, Jack Merrit. Mr Wright just told you.'

'Did he? Did you, Jimmy? Why didn't you say so?'

'You are with us this evening, aren't you, Doc?' Jimmy smirked, and with no thought for politeness, said, 'Doc Markland is a genius, but he lives in a world of his own unless he's saving a life or is in his box at Lords. You'll get used to him.'

Jack wasn't so sure about that.

'So, you have a man driven to self-starvation by concern,' the doctor said, picking up a conversation he must have left off before Jack arrived. 'Insomnia caused by worry is common. Unable to eat? Yes, well, when someone is in deep concern, something happens inside the body to restrict appetite or increase it, and we have yet to understand why or how. There may be another cause for his condition, of course.'

'According to him, it's pure concern,' Jimmy said. 'There's no reason to suppose otherwise. I just want to know I am not dealing with a lunatic.'

'Is he a politician?'

'No.'

'Then at least you're batting on a smooth wicket.'

Max appeared from the hall, tall and elegant in his uniform. 'Mr Havegood be on his way,' he said. 'Straight to the dining room?'

'Yes, I think so,' Jimmy replied, but before he led the doctor out, said, 'Remember, men, it's informal. We want to encourage him to talk.'

Earlier, Jimmy had said something about not taking sides or showing sympathy, and Jack told himself he would do well to remember the advice. *An open mind is better than an open book*, was one of Granddad Reggie's odd expressions, and also seemed apt as they crossed the hall to the dining room. *Keep quiet, watch and remember;* that was all he had to do.

Will was taking a slow walk around the dining table, straightening the cutlery and touching the wine glasses with a finger to move them a tiny distance to bring them in line. On seeing the men, he stood back, and neatened his already neat lapels, appearing to be half a waiter and half a dinner guest. Whatever he was, he didn't look out of place.

The men talked about the weather, and Jimmy asked after the horses, so when Havegood arrived, he walked into a congenial atmosphere of men discussing nothing of any importance. Jimmy introduced him to the doctor, and Havegood regarded him suspiciously at first, as if he had been expecting an instant medical examination and was waiting for criticism. After they had shaken hands, Markland asked him if he enjoyed cricket, and as it was something Havegood was keen on, any uncertainty he'd shown evaporated. Although he relied on his cane, and his suit hung from his body, he was no longer unsteady on his feet, and when Jimmy asked if he had rested, he said he had, and admitted to being less agitated than before.

'You really have been most kind and understanding, Mr Wright,' he said. 'I feel as though I am at a hotel.'

With the amount he'd agreed to pay for Jimmy's services, Jack wasn't surprised. The excess of entertainment continued when Max appeared with a maid, and the men sat to be served with a fine meal that put even Joe's cooking to shame.

'The doctor runs Lord Clearwater's charitable mission in Cheap Street,' Jimmy explained once they were into their first course and the mundane niceties had been exhausted. 'He has some knowledge of the conditions you are suffering, and the behaviour you described in your friend Mr Stape. Do you mind if I show him the letter you received?'

'When helping Mr Wright with a case, I apply the Hippocratic oath to evidence as much as I do to patients,' the doctor said. 'Confidentiality is my middle name. Actually, it's Cedric, but I think you see the end I am bowling from.'

Havegood smiled at the man's eccentricity. 'I have no objection,' he said. 'Let's to business.'

Jimmy handed the letter to Markland, who spent some time searching his chest and pockets, until Will, beside him, lifted his spectacles from his ear, and placed them on his nose.

'How kind,' the doctor said, and read the page. 'Fascinating,' was his verdict as he passed it back.

'Fascinating, why?'

Markland didn't answer, but aimed his attention across the table to Havegood. 'I can see why you are concerned for your friend's state of mind, but can you tell me your thoughts?'

'I can, Doctor, because I have no-one else to turn to.'

'You have all of us,' Jimmy said. 'Please, be as open as you can.'

'I have little to go on,' Havegood continued. 'Only the way the letter is written. Such writing is out of character for Mr Stape, a man usually of the most positive nature.'

'Have you met with him recently?' Markland persisted. 'Have you seen any physical signs of melancholia?'

'Sadly, I have not seen him for some time. When last we met, he appeared as happy as he always was, but that was before the family tragedy.'

Havegood recounted the story of how the wife and child had died in childbirth, and as he listened, Markland's top lip tightened in thought, and half of his moustache disappeared into his mouth. The meal continued, and Jimmy asked questions, diverting Havegood's attention from Will who was picking apart a bread roll and arranging the pieces at the edge of his plate. Even when Jack nudged him, Will continued to reorganise his food before eating its components in alphabetic order.

Havegood ate a reasonable amount of the first course, but refused the second, stating he had never been keen on braised beef, and preferred to keep his appetite for the dessert. Jimmy let him ramble when Markland asked more questions, and as Havegood's dialogue became more liberated, Jack noticed his hands no longer trembled, and his voice became stronger. By the time the dinner was complete, he said he had given as much information as Jimmy and the doctor could extract, and at no time did he appear unnerved or reticent in telling his story.

'I must say, Mr Wright, I have never attended such a relaxed evening,' Havegood said, putting aside his pudding after one spoonful. 'I feel... hopeful. I must admit to arriving as a sceptic with my heart as hopeless as my appetite, but as I have been made welcome enough to pour the angst from the depths of my soul, I can think of no-one better to turn to on this matter.'

'You have nothing to worry about,' Jimmy said. 'We'll report back to you immediately we have confirmation of Mr Stape's address. Mr Merrit the younger is already working on it.'

That was news to Jack who thought Will had been investigating the school.

'I have directories lined up ready to investigate, and I came across what I can only call a hoard of newspapers dating back some time. They won't be of much use unless Mr Stape did anything newsworthy...?' The question was aimed at Havegood, who shook his head. 'Then, it will be the various listings to check, and visits to family and friends to make. Correct, Mr Wright?'

'Correct,' Jimmy said. 'But that's for me and Jack to see to.' To Havegood, he said, 'Maybe, as we have finished in here, you would like to sit in the drawing room with Will and give him the list of names of family and friends. You wrote them down?'

'I did.'

'Excellent. We'll join you in a minute.'

'As I said, Mr Wright. My life is in your hands, I will do whatever you ask.'

Max held his chair for him as he stood, and Will assisted him from the room, carrying a casebook under one arm, and his confidence caused Jack a tentative smile. If anyone should have been Jimmy's assistant, it was Will.

Jimmy waited until they were out of sight before asking for Markland's diagnosis.

'I don't want to cloud your judgement, Philip,' he said, pouring the doctor a lavish measure of port. 'But you must understand that although I don't know Havegood, I do care about the man. He is batting for our team if you take my meaning, and I fear he has suffered with crippling anxiety since hearing news from a man he used to be in love with.'

'Still is,' Jack put in because he wanted to contribute something.

'Indeed. Do you agree, Philip?'

'Not necessarily.'

Markland's reply took Jimmy by surprise, because he said, 'Oh? You think he has a wasting disease?'

'No. If it were that, he wouldn't be able to hide it. I agree, if he were an alcoholic the yellowing of the eyes might be associated with a dysfunction of the liver, but he only took four sips of wine through the meal, and he grimaced at each.'

'Bloody cheek,' Jimmy joked. 'Maybe he has no idea about wine. Go on.'

'The trembling you mentioned was not so evident, and if what you saw earlier today was delirium tremens, as seen in men addicted to alcohol, I would also expect to see fever-like symptoms. Sweating and confusion, at least. There is none of that, and no foul smell to his skin that I could detect.'

'But it could be something else?'

'There are many things that can cause a loss of appetite, Jimmy,' the doctor said, staring at his glass in thought. 'Many of which we don't yet fully understand. But discounting addiction to drink or opiates, which we can do because there are no physiological signs, and assuming he is not pregnant...' The doctor looked up to gauge Jimmy's reaction and found him amused. 'Thought not. Having seen no symptoms of the failure of the liver or kidneys... Oh!' Breaking off, he pulled a pocketbook from his jacket and scribbled a note.

'What is it?' Jimmy asked with hope in his voice.

'Shopping list. What were you asking?'

Markland might have been a genius doctor, but was one of the scattiest people Jack had met, and one of the funniest. Jack liked him, and Jimmy obviously did, because he wasn't annoyed as he put the doctor back on course.

'Ah yes,' Markland said, stroking his moustache and talking to himself. 'Whipworms would do it, but they are only found in dogs.' A few more seemingly random ideas were offered to his glass before he shook his head. 'No. Nothing. In fact, after his initial nervousness, which is understandable because we are strangers, I can see no physical cause for his weight loss. It is not attributable to a disease. I would need to conduct a thorough examination, of course, and I was only able to feel his pulse briefly as we shook hands, so I cannot be as accurate as I would like.'

'I understand, Philip. But what is your diagnosis?'

'Has his hair thinned recently?'

'I didn't ask.'

'While you were concerned at the yellowing of his sclera, did you notice the depth of shadows beneath the eyes?'

'I did.'

'His skin was cold to the touch?'

'Yes.'

'And you found him irritable, lethargic and unconcerned about what is happening in his life?'

'No, not at all. He was nervous but congenial, though he did drift into melancholia. I assume that was because of his concern.'

'It's strange.' Markland took a sip of port. 'He shows some of the signs of malnutrition but not others. He shows physical symptoms which don't match his emotional condition. In my experience with the street boys of the East End, when one has no option but to starve, one of the first things to fail are the abilities to communicate and think.

Things Mr Havegood is more than capable of doing. Therefore, my diagnosis can only be...'

The doctor put down his glass and ran a finger over his moustache from one side to the other. It continued its journey, travelling over his cheek to his ear, and ending up digging into his temple. Jack assumed he was thinking how to describe Mr Havegood's condition, but Markland twisted his finger back and forth, and grinned like a lunatic.

'And that is your considered opinion is it?' Jimmy laughed. 'That the man is heading for an asylum?'

'No, sorry.' Markland's hand dropped to his lap, and the grin evaporated. 'In my opinion, Jimmy, Havegood is quite sane, but consider this. According to what you told me of his past, Havegood was a man built for naval gun running, but the person who shook my hand could hardly lift a pistol let alone the wheels of a cannon. Discounting a physical illness, and seeing no signs of madness, only leaves an emotional incapacity. His heart was as hopeless as his appetite? He was able "To pour the angst from the depths of my soul"?' Markland shook his head. 'I don't know why, of course, and my opinion is based on a visual examination only, but to me, Jimmy, that man has been starving himself for longer than a few weeks.'

EIGHT

Jack was late.

'Morning,' he said, as he hurried into the office. 'Joe had to leave early, so I did both mucking outs and feeding.'

'Only five minutes, Jack. Have a seat. There's coffee.'

Jimmy didn't look up as he scribbled away at his desk, and Jack apologised for his lateness as he helped himself to a cup.

'Joe's soon to be away on a lengthy excavation,' Jimmy said. 'Dalston's got a commission up north near the dig, so they'll both be off. If you need someone to help in the stable, just say the word.'

'Really?'

Jack had had stable hands and waterboys at Harris' yard, and it was only since coming to Delamere that he'd appreciated how much time it took to keep the horses. Even at the docks, there had been horse masters and their crews to look after the animals, and he'd taken them for granted. It wasn't because he was lazy, far from it, but if he was to help Jimmy and run the stables, an extra pair of hands would be useful.

'We have someone who covers for Joe, and he wants a more permanent position,' Jimmy said, putting aside one piece of paper and dragging across another. 'Young chap from Cheap Street. One of us. I'll have him come in and work under you.'

'Yeah?'

'It's your stable, Jack, and there's a budget for it. Besides, Joe's away more and more these days and just as occupied as you're going to be. Leave it with me.'

A terrace to cross, and now a stable hand to work for him and look after his horse? Sometimes Jack had to stop and wonder what he'd done to deserve such good fortune, and all he could come back to was, nothing.

'Are you ready, Will?'

'I am, Mr Wright,' Will beamed from his place by the chalkboard, looking every inch the eager young clerk.

'Right, gentlemen,' Jimmy said, opening his casebook. 'To this morning's business. Will has chalked up our plan of action. It reminds us of what we have to do, how we are to do it, and, should anything change, it's easy to rub out.'

Will had divided the board into columns, and given them headings underlined twice, with each line being perfectly straight and the same length. He'd even placed the chalk symmetrically in the tray.

'The Route to Stape.' Jimmy read one of the titles. 'The first thing is to question the mother, and I have written asking for a visit. I've already dispatched a telegram to America to contact the brother, though I doubt he will be of any use, and I have a letter here to the neighbours in Clapham Park. Apart from his workplace, these are all the contacts Havegood was able to provide. Hopefully, we will have replies in a day or so and can make the calls.'

'I have left spaces so the results of your investigation can be noted,' Will said, bolt upright like a churchgoer standing for a vital sermon. 'I trust that is acceptable.'

'Of course. Jack and I will make the visits when we have the replies.'

'What if they don't write back?' Jack asked.

'We'll visit anyway.'

Will had written, *Inspect* beside Mr Stape's address. 'You want to get into his house?'

'Yes.'

'Alright.' Jack wasn't sure how they would do that if the man was no longer living there, but Jimmy knew his business.

'We can't do much else to locate Mr Stape until we have more information,' Jimmy went on. 'However, Will has been looking at directories and other records, and I'm going to call at his old workplace to see if they'll give me any information. If not, I might have to speak to Lord Clearwater.'

'Why?' Will asked.

'Because Stape worked for the Bank of England, and Clearwater is the fifth... No, sorry, since Lady Marshal died, the third richest nobleman in the country. If he asks the bank's board for a favour, he'll get it.'

'I don't understand how that works.' Will had started making notes in his casebook. 'All we want to know is if anyone he worked with might know where he is, correct?'

'Yes.'

'How would they? Unless he was on the board of directors, perhaps. Was he in a high position?'

'Sensible questions,' Jimmy smiled. 'And things for us to discover as soon as we can. The point is, our patron will help out if needed. So, unless either of you have any questions about those leads, we'll look at the history.'

The detective left a pause, and keen to prove he was capable of more than mucking out a stable, Jack tried to think of something sensible to ask, but came up blank.

Will said, 'No questions at this exact moment,' and Jimmy continued.

'Then, let's consider Mr Stape's letter.' It was beside him on the desk. 'Havegood also left the envelope, so I can read the postmark, and it wasn't sent from within London.'

'Oh!' Will exclaimed. 'That's a good idea. You can see where it came from, and that gives you a clue to where he is.'

'Almost right. A postmark would only tell us where it was posted from, and that's not necessarily the place the sender lives. Mr Stape knows this, but because he doesn't want to be found, he sent it within another letter via persons unknown.'

Jack was already becoming lost, and asked Jimmy to explain.

'First, the envelope.' Jimmy held it up. 'Addressed to Havegood, and sent from London West Central. So, that's no help, but then there's this.' Turning the envelope around, he used his pen to point to two small letters. 'P and F, standing for Please Forward. This tells me that this envelope was inside another, and I'd guess, one that held not only this, but a letter to the receiver asking them to drop the enclosure into a post box. Who that recipient was is anyone's guess, and we have no way of knowing.'

'But someone within the West Central area,' Jack suggested.

'Which is a large section of the city with thousands of addresses from Chancery Lane to Finsbury,' Jimmy countered. 'On top of which, the person who forwarded it might live outside the city, and happened to post it when they were in town for a day, or on their way to work. It might as well have been posted from Inverness.'

Jack felt himself blush, and decided to keep his ideas to himself.

'The envelope only tells me it was addressed in the same hand as the letter it contained.' Jimmy put the envelope aside, held up the letter, and sniffed it. 'The writing paper is no help. It could have come from any number of stationery shops anywhere in the country, and all I can tell is the words were penned sometime in the last five years. I'd need Henry Hope to run a test on the ink, but it smells metallic and smudges like Nigrosine, and that's been in use since the late sixties. The paper, however, was first produced in eighty-seven.'

'That's incredible,' Will said. 'How do you know?'

'I can tell from its watermark. Paper is one of my specialities, what with working for the post office for more years than I care to remember. The point is, we have no clues from this correspondence apart from the words. Even if I had Hope and Hyde take impressions of the fingerprints, it would only tell us if Stape touched it or not, and we have to assume he did because there are clues outside of the text.'

Jack kept his mouth shut. He'd ask later what Jimmy meant by fingerprints.

'One of the words was erased with an erasing knife,' Jimmy said. 'Erasing knives went out of fashion after the invention of vulcanised rubber in the fifties. These days, there are things that will rub out ink, although they tend to leave a mess, and rubber hasn't been used in this instance. That, gentlemen, raises another couple of questions.'

'Which are...?' Will prompted after a lengthy wait during which Jack pretended to study the chalkboard.

'Why didn't the author simply put a line through the word he wanted to change?'

'Before I guess, can you tell what that word was?'

'Actually, Will, I can.' Jimmy held it to the light. 'It is vague but still visible. Where Mr Stape wrote *my devotion of that time*, the word devotion was originally *foolishness*. Perhaps he thought Havegood would be upset at being told their relationship was foolish, and changed his mind.'

'I doubt it,' Will said, and tutted as if he was putting Jimmy down a peg. 'Mr Havegood would have been devastated to learn his lover was to take his life, so one word here and there wouldn't lessen the blow.'

'Will. Watch your tone.'

Jimmy cleared his throat and looked at Jack as if Will's forwardness was his fault. Jack raised his eyebrows and grimaced an apology as if to say, 'That's Will for you.'

'Quite,' Jimmy said. 'That's one extra clue, though. The other isn't really a clue but a confirmation. The writer was tutored in letter writing in the old-school fashion, and I say this because of the style of handwriting and the use of the erasing knife. Apart from there being no reason for anyone else to write such a thing, Stape attended the same school as Havegood, and this correction is similar to one Havegood made in his initial letter to me. They both used erasing knives instead of rubbers to make their corrections, and neither of them is in favour of crossing out. So, we can be sure the letter is genuine.'

'It looks to be an easy script to reproduce,' Will said.

'Ah, so it could be from Havegood copying his mate's handwriting,' Jack put forward without thinking.

'And what would be the point of that?'

'Just trying to help.'

'All ideas welcome at this stage,' Jimmy said. 'But I can't see why anyone would invent the potential suicide of a friend.'

'Maybe he's got another reason for trying to find him, and thought getting us to do it was the best way,' Jack countered.

'What reason?'

'I dunno. Because he wants him back.' Neither Will nor Jimmy looked convinced, so he added, 'If you love someone and they disappear, you want them back even more.'

'And you'd know this, how?'

'Because, Will, when I went to find you that morning and discovered you'd gone, I spent the rest of the day mad with fear. When the thing most dear to you vanishes without reason, you can't help but imagine the worst and make yourself sick. How did Havegood put it? Not knowing is the worst punishment of all. I know from experience, alright?'

Shamefaced, Will concentrated on his casebook, and said nothing.

'Then you understand how Havegood feels,' Jimmy said. 'That's a good thing.'

'Yeah, I do, and it ain't a nice feeling. Poor bloke, no wonder he's ill. Any longer without knowing what had happened to Will, and I'd have been the same.'

'It wasn't my fault,' Will muttered.

'Meanwhile...' Jimmy drummed the desk, bringing the exchange to a close. 'We must assume the letter is genuine. The timing of this forthcoming and alleged suicide interests me. So, while we wait for and make our visits, I want to understand more about Sinford's School, and who was there at the time Jacques Verdier died.'

'There are no listings of pupils in anything I have found,' Will said, with his eyes still in his book as if he was embarrassed to look up. 'I suppose that kind of information is private.'

'Probably,' Jimmy said. 'So, we need to find a way of tracking down Mr Hunter and anyone else who would have known Mr Stape. Perhaps he was in touch with other old boys, and one of them may have an idea where he might be.'

'How do we do that?'

'Good question,' Jimmy said, and Jack felt more useful. 'We know the school closed in...?'

'During August of eighteen-eighty,' Will said.

'And we assume the masters found other work, while the pupils were found other schools. However, those who left in the summer, like Havegood and his chums, went on to university, and he mentioned Cambridge. They must keep records of their students, and they might be of some use. That's a job for Will. I know ordinary schools are required to keep lists of pupils who come in, go through and leave, but I'm not sure about private places like Sinford's. If they exist, they may tell us how to find out what happened to this Mr Hunter and others in the same year as Stape. Perhaps he's been in touch with them. I'm also interested to know why the school closed. It's probably of no consequence, but again, any papers associated with the closure may mention people there in eighty-eight who we can also contact.'

'Water,' Will said, and pulled a wad of documents from a briefcase by his feet.

Jack hadn't noticed it before, and wondered how he'd come by it. Probably in the same way they had come by the means to hire a new stable hand; Jimmy's apparently endless supply of money.

'I don't know why the old lady who had this house kept all these in your library,' Will said, heaping yellowing newspapers on the table. 'They go back some way, and they all appear to be The Times.'

'Lady Marshall's family owned it.' Jimmy came from behind his desk, to sit closer to the table. 'She gave me the collection a couple of years back when I was investigating a case. Should we ever need them, there's a copy of most editions for the last ten years. Most are in trunks in the coach house, because they were taking up space in the cellar. What did you find?'

Will opened one of the papers and folded it back. 'The school closed at the end of summer term, eighteen-eighty,' he said, referring to the page and his casebook. 'It fell foul of the Public Health Act of eighteen seventy-five and the supply of wholesome water. According to this short report, Sinford's grounds were so remote, they took their water from a well rather than enter into the expense of running pipes from somewhere else. They had done this since the school was founded. However, the well was drying up, and there was no way of maintaining a fresh supply. They might have found a way around that, but the accident of July that year shone a torch on the place, and it came to the attention of the water authorities. The school was to be sued if it didn't adapt, and they couldn't afford to do anything but close. The report quotes some students saying how brackish the water was. Before you ask, Mr Wright, those boys aren't named, so there are no leads. There is, though, a mention of a Mr Hogg who retired when the place closed, and went to live in the nearby village of Biddenden.'

'He was a teacher, wasn't he? Havegood mentioned him.'

'He did, Jack. The housemaster of Grace Tower. It will be worth asking if he kept in contact with any old pupils or knows someone who did. I'll add him to my list of people to visit. There can't be that many Hoggs in Biddenden, wherever it is.'

'Shall I write another visit on the board, Mr Wright?'

'Yes, Will. In fact, thinking about it, instead of heading to the Bank of England today, I'll write on Clearwater paper and ask the manager if he can tell me why Stape left and when. That would probably give a better result than turning up without an arrangement. While we wait to hear, I can see if we can find this Mr Hogg.'

Will added notes to the chalkboard, and Jimmy took a large book from one of his shelves and opened it on his desk. With nothing to do but wait, Jack sat in silence, sipping his coffee and watching the detective at work. Not only had he removed his jacket against the heat of the morning, but he'd also taken off his waistcoat, and hung both at random over the back of chair. His braces hoisted the seat of his trousers as he leant over the desk, and in turn, the trousers pulled tightly across his backside, revealing curve and crevice alike. Above, his strong back arched to his wide shoulders, and the straight cut of his hair across his neck. A lighter blond than Jack's and shorter, it was the crown on a worldly and clever man. Jimmy had about him none of the raw and rough edge of a Limehouse man, not even one who managed a factory or office. There was no impatience, only understanding and kindness, and even though he was the boss, he was also the one who'd seen abilities in Jack beyond driving a cab. Whether Jack was able to live up to his expectations remained to be seen, but otherwise, what more could he want?

'Me?'

Jack's daydreaming came to an end when he realised Jimmy was talking to him.

'Sorry, what?'

'I said, want to come with me?'

'Pay attention, Jack,' Will tutted, still scratching on the board.

'Yeah, of course,' Jack said, not knowing what he had agreed to.

'Excellent. Then, you'll need to pack some things for the night, and we'll head down after lunch. We'll be back tomorrow.' Jimmy looked at his watch. 'Which means, I need to contact Cheap Street, and ask Baxter to come in to look after the stables. You can meet him when we get back.'

'Yeah, right, but sorry. What are we doing?'

'Head in a cloud,' Will said, dusting off his fingers. 'My brother's mind travels more than the hansom he used to drive.'

'And wouldn't we all like to know the destination,' Jimmy said, but Jack didn't understand. 'We'll go to Clapham Park on the way to Biddenden, and see if we can find a neighbour at home, if not, I'll drop off this letter. If we're lucky, they may know where Mr Stape is. If not, at least that's one line of enquiry crossed off the board. After, we'll go to Kent and see if we can find this Mr Hogg. We'll have to stay over, but we'll travel light and be back by tomorrow evening.'

'Is that it for now?' Will asked, dusting his hands for a second time.

'It is,' Jimmy said, returning to his chair. 'Let's meet again at lunch, and Jack and I will set off straight after. Ever been to Kent, Jack?'

'No. Never been out of London.'

'Countryside, fresh air, a village pub with private rooms.' Jimmy gave one of the biggest smiles Jack had seen him award anyone, and it was followed by a wink. 'We'll have an adventure.'

NINE

As the cab took them south towards the river, Jack did his best to ignore the idiotic way their driver dealt with junctions and corners, took a longer route than necessary, and cracked his whip more than he needed to, and waited for Jimmy to tell him what they were to do once they reached Rodenhurst Road. He'd still not said anything by the time they rolled onto the Albert Bridge, and with their destination approaching, thought it was time he asked.

'Have you done this much before?' he began, and realised it was too vague a question. 'Turn up at someone's house without warning, I mean.'

'Oh, yeah. It's simple enough. I show them my card and my letter of authorisation from Inspector Adelaide at the Met. There's never any problem.' Jimmy regarded him with a puzzled expression. 'You nervous?'

'Nervous? No.'

'You look it.'

'No, just... Well, it's all new to me, ain't it? I'm a cabbie not a copper.'

There was a companionable silence for a few hundred yards while they admired Battersea Park, then Jimmy looked at him again, and said, 'Did you mind?'

'Mind what?'

Jimmy took off his newsboy cap, ran his fingers through his locks, and frowned. 'I'm aware I made my proposition at a time when you were down on your luck,' he said, leaving Jack to wonder what proposition he was talking about. 'When I said you and Will should come and work for me, you'd only just saved your brother, he'd had a hard time, and you'd been in court. You were worried about the Flay family coming after you. I should have waited.'

'No, you're alright.' Jimmy had been good enough to show his concern, and Jack repaid him with his honesty. 'You made such an offer, of course I were going to say yes. Even if it were only to work your stables. You've given us so much else, I ain't going to throw it in your face and say, no thanks, mate, not for me. Me and Will spoke about this that first week when we was making up our mind for sure. I told him what I'll tell you; I might not be no good at it, but I'll give it me best.'

'You already are,' Jimmy said, and his eyes glinted in a stray sunbeam. 'Obviously, we're still getting to know each other, but your brother's got a fine head on him with a memory that reminds me of Clearwater's housekeeper, and you've got guts. Like I said when I hired you, this detecting lark is mainly about common sense.'

During the first week at Delamare, Jack had crept around the house not wanting to disturb anyone, and afraid he was going to do or say something wrong. Since then, however, he'd learnt to treat the house as his home, and not worry what anyone else thought of how he spoke or behaved. Except, he'd never met so many others who, like him, preferred the company of men. With so much that was new, he remained wary, and was content to watch and learn. Part of that involved asking questions at the risk of sounding foolish, a thing he was reluctant to do in front of Will, but when he was alone with Jimmy, he had no qualms.

'What's that about Clearwater's housekeeper? You mean she's as mental about being tidy as Will is?'

Jimmy gave a short laugh. 'He, not she, and yes and no.' Seeing

Jack's confusion, he explained. 'Jasper's a man about Will's age, and he's got a memory like a new Kodak, especially when it comes to music. He's just one of several talented men who live and work at Larkspur Hall, and yeah, he does keep the place well. It's more than that, though. Like Will, he has a mind for precision and observation.'

'Larkspur's your boss' country house, right?'

'Larkspur Hall is Lord Clearwater's country estate,' Jimmy said, adding, 'One of them.'

Without a thought for etiquette, because he'd never learnt any, and not bothered that the cabman above might hear, Jack said, 'That's where your special man lives, yeah?'

As soon as he'd said it, he expected Jimmy to take offence, but he simply clicked his tongue, tipped his head, and returned his gaze to the view.

'Yes,' he said, and sighed. 'But that's another story.' As if an idea had struck, he whipped back to Jack, and said in a much lighter tone, 'What's happening with you and Mr Chase?'

Jack's heart skipped at the mention of the name.

'What d'you mean?'

'Only wondered if you'd heard from him. You were getting on well when I first met you.'

'Were we?'

Jimmy said nothing, and his silence suggested Jack had to say more.

'I suppose we were,' he admitted. 'He wrote and said I was welcome any time, but I got other things on me mind. What we're doing, for a start.' A quick look at where they were, and not wanting to talk about the difficult subject of Larkin, he added, 'Not far to go.'

'Just me being inquisitive,' Jimmy said. 'Didn't mean to pry.'

'Nothing to pry into. As soon as I get paid, I'll send him the money for the togs he bought us, and that's that.'

'Send? You won't take it to him?'

'No. He won't want to see me.'

'Are you sure?'

'Yeah.' The afternoon was warm enough without suffering the heat of embarrassment, and Jack tried again to change the subject. 'So, what do we do once we get to the house?'

Jimmy gave a brief smile. 'Fair enough,' he said. 'You can talk to me anytime about Mr Chase, you know that. As for the visit, leave it to me. I'll ask the questions. Your job is to listen, observe and remember.'

'I'll give it a go.'

'You learnt the London knowledge in a year when it takes most men at least two. I think you'll be alright.'

They left the railway arches and viaducts behind, and crossed the common with rows of tall trees either side, families taking picnics beneath, and men wobbling their way on bicycles. After the open space, the houses gradually thinned to leave fewer well-kept roads with less traffic. It was easy to see why the area was called Clapham Park, because they passed more green spaces than they did houses, and many of those they saw stood alone in grassy grounds. Some were cottages, some were larger, and the buildings were packed less tightly than those closer to the river. Even so, it looked like the city was spreading ever southwards, eating up green spaces and replacing them with newer dwellings, but hadn't yet started to feast on the Clapham fields. Where one home had a paddock, a cart and a horse in front like a farm, the next had a well-kept garden, a Brougham carriage, and a stable to the side. They took one road where a row of houses stood in pairs, each the mirror image of the one it was attached to, with a gated alley between them, and even though these had been built by the road, there was still the sense of being in the country, not the city.

Rodenhurst Road was a place Jack had only seen on a map, and he couldn't remember having driven there. The houses were like others they had passed, with two properties joined, each with three storeys, an open area at the front. Railings protected front gardens, and the buildings suggested luxury that would have been beyond Jack's imagination until he came to Delamare.

'People with good incomes live here,' Jimmy said, having paid the driver. 'Men with decent jobs and plenty of money, but not enough to allow them to live without working. Maybe a few private incomes, but orwise, we can expect snobbish neighbours, mistrusting residents, and men keen to protect their little castles.'

'You can tell all that from one rhododendron bush and a few

windows, can you?' Jack joked as they stood looking at the house attached to number twenty-two.

'The flagpole gives it away,' Jimmy said, and pointed to the roof where a union flag flew.

'Who has a flagpole on their house?' Jack scoffed. 'What, they think they're the bleedin' royal family or something? Bloody toshers.'

'Like I said, Jack. Leave the talking to me.'

Jimmy hoisted his knapsack, marched to the porch, and tugged the bell pull. He was taking a wallet from his pocket when the door opened, and they were confronted by a white-haired man with a red nose. His cheeks were crisscrossed with broken veins, and resembled a map of the railways, while his shock of thinning hair must have been his pride and joy, because although there wasn't much of it, it was combed across his liver-spotted scalp and kept down with grease.

'Yes?' he said, small eyes boring into Jimmy. 'Can I help...?'

The eyes fell on Jack, and the words ended with a change of expression. Where he had shown initial wariness, he bit his bottom lip, and became coy. Jack was sure he gave a slight curtsy, but he might just have been unsteady on his feet.

'My, my,' the man said. 'What have we done to deserve this come to our door? Are you selling?'

'No, Sir,' Jimmy said.

'Shame. I'd buy it, no matter what it was.' A girlish laugh split the afternoon.

'Detective James Wright. The Clearwater Detective Agency. My card.'

'Hmm?'

The eyes continued to wash Jack with approval, and Jack looked away as Jimmy repeated his credentials.

'Oh, detective?' the man said, finally paying attention. 'Come to arrest this naughty boy, have you?'

'Er, no. That would be the police.' Jimmy threw Jack a look which, had it been words, would have said, *We've got a right one here.* 'I'd like to ask you about your neighbour.'

'I see.' He looked Jimmy up and down with such intensity, he might as well have used a magnifying glass. 'Mr Wright, you say? Hm.

Sure to be some lucky lady's Mr Right, but this vision beside you is...?'

'My assistant, Mr Merrit. I hope it's not inconvenient, Sir, but may we come in?'

'In? Well now...' The man dipped a hip, put a hand to his chin, and resumed his intrusive appraisal. 'It depends on what you mean by come in. There are many things here you could come into, if you had a mind to enter something.'

'Or we could talk here on the step.' Jimmy's voice was firmer and louder. 'But people passing by might wonder why you had two detectives at your door.'

'Oh, Mr Wright, they already wonder about a lot of things.' Another laugh lasted long enough to send a crow complaining from a tree. 'Let me ask Her Ladyship,' the strange man said, and shut the door in their faces.

'Bold,' was Jimmy's assessment. 'And rather keen on you.'

'Leave it out.'

'No, it's good. We might have to use that to our advantage.'

A curtain drew back, and the same piggy eyes peered from within.

'How?'

'I mean, look at him. As womanish as a pair of bloomers. He's already undressed you, got you into bed, and had you bugger him to oblivion.'

'Shut up,' Jack hissed, laughing. 'That's just nasty.'

The eyes vanished, to be replaced by another pair, shadowed and darker.

'Poor old duffer. Her Ladyship's probably an original Piccadilly Mary-Ann.'

There was no time to ask what that meant, nor who Her Ladyship might be. The door swung open and the same map of the London and South Western Railway was back and beaming.

'She'll see you,' it declared. 'Please wipe your feet, and follow me.'

The commands were aimed at Jack, as if Jimmy didn't exist, and having wiped their already clean shoes on the mud scraper, they stepped inside to be met by the smell of cinnamon and cloves. It reminded Jack of the warehouse at West India, but without the tang of sweat and horse dung. His boots sank into a purple rug as they skirted a marble table on which stood the source of the unusual, feminine smell; a brass flower holder with a thin plume of smoke rising from the centre. The servant wafted the fumes towards himself as he passed, and led them through a door and into unexpected grandeur. The drawing room at Delamere was smart enough, but made homely by the men who lived in the house because they left their jackets hanging over the furniture, and books scattered around the tables, but the room the servant invited them into offered no such informality.

Two settees stood on twisted gold legs, had thin cushions for seats, and straight backs. The fireplace was white marble, and the mantlepiece held a gold clock framed by figures of two men dancing. Every picture was a portrait of someone's young nephew or son, and each was framed in gold. The many surfaces held pointless ornaments of, by the looks, great value, including statues of naked or semi-naked men in various theatrical poses, and a massive, framed poster dominated one wall. It displayed a theatrical advertisement which screamed, 'Phineas Ashton *Is* The Blackmailer!' Above it was an image of a man with half his face covered by a cloak, and the eyes were the same as the second pair that had peered from the window. Melodramatic didn't cover it, because other words suggested something even darker. 'A work of deep resonance by Raffalovich and Gray,' said one splash, while another warned, 'The Dean Street Theatre Club is *Not* for Women!'

Beneath it was an armchair whose wings rose several feet above the man seated in it, and the man himself was as upright as the plant stands and pillars that displayed more naked dancing boys. Jack assumed this was Her Ladyship's husband, and he'd sat himself in just the right place to be lit by a single sunbeam as if he was caught in a policeman's lantern.

'Two detectives to see you, M'lady,' the servant said, and lathered Jack with a stare which hung lasciviously above a thin-lipped, pale smile.

M'lady?

'Thank you, Ricketts,' the seated man said. 'That will be all.'

'Oh, no. I have to stay and hear this. You been a naughty boy?'

'Do be quiet.' His Lordship dragged himself from his chair. To Jack's surprise, he offered his hand, saying, 'Phineas Ashton at your service. Take no notice of the tramp.'

While Jack shook his hand, he passed a sideways look at Jimmy, who, having glanced at the theatre poster, seemed equally confused.

'Detective James Wright,' he said, but his offered hand was ignored.

'Seat yourselves, do,' Ashton said. 'Ricketts was about to make tea.'

'I wasn't.'

'Would you care for some? It is Indian.'

'No, thank you,' Jimmy said, pointing to one of the settees as an instruction for Jack to sit. 'Very kind, but we have a train to catch. I won't keep you long. I just wanted to ask the homeowner...'

'How we survive in such a heartless world?' Ashton slapped the back of his hand to his forehead, and fell into his armchair. 'The tragedy of life, Mr Wright, is that I must suffer its slings and arrows. Slings *and* arrows! Oh, life! Where is thy sting?'

Certain that the man thought he was still on the stage, Jack covered a laugh with a cough, and received a glare from Jimmy.

'Yes, well...' Jimmy was also trying to suppress a grin, but it was only there for a second. 'Sorry to call unannounced, but I need to ask you or your wife about your neighbour.'

'There is just me,' Ashton sighed.

The settee creaked as the railway map sat beside Jack, and continued to stare like a dog waiting to be fed from the table.

'If you can tell us anything, it will be of great use to the case,' Jimmy said, producing his casebook and pen. 'Anything you say will be treated in confidence. There has been no crime, so you will not be implicated in any way. Perhaps I should start by showing you my credentials.'

'Oh, yes,' the railway map cooed, and his leg shifted closer. 'Do present your credentials, Mr Merrit.'

'My man has seen your card,' Ashton waved it away. 'It is enough for me.'

'Been his man nigh on thirty years,' the rail map whispered. 'Not just any man either.'

'Do keep it to yourself, Ricketts. The detectives don't want to hear of your sordid past.'

'I once sat on the lap of a crowned head of Europe,' Ricketts persisted. 'The Duke of Vendôme was also a lovely boy.'

'The last Duke of Vendôme died in seventeen twelve,' Ashton said. 'Ignore him, Mr Wright. The man has always been a hopeless prattle-whore.'

Jimmy made no comment on the statement as he flipped open his book, but whatever noise it was that sprang from Jack's throat had to be covered, and he coughed again, while trying to ignore the creeping leg and advancing fingers.

'We are keen to speak to Mr Simon Diggory Stape,' Jimmy said. 'I understand from a friend that he lives next door. Do you know him?'

'Not as much as he'd like,' Ricketts drawled, imparting a secret Jack didn't want to know.

'Yes, actually,' Ashton said. 'Quite well. Is he in trouble?'

'No, Sir, not at all, but his friend is eager to find him because he has been out of contact for some time. This is unusual, and the friend is concerned.'

'Oh dear.' Ashton waved a languid hand towards a desk beneath the front window. 'Ricketts, my appointment diary,' he said, and his arm flopped back to his side.

'Treats me like a servant,' Ricketts muttered, and left Jack alone while he collected a book from the table not twelve inches away from where Ashton sat. Having dropped it in his lap, he retook his seat so close to Jack he might well have been sitting on him.

'Leave the young man alone,' Ashton said, and flicked through the pages. 'Ah, Mr Stape. Dined with us not long before his wife shuffled onward to the immortal coil, poor man. We had the Bishop for dinner that night.'

'No we didn't, we had salmon.'

Ricketts laughed at his own joke, but Jack didn't see the funny side of it. Neither did Ashton, who closed his eyes, and said what sounded like, 'Kyrie Eleison,' with a heavy sigh.

'Was that when you last saw him?' Jimmy asked.

'No.' Ashton turned more pages, and frowned. 'That was the last time he was here with us, but I am sure I called on him recently.'

'How recent? Do you know?'

'Let me look...'

'Always happy to visit next door, he is,' Ricketts confided, his breath hot and unwelcome in Jack's ear. 'If you'd met Mr Stape you would know why. He's the age of your colleague, I would say. Ripe-for-plucking. Old enough to know better, but doesn't. Thirty? So tragic. That he came with a wife attached, I mean. Such a waste.'

'Would you say you knew Mr Stape well?'

'Not as well as we would like,' Ricketts said. 'Not as well as I would like to know you,' came next on lewd breath, and Jack's stomach turned over.

'Ah, here we are.' Ashton offered Jimmy the open diary. 'I keep notes of who calls, and who I visit. When invited to dine, I ensure the etiquette of a written thank you note in the manner of the Reverend Collins, but without the obsequiousness. For Mr Stape's benefit, I also note when I last dropped in to mind his plants and do his dusting.'

'Hark at the madam,' Ricketts scoffed. 'Just tell them what they want to hear, you old ponce.'

'Dear God.' Ashton smiled apologetically at Jimmy, but did nothing to admonish his servant. 'Please, take no notice. One becomes quite accustomed, and he is rather wonderful in the hammock. As we said in the navy, he's better than get-out.'

'Serviced all the boys from Plymouth to the Indies in my day.'

'Yes, Ricketts, they don't wish to know.'

'Oh, Mr Merrit, if I was thirty years younger.'

'And if you were anymore forward, you would spend the rest of your days behind bars, you old tart,' Ashton complained.

'Done that,' the unstoppable Ricketts preened. 'Had every single lag in the place. Of course, when the boys are locked up, they hanker for a little comfort, and who better to give it than Babs? That's what they called me, Mr Merrit. Brighton Babs...'

The appointment diary flapped across the room and landed squarely on Ricketts' chest. He caught it and put it aside as if being attacked was nothing.

'You tend to his plants and housework?'

By some miracle, Jimmy was keeping a straight face.

'I do when he is away, Mr Wright, indoors and out, and a fine collection our neighbour has.'

'The biggest staghorn you've ever seen, Mr Merrit,' Ricketts confided. 'Quite the thing. Unyieldingly rigid when...'

'Ricketts, enough!'

Although Ashton rolled his eyes, Jack was convinced he was enjoying the outrageous display. Jack on the other hand, was growing impatient, and knew if the letch didn't stop his letching, he'd have to sort him out.

'I'll get to the point,' Jimmy said, snapping shut his casebook. 'When did you last see Mr Stape?'

'A little over four weeks ago.'

'Not since? Are you sure?'

'I am, Sir. I have been watering his collection thrice per week since he left for the Levant.'

'For the...?'

'Levant. It's Western Asia.'

'Yes, I know where it is,' Jimmy said, glancing at Jack. 'And he left a month ago?'

'Not long after the double funeral. They were buried together, the wife and child. It is in my book.'

'Do you know when he will return?'

'Next month, he said. At least, sometime after the end of July. He couldn't be sure.'

'Why?'

'Why? I assume because it is not that easy to make travel arrangements from Damascus to Dover so far in advance. There was also the mention of not coming back until something was known. What was it, Ricketts?'

'The truth.'

A finger brushed Jack's ear and he darted his head away, giving Ricketts a sneer, which only seemed to inflame the old man's interest.

'The truth,' Ashton repeated. 'He wouldn't be free of his journey until the truth was known.'

'The truth about what?'

The truth that Jack was being flirted with by an outrageous railway map who stank of spices and couldn't keep his hands to himself. He gave a threatening growl, but it still didn't help.

'I cannot tell you,' Ashton shrugged. 'I don't mind, of course. We are always happy to help all and any of our neighbours. My service in caring for their plants, cats, even pond fish is a small price to pay for their... understanding.'

The couple's behaviour left Jack in no doubts what there was to understand. He still wasn't sure if Ricketts was a servant, lover or ancient boy-whore kept for sexual favours, possibly a mix of all three, but that the couple was a pair of something odd was undeniable. Lunatics, probably.

'You gain access with a key?' The way Jimmy continued to probe was impressive.

'No, love. He shins up the drainpipe and drops down the chimney.' Ricketts had no time for Jimmy, and made no secret of it. 'Yes, we have his key. Oh, My Ladyship. The youth these days.'

'Stop it, Babs,' Ashton said with a grin. 'You have been quite outspoken, and will receive your preferred punishment as soon as we have helped Lord Clearwater's men.' Seeing Jimmy's expression change, he explained. 'It is on your card, Mr Wright, and I am great admirer of Lord Clearwater. I followed that business in the newspaper late last year with great interest, and was glad to see he got one up on the Earl of Kingsclere. I am also a great admirer of his work with the poor.'

'Especially those boys from the East End,' Ricketts enthused. 'All those young men on the game and in need of guidance. I'm tempted to volunteer. I could certainly teach them a thing or two about how we did it in the old days.'

'You will go nowhere near that charity,' Aston barked. 'Not after the last time.'

'Do you know Lord Clearwater from the House, My Lord?'

'The House? Oh, I see!' Ashton laughed, and leant forward to tap Jimmy's knee. 'Merely my man's affectation. I am no lord, nor am I a lady. That title was awarded to me many years ago when I first began my on-stage odyssey.'

'The diva treats me like a servant, so I treat him like a lady,' Ricketts said, and pressing on Jack's shoulder, added, 'Like I treat all my men.'

Jack was considering breaking the man's fingers, when Jimmy saved him from committing the offence by distracting Ricketts with information that sounded like a threat.

'Inspector Adelaide of Scotland Yard is a personal friend, Mr Ricketts,' he said. 'As is Lord Clearwater, Mr Ashton. Both will vouch for me if you have any qualms, but would you be willing to let us into Mr Stape's property with your key? As I have said, we are concerned for him, and, as far as we know, he is not abroad. To take a quick look inside might offer us useful clues.'

It took Ashton a while to make up his mind, during which time Jack suffered an inappropriate probe from Ricketts' little finger, and more whispered flirtations. It looked as though Ashton was about to refuse the request, when out of nowhere, Jimmy added, 'You might like to know, one of my personal missions is to investigate the offences raised by the Labouchère Amendment of eighty-five, and see moral justice brought to those who break the obscenity laws.' It was said with a glare at Ricketts, who pouted right back. Whatever the strange statement meant, it worked some magic, and Mr Ashton agreed.

'I am happy to show Mr Merrit the house on his own,' Ricketts offered, brushing the nape of Jack's neck.

Without thinking, and forgetting where he was, Jack said, 'Over your dead body, mate,' and leapt to his feet, making sure the heel of his boot landed on Rickett's silk slipper. 'Shall we get on with it, Mr Wright?' he said, ignoring the squeals from the settee. 'My wife and kiddies will be expecting me home soon.'

TEN

'Bloody hell, they're shameless,' Jimmy whispered as they stood in the front garden waiting for Ashton.

'Bleedin' mad is what they are. Never seen it so obvious.'

'Behind closed doors is safe, but in front of strangers? I didn't think he was going to agree, but the threat got him.'

'That law thing?'

'Yeah. Mr Ashton... Sorry, Her Ladyship...' Jimmy sniggered, while Jack shivered. 'He knows what he's about. Soon as I mentioned the act he knew I was serious.'

'Don't get you.'

'How their blatant showing off would land them in trouble if they didn't agree to let us in. There's a law that makes gross indecency between men illegal. And if anything is grossly indecent it's their behaviour.'

'Never seen nothing like it.'

'Lucky you. I can't say that kind of effeminate stuff does anything for me. A man's a man in my book, and the more manly the better.'

Convinced that was a hint, and feeling a mild thrill of flirtatiousness more welcome than Ricketts' attempts, Jack was about to ask him how manly he liked his men, when Ashton appeared from the house. The sun was on its way down, but had a few hours to go, and the afternoon was warm, but that hadn't stopped him donning a scarf, gloves and overcoat. He carried a watering can, and if Jack wasn't mistaken, had put powder on his cheeks. Ricketts was watching from the window like a hound awaiting its master, and Jack enjoyed turning his back on him as their host led them from one garden gate, a few yards along the road and through another.

'You intimated that dear Mr Stape might be in distress?' Ashton said, as they approached the identical property.

'Only that a friend is concerned,' Jimmy said. 'We've been charged with discovering where he is, that is all.'

'But you want to see inside his house? That, to me, suggests foul play.'

'Not at all, Sir. If he has gone abroad, there may be some evidence to substantiate the fact, and we can show it to our client to put his mind at rest. Nothing sinister.'

'I was in a play once,' Ashton mused, inserting the key. 'It was actually titled *Foul Play*, and it was. A totally foul play. Badly written, terribly directed. The only thing that saved it was my performance.'

'I'm sure,' Jimmy said, and as Ashton entered the house, rolled his eyes.

'How does this work?' Ashton collected letters from the doormat and put them on a table. 'I suppose I should accompany you. I am reticent enough letting you in without having you rummaging through my neighbour's belongings on your own.'

'No rummaging, Sir. We will be discreet and gentle. Here...' Jimmy showed him a piece of paper he'd taken from his pocket. 'Authorisation from Inspector Adelaide of Scotland Yard. Does this help?'

Ashton examined it, and said it did.

'There is little in the property. The couple had not long moved in and were still finding their way, what with Mr Stape at work, and Mrs Stape with child. His study is through there, the usual reception rooms this way, bedrooms upstairs. I will attend to the plants. Should I be looking out for anything that might help?'

'Only if you see anything suspicious,' Jimmy said. 'Or notes about travel.'

'Happy to keep you happy and remain discreet,' Ashton said with a hopeful expression to which Jimmy replied with a nod. 'Then call me if I am required.'

Jimmy thanked him and waited until he was out of sight before putting his letter away and picking up those from the table.

'The Scotland Yard thing.' Jack said. 'That's official, is it?'

'No. It's a forgery Silas put together. I've got a stack of them. Right, we'd better stay together in case Mr Stape finds out we've been rummaging, and we need to vouch for each other's whereabouts, or in case your admirer comes after you.'

'That's not funny. What you got there?'

'His post.' Jimmy sifted through the pile, putting one after the other back where he'd found them, but keeping one. 'From Havegood,' he said, holding it close to his eyes at the window. 'I think the postal date is three weeks ago, but I'll have to open it to be sure.'

'You can't take that,' Jack protested when he put it in his inside pocket.

'Take what?' Jimmy winked. 'Come on.'

Jack followed him to the back of the house where Ashton had pointed out the study.

It was much as Jack had expected from having seen Larkin's workroom in Kingsland, and Jimmy's at Delamere, but the furniture wasn't as luxurious. The chair cushions were threadbare, the rugs too, and the desk reminded him of the one Harris had in his cab yard office, not the leather-topped, dark-wood ones Jimmy and Larkin used. There was no padded desk chair either, just a dining-room one pushed into the well. The desk was clear of clutter, though, and only an oil lamp stood on it, while the bookshelves either side were stacked with spines in a neat order that might even have satisfied Will. There were a couple of clocks, but they'd stopped at different times of the day, and what pictures there were hung at unmatching angles. A window looked out onto an overgrown back garden that wasn't a patch on Delamere's, and the windowsill housed a line of free-standing picture frames.

Jimmy stood in the middle of the room, taking in the sight, and frowned.

'I'm not totally sure what we're looking for,' he said. 'Anything I suppose.'

'Anything like what?'

'Something to tell us where he is would be good. Failing that, anything the tells us why he might be about to kill himself. A receipt for a boat train abroad would be handy, but if he is in Asia, we're not going to be able to stop him taking his life. Have a look around while I check the desk. We'd best be quick.'

Jack did as instructed, and started with a bookcase, aware that this was the first real test of his new job. To Jimmy, examining a room for clues was an everyday thing. For Jack, it was an entirely new adventure, and he took furtive glances at his boss to see how he went about things. With care, he noticed, and with great respect for someone else's belongings. Jimmy was also meticulous as he opened drawers, crouched to see right into them, felt underneath the desk, and when that was done, even examined the inside of the fireplace.

Still not sure what he was looking for, Jack gave the bookshelves the same treatment.

'He ain't used these much,' he said, wiping a finger of dust from the shelves. 'There's a book missing, but the rest are as dusty as a corpse.'

'Any idea what book?' Jimmy asked, kneeling by the hearth, and running his hand over the tiles.

'How would I know that?'

'Is there an obvious collection? Are the ones around it all about the same subject? Think like Will, Jack.'

'Oh, right. Um... There's a few books about maps here. Greenwood's Map of London, a Reynolds atlas, and a few ordnance survey sheets. Some are out of date. The next lot's all about banks. *A Practical Guide to Banking*, by a bloke called Scratchley. *The Theory and Practice of...*'

'Yeah, alright. Havegood said Stape had an interest in cartography. There's a book of maps in the desk drawer. That's probably your missing one... Oh. What's this?'

Jack found him crouched beside the log basket.

'What you got?'

'Not sure. A lot of kindling, scraps and... Keep looking, mate.'

Jack returned to his task, and with the bookshelves examined, and while Jimmy sat at the desk and turned the pages of a book, Jack took on a sideboard. Its cupboards revealed only glasses and a bottle of Scotch, and the drawers were empty, as were most of those in a tall cabinet which had trays for shelves. Some had documents to look through, but they were to do with Mr Stape's work; notes from his bank, receipts for purchases made several years ago, and a few statements, and when he asked Jimmy about them and they'd been through them together, Jimmy decided they weren't of value.

'There's nothing much here at all,' he said, kicking the log basket aside, before crouching to scout the grate with a frown. 'Something's missing, but...' A shake of his head, and he said, 'One more cabinet to do, then we'll move on.'

Jack waited at the window, and while watching Ashton refilling his watering can in the garden, nudged one of the frames. Trying to save it from falling, he managed to knock it to the floor, but when he picked it up, was pleased to see he'd not broken the glass. More pleasing to see, however, was the image.

Jack had only ever held postmortem photographs of his grandparents in their coffins. Both had been framed and hung in the Limehouse parlour, and both had perished in the fire. The one he examined by the last of the afternoon sun, could not have been more different. For a start, the people in it were very much alive, and very much younger than Reggie and Ida, and they were better dressed. The picture showed four young men, schoolboys by their uniforms, with three facing the camera, their arms about each other's shoulders, and the fourth, also attached, but bent over as though laughing. Where his face was hidden, the others were on full display, and he didn't have to think like Will to work out who they were.

Next to the doubled-up man stood another with the same build as Jimmy; fit for football, Ida would have said, or right for rugby, and his features were those of Marcus Havegood. The man on the other end was darker, almost as tall and equally trim, and both of them wore top hats and frock coats, ties and wide collars. However, the man in the middle wore only a pair of bathing shorts, not even a full suit, as if proud to show off his fine physique. All three had the look of the carefree young about them, and behind them stood a long, dark building with a central tower.

'What's on the back?'

Jack jumped at the voice so close to his ear. Jimmy's chin was almost resting on his shoulder.

'Nothing,' he said, turning the frame.

Jimmy took it from him, and examined it close-up before sliding the back free of the surround. Removing the photograph, he flipped it and said, 'Ah ha! Now we know who we are looking for. At least, we are if we can add twelve years.'

Across the paper in a fancy script was written, *Hunter, Caesar, Jacques and Diggs, June '80*. Jack had been admiring the body and face of a man who would be dead a few weeks after the image was captured, and the face of another who might be dead by the end of the month. His flesh crept with the thought, and he hurried to put the photograph back in its frame.

'No,' Jimmy said. 'We need it.'

'We can't steal from a man's house.'

'We're not. We're collecting evidence which will be returned. We need to know what Diggs looks like, else how will we know if we find him?'

'We're not meant to find him. Just find out where he is.'

Jimmy ignored Jack's protests, took back the photograph, and put it in his pocket. 'Anyway, it's not the only thing I'm taking away,' he said, and placed a finger on his lips. 'Mr Merrit, would you like to come up to the bedroom with me?'

'You what?'

Where had that come from?

'If we've finished searching in here, let's make our way to his bedroom. It's the second most likely place for a man to keep secrets. I know my bedroom has many.'

With that ambiguous statement stirring his imagination, Jack followed him to the hall and up to the first floor.

'Odd,' Jimmy said, as they climbed.

'What?'

'No trace of his late wife. No silhouette, photograph or portrait. This is very much a man's house.'

'They'd not long moved in, the ponce said.'

'Ponce?'

'Yeah, well...' Jack sniffed. 'Left a nasty taste in me mouth.'

'I doubt you're the first person to have said that about Phineas Ashton, and you won't be the last.'

'Oh, you're vile.'

Their sniggering stopped when they entered the main bedroom and found two stripped beds and an empty cot. Perfume bottles stood on a dressing table, where the mirror was draped in black crepe, and when they investigated the wardrobes, they found dresses and stoles Jack was unwilling to touch.

Of all the many new sensations and experiences of the past few weeks, walking through a stranger's house and examining his personal items was one of the most uncomfortable. It wasn't so much the act of opening drawers and cupboards that unsettled him, because all he was doing was copying Jimmy, and that was his job, it was the silence in which they carried out the search. Apart from the occasional creak of a floorboard, and clunk of something being closed, the rustle of material and scrape of coat hangers on metal poles, all Jack had for company was his breathing. It mixed with the faint smell of another man's life, a hint of perfume, and the muskiness of clothes that had gone unworn for some time.

The rooms they examined were as unfamiliar as the act of searching them, but he carried out his instructions on all three floors, until Jimmy told him he'd seen enough.

'We should get a train before it gets too late,' he said, once again in the study and looking from the window. 'Looks like Ashton's finished pissing about in the shrubbery.'

They met the neighbour in the hall, and Jimmy told him they had seen what they needed to see.

'I hope I have been of use,' Ashton said. 'According to my meticulous schedule, I am due to return and dust in a day or so and I will continue to keep these tired old eyes open.'

'That would be very useful, Sir,' Jimmy said. 'If anyone comes to call for Mr Stape, or if you hear any news of him, if you see, find or can think of anything that might be of use, however trivial...'

'I know the plot, Mr Wright. I was a sensation in *The Missing Mistress of Margate Manor* where I played Detective Dick Tingle.'

Jack laughed and received a dramatic glare in return.

'It was a very serious piece, Mr Merrit. The critics were in awe,' Ashton said through pursed lips before awarding Jimmy a smile. 'I still feel guilty for letting you in, but if I can help you find dear Mr Stape, I suppose I shan't be in too much trouble.'

'You won't be in any,' Jimmy said. 'I am sure he's safely on his travels. We can report to our client that we have found nothing for him to worry about. When Mr Stape returns, and if he wants to know why we have been, you can direct him to me, and I will explain. Will you contact me or Mr Merrit the moment you see him? His friend is very concerned.'

'I shall do so without hesitation. I have your card.'

'Thank you, Mr Ashton, and I wish you well in your theatrical career.'

'Kind of you, Mr Wright, but I fear it is all but over.' Ashton let them out into the normality of the late afternoon. 'There are those who seek to keep me from the London stage, and it is proving a battle of Biblical proportions to find work.'

'Is that because of your man friend?' Jack asked, thinking it was polite to say something.

'Man friend?' Ashton was taken aback. 'I can't think who you mean.'

'Mr Merrit's father was in the theatre,' Jimmy said, to cover. 'Music Hall wasn't it, Merrit?'

'That's right. A bit of comedy, bit of singing and foolery.'

'Oh?' Ashton paid attention. 'Not Samson Merrit?'

'The very same, Sir. I didn't know him well, and only saw him perform a few times, but he was me dad.'

'A terrible act who met a terrible end,' Ashton said, as if to get Jack back for anything he might have said out of turn. 'Never mind, Mr Merrit. I am sure your detecting is of more worth than your father's ditties. If there is nothing else, Mr Wright...?'

'No, nothing, Sir. Once again, thank you for your help.'

Ashton's man friend was still pressed to the window as they passed by the house, and much as Jack wanted to leave him with an insulting gesture, he thought it best not to, and carried on towards the end of the street in search of a cab, glad to have turned his back on the pair.

* * *

It wasn't until they were boarding a train at Charing Cross that nervousness set in. Not only was he to ride on a train for the first time in his life, but it was also the first time he'd travelled outside of London, and he was leaving Will to his own devices for longer than ever before. The Hackney Marshes and Epping Forest might have been considered by some as 'out of town', but a village in Kent was further still. Some in his street regularly took holidays in Kent at hop picking and harvest, spending two weeks in the clean air, where they worked up to eighteen hours a day. A holiday for some, cheap labour for others, but not something Jack had ever done. Also adding to his apprehension, was wondering if he and Jimmy would have to share a room at whatever place they could find. Jack had only shared a room with Will and their grandparents who'd slept behind a curtain for privacy and dressed and washed before the brothers woke. To undress and sleep close to Jimmy would entail unfamiliar intimacy, and he didn't know how he was expected to behave.

Compounding all that was the memory of the house they'd just visited, and the unusual couple they'd met. They pair had left him with the unsavoury feeling that such behaviour was what was expected of men like himself, but then he looked at Jimmy, reading the thing he'd taken from Stape's study, and told himself men like himself were also men like the detective; not a hint of womanish about him, a sturdy, reliable and manly man's man.

As the train shunted and groaned from the station, he wondered about Larkin and where he fitted into an imaginary row of hansom cabs waiting on a rank, each one a man, and arranged in increasing degrees of manliness. At the back were the likes of the pair at number twenty; outrageous, uncaring of what strangers thought, and proud to be unacceptably different, as if their life's mission was to shock. At the front were men like Jimmy and himself; fit and strong, just as the world expected a man to be. Somewhere in the middle was Larkin with his fancy words and pleasant house, his education and larger-than-life way of moving around his fine furniture and clever books. Not womanish, but not overly masculine either, unless he was standing in his undershorts in front of a mirror, in which case, Jack remembered, there was no denying he was a man. In bed too, during that easy-to-recall half an hour when they explored each other's bodies as two men made equal by their nakedness and shared desire.

If men were the queue of cabs, Jack would remain closer to the front than the back, no matter if anyone thought he should be elsewhere. If Jimmy could remain masculine and dignified while in love with another man, so could Jack Merrit.

That was that, and he put thoughts of the outrageous pair at number twenty from his mind, and watched the scenery until Jimmy finished reading.

'You want to see this,' the detective said, when he closed the book. 'I found it wedged in a gap between the mantlepiece and the fire surround.'

'What is it?'

'Notes by Mr Stape. More like the beginning of a diary. There's nothing that might suggest where he is, but it throws some interesting light on what Havegood wrote about him, and there's a page missing.'

Jimmy handed him a thin notebook, and with the light fading outside, Jack shifted beneath the overhead lamp to see more clearly. The handwriting was the same as Havegood's, suggesting both men had been taught by the same teacher, and had written as their school expected. No doubt they had paper to practice on, where, during Jack's limited schooling, he'd only had a slate.

'Are you sure it was alright to take this?' he asked, flicking through the pages, until he came to the rough edge of one that had been ripped out. There was nothing after it. 'Ain't it stealing?'

'It's a fine line. Our job is to act on the wishes of the client, and because he seems genuinely concerned that Mr Stape will do himself harm, it's reasonable for us to take any action we see fit. I was looking for a suicide note, or anything that might suggest a location or a reason, but there wasn't much. What you've got there isn't exactly a farewell, merely a few pages of ravings, but there might be a clue in it, and I'd value your opinion. It was all I could find, and there was no sign of the missing page, which, my instinct tells me, could be important. In fact, there was very little of anything personal in his house, don't you think?'

'His clothes and a few photographs.'

'Yeah, but not much else. Nothing from his parents, no letters other than official ones, and no souvenirs.'

'There was a letter from Havegood, you said. You nicked that too.'

'Borrowed for the sake of the investigation.' Jimmy waved the envelope. 'I'll read it next.'

'Yeah, alright,' Jack watched the scenery roll by. 'What's the plan for later?'

'Find somewhere to stay, and tomorrow, visit Biddenden and see if we can find the old housemaster. If we can, and if he is willing to talk, we need to ask him where Stape might be.'

'How will he know that?'

Jimmy shrugged. 'He probably won't, but we have to explore every lead. You never know, he might be in touch with one of the others from Stape's class. One thing can lead to another in this job, mate. Oh, remember, we won't tell him why we want to find his old pupil, though.'

'Right. And after?'

'Get home tomorrow, see what we've got, pull together any information Will might have found, and with any luck, one of the other leads will come up with possible locations. We can then verify he's at one of them, and send a message to Havegood, expecting a large cheque by return of post. That's all this case is, Jack. It's not the most thrilling I've handled, but if we please the Honourable Marcus Havegood, then who knows what other work it will lead to.'

Who knew where the train would take them, where they would stay, and what the sleeping arrangements would be? Not Jack, that was for sure, and with the Kent countryside fading into the night, he arranged Stape's book and began to read.

ELEVEN

Simon D Stape's Journal

June 7th, 1892

The memory of Jacques Verdier came to me this evening on my return from Threadneedle Street. There was no reason for the man to enter my thoughts, in fact, he has been absent from them for many months. It is only towards the end of July when they appear, as that is when I prepare to meet with Caesar. The two go hand in hand, although they never did, nor ever should have.

Perhaps next month's meeting was playing on my thoughts as I took the omnibus for my usual journey from the City, because it is around the end of July that dear Daphne is due to deliver our child. She has been most tired of late. The unusual summer heat is causing her some distress, as is being confined to her rooms from where she may only listen to the public in the street and hear children playing. How she wishes to be among them, but she must remain indoors in confinement on the doctor's orders, and at the will of her mother.

I was on the open-top omnibus, passing the Lyceum Theatre when I read their notice. Henry Irving was playing Cardinal Wolsey, and

Miss Ellen Terry, Katherine, in Shakespeare's *Henry the Eighth*. On seeing the poster, I remembered a night at Sinford's and the great tower where the Triumvirate lived and worked in pleasant harmony. On that occasion, Caesar was rendering some of the speeches from the play, and Jacques was listening in rapt contemplation. I was unbothered as I still am about such frivolities, being a man, even then, more interested the economics of a country, not its literary output. I don't recall the speech, but I suppose the connection was made; the play, our rooms at Grace, July approaching, and they all led to Jacques.

From there, my mind opened to the dark happening of the time which I have refused to entertain since it occurred, but not even the thought of Daphne's impending birthing and the joy it would bring could dislodge it. By the time I changed at Trafalgar Square, the memories of Sinford's had darkened further, and I had to make a conscious effort to concentrate on something else as I journeyed homeward.

June 9th

Jacques has remained with me, and I am unable to shake him from my tree of thoughts. Not his face, not the joy I felt back then when in his presence, not the hold he had over me because he had the same hold over every one of us, but because of where he is now—walking with the angels he so deserves to walk with through endless rapture beyond Heaven's gates. It is a place to which all good Christian men must aspire, and I am among their company. My work may lead me to be ruthless with some, but that ruthlessness is borne from wanting to do good by them, and in my working life, I am as the scripture directs me to be; compassionate. At least, I try to be.

Loyalty. To love one's friends, neighbours and self. To do what is best for others while respecting the laws of the Good Book. This is how I have kept myself on the right path for all these years.

This is why I must turn my back on the darker lane along which I have wandered.

This is something I must contemplate further.

June 11th

He was there again in a dream, and it was as clear as if I had lived it in my waking hours. We were back at Sinford's, and in our last days, locked away in our casemate with the lantern lighting the peace we always found there. He was anguished by attentions, and by the impending end of our time at school, worried about what would happen next, and how our superstitious and sometimes arrogant friend was behaving. I reminded him that our friend was also compassionate and could be reasonable, but in my dream, Jacques would not be appeased.

When I woke, it was with the sense of still being there among the dank and dripping walls, with the gurgle of the dying well a way beneath our feet. Despite the conditions, it was our safe place, and a place we would go to hide from the world. A bastion from which we would fire volleys at the injustices around us, and, for him, a place where he could safely share with me his secrets, and me, mine with him.

My mental state persisted through the day, keeping me distracted from my work, and I resolved more and more to consider firing one last volley from that safe place. Considered only, because if fired, the shot would be so great as to shatter the worlds of many.

June 25th

How ominous it was that I should write of shattering worlds, for no sooner was the ink dry on this page than my world was blown apart by a volley from an unseen enemy. The enemy is God, it can only be, for it is only He who could have decided to rob me of my love and my child in one swoop of his unforgiving sword.

A FALL FROM GRACE

Gone, both!

And leaving me with nothing but the truth.

It shall be known, for as I sit here with even the candle dying beside me, I see no other way but for the truth to be known. I pray that by sharing it, He will see me repented and allow me to enter His gates to walk beside my boy and my love in the steps of Jacques and the angels and all that is good in the world, because I, wretched and alone, have been anything but good. God knew, and I have suffered his punishment.

It will happen, and Jacques will at last bear witness on his day, and the man of superstition and reasonableness, like the rest, will know the truth.

But how and from where does the truth come?

I must plan. If my fevered mind will allow me to walk through the paper streets and cross the black lines of rationality beside me, I may be able to see my way. For whom do I leave my next page? For anyone who may, after missing me, want to find me in the dried-up chasm of the past. Or, for him, to face the truth as a man.

* * *

The clattering and vibrations, the jolting, the screaming whistle, the hard seats, and waxy lantern light were over, and he was standing in the dark surrounded by the smell of grass made damp by dew. At least, that was how Jimmy explained the scent, as they stood outside Headcorn station hoping to spy a cab. There weren't any, and if they hadn't asked, they could have been standing there all night.

'The porter says it's not far to walk to the Station Hotel,' Jimmy reported on returning from the ticket office. 'This way.'

It was an unlit path into the unknown, and Jack couldn't help thinking that was a way to describe his time since starting work for the agency. The way was lit by the stars and the moon, and a distant light ahead guided them towards their destination. No-one passed, and there was very little to hear, just rustling in the bushes and an occasional screech Jimmy said was an owl. Apart from that, their only company was their footsteps, and the only talk was a brief conversation about Stape's diary.

'Sounded like he got more and more upset about something,' was Jack's initial observation when questioned.

'Yeah, don't know what to make of it,' Jimmy said. 'It was the only book, and he'd only used the first few pages. Suggests to me he'd kept a diary in others, but if so, they were either well-hidden or not there.'

'Doesn't help us find him, though.'

'No. But raises some questions about his state of mind. All that rambling about bearing witness, secret rooms, people knowing the truth, and the chasm of the past. I suppose the truth is, he decided to top himself not long after his wife died.'

'Reads that way.'

'So, wherever he is, he planned to leave behind a suicide note. Least, that's one possibility.'

'I can see why Mr Havegood's worried,' Jack said.

Although his contributions were minor compared to the things Jimmy had said and discovered, Jack felt he could give himself a pat on the back for his work so far, and his pride was further boosted when Jimmy agreed with what he'd just said.

'Yeah. Can't imagine what it must be like to know your friend plans to kill himself and yet not be able to do anything about it.'

'Terrible,' was all Jack could come up with, but he might have been talking about the condition of the road, because he stepped in a pothole and nearly stumbled. 'What about the letter? You've not said nothing about that.'

'Mundane,' Jimmy replied through the darkness. 'A note from Havegood reminding Stape of their meeting. Midday on July the thirty-first, at a hotel off the Strand. Nothing else. No clues. Dead end.'

'Ah, but is it worth going there and asking at the hotel? Maybe someone there knew Mr Stape. Maybe that's where he plans to do himself in.'

Jack thought that was a mightily fine suggestion and preened because he'd thought of something Jimmy hadn't.

There was, however, a reason.

'Havegood said they never used the same hotel twice,' Jimmy said. 'I guess that was for anonymity considering how they'd get up to sex. Least, that's how I read between the lines. I don't think knowing the hotel would help. We're nearly there.'

The mention of sex reminded Jack that they might have to share a room, but why he should assume a shared room would lead to anything but sleep was a mystery of his own making and one he could only solve with honesty. Jimmy had given him messages in winks, looks, and words with two meanings, in the way Larkin had done when they first met. That, clearly, was some kind of code that men of the same inclination used, and as Jack was learning the business of detecting from his boss, so he was learning the ways of men who liked men. It was quite possible Jimmy had asked him to come on the visit so they could be alone, and if Larkin had found Jack attractive, why wouldn't Jimmy?

The question was what to do about it, and he decided the best thing was to wait and see. After all, Jimmy was his employer, and as much as he might have been 'the same', and as friendly as he was, he was still the one who paid the wages. A wrong move from Jack, and that might come to an end.

It was with that in mind that he surveyed the one bed in the only room the Station Hotel had available. The landlord hadn't asked questions as to why two men would agree to share. He must have known or thought there was no other accommodation to be had in the village at that hour. Maybe he assumed two men *could* only sleep together and weren't capable of doing anything else. Whatever the reason, he showed them the room and took their money.

It was gone half past nine when they sat down to eat. Jimmy took the opportunity to ask if anyone in the bar knew a Mr Hogg who used to work at Sinford's, and it wasn't until the last customers were leaving, that he had any success.

'You might find him at Rose Cottage,' someone told them. 'If it's the couple I'm thinking of. Moved in years back, and no-one's taken much notice of them since. Nor them of us. The cottage is about four miles, on this side of Biddenden.'

It wasn't much, but Jimmy called it a lead, and it gave them hope that they might learn something new in the morning. With that being the end of the investigating for the day, they returned to their room and surveyed the bed.

'I'll have that side,' Jimmy said. 'If that's alright with you.'

'I'm used to being kicked out of bed by Will's strange dreams,' Jack told him, as he began to undress. 'Don't bother me where I sleep.'

'Must be a change, then, having a room to yourself at Delamere.'

'Everything's been a change this last month.' Jack turned his back to wash at the stand. 'A good one, mind.'

'Glad to hear it. I knew you were the right man for the job.'

'Me?' If Jack had to name anyone he thought would make a good private investigator, it wouldn't have been him.

'You're doing alright, Jack. As long as you're enjoying it. You know, you can return to cabbing anytime you want. I'd be happy for you to stay at Delamere while you got things together.'

'That's good of you, but I think I'm alright. As long as you're happy with me.'

'More than happy,' Jimmy said, and the way he said it caused Jack to look up from the bowl and into the mirror.

Jimmy was naked apart from his undershorts, and was turning back the bed. He carried not an ounce of fat, there were no rolls at his stomach, and Jack made out the shape of his muscles on his hairless chest. His flesh glowed white beneath the lamplight, which caught his blond hair and gave it a halo, and when he glanced across, he was smiling.

On being caught, Jack looked away and mumbled, 'Sorry. Wasn't staring.'

'Stare all you want, mate,' Jimmy said, and Jack was about to take it as a flirt when he added, 'There's no harm in looking.'

To add to the new experiences of travelling on a train and staying in a country inn, Jack climbed into bed also dressed in his undershorts, and lay less than a foot away from a man he had known only a few weeks.

Jimmy turned down the lamp until the room was as dark as pitch, and Jack waited for something to happen. He had no idea what, or whether Jimmy would move closer, or ask him to, but what he said, after some time, was unexpected.

'This reminds me of when I met Tom.'

What was he meant to say to that? If what Max had told him was right, Tom was Jimmy's special man in Cornwall.

'Oh?' seemed like the easiest thing, and Jack waited for an explanation to come through the darkness.

It didn't take long. 'Yeah,' Jimmy said, his voice amplified by the otherwise silent night. 'He'd been fired from his job and was waiting to buy a ticket home. I was waiting for a reply to a message. I was a telegraph runner then. We'd met a day or so before when I'd delivered a message off my patch. Tom answered the door and that was that. Anyway... With no job, he had to go home, but he wanted to stay in London, so I invited him to lodge at our house, and he did.'

'Oh?' Jack said again after waiting long enough for the story to continue.

'Was just remembering it because we were happy then,' Jimmy said, and his voice dropped to a whisper. 'Both of us were nervous, sharing my bed, because it was small, and Tom... We'll, he's about your build, but not as wide. More slender.'

Jack wasn't sure if that was an insult or simply information, but didn't dare ask.

'We both knew what we wanted, because it was pretty clear we fancied each other from the moment we met on the steps of Clearwater House. But it was a new situation for both of us, lying there in our unders, both—I found out later—as hard as nails and hoping the other would make a move first.'

The thought of it was pushing Jack towards the same condition. Or maybe it was because he was sure Jimmy was telling him this in the lead up to something else. A reliving of the event, perhaps.

He'd be happy with that.

'We had a chat, and nothing else, but things moved on from there.'

That appeared to be the end of the conversation, or flirt, or hint, or whatever it was, and it seemed like Jimmy was waiting for Jack to say something, or to make the next move, if moves were to be made. If that was the case, it wasn't fair. Jack had no clue what to say, but feeling the pressure of the darkness, listening to Jimmy's breathing a few inches away, and knowing his naked body was within touching distance, he at least had to find out if he was imagining something was happening, or if it really was.

'So, being here like this, is like it was being there like that?' he said, with his quick breathing fighting against his desire to speak.

'In a way,' Jimmy said, with a mild laugh. 'Two near strangers in the dark, in bed, both male.'

Nails. Hard as. Jack was the same, and neither of them had done anything to get him that way. It was simply the proximity and the possibility.

'What? You're like nails, are you?' he said, trying to sound light-hearted.

The silence that followed told him he'd put his foot right in it, but the silence only lasted so long. Jimmy shifted, and Jack felt the mattress tip as he moved closer. So close, that when he spoke, his breath was on the side of Jack's face.

'I am, Jack,' Jimmy said. 'But only because I was thinking about Tom.'

Had they been haggling over something at the Limehouse market, that would have been what Grandad Reggie called an opening gambit. The first offer of a trade. A position from which to negotiate up or down, and it was Jack's turn to make a bid.

'If the thought of him gets you hard as nails, I wonder what the sight of him does,' he said, his throat dry.

'Yeah, well, you can imagine.'

A blocker, Reggie would have called that. A dead-end street, in cabman's terms, where you couldn't go any further in that direction, but you could go back and find the same destination through a different route. Jack was expected to better his offer.

'Got a good imagination, me,' he said. 'And I like what I imagine, mate. Being like that must leave you wanting to do something about it.'

He'd passed the blocker and was on the open road towards his destination, but the route was up to Jimmy.

'It does,' Jimmy said, and in doing so, directed Jack towards the inevitable.

'And do you need any help with that?'

'With what?'

That was a bump in the road, either an unseen pothole, or Jack had run over a cat.

'With your...er, nail?'

The atmosphere changed as a wheel fell off the cab, and Jimmy rolled away.

'Ah,' he said. 'Sorry.'

'About what?'

'You thought I was...?'

'Eh? Oh, no, mate. Nothing like that.'

The room was hotter, the blankets too thick.

'Sorry,' Jimmy said again. 'Didn't mean to...' A growl followed by a tut. 'Oh, to hell with it. The thing with me and Tom is complicated,' he said. 'I love the man like he's my right arm, but we don't see each other much. When we do, it's perfect. When we don't, I can't help but wonder what he's doing. It's like I don't trust him, but I do. Only... Ah, you don't need to hear all this.'

Hearing anything would shift the heavy quilt of embarrassment, and Jack said, 'Go on. If you want, tell me. I don't mind.'

Jack had said just the right words, because Jimmy let go a story that must have been festering beneath his skin like a sore.

First, he told Jack how Tom had always been in love with his master, Lord Clearwater, and how the earl had always had a thing for Tom. How they'd grown up together as servant and nobleman, how they'd been the best of friends and still were, and how the lord was Jimmy's best friend, and even how he and the man had done what he and Jack were now doing, and shared a bed in a country inn. Nothing had happened there, but that had been when Clearwater told Jimmy he was his best mate, and then encouraged him and Tom to get together, and how everyone was one big family, except the men could love each other like a man loves a woman, including all the sleeping together, because they were safe. Like Jack and Jimmy were safe to speak like Jimmy was speaking, because there was trust and comradeship.

The telling lasted for several minutes, and Jimmy hardly drew a breath, only slowing when he came to an end, and gave a deep, long sigh.

'Couldn't live without him,' he said. 'But I have to for great long periods of time, and sometimes it's hard, and not like your nails are hard.'

They had been Jimmy's nails, but Jack kept quiet. His ardour had softened, but his heart had swelled, because he was flattered Jimmy trusted him enough to admit all he had confessed.

'Don't know what I'd do if anything happened to Tom,' Jimmy said. 'So, I pay the price. I suffer my own imaginings when we're apart, but I know he feels the same, so I shouldn't get wound up, but recently...' Another sigh. 'No, I've said too much. I'll sort it out with him next time I'm down at Larkspur. Don't you worry about it.'

'Oh, ain't worried,' Jack said, because he wasn't. If anything, he was confused. 'As long as you're alright.'

'Yeah.' Jimmy moved again. When he spoke, he sounded further away, as if he was on the edge of the bed and facing the wall. 'Won't keep you up any longer. Forget I said anything, and we'll get on with the case in the morning. Goodnight, mate.'

That, it seemed, was that, and feeling as though he'd been knocked down by a coalman's cart, Jack faced away and did his best to sleep.

TWELVE

The next day, Jack woke to find Jimmy sleeping soundly on the far side of the bed, and embarrassed about what he'd assumed, crept to the washstand to douse his face, and put together an excuse. As the cold washed the sleep from his eyes, it also washed away the shame, and replaced it with realisation. Not only did Jimmy think he was capable of his new job, but he also trusted Jack enough to confide in him. The trip down to Kent wasn't an engineered excuse to be alone, sharing a bed had been a necessity not a desire, and even though Jack had made a fool of himself, Jimmy had reacted as if he'd been the one to make a mistake. 'One of those things,' Grandad Reggie would have said. 'Chalk it up to experience, and move on.'

Jimmy must have been of the same opinion, because as soon as he woke, he talked about work and not Jack's lack of judgement.

'I'd like to see this man in time to catch the midday train,' he said, washing at the bowl, as Jack tidied the bed. 'It'll be at least two hours back to town, and I want to check if there are messages. We're against time with this one.'

'Right you are.'

Jack was also keen to be on the move and see how Will had managed being at Delamere on his own, but what he needed to concentrate on first, was finding Mr Hogg and seeing what he had to say about Mr Stape. So intent was he on his new job, it was him who began the conversation over breakfast, where the landlord slapped down plates and tin mugs from time to time, but otherwise, left them free to talk.

'Let me get this right,' Jack said, having thought about everything he'd heard in the last two days. 'So far, we got a date Havegood thinks Stape will kill himself, a few words in a diary, and not much else. That's it, yeah?'

Jimmy blinked his blond lashes, and his cheeks pinked as he smiled.

'That's basically it,' he said. 'Except, we don't know Stape's exact intentions, and we only have Havegood's theory. I admit, the diary suggests he was down in the dumps, and who can blame him, but there's more in there than you mention.'

'Like...?'

'What is this truth thing? It was important enough for him to mention the word to the neighbours.' Jimmy fished the diary from his knapsack, and pointed to the page while chewing bacon. 'There, in the last bit. *Jacques will at last bear witness on his day, and the man of superstition and reasonableness, like the rest, will know the truth.* There's also something about his wife's death being God's revenge. You can tell he's distraught, but is he also guilty? If so, of what?'

'I suppose he might sound a bit guilty,' Jack conceded. 'But then, ain't we all? I had to listen to the prattle-box preachers on a Sunday down St Anne's, because Ida insisted. They was always going on about truth this and guilt that. Then, we'd all sing about it, and everyone would go for a pint like none of it mattered. Still left you feeling like you'd done something wrong. Worse if you're a bloke fancying another bloke. Stape had been living a lie, and he sounds like a God botherer, so there's your guilt.'

'Not a churchgoer, Jack?'

'Was until they started telling me I shouldn't do things which came natural. You know, like... Well, like you and your friend.' The last part, he whispered, even though the landlord wasn't nearby, and to change the subject, added, 'Who's the other bloke?'

'Other bloke?'

Jack turned the diary and found the entry.

'He talks about him and another bloke being in their casement, which I suppose is a window, and they're talking about someone who's superstitious and the way he was behaving.'

'For a start, the word is case*mate*. Unless it's a spelling mistake, it's the name of a place. I don't recognise it, but we're talking about a posh school here where they have strange words for all sorts. As for who he met there and who he's talking about, I imagine it's the other in the Triumvirate.'

'Which is a what?'

'Three something. I'd have to look it up, but I reckon it refers to the three of them who were good mates in the tower. The diary's only really useful for proving Stape was in a bad way around the time he cancelled his meeting with Havegood. Havegood's letter I took was sent not long after the last entry. In it, he begs him to reconsider and to make the meeting.'

'And through all of it, there's no clues to where he plans to do himself in.'

'You have a nice way of summarising, Jack. That's a useful thing. As we investigate, it's a good idea to remind ourselves where we are, so we don't miss anything, and we make sure we stay on track. That's why I had Will set up the chalkboard.'

'So, I'm doing alright so far, am I?'

Jack wasn't looking for praise, he wanted to be reassured he was being of use. So far there had been a lot of thinking, where he was more used to driving, a skill which, once learnt, came as easily as breathing.

'You're doing fine, mate,' Jimmy said. 'But unless you're going to scoff another six eggs, we should get started.'

The first thing to do was find transport to Biddenden village, a distance of five miles, the landlord told them. That would have been a two-and-six cab fare in London, but things worked differently out in the country, and Jimmy paid a delivery man to drive them. It meant sitting among barrels in the back of a cart, but it only cost a shilling, and the sun was out.

So were birds, flowers along the hedgerows, and the farmers

tending their fields, wandering among corn, or herding sheep. The route took them past children picking berries, and fishing in a narrow ditch that ran alongside the lane. The land was flat all the way to distant hills, but the view was interrupted by leafy trees and the occasional house with cone-shaped chimneys topped by slanting white hats. To Jack, they looked like rows of nuns in capes, but Jimmy said they were kilns used for drying hops to make into beer.

'Here be,' the cart driver called as he drew his horse to a stop.

It was a grey Percheron with a white flash on its nose, a sturdy draft horse that would have no trouble working long hours pulling heavy load. Jack thanked it more than he did the driver as they waved the cart away and turned to a sign that read, Rose Cottage.

'Nice,' Jimmy said, admiring the white, weatherboarded house.

Simple in design, but decorated with creepers and all things flowering, it reminded Jack of the lid of the cake tin Larkin had brought when he called at their tenement to persuade Jack to track down the Flay brothers. That meeting had somehow led him to a cottage in an ideal setting in the middle of nowhere.

'I'll do the talking,' Jimmy said, giving the front garden a once over.

'Yeah. I know me place, Boss.'

'Oi, don't start getting all servant and master on me,' Jimmy smirked, and cracked the iron knocker against its plate. 'We work as a pair, Mr Merrit. We are equal.'

'Except, you're in charge.'

'Quite right.' Jimmy cleared his throat as something rattled on the other side of the door. 'Polite and professional, Jack, and we'll do well.'

The door was tiny and creaked as it opened a fraction, revealing an even smaller person peering through the gap.

'I have already given.'

At first, Jack thought it was some kind of wrinkled fairytale creature, but when Jimmy introduced himself, and offered his calling card, the door opened further to reveal a woman Grandma Ida would have called as ancient as the hills and just as craggy. The poor old thing was half blind too, by the looks, because she pressed the card to her nose to read.

'From London?' she said, her voice sounding like the high and piercing train whistle of yesterday. 'Oh, I say. Will I need my hat?'

'Hat? No,' Jimmy said, putting on a broad smile. 'We were hoping to chat to Mr Hogg who used to work at Sinford's School. Is he here?'

'Mr Hogg?'

'Yes, Madam. We were told he might be found here.'

'Sinford's School?'

'Yes.'

'Dirty water.'

'So I understand. Er... Mr Hogg?'

'You want to speak to my husband?'

'If you are Mrs Hogg, yes, please.'

Jimmy had raised his voice because the old dear craned her neck as high as she could to hear him, and still her ear only came level with his chest.

'Speak to Arnold?'

'If that is your husband's name.'

'He's at the church.'

'Oh, I see.' Jimmy glanced up the lane. 'Towards the village?'

'I'll need my hat,' the woman decided, and closed the door.

'Not the most eccentric person I've encountered during an investigation,' Jimmy said.

'Ah, she's sweet. Reminds me of Mrs Wise at number thirty. Lovely old dear who used to make everyone cakes on Saint Swithin's Day, bless her. She had a public affair with the postman, caught the French disease, and died a lunatic.'

'So, not that wise then.'

They stepped back from the door, chuckling and expecting Mrs Hogg to make an appearance, but after a few minutes it became clear she had either forgotten they were there, or couldn't find her hat. Jimmy was about to knock again, when the sound of an approaching horse stopped him, and a moment later, a sturdy Cleveland appeared from the side of the house pulling a buggy. Beneath the canopy, Mrs Hogg sat wearing a massive straw hat with the widest brim Jack had ever seen. The top was decked out in an array of foliage so diverse she looked like a Covent Garden fruit stall.

'One of you will have to walk,' she said, taking the two-man trap up to the lane.

Jack volunteered, so Jimmy could talk to her on the way, and prepared himself for a long trek in the morning sunshine.

It was more of a dash than a trek, and lasted for two minutes during which time Mrs Hogg managed to mount the verge three times, swerve cross the lane twice, narrowly missing the ditch on the other side, and scare a flock of birds from a bush. She took the corner into another lane so fast, Jimmy nearly fell out, and bounced the trap through a gate and into a churchyard until then disguised by tall trees. The church was as unexpected as it was impressive, and as he approached, Jack wondered if Mr Hogg was the vicar, and reminded himself to mind his language.

Mrs Hogg, however, didn't stop and get down as he expected, but drove alongside the building over grass that was more like straw after the long summer, and despite heading directly for a clump of trees and knocking over vases of dead flowers, kept going. With no regard for where the dead were sleeping, she continued over the graves, somehow avoiding the tombs and headstones, and didn't come to a halt until they were beneath the furthest trees. There, she leapt down as nimbly as you like, tied the horse to a bough, and sat on a coffin-shaped slab swinging her legs.

Jimmy, shrugging, joined her, and when Jack arrived, seemed as confused as he was.

'Does Mr Hogg keep the grounds?' Jimmy asked.

The old woman was peeling an orange she'd fished out from somewhere. 'Keep the ground, dear? No, he's under it. There.'

She pointed to the adjacent grave, a simple, new headstone and a body-shaped mound of grass as dead as the man beneath.

'What do you want to ask him?'

Jimmy's face was a picture of laughter held in check by disbelief, and behind her back, he raised his arms in a gesture of hopelessness.

Jack, on the other hand, had experience of dealing with the syphilitic Mrs Wise, and other old Limehouse ladybirds, and held up a finger telling Jimmy to wait. Sitting beside the old woman, and accepting a slice of orange, he put on a sympathetic voice, and spoke slowly.

'I expect you come to talk to him a lot.'

'Every day, dear. We were married thirty years, but it's only since he's been dead that I can get a word in. I make the most of it.'

'Did he talk much about his days at the school?'

'And not much else.' Mrs Hogg, sensing an ally, leant into him, and whispered. 'You should look out for your friend, dear. Him. He's a bit touched isn't he?'

Jack said nothing, it wouldn't have been loyal to do so, even if Jimmy had been touched. If anyone was mad, it was her, smelling of oranges and something less pleasant that reminded him of Mrs Wise's deathbed.

'I can see you are a clever old bird, Mrs Hogg,' he said. 'And I bet you got a memory like the best of them. Am I right?'

'Maybe.'

'Ah, for sure. There's a lot of knowing in the noggin beneath that gorgesome hat of yours.'

'You come from East London,' she said, pulling away and staring at him as though he'd insulted her.

'I do. Limehouse.'

'I know from your voice. I read people as easily as I read the parish news, you see, Mr...?'

'Merrit.'

'You call me clever. Why d'you say that? Is it because you are uneducated.'

'No. Because you have a Cleveland to pull your buggy. The best temperament, and very loyal.' Jack was reminded of Shadow, at that moment no doubt deep in conversation with Emma and Shanks about the luxury of the Delamere stables. 'And, as a wise old bird, what can you remember about the boys at your husband's school.'

Maybe Mrs Hogg was impressed with Jack's nature, or maybe she was charmed, but either way, she settled in to chat as if she had known him for years.

'Mostly a rowdy bunch of rich men's sons,' she said with orange juice running in rivers down her powdered chin. 'Don't remember their names, of course. Arnold was housemaster there for forty years. He loved his job, especially working with the older boys. They were clever students by then, and wanted to learn.'

'It's the older ones I wanted to ask about, actually. The last ones of the school.'

'How do you mean, Mr Martlett?'

'It's Merrit. The last ones who lived in the tower before the school shut. That would have been when your husband retired.'

'Correct, it was. It was the water, you see. Went bad. Dried up. The school was so poor they had to close it. That's how I came to move away from the stink of boys' socks, their passion for games and hatred of academics. Well, the younger ones. What about them?'

'Do you remember one by the name of Simon Stape? His friends in Grace Tower called him Diggs.'

She thought while Jimmy hovered behind her in silence, giving Jack encouraging but unnecessary prompts.

'I'll ask Arnold,' Mrs Hogg said, and swung herself from someone else's grave to kneel at her husband's, where she mumbled to herself for a long time.

Jimmy had just waved his pocket watch, and Jack had just nodded in return, when Mrs Hogg scrambled back to her perch.

'He says that was the year one of the boys fell from the roof,' she said.

Either she had a better memory than she'd let on, or she really could talk to the dead. Even Jimmy looked impressed.

'No, he didn't really say that, because he's dead,' she continued. 'I just happened to remember the fact because it was such a tragic accident. No, my husband said to ask you how is he supposed to remember any of the men from that place when he saw so many? Then he said, the school shut because of the dead boy's fall, but of course, he wasn't dead when he began the descent. The accident and the water were the two main reasons. The accident caused what Arnold called bad publicity. Parents withdrew their children over the summer, thus, there was little income to use for the extensive works needed on the water pipes. Even the rich ex-pupils vanished into the woodwork like beetles, so there was no money, you see. The bursar told me all this. He was an old, old friend, in fact, so old, the boys called him Meths, short for Methuselah. He may even have drunk it. There were always rumours, but there is one lasting fact, Mr Mullet. Sinford's had had its day long before it closed, and nobody wanted to know.'

'So, nothing about a Mr Simon Stape? A friend of the boy who fell. One of Mr Hogg's last boys. No?'

'Very sorry, Mr Millet, not even dear old Arnold can help you. Have you tried visiting the place?'

'It's open again?' Jimmy slipped in beside her.

'The touched one's back,' Mrs Hogg whispered, and nudged Jack further along the tomb. Ignoring Jimmy, she said, 'Arnold had a few favourites, and he was keen on his last boys. His last lost boys, he called them, but then he called all last-year boys lost, because they left not really knowing where they were going. If he remembers correctly, the boy who died had three good friends, two in particular, and a Stape might have been one of them. There was definitely an honourable someone, but then, there were many.'

'The Honourable Marcus Havegood,' Jimmy said, but Jack had to repeat it before she would speak again.

'Might have been,' she frowned. 'You can't expect the man to remember everything. He's been dead a while.'

Obviously, she'd not taken this information from the man rotting at their feet, and Jack suspected she knew more than she was letting on.

'Anything more about this Mr Stape?' he asked. 'We are trying to find him, you see, but he is not at his parents' house, or his own.'

'And you thought one of his teachers from twelve years ago would know? Who came up with that daft idea? Still...' She produced a pear from the display on her hat, and Jack realised the foliage was real. 'Makes for a nice outing. Have you thought to look at the school?'

'Has it reopened?' Jimmy repeated, and this time she answered.

'No, it is abandoned, but if you're asking a dead man and his wife to tell you where one of the old boys is today, you'd have just as much luck asking a pile of old stones.' To Jack, she hissed, 'I told you he was touched.'

'But what's the point of looking at the school if it's closed?' Jack said.

'Not the actual building, Mr Muddit, its records.'

'Are they still there?' That was Jimmy, trying his best to gain the woman's attention.

Mrs Hogg twisted her mouth, and like a conspirator, leant in to say in a hushed voice, 'The man is completely unhinged. He asks such questions.' Louder, she said, 'I know much of the place is as it was, furniture and all, but I expect the records have been taken away. If anything will tell you where the boys went after they left, it will be them. Mind you, most went on to university, the priesthood or the army. I expect they are teaching, preaching or dead.'

Boosted by Jimmy's furtive looks of encouragement, Jack persisted, feeling more like a detective with each question. 'Where would they have put these records?'

Mrs Hogg bit into her pear, but finding it too hard, dropped it back into the shrubbery on her head. 'Now, that's a good question,' she said. 'One moment.'

With that, she slid from the tomb and knelt at the grave like a woman keening over a deathbed, but without the wailing.

'This was a pointless exercise,' Jimmy said. 'We should get back to Delamere.'

'Yeah, I agree, but let's give her a couple more minutes. You never know.'

Mrs Hogg made a fuss of righting herself, using her husband's headstone for support, and adjusting her hat as she regained her balance.

'Arnold says you could try the Temple. Not in any religious sense, but as in the place near the Thames embankment. You see, private schools such as Sinford's are not required to keep records like the dear little schools of poor people, but they may if they wish. Sinford's did, because it was mainly a decent place. If the school records went anywhere, it would have been with the headmaster, Mr Marsden, and he went to work at the London School Board. I don't know why. Probably insane, but that was all Arnold was willing to share.'

Jack still couldn't see how any such records would tell him where Mr Stape was so long after leaving school, but perhaps the records contained an address other than his parents' home. Maybe he had more family than Havegood had mentioned, or even, like Jack, had an 'Uncle' Bob who wasn't an uncle, but someone he could go to when he was in trouble. If such a man or woman existed, it would give them another lead.

'You are thinking deeply,' Mrs Hogg observed, staring at him too closely for Jack's liking. 'That is a good sign in any man, for so few bother to think these days, don't you agree, Mr Muggit?'

'Merrit, and yes, I was thinking.' To Jimmy, he said, 'We should follow this up. We ain't going to get anything else by sitting here.'

'I agree, Mr Madlett,' Jimmy gave him a matey grin. 'Time is moving on, but our investigation isn't. We should get back to Headcorn and then London.'

'Too far to walk,' Mrs Hogg said, and tipped her head to look at the sky. An apple dropped from her hat and rolled across the tomb to fall onto the dried grass. 'As I have been of so little help in any other way, and as it is a lovely morning, I will drive you there. It will make another outing, and it has been too long since I had one.'

Jimmy tried to dissuade her, but she insisted, and Jack didn't fancy sprinting alongside her wayward driving for four miles.

'Thank you,' he said, taking the final decision off his own back. 'We'll accept the offer, Mrs Hogg, but I ain't running. Your horse is strong enough to pull the three of us, so we'll squash in, and this time, I'll take the reins.'

THIRTEEN

Jack had harboured a concern since meeting with the unusual Mrs Hogg, and thought it best to tell Jimmy before they reached home. They were alone in their compartment, but were pulling into a station with a crowded platform, making time limited.

'There's something I don't understand,' he said. 'I'm new to this, and you know what you're doing, but I don't get how Mr Stape's past can tell us where he might be now. I ain't a clue what these school records have in them. It might be useful if they had the name of someone from his family we don't know about, but otherwise…?'

'I've got a reason,' Jimmy said, and gave a wink which Jack though unhelpful.

'And what is it?'

'You get a nose for these things after a while.' Jimmy touched the side of his, suggesting he was going to keep the information to himself, but when Jack rolled his eyes, he picked up on his annoyance, and said, 'Something doesn't smell right.'

'Like what?'

'Like all of it. Give me a little more time, and I'll tell you about it when we get home. I want Will to be there.'

More passengers crowded in, including gentlemen with unnecessary umbrellas, a woman with a massive portmanteau, and two vicars who immediately lit up cigars. Jack pulled down the window, and stared at the back of drab buildings until they crossed the river. Eyeing the cabs amid the traffic over on Waterloo Bridge, he couldn't help wondering if he wouldn't have been better off remaining as a cabbie. At least there wasn't so much thought involved. Then, he remembered the food at the inn, the countryside, the amusement of an eccentric lady, and the praise Jimmy had awarded him over the past three days. There was very little praise as a cabman, and not much excitement. Although his new job hadn't brought much intrigue, it had brought some. Apart from that, and Jack's concerns about Will, his brother was having the time of his life, fitting into the household, enjoying its books and his tasks. The thought brought a smile, which Jimmy questioned with a look, but Jack said, 'Nothing,' and turned his mind back to the case and what Jimmy had meant about something not smelling right.

Whatever it was couldn't have been as bad as the smell of people and oil, steam and smoke, as they bustled through Charing Cross Station, with its aromas more powerful than those of the country and far less pleasant. What was pleasant, though, was hailing a cab, and telling the driver to take them to Bucks Avenue. Better still was fixing the fare.

'Four shillings, Sir.'

'Rubbish,' Jack countered. 'One. It's only two miles.'

'Oh? Got the knowledge, have you?' The driver sneered down from his perch.

'I have as it happens, mate. You don't want to go through Westminster at his time of day, and nor do we. The Mall, Constitution Hill, Halkin Street, Belgrave Square, Wilton and into Bucks. Two miles on the nose. One shilling as standard for this time of year. Quick as you like if you want a tip.'

Once in the hansom and underway, Jimmy said, 'You're sounding more like a gent every day.'

'Sounding more like a toff, you mean. I'm learning from the best.'

'Thanks, I think, but probably not the best. Say, can you tell your man to stop by the church at Wilton Place? I want to dash out and get something.'

Jack knocked on the ceiling, and when the hatch opened, took up the voice of a toff, and said, 'A quick stop by St Paul's on Wilton if you will.'

'There'll be waiting time.'

'I wouldn't expect anything less.'

Wilton Place was a residential street of town houses, expensive ones at that, and Jack couldn't think what Jimmy was up to. When the cab stopped, he hurried around the corner into Kinnerton Street, and returned five minutes later with a box. Back in his seat, he said nothing except to order the cab onwards, and a few minutes later, they were home.

Jimmy still hadn't explained his action as they let themselves into the hall to find it quietly abandoned with new flowers on the table, and the doors to the drawing room wide open. Beyond it, further investigation showed them Will pacing in the office, and, as soon as they walked in, he stopped, and carried on a conversation he'd been having with them only two minutes before. At least, that was how it sounded.

'I put up a second board because of it,' he said, and indicated a duplicate chalkboard by the first. Both were covered with writing. 'There was more to what you left me than I think you have seen, and this is the best way to work through the information. I have also done some calling, and found some information, but sadly, nothing yet of any great use. Mr Pascoe says Mrs Norwood from next door has made supper for tonight because Joe and Dalston have left for the north. Jack, you are still wearing your bowler, and you are inside the house. Good afternoon, Mr Wright.'

'Er, good afternoon.'

'Sorry, this is how Will is sometimes,' Jack said. 'Are you alright, brother?'

'I am. Your machine, however, is not, Mr Wright. In fact, were it human, I would say it is quite sick. It has been vomiting all morning. I have put the strips here on your desk in the order they arrived. Beside them, as you will see, I have arranged your post. Between yesterday afternoon and just now, you have had four telegrams and three postal deliveries comprising sixteen letters between them. Here, arranged in arrival order by size. You have also had one newspaper delivered and a copy of the Police Illustrated, which, I'm sorry to say, I was unable to prise from Mr Pascoe before he ran off with it. Meanwhile, something terrible is about to happen.'

Jimmy dropped his satchel and the box. 'What?'

'I don't know yet.'

'Will...' Jack took him by the shoulders, and in a routine practiced over many years, looked directly into his eyes. 'Slow down, mate. I'm here.' He brushed his fringe from his face, and cupped his cheeks. 'Take a breath, put your mind in order, and remember, not everything has to be exact. Slowly, yeah? You're behaving like a puppy what's not seen its owner all day.'

Will's green eyes lost their agitation, and he blinked himself to a calmer state.

'What a strange analogy,' he said. 'Next, you will be accusing me of leaving puddles behind the furniture, and that is something I have not done since I was seven.'

'What d'you mean something's going to happen?' Jimmy was at his desk, and much to Will's consternation was reordering his letters.

'I have a feeling,' Will said, his fingers dancing by his sides.

'Are you settled, Will?'

Will nodded. 'I have much on my mind. This, mainly.' He threw his hand to the chalkboards. 'And that...' He pointed to the safe.

The door was open.

When Jimmy noticed, he shot to his feet and dived for the thing to check its contents.

'We've been robbed?'

'No, Mr Wright. I opened it.'

By the look on his face, Jimmy was either outraged or impressed, it was hard to tell, but he was certainly dumbstruck.

'How the hell did you do that?'

'Via logical thinking and with a little help from Mr Pascoe, who is not to blame, because he didn't know what I was about.' To Jack, he said, 'You don't have to hold me as though I were a lunatic. You may let me go.'

Jack ruffled Will's hair, earning himself an annoyed tut and a shove, before he suggested they all sit down and start again.

Jimmy was the last to take his seat, and when he did, his narrow eyes transferred displeasure from the safe to Will.

'What have you been doing?' he said, and loosened his tie.

'Lots,' was Will's unhelpful reply, but before Jimmy could take him up on it, he explained. 'The safe was easy. A combination lock demands numbers and directions. I read about that in *The History Of Pollacks, Security and Sensation*, a tiresome little work you have on one of your shelves. The safe was built by Pollacks of Hatton Garden. The book explained how each combination for this model requires a three-directional number combination, with the numbers being set and reset by way of an internal mechanism. Your birthday, Mr Pascoe told me, is the tenth of January and the year, eighteen sixty-three. Strangely, you were born on the same day as the first underground train arrived at Farringdon Street station. The number of the locomotive was fifty-six, its first journey, four miles. The station was relocated two years later in December sixty-five. I concluded you are too clever to simply use your birthday as the combination, even in reverse order, but would use something more obscure. After three trials, I combined the day of your birth, Saturday, the sixth day of the week, the distance the train travelled, four miles, and the year of relocation, sixty-five. As the first train travelled from west to east, I began clockwise. As I know the current code, I suggest you reset it.'

Jimmy was open-mouthed, and even Jack was impressed. He'd seen Will's display of what some would call madness on many occasions, but this was exceptional. If his mind was a racehorse, it had just won the Derby.

'Why?' Jimmy said.

'Ah, yes. That is a little more ambiguous,' Will replied, and crossed his legs, his eyelashes fluttering. 'I felt you had kept something from me, and I wanted to be sure. With you and Jack off on an adventure, I sought one of my own, and although the shelves of your library are well-stocked, I craved something more practical. Something of more use to the case.'

'So you broke into my safe?'

'Mr Wright. You have employed my brother and I to work for you, and I can't do that if you keep information from me. I am either part of your investigative team, or I am not.'

'Can't argue with that, I suppose,' Jimmy muttered, and Jack sensed he was more impressed than angry. 'Go on.'

'I have yet to read the file you have prepared on this missing man. I was going to do that directly, but as soon as I retrieved the folder, I felt that something was about to go wrong. It was at that time your machine vomited another strip of paper.'

Jimmy picked up the strips to glance at the stream of dots and dashes.

'Will's had these feelings before,' Jack said. 'They usually lead to nothing. Grandma Ida took him to a medium once, but that didn't help.'

'It is not supernatural, Jack,' Will chided. 'It is part of my preciseness. Anyway... Before any of this business with the safe, I rearranged the information on the boards, as you can see. I have put together facts about the school, and discovered that its records are kept at the London School Board's offices at the Temple. Apparently the last headmaster took them there when he became an inspector, and they found a home in the storage department. I thought I might go and see if they are still there.'

'Why didn't you tell us this before we went to Kent?'

'Because I didn't know, Jack, and that was because you'd not let me in on all the facts of the case.'

'To be fair, that ain't my decision.'

'To be fair would have been to ask me to sit in on the interview with Mr Havegood.'

'Your job's in the book room.'

'My job is to assist you two, and it's called a library. You'd do well to use it.'

'Oh, give over on your prattle-nagging...'

'Right!' Jimmy slapped his desk and stood. 'Like I said on the train,

Jack, there's more to this case. After dinner, I want us to get around the desk and talk it all through. We've got nowhere, and we're only a few days away from a suicide.' He fiddled with his safe as he spoke, and when he turned back, slammed the door and spun the dial. 'I'd appreciate it if you asked next time, Mr Merrit.'

'I shall if you are here. Are you going to look at the letter from Mr Stape's mother?'

'What?'

'It was in the second pile, but you have since ruined the arrangement.'

Jimmy searched through the letters. 'How do you know it's from her?'

'Her name and address are on the back. What did you learn in Kent, Jack?'

'That some old women like to keep fruit in their hat,' Jack said, still scowling at his brother. 'Apart from that, nothing much. She also suggested these records you just talked about, but I still say they ain't going to help us find the man. It's been too many years.'

'Agreed,' Jimmy said, holding a paperknife in one hand while reading the letter. 'And Mrs Stape is no help. She's had no word from her son since June. No other address for him... Last seen at the funeral of wife and child... Not unusual for him to go abroad without warning... Will contact us if and when she hears, but thinks there is nothing to worry about... Despite his recent tragedy, he is a sensible man with a devout faith that will see him through... etc. We're not welcome to visit while she is in mourning.'

'Understandable.' Will was already at his boards, noting the details in the box beside Mrs Stape's name.

'More like she's not concerned,' Jimmy said. 'Which suggests there's nothing wrong.'

'Or she don't care about him,' Jack put in. 'I mean, he lost his wife and kid only a few weeks ago, and you're telling her you want to find him. She don't know where he is and don't sound in the least upset. What is it with these rich nobs? When Will went missing, the whole street was out looking.'

'I wasn't missing,' Will protested. 'I knew exactly where I was.'

'And we can add to that, the brother doesn't know or doesn't care either.' Jimmy held up a strip of paper. 'From America. *Unable to help. Not seen brother for years. No family contact. Have a nice day.*'

'How many more dead ends?' Jack said. 'What now?'

'I think it's time we had another word with Mr Havegood.' Jimmy slumped into his chair. 'Oh, that's for you, by the way,' he said, waving towards the box. 'Will already has one.'

'For me?'

Inside was a leather satchel with shoulder straps, not dissimilar to the battered one Jimmy carried everywhere.

'You mean it?'

'I do.' Jimmy put on a brief smile, but Jack had no doubt it was false, because his face remained otherwise strained. 'You can't be a Clearwater investigator without a decent satchel,' he said. 'I keep everything in mine.'

To Jack, the gesture affirmed his place in the house and in the company, and he allowed himself a moment of pride.

'Thank you, Jimmy,' he said, brushing his hand over the polished leather and drinking in its raw smell. It was probably the most expensive gift anyone had given him, but it meant more than its cost.

'Why?' Jimmy said, drawing Jack's attention away from the brass clasp and buckles.

'Why what?'

Jimmy swapped the strip he was reading for another, and then reread the first. 'What's this all about?'

'Is it the case?' Will asked, wiping his hands free of chalk.

'No. Something else... Where were we?'

'Nowhere,' Jack said, thinking it was funny, but realising it wasn't. 'I mean, still not much further down the road. You said we should speak to Mr Havegood again.'

'Yes... Possibly... Make a note, Will. Things to do. See the school records for possible contacts, chase up Stape's workplace, see if he has other friends, because those neighbours will be no more help. There's something else though....'

His thought hung in a stream of afternoon sunshine, and he stared blankly at the far wall, while Will's chalk scratched, and a carriage rolled past the window.

'No. Can't put my finger on it,' he said, and took a deep breath. 'So, after dinner, meet in here and start from the beginning, yeah?'

'If that's what you want,' Will said. 'I am happy to talk more now. My mind is constantly at work.'

'No, Will,' Jack said. 'There are times when you need to slow down. Otherwise, you'll be like a horse working too many miles, and end up in the knacker's yard before your time.'

Will's face tightened with annoyance, but Jack ignored the glare. Will couldn't see his own shortcomings, and older brothers always knew best.

'I, for one, want to wash and change,' Jimmy said, reading a note. 'Jack, you'll want to meet Ben Baxter.'

'Will I? Who's that?'

'The Cheap Street man currently looking after the horses. With you working on this, you won't have time for stable duties.'

'Oh.' Jack suffered a pang of annoyance. Yesterday, he'd liked the idea of having someone to work under him, but now that someone was there and looking after Shadow, it was as if something had been taken away.

'He's a good chap. You'll get on well.'

'What about me?' Will hovered hopefully at the boards.

'You might want to take a look at what we found in Clapham,' Jimmy said, and passed him the diary. 'There's not much in it, but seeing as how you've raided my safe for the rest of the evidence, you might as well have a look at this.'

Will took it, and thanked him.

'Right then...'

'Oh dear.' Will interrupted whatever Jimmy was about to say next.

'What is it?'

'That strange feeling.' He hurried to the window to look out. 'No. Not there.'

'Will?'

'Mr Wright says something doesn't fit with this case, and I agree.' Will was fussing again, his hands flicked over each other, and his eyelashes twitched more than usual. With his gaze settled on the chalkboard, he put two of his dancing fingers between his lips as if about to whistle. 'It's on there, but that's not what is worrying me. No, no...' The mumbling continued as he returned to his seat. 'It is not superstitious, but by the pricking of my thumbs...'

Jimmy threw Jack a look of annoyance, but equally concerned, Jack had no answer. Will had been in many states ranging from overexcited to silent and stubborn, but this was unusual.

Jack touched his arm to calm him, just as a woman appeared in the doorway.

'Sorry to interrupt, Jimmy,' she said, glancing between the brothers. 'Mrs Norwood. Hello.'

'Yes, hello, oh, and hello to you. The other Mr Merrit I assume?'

'Yes. Jack.'

'Lovely.' The woman was more interested in Jimmy. 'They've been trying to reach you all day. You had messages.'

'I've seen, but they only said to contact them as soon as I could.'

'Yes, well, the situation is worse than first thought. Mr Nancarrow messaged me. Here, I'll let you read it.'

She handed Jimmy another strip of paper, and as he read, the colour drained from his face.

'I know, Jimmy,' the woman said. 'I am sure it will be alright, but Mr Nancarrow thought you should be there. They have sent for Doctor Markland.'

'It's that bad?' Jimmy stood a moment like a statue.

'Jimmy?'

'Sorry, Mrs N. Yes. I will...' Stumbling for words, he looked at Jack and then Will. 'It's the timing... Damn. I can't just...'

The woman took him by the arm. 'Jimmy, you've had it before, and the doctors say you can't catch it a second time. Whatever you are doing, you must leave it and go. Who knows how much time he has? Remember Mrs Baker and Her Ladyship?'

They might have known what and who they were talking about, but Jack was in the dark until Jimmy found his resolve, and squared his shoulders.

'I have to go to Larkspur,' he said, and began emptying his

knapsack. 'Tom is gravely ill.' Breaking off, he froze again, and his eyes became moist.

'Mr Wright?' Will whispered, and brought him back to life.

'What? Yes. Mrs Norwood, can you book me a ticket on the night express?'

The housekeeper examined the watch pinned to her dress. 'It leaves in ninety minutes. Baxter can drive you.'

'I can do that,' Jack said, affronted.

'I'll write to Havegood as soon as I arrive.' Jimmy ignored him. 'I'll send apologies. Tell him we can't take his case any further.'

'Being with Tom is far more important,' Mrs Norwood agreed. 'I will make you a basket for the journey.'

She swished from the room, leaving Jack confused and Will open-mouthed.

'You can't leave this case, Mr Wright,' he said. 'The poor man is beside himself, and we are the only ones who can help.'

'*I* am the only one,' Jimmy said, as Max appeared from the next room.

'Anything I can be doing?'

'Yes, Max. Help Baxter get the trap hitched up. I'll be ten minutes.'

The butler left as Jimmy repacked his knapsack with writing materials.

'I apologise if this is bold, but we can continue the case,' Will said, his fingers still fiddling with each other, but his face solid with determination.

'No. You've not been with me long enough. You don't understand the business.'

'The business is all on the board, Mr Wright. It is a case of asking a few people a few things, noting what they say, and, sending a letter to the client to tell him either where his friend is hiding, or not.'

Jack said nothing. Part of him agreed with his brother, another part saw sense in Jimmy's decision, and yet a third part smarted at the thought that Jimmy didn't, after all, think he was capable. If he had any parts left, one of them was annoyed that Max had been sent to hitch the vehicle and not him.

'No, Will. I can't risk having two untrained men left alone to conclude an inquiry, not for the son of a viscount.'

'Untrained?' Will was exasperated. 'Sir, I have read Poe and Collins. I invented my own satisfactory ending to *The Mystery of Edwin Drood*, and recently digested *A Scandal in Bohemia* from the Strand Magazine. I had the answer long before Mr Holmes. The Havegood case will be safe in our hands.'

'This isn't storybook stuff, Merrit,' Jimmy snapped. 'It's not children's fantasy.'

Jack took a sharp inbreath. Had it been him on the receiving end, he would have hit back, but Will remained composed.

'Put what we have in a report in case Havegood wants to see what we've tried,' Jimmy said, marching to the door. 'I'll have to charge him for time spent, and he'll want evidence. Write it up, and wait for me to return. Max will open my letters. Goodbye.'

He was gone.

'Bloody cheek,' Jack said under his breath. 'Don't take it to heart, Will. His man's dodgy sick by the sound of it.'

'This will not do,' Will said, looking at Jack for agreement. 'We must carry on.'

'I'm a cabbie, Will, not an investigator. We're lucky to have these jobs, and if they mean doing nothing for a few days, then that's that.'

'You don't mean it.'

'I can help the new bloke with the horses. Get Shadow out for a few runs...'

'Oh, do stop it. You know as well as I that we are more than capable. You are fuming at Mr Wright for what he just said, and apart from anything else, neither of us can leave Mr Havegood pining for his missing lover just because Mr Wright has flown to the bedside of his. What kind of hypocrites would that make us?'

'I don't get it.'

'You don't need to. It was a hypothetical question. Go after him, tell him we will continue the case, and ask him for his letter of authorisation. That's all you need to do. Go.'

'You think we can?'

'Of course. Now, if you would,' Will prompted, waggling a finger towards the door.

The part of Jack that agreed with his brother joined forces with a slice of him keen to prove himself, and together, they won the battle against doubt. Calling, he raced after Jimmy.

There was no point trying to persuade him against his decision in the same way there was no point trying to force a horse into a cab's traces. There were other ways of doing what needed to be done, and his experience at the Harris yard had shown him honesty was not always the only option.

'At least leave us your made-up letter from the police,' he said, catching Jimmy's arm at the top of the stairs. 'In case you get a reply from Mr Stape's work, and they ask for it, or something.'

Jimmy stopped on the landing, and spun to him, his eyes now more than moist.

'There are copies in the desk,' he said. 'But you won't need them.'

'Will you be alright?'

Jimmy swallowed as his eyes searched Jack's face. 'I told you about Tom last night,' he said. 'I didn't tell you just how much he means to me. They all do. If they've sent for Doc Markland, it's bad.'

'What is?'

'Russian flu. It killed Prince Eddy in January, it killed Clearwater's mother before that, and his housekeeper, and others on the Larkspur estate. It's back, and Tom's the worst affected.'

Jack knew how bad the illness could be, they'd lost several neighbours because of it. Granddad Reggie had caught just a mild case, but the doctor's said it was one of the things that contributed to his decline. There was no time to sympathise, though, because Jimmy set off towards his rooms.

'We'll keep an eye on things,' Jack said, following. 'We can message you if anything happens.'

'You can't solve it on your own. I'll let Havegood know.'

'That won't do the business no good.'

'I don't care about the business.'

'Alright then. I'll send the letter tomorrow. You don't want to be worrying about work.'

'Yeah, alright, but write it politely. Ask Mrs Norwood to help.'

'I ain't an idiot, Jimmy.'

Jimmy swung into his room. 'All I care about is finding Tom still alive.' Hearing himself, he froze, and said, 'Oh, God.'

Jack stood speechless in the doorway as Jimmy gripped the end of his bed.

'I'm sorry, Jack,' he said, his voice quieter but not quite under control. 'I have to be with Tom. Imagine if Will was dying three hundred miles from here. What would you do?'

Jack understood, but Will had been right. They were capable, and they needed to show the boss they could do the job. Jack might have been a cabbie four weeks ago, but now he was a man determined to find an answer, even if that meant going behind Jimmy's back.

Kicking the door shut, he said, 'I'll help you pack.'

FOURTEEN

'There is good news, and there is bad news,' were Will's first words when Jack found him the next morning already at work in the office.

'Wondered why you weren't at breakfast,' he said. 'What time did you get up?'

'Six. You wanted an early start.'

'Yeah, I meant like, nine or something.'

Will was examining his chalkboards with a book in his hand, and having found a place to write, scratched some words in white against the black. Unsure where to go, and not wanting to take Jimmy's leather chair, Jack sat on one of the hard-backed ones within reach of the desk, and put his new satchel at his feet. From it, he took Jimmy's casebook and opened it in his lap, ready to start.

Now what?

Will answered for him. 'Which do you want first? Good or bad?'

'Er, bad, I suppose. Hell, it's not Jimmy is it?'

'No.' Will had finished his writing and drifted to the large reading table, placing his notes to one side. 'Mrs Norwood called in and said he arrived safely in Cornwall, and was with his Tom. At first, I thought she was talking about a cat, but then the fog cleared. This Tom person, apparently, is no better and no worse, but several of the maids are down with it, no-one else is allowed in or out of the grounds, and the doctor is seeing to everyone. She also said something about a chemist coming down from... I think it was Stoneridge... An academy, at any rate. A Mr Hope was bringing hope of, if not a cure, then a treatment. The upshot was, Mr Wright won't be back for some time. I can now tell you the bad news. Boss.'

The last word came with a grin, and Jack told him not to call him that. If anything, with the way Will was behaving, it should have been the other way around.

'Go on,' he said. 'Better get started on something. What you got?'

'A letter from the dead wife's father. It was addressed to Mr Wright, but he gave Max permission to open his correspondence, and Max passed on all the relevant letters and messages to me. He would have given them to you, but you were still asleep.'

'Alright, don't go on. I was tired. What's the letter say?'

Will picked up what he had been reading and passed it over.

Dear Mr Wright,

Thank you for the gentle way you approached this subject, and for your condolences. I can inform you, neither my wife nor I have seen or heard from our son-in-law since the day of the funeral.

As for his possible whereabouts, I can only tell you this:

As we parted on that terrible day, I asked him of his plans for the future. We had not known each other long, but I had known him to be a good man, a sensible one, and one able to contain his sensitivities. Throughout the terrible proceeding, he had remained stalwart, and not given way to grief, as others had. My concern was for his well-being, and I offered him respite at our house; an offer he declined. Travel was on his mind, he said, once a suitable period of mourning had passed. I told him, we would not be in the least offended if he wanted to travel before the customary year had passed after his son's death, nor even the six months' mourning usually expected following the passing of our daughter. With my permission, he intimated he might leave immediately, and as his friend, the Hon. Mr Havegood is unable to locate him, I can only assume that is what he has done.

This is all the information I can impart at this time.
I remain, your servant,

F. G. *Arrowsmith Esq.*

'So, the bad news is, the in-laws don't know where he is or might be, apart from abroad, which is what his neighbours said.'

'I've already amended the board.' Will pointed. 'This only leaves his workplace, and we have yet to hear. No luck with the neighbours, you said?'

'Yes. I mean no, no luck, though one of them, Mr Ashton...' Jack grimaced at the thought of the other, 'sounded like he knew Stape well. He looks after the house and stuff, and was happy to let us poke around if it meant finding the man. Said he'd be in touch if he saw him, but I can't see him telling us nothing else, and there's no-one left in the family to ask.'

'Other school friends? Any other friends, come to that. Did Mr Havegood say?'

Jack flicked pages in the casebook, and silently thanked Max for his help. During breakfast, the butler had sat with him and helped him understand Jimmy's handwriting. Along with all manner of notes and diagrams, there were lines of strange dots and dashes, and Max said they were Morse code, which Jimmy often used as shorthand. Impressive, but not much use to Jack. However, Max said, if necessary, the housekeeper next door could translate, or there was a book he could use, and Jack's day began with the same bemusement as the previous one had ended.

Jimmy had left in a carriage driven by someone who'd come from a mission for renters. The butler was an actor, the housekeeper next door understood telegraph code, and now, a cabbie was a detective. Throughout the last evening, and part of the night, he'd bounced between the thrill of what he might do, and the fear of having to do it, and had woken with the same confusion. The only steady light was Will, waiting for him to answer.

'School friends? Er, no. Havegood's list only mentioned them what we've already contacted.'

'I thought as much. Still, we have plenty to go on, and I have put what we have in order, but first, there is the good news.' Will pulled out his pocket watch. 'I will be leaving in a few minutes.'

'To do what?'

'To visit the London School Board. I messaged them while you were in Kent, and the reply came early this morning. I am invited to meet with a Mr Salisbury. The secretary of the board said...' Will collected another letter from an ordered line on the table, and read aloud, '"I await your good self with everything at my disposal of which I hope will be assisting to the investigation."' Screwing up his nose as if the paper smelt bad, he put it back in its place. 'You would have thought anyone who worked for the School Board would be able to construct a better ordered sentence,' he said, and sat on the settee.

It had sounded fine to Jack, who said, 'I should go with you.'

'Why?'

'Well... D'you know where it is?'

'I have the address.'

'Is the boy going to drive you?'

'You mean Master Baxter? No. I shall take the omnibus.'

'D'you know how?'

Will regarded him with sadness and let out a long breath. At the same time, he twisted his fingers together, and his brow wrinkled.

'I'm not a child, Jack.'

'I know, mate, but...'

'No. Don't give me any of your buts. I am no longer eleven. You no longer need to watch over me as if I were an imbecile...'

'I weren't saying that.'

'It's how it sounds.'

'But you've never been further on your own than 'round Millwall.'

'That's not true. Listen...' Will leant forward with his forearms on his knees, and his fingers still worrying each other. It looked as if he was about to say something vitally important, because his eyes and lips narrowed. 'I am becoming cross.'

There was no hint of anger.

'Why?'

'Just because I am precise, doesn't mean I am an idiot, or going to get lost, or blithely wander under the wheels of a tram. I am twenty-one years and eleven months old, and I am far better read than you. I have most of the street atlas of London imprinted in my head from when I helped you learn the knowledge, and I can't help but count and remember every turn and pace of my pacing when I walk anywhere. I've had to take care of myself for days on end. Yet, you still take me for a boy.'

'Will...'

'After years of being stuck in the house, stitching your clothes, counting your pennies, cleaning our floors, and doing nothing of any use to anyone, I am considered an adult. Not by you, but by strangers who have seen abilities in me you are too blind or too proud to acknowledge. It should have been you who did that.'

Jack was too stunned by the outburst to know what to say. Will wasn't looking at him, he was watching his hands, where the fingers of one clamped and clawed the other in turn, writhing and pulling like live eels on a pie shop slab.

Jack bounded from his chair, and knowing better than to try and tear his hands apart, took his wrists, and repeated his name until Will looked him in the eye. From then, it was a case of repeating calming words, 'Easy, mate. Slowly. You're doing good...' until the anxiety left Will's fingers.

When they were still, Jack took his hands and clamped them gently to Will's knees, and eye to eye, said, 'Did I cause that?'

Will nodded.

'I'm just worried,' Jack said.

'No need.'

'What if you got distressed when I weren't around?'

'I would cope with it on my own. Besides, it only happens when you *are* around.'

'They'd try and take you in like last time.'

'And they would not succeed. I am calm now, Jack. Thank you.'

'You see why I worry?'

'I've not done that for some time, and it only happened because...'

'You were angry with me.'

'No. I was frustrated, because I can't make you see. You worry about me too much. This is the problem, and it is one that can be avoided in future.'

'How?'

Will gave another sigh, but this time it was shorter, and he pulled his hands free so he could wipe his face.

'By accepting I am nearly twenty-two, and you cannot mother me for the rest of my life.'

'I worry...'

'I know, but there is no need. Agreed?'

It was a lot to let go of. Now they were away from old routines and without their grandparents, Jack had assumed Will would need him more, but the opposite was true. Apparently no-one needed him. Not Will, not Jimmy who didn't think him capable of continuing with the case, and not even Shadow, not now the renter was living in the stables.

'Agreed, Jack?'

There *was* someone who needed him. Two people, in fact. The client, and the missing man, and if the only way to help them was to allow Will a little freedom, that's what he'd have to do, no matter how much concern he might suffer.

'Yeah, alright. But if you get lost, or have any trouble on this visit, I'll be coming with you next time.'

'Might as well put me in the traces and crack your whip,' Will muttered as he returned to his table.

'Oi. Don't get arsey.'

'Your top waistcoat button is not done up as you usually have it. You might want to see to that,' Will said, bringing the subject to a close, and having collected his casebook, took up his seat and smiled as if all was well with the world.

'So, what do I do while you go to the school?'

'It's not a school,' Will chuckled. 'It's actually a committee, and one that is in charge of improving schools and schoolchildren across the city. However, there is an office. The secretary of the board confirmed that even though Sinford's was in Kent, its ledgers are in the collection because they were left there by the headmaster. As this, rightly or wrongly, makes them public, he must show them to me.'

'And what are you looking for?'

'To be honest, Jack, I don't know what to expect, but I will be vigilant. I don't know how long I will be away either, but you have no need to worry.'

'I know,' Jack said, trying to sound convincing.

'Except you will. Now, for what you must do.'

Like a cat unable to sit still, Will was on his feet again, trotting back to the boards and picking up his chalk.

'I was wondering when I'd get my instructions,' Jack said. It sounded sarcastic, and he added, 'What am I doing while you're out?'

'Fish,' Will said, facing the board and comparing it to a list.

'Fish?'

'The smell of.'

'I thought we'd left that behind in Limehouse.'

'Not quite. As Mr Wright said, as and we were going to discuss before he was called away, there is a rank smell of it all over this, and I think it would be a good idea if you tried to find out why. Of course, we are working on this together, so I am open to your suggestions.'

'In that case, I'd suggest you tell me what the flip you're talking about.'

Will was back in his seat in a second, his casebook open in his lap, and comparing the list to the pages.

'Good,' he said to himself. To Jack, he said, 'What is on the board is copied into my book, and I have made a note of what we need to do, because something is as off as a week-old haddock. I wrote everything down before it slipped my mind, and it would be a good idea if you looked through it and had a long, hard think.'

'Yeah, and...?' Still unsure what Will was driving at, Jack left the words hanging.

'You'll see,' was Will's unhelpful conclusion. 'There are also suggestions for things you can do while I am out. Time remains against us, and I should go. The first job is to write to Mr Havegood for any other contacts, and to tell him our progress. If you can do that now, I will post the letter on my way.' Crossing to the door, he stopped to drop the list into Jack's lap. 'Just so you are aware, Max knows we are continuing with the case, and he says he won't tell Mr Wright. No point in worrying him in Cornwall, because you already worry enough for everyone.'

'Yeah, alright, no need to go on.'

'I will fetch my hat and be down in five minutes.' Will left, calling back, 'There is writing paper in the desk.'

'Ah, well...' Jack dragged himself to his feet. 'He's taken charge alright, and you agreed to do this, so better get on with it.'

The thought of having to think about something other than cabs, horses and routes was another new experience, as was sitting at Jimmy's desk, pulling out a sheet of headed writing paper, and trying hard to remember how Grandma Ida had taught him to write a letter in his best hand. There was no need to put his address because it was already printed, but the date had to go somewhere, and, that done, the man's name went on the left. *Dear Mr Havegood...* Or was it Sir? Maybe Dear Mr Honourable Havegood Esq...

'Just do your best and think toff,' he said, and dipped the pen, only to discover it didn't need dipping, and when he used it, the date came out as a lake of ink. 'Bugger it.' Another sheet of paper, no dipping, and with his tongue set between his teeth, he concentrated on making neat letters and keeping straight lines.

Dear Mr Havegood,

We want to know if you can think of anyone else who might know where Mr Stape has gone. I know you've already said you can't think of no one else, but I thought, by now, you might of.

If you can, please tell me (Jack Merrit) quick as you like.

We are doing what we can, and it's going alright. I think we will find him by the right date.

Jack Merrit (Assistant to Mr Wright, Detective.)

The first attempt was more crossing out than anything else, the second was a little better, and so was the third, but it was the fourth he was most proud of, and that was the one he put in an envelope, and addressed.

'I will see you when I return.'

Will had crept back and was waiting by the desk. Jack handed him the envelope, but before he could say goodbye, Will was gone.

'Bloody hell,' he sighed, and able to relax for the first time since walking into the office, rested back in the chair.

Relaxation, however, was not what Will had on his mind. That was clear after Jack took a brief glance at his instructions.

The page was headed, *Things To Do (Jack)*, and beneath the title was a list.

One. There is something unsettling on the chalkboards, as if we have missed a vital thing. I cannot say what. Please have a look and see if what is there makes sense to you.

Two. Reread Havegood's memorandum about his days at Sinford's because it niggles me. It is in the safe. (Jimmy reset the combination: Clockwise (to the right), eighteen. Anticlockwise four. Clockwise seventy-two. His reasoning was rather simple. The ages of the Sinford's 'triumvirate' at the time. The number of men living on the top floor of Grace Tower. The combined ages of the four men.)

'I know which way is clockwise,' Jack tutted.

Will had also listed what and who they had tried, and Jack wondered if Jimmy had given him the same advice; to stop now and then to consider where they were with the facts.

The list continued:

Three. Who is/was Mr Hunter? Where is he? Would he know a place Mr Stape might have hidden himself? I hope to find more details of him in the school records.

Four. We also need to consider what is meant by 'Stape's truth.'

Five. (A note.) I have looked through all the directories available to us and can find no mention of another address or business for Mr Simon Diggory Stape. End of lead.

Six. Unlikely to help but worth considering: The headmaster, Mr Marsden (I will make enquires at the School Board), Mr Stape's work; we wait to hear.

Of interest for background: The inquiry into Mr Verdier's death. I suggest this because Mr Stape intends to end his life on the anniversary. Mr Havegood said they had made statements. I would be interested to know if any other pupils did the same. If so, there should be more names we can research.

Mr Pascoe tells me that there should be a report of the inquiry in newspapers dating from 1880 (August), and that these newspapers are in the coach house. He suggests Ben Baxter might help you as Mr Pascoe is to be out most of today.

Jack considered the list again. There was something 'unsettling' on the chalkboards, but as Will had written all the words, it couldn't have been the handwriting, and after reading all the information, he couldn't think what he was talking about. Another read of Havegood's blather about his school days could wait until later, and he was already sure that Mr Stape's "truth" was the lie he had lived, and the sex he and Havegood did at school, so that job was done. He couldn't say he was excited by his instructions, and he certainly wasn't as enthusiastic as his brother, but then he came to the part about the inquest, and the thought of visiting the stable lad eased his reticence.

At least it would give him an excuse to visit Shadow and meet the man who'd taken his job.

FIFTEEN

The stable was empty. The animals had been fed and watered, Jack could tell that from the remnants, and the stalls had been mucked out well. There was nothing to complain about the way Mr Baxter was keeping the place, and there was nothing out of the ordinary, except, there were no horses and both the trap and the carriage had gone. Jack was a fair driver, but not even he could handle two vehicles at once. Even if it was possible, what would be the point?

Unable to work it out, he was about to head back across the yard, when the trap pulled in through the gates with a girl at the reins.

At least, from a distance the driver looked like a young woman, with long blond hair, angelic, feminine features, and sitting high and straight, but as the vehicle came closer, he saw it was, in fact, a young man. Ben Baxter, he assumed and leant against the stable wall to watch and see how he handled his parking.

Very well, was his verdict when the lad turned Shadow and backed her so the trap was under cover. Shadow was a docile creature and took to instruction well, she always had, and she was intelligent too. Recognising Jack as he approached, she dipped her head twice, and when he unclipped her blinkers, she shook out what there was of her mane as she always did at the end of a drive.

'Mr Merrit are you?' the lad said as he jumped down. 'Ben or Benny, prefer Benny or Bax, as it happens, but as you like it. Makes no feather to a lame duck. Fine horse.'

'Yeah, she is, ain't you, girl?' Jack stroked her shoulder as he tried to process what the lad had said.

'Just took her out for a trot about. Gotta keep them moving, else she'll get the founder round her hooves, yeah?'

'She were used to cabbing twenty miles a day. She likes being on the road, but not all the time. How's her shoes?'

'Smithy came in only last night. Soon as I got meself back, saw Deaf Joe's books, and thought, now there's a girl needing a new couple a hoof boots.'

The lad was unfettering the traces, and doing them in the correct order, while Shadow nudged Jack in the way she did when she wanted a treat. He gave her an apple he'd taken from the pantry on his way down, and joined her by eating one of his own.

'So what is it?' he asked as he munched. 'Ben, Benny, Bax or what? And while we're at it, how old are you, and where d'you learn to back in and untack like that?'

'Bax, if you want,' the lad replied, too intent on his work to look Jack in the eye. 'Nineteen, as you ask, and been around horses all me life. Me dad were a coser up in Scotland, weren't he? Came down to London years before I got sloshed out on the side of a street, but they kept me on. First thing I remember were a yard full of the beasts and me dad buying and selling. 'Course, that were before they carted him off, me mum got murdered, and I had to peddle me pinker for pennies. What's your story, mate? Cabbie weren't ya? Got a right smart brother in the big house, ain't it?'

Bax not only enjoyed working with horses, he also enjoyed talking, and by the sound of his friendly tone, had already taken to Jack as much as he had to Shadow.

'Yeah, cabman, but not for long.'

'What, you learnt all that knowledge and now you don't need it?'

'Something like that. You softened that strap today? She's got a rub.'

'You're right, mate. I'll get some Sloan's on it.'

Bax ran his fingers over Shadow's flank, nodding in thought. They were long and delicate fingers, as slender as the rest of him, and just as feminine. Yet the lad had a deep voice, and when he threw off his jacket and rolled up his sleeves to protect them from the ointment, strong muscles showed on his arms.

'What you done with the others?'

'Emma and Shanks?' Bax threw his head towards the house next door. 'Mrs Norwood took them out. She's gone shopping with Max.'

'Oh? Does he drive?' Jack wouldn't have been surprised to hear the butler could handle a rig as well as a disguise.

'Nah, he's as useful as an honest beak when it comes to horses. Mrs N's the driver.'

'The housekeeper? But she's a woman.'

'Don't let her hear you say that, mate, truth though it is. Anything I can do for you, or you just come a gaze at me and your nag?'

'Shadow's no nag, mate. She's a princess on the streets.'

Bax roared with laughter at that, his deep speaking voice strangely high as he cackled. Whatever he found funny didn't put him off his delicate strokes as he rubbed the Sloan's into Shadow's flanks. She'd have let him know if he was being too rough.

'What's the joke?'

'Princess on the streets.' Bax's laughter subsided and ended with a long, 'Ah. That's what they call me,' he said, wiping his hands, and giving a final chuckle. 'Least, that's how it was before I got fed up with the lark and got meself into Cheap Street.'

'You don't do that no more?'

'Only for pleasure, not for pennies. Got too dangerous, what with that Russian flu, all them foreigners bringing over their new diseases, the rozzers getting the hump and such. Anyways, you didn't come down here to talk about me, I fancy. What you after, Mr Merrit? Need to go out?'

'If I did, I'd drive,' Jack said, looking for somewhere to throw his apple core. It gave him an excuse to turn away from the younger man he was now finding intriguing as well as attractive, because it didn't seem right to be thinking of that kind of thing when he was on Jimmy's business. Then again, the house was empty, the lad said he did it for pleasure, so he was obviously 'one of us', and much as Jack had tried, he'd been unable to put the night at the inn from his mind. Jimmy beside him, himself hard and wanting to do something with it, hopeful that Jimmy might...

'Well?'

Had it not been Jimmy, it could have been any other man, as long as Jack was safe with him. Maybe, when he got his wages, he'd take a night out and find someone like the angelic nineteen-year-old brushing Shadow with supple fingers but strong arms and looking at him with a mixture of admiration and curiosity.

'Well, Mr Merrit?'

Shadow nudged him on the back, jolting him forward a step.

Nineteen was too young, and the lad wasn't manly enough.

'Yeah, what?'

'Can I help you?' Bax passed him, and began brushing the horse's other flank.

'Sorry, yeah. You're staying in the coach house, ain't you?'

The loft is what Jack used to call it, but they spoke differently in Knightsbridge than they did in Limehouse.

'I got a room, privy and water upstairs, yeah,' Bax said. 'Very nice it is too. Better than the shared hall at Cheap Street, and much better than Miller's Court off Dorset. What's it to ya?'

'Blimey, bet that was rough,' Jack said, stepping into the sunlight to look above. 'Jimmy says there are boxes up there, and I need to see some. He thought you'd help me look.'

'Trunks, mate. Yeah, loads of them in the other rooms. Pascoe asked if I wanted them out, but I said no. Deaf Joe never needed the rooms, he said, but if I do, I can have them. I went, "You barmy or something, Mr Butler? What's a street rat renter like me want with four rooms when I'm used to a space under a mate's bed when I ain't in a stranger's?" Anyways, you're the coachman, ain't you, Mr Merrit? I'm only here while you work on one of Mr Wright's jobs, so I don't need no parlours. What d'you want them for, these chests and stuff?'

It was like listening to Johhny Clarke when he'd been on the tipple, all free-flowing words and hardly any room to breathe. Jack smiled and told him to call him Jack. The lad took that as a great compliment, and his smooth, unblemished face swelled into a massive grin, which only enhanced his appeal.

'You're a gent, Sir,' he said, and hung his brush. 'Reckon she's cozy, ain't you, girl?' Shadow didn't react, because her eyes were on her trough. Bax noticed and said, 'Right-o, just a little, as you've had your morning's.'

'She can be greedy, aye,' Jack agreed, and put in just enough feed. 'So, Bax, I want to get into your trunks,' he said, and for some reason, the lad fell about laughing for a second time. 'What?'

'It'll cost you one and six,' Bax howled, clinging to the stall to keep himself upright.

Jack blushed. 'Not them trunks,' he said, unable to hold back his own mirth. 'Them's as upstairs.'

'Shame.' Bax became serious in the blink of an eye. 'I'd not've charged a fine man like you. Upstairs then, and I'll show you where they is.'

'You're bloody bold.' Jack used a serious, gruff voice as he followed. 'You always so brazen?'

'Habit from the streets, ain't it? Didn't mean nothing by it. This way.'

Would that he had meant something. Bax hadn't put his jacket back on, leaving his tiny arse to plant itself right before Jack's eyes as they mounted the stairs to the first floor. Under other circumstances, he would have thought the two firm mounds within the lad's breeches were being handed to him on a plate, but Bax was a colleague. Besides, with his inexperience, Jack wouldn't have known what to do with the things.

Then again, Bax was a professional, so he'd lead the way.

It was that thought that put him off. Even if there was no one and six involved, he'd feel like he was going with a prostitute, and that was something he'd never do.

Not a female one, but this was a male one, and that was somehow different.

The arse swayed beneath slim hips that lead to strong shoulders, partly hidden by the long hair, and...

No. Still too much like a girl. Besides, although his lob was starting to strain his drawers, and he was unable to look away, he had work to do.

Even with that decided, he was sweating when they reached upstairs and Bax led him into a simple sitting room with basic furniture and a fireplace.

'I got a whole kitchen through here', he said. 'That one's me bedroom, and your boxes are that way. Don't need me to come with you, do ya?'

'I was...' Jack had to stop and clear his throat. 'Sorry,' he said. 'A bit dry. I was hoping you'd help look. They've got newspapers in them, and I got to find one month out of I don't know how many years.'

'Ah, you'll be alright, mate,' Bax chirped, and strode into the passage. There, he picked up a book from a shelf. 'Mr Fairbairn had it all recorded before he left. He were a decent bloke,' he added, and stepping close, added more. 'Scottish, redhead. Massive lobber what nearly split me difference, if you get me.' Louder, he said, 'All set out by what years and months are in what pile inside what trunk. Reckon it'll take you not two shakes of a gent's gonads to find what you want, but if not, give old Bax lip fingers and I'll be right there. Alright?'

'Er... Right,' Jack said, and taking the book, watched as the lad stomped back to the other room.

There was nothing womanish about the way he walked, and his boots hit the floorboards with heavy thumps, but still, there was definitely a charm about his face that, had he been a girl, normal men would have found attractive.

'Oi,' Jack whispered to himself. 'Mind on your work.'

The work, as Bax had predicted, was easy. A book filled with lines of exact writing, easy to read and arranged in a sensible order, soon told him that copies of the Times from August eighteen-eighty were in trunk two, righthand side, and the pile was marked July to December. What was not so simple was locating the correct edition, and by the time he found what he was looking for, his legs were numb from sitting on the floor. His hands were black with ink, he was surrounded by piles of newspapers, and he was sure he'd seen a flea jump from the pages. Through the floorboards came the sound of Bax singing music-hall songs accompanied by the clank of brass as he polished the harnesses, and with the temperature rising as the morning wore on, Jack was keen to be back in the cool of the house.

'Best to make sure this is what you want,' he told himself, as he imagined how Will would deal with the task.

A report in the first newspaper only said there had been a tragedy at Sinford's and there would be a full report after the inquest. That report gave the inquest date, making it easier to find the correct later edition, although the report turned out to be a copy of one filed by a Kent newspaper, and the passage wasn't too lengthy. To be sure he had everything, he also scanned a few more editions on later dates, but after the main article, dated August the fifth, the news had dropped from the London papers.

Unsure why Will and Jimmy were so interested in what happened when Stape was eighteen, rather than where he was now, Jack sat against the wall to read with his legs stretched out in front, and his arse planted on a cushion he'd borrowed from Bax's sitting room.

The initial section of the report dealt with the names and addresses of witnesses, the size of the panel, and who was saying what, and Jack found it dull, because it didn't offer any new names. It wasn't until later in the story that he became more interested.

The Times
The inquest into the tragic death of a public schoolboy.
(From the Kentish Gazette.)

It having been decided that the students of Sinford's School would bear unnecessary suffering were they called to give verbal evidence, their previously recorded statements were read out by Mr Marsden, whose testimony had already been heard.

The evidence came from three students housed on the upper floor of the tower in shared studies known as A-one and A-two. The evidence from the boy who shared the A-two study rooms with the deceased was brief, due to the boy being quite asleep from mid-evening until the following morning, as, the headmaster attested, was his wont. The depositions from the other students verified this, and Mr Troutbeck thanked the young man for his statement, and recorded his evidence as nil.

The second statement, that of Master Simon Stape, was also brief, but in it, he stated that Mr Verdier, a well-liked pupil with no enemies, had begun the term in a state of glumness, but, as the term progressed, so his humour improved. During the days leading up to the incident, Mr Verdier had shown no signs to indicate he was considering taking his own life, but the statement also reported that the man, being of French descent, was prone to unpredictability. That said, the last evening of his life passed in the usual fashion of that of such a school, with reading, ablutions, talking amiably with his fellows, and retiring to bed at a sensible hour. Mr Stape had done the same, being abed without candle by eleven o'clock, as was his study companion.

When asked if he knew of Mr Verdier's nightly routine and whether it included visiting the tower battlements, Mr Stape had stated the deceased often took a pipe on the roof, and returned to his room well before candle-snubbing in order to compose a journal he kept meticulously throughout his school career. Asked of the whereabouts of this journal, the witness was unable to answer, and the matter was taken no further in his report.

Mr Troutbeck referred back to the statement from Mr Verdier's study companion, only to find the same evidence; that the deceased was known to record his daily life, but the witness was unable to say where it was kept. It was a shame, the chairman said, that such a book was not listed on the inventory of the man's quarters following the tragedy, as his own words might have cast some light on his state of mind. (At this stage, suicide had not been ruled out.)

The Hon. Marcus Havegood, eldest son of The Viscount Beresford, had also given his interview and written testimony in the presence of his headmaster. He stated that Mr Verdier showed no signs of behaving in an unusual way. He knew of the journals, but not where they were kept, and could think of no reason why the deceased would want to end his life.

On the penultimate day of July, the students who had stayed behind for two weeks of 'Praemisit' enjoyed a final meal with their masters where, Havegood said, the atmosphere was jovial, and after it, retired to their rooms to complete their packing. At ten thirty that night, he reported, on returning from his bathing, he discovered Mr Verdier in study A-one in discussion with Mr Stape. They were discussing letter writing and staying in touch with each other through the summer until they went up to Cambridge. Mr Verdier retired, as did Mr Havegood, and there was nothing to suggest an unbalanced mind of any student.

Mr Havegood then described being woken early in the morning by the sound of the ambulance bells, and stated that his study companion, Mr Stape, was woken by the same.

With nothing more to be added by the statements, the inquest turned to the medical examiner, whom Mr Troutbeck questioned at length. Death occurred at the end of the fall, and there were no signs of foul play or intoxication. Sergeant Lawless for the Kent Constabulary, investigating, reported there was nothing sinister to be found on the tower roof. All that was there, he said, was a tobacco pipe, which the housemaster, Hogg, confirmed at the time as belonging to Mr Verdier. Tobacco matching that from the bowl was found in his room. It was not unusual, Mr Hogg said, for the 'Gold' students to visit the roof to view the stars and better their astronomy. This was permitted once they had passed the age of eighteen. The battlements were of significant height and width as not to present a danger to falling, and in all his years, there had never been an accident.

The rest of the report was dull, because all the gruesome elements had been left out. All it said was the condition of the body was consistent with that of any other which had fallen from a great height, and no evidence was found on it to suggest either suicide or foul play. The inquest concluded it was most probably an accident.

'So why's Jimmy so interested in what happened back then?' Jack muttered as he replaced the newspapers, saving only those that mentioned the case. 'What's on that board that's got him and Will wondering?'

The thought occupied his mind as he made his way downstairs, but moved out when he saw Bax washing at the standpipe.

Bent over, his wet hair shielded his face like a pair of curtains, leaving the sight of his naked, pale torso, but when he stood upright and threw back his head, water arced from him, catching in the sunlight like a shower of diamonds. More interesting was his completely smooth chest, with the lines of his muscles defined, and his slim frame narrowing to his flat stomach and the band of his half-undone breeches. After wiping the water from his face, he noticed Jack, and pulled his hair into a tail, fixing it with a ribbon, and in doing so, revealed golden tufts beneath his arms.

'Find what you need?'

'Er, yeah,' Jack stammered, and waved the newspapers.

'Nice one. Bleedin' hot, ain't it?'

'Yeah.'

If Jack was hot, it wasn't only because of the sun, and he averted his eyes to Shadow, slurping at her bucket in the shade of her stall.

'There's talk of a storm,' Bax said through the towel as he rubbed his face. 'Good to know I'll be in the dry for a change.'

Half of him wanted to leave, but the other half wanted to stay and see more. Jack had experienced the sensation before, but this time, he reminded himself, he was in charge of Jimmy's work, and Will would demand answers when he returned.

'See you,' he said, and was making for the house when Bax called him back.

'Do us a favour?'

'What's that?'

'Put in a good word with Mr Wright, will ya? I only ever been needed now and then. Would be good to be permanent. That's if you like what you see.'

'I do,' Jack said, giving the words a double meaning without thinking.

'Yeah, me an' all. You're a proper horseman, I can see that, so a word from you'd go a long way.'

The lad was talking about his job, nothing else.

'See what I can do,' Jack said. 'I've only seen you working a few minutes, but I like the way you handle Shadow. Means a lot to me, that horse.'

'Kind of ya. Tell you what, if you're stuck for something a do come the evenings, why don't you come down? It'd be good to hear what you go to say on the horses and waggons. Reckon I could learn a lot from a man like you, Jack.'

Was he still talking about work?'

'We could bustle up me gaff, share a beer, and get along. Gets a bit quiet here at night. Mr Pascoe says I can come into the house, but it don't seem right, not for a Millwall lad, know what I mean?'

'Millwall?'

'Yeah, down your way, ain't it? We got a lot in common. We could banter for hours if you like. Banter and other stuff, anyways. Come and be cosey, mate. Anytime. We can do whatever you want.'

Bax was not talking about work; a man didn't need to be Will to read those signs. No shirt, hair back, the casual way he threw the towel over the rail, the delicate fingers hiding the white of his shorts as he buttoned his breeches, and all the time, his endearing eyes fixed on Jack, and magicking his pulse up a notch.

'Yeah, might do that,' Jack said, and turned away.

'Even better from the back,' were Bax's last words, as Jack hurried across the yard muttering, 'Brazen or what?'

Brazen for sure, but also cheery, and somehow mysterious. Definitely interesting, but for all the wrong reasons—or the right ones, depending on what Jack wanted, and clearly, whatever he wanted was available.

'Don't want nothing but to show Jimmy I'm up to his eighty quid a year,' he told himself as he entered the cool of the house, and shut the back door on the yard and its temptations.

By the time he reached the office, the conversation with Bax was a memory; a strong one, but one he had to put aside if was to follow Will's instructions.

This, he did for the rest of the morning, and after feeding himself from the pantry, for most of the afternoon. He was rereading Havegood's pages as the clock struck two, comparing them to the inquest reports and writing notes when it struck three, and dozing when it struck four. The memory returned in broken images of Baxter half naked, his thin eyebrows that seemed to speak as clearly as his voice, his fingers like the soft bristles of a brush, and, almost as if it had taken physical form, his availability should Jack ever want to investigate the two rounds of his arse.

Maybe it was what he had seen, or what Bax had intimated so boldly, or it could have been the stuffy heat of the afternoon, but when he stirred from his slumber, stretched out in a chair, and his eyes fell on the front of his trousers, there was no denying something had put him in the mood to release his frustration.

Its outlet was waiting for him in the coach house, and there was little doubt all he had to do was arrive; he'd probably not even have to ask.

'No.'

It would be sex for the sake of it.

'So?'

Hadn't he told himself not three weeks ago that he was on the path for love? That was his destination, and he wouldn't reach it with a quick fumble it in a stable.

'Maybe more than a fumble. Never done the whole thing before.'

Jack Merrit had never done a lot of things, certainly not when it came to the base desires of sex, but now, he had the chance to experiment, to let loose without fear of getting something wrong. Love was alright, but he'd never known the love of another man in that sense, and he'd waited so long, he could wait a while longer.

For whom?

It was a hot afternoon, the house was empty, Bax was there, Jack was hard.

The carpet gave beneath his feet more than usual as he made for the door, and the air was lighter, or his head was, because he knew where he was going, what was about to happen, and he was unable to stop himself. His lob itched for the touch of new knowledge, and although his limbs were weak and his breathing shallow, he knew he'd be strong when the time came, and that time was soon. Passing through the drawing room with his skin tingling, he approached the hall knowing exactly what was to happen next.

Except he didn't.

As soon as he stepped into the hall, Will burst through the front door, and launched into a conversation they'd not been having.

'I'd never have guessed it,' he exclaimed, his face radiant with excitement.

'You what?' Caught off guard, Jack pulled the front of his jacket across his crotch, and took a sudden interest in a painting.

'Jack, you will never believe it.'

Will was at the hat stand, arranging his cap and coat just so, and Jack took the opportunity to stand behind the flowers on the centre table.

'It took a while to find, but I got it.'

'Yeah, alright,' Jack said, doing his best to sound as though his balls didn't ache. 'Can it wait? I need to see Shadow.'

The mention of his horse's name deflated his ardour, and picturing her listening while he and Bax romped in the hay finished it off. Bax and what he had to offer would have to wait. Release was there anytime he wanted it, and it would come without the complication of love. Sorted.

'You want to know?' Will was bouncing from one foot to the other. 'We can talk to him immediately. He's bound to know something. I bet he knows where Mr Stape might be.'

'Yeah, calmly, Will. What you on about?'

'The mysterious Mr Hunter, named as one of the four great friends of Grace Tower. Not one of the Triumvirate, admittedly, but one who knew all three well. He's alive, nearby and...'

'Calm, Will.' Jack waved his brother down until he had stopped bouncing. 'Where's this bloke live then?'

'It's not where he lives, it's who he is,' Will enthused. 'Nicknames, Jack. Rife at Sinford's as we know. Caesar, Diggs, Hunter...'

'Yeah, yeah. So?'

'Hunter. The fourth friend, the third witness, the man we need to see, and by the looks, our last chance of finding Mr Stape in time.'

His smile prevented him for saying more until Jack gave a growl of impatience. It did more to expel the last of his passion than it did to hurry his brother, but when Will finally took a deep breath, and his wide smile fell, he said:

'Hunter was the nickname for a Mr Chase. Mr Larkin Chase.'

SIXTEEN

Larkin bloody Chase. The only man Jack had intimately explored, and the only one who had stirred more than lust. There was his name, tripping from Will's lips like a magician's rabbit appearing from nowhere. An unwanted rabbit because it got in the way of what he thought he'd be doing at that moment, but also, was not in the way because Chase offered the same as Bax, but with additions. A fine house, discretion, a more suitable age, and more familiarity. At the same time, he also came with the likelihood of more than a grope, and talk of love adding more complications.

'We can go immediately,' Will said, passing him on his way to the drawing room.

'Hold your horse, mate.' Jack grabbed his collar as the only way of preventing his brother from escape. 'We can't just turn up. It's nearly dinner time, and we don't know what we'd say to him.'

Jack did, but it wouldn't be words about the case. It would be something about asking to use the bedroom opposite his for the night and seeing where that led. However, a visit to Larkin for that purpose would be as unsuitable as a visit to the stables, and much as it hurt and confused, he turned lustful thoughts aside, and put his mind to work.

'We should write first and ask for an appointment,' he said, releasing Will who spun to the mirror to make sure his clothes were still correctly aligned.

'Then I will write and hurry to the post. With any luck, we will hear back tomorrow.'

'And if we don't?'

'Then we will be forced to arrive without an appointment.'

That was the job, Jack reasoned, and told Will to go ahead. At the same time, the tall clock started to chime a sad six; the time Jack needed to go below and make a start on dinner.

Stable boys, inquiries and even Larkin Chase set aside, he found Max in the kitchen happy to help, and the two of them were sitting down to eat when Will returned. Strangely, he didn't come down from upstairs, nor did he come from the back door, but he appeared from the passage adjoining Delamere to Clearwater House and he was carrying a book. Seeing the dinner was set out, he hung his coat and cap, and put the book beside him as he sat.

'All done,' he said. 'I asked to see him at his earliest convenience, and gave him our telegraph number.'

'Why?'

'For alacrity. The post office assured me my letter would arrive first thing in the morning if not tonight. This was fortunate because I wrote to ask if we could call tomorrow afternoon, evening at the latest. I said it was on a business matter, and I would come alone if it would be awkward for him to see you after what happened.'

Jack spluttered on his gravy. 'You said what?'

'I wrote no detail, Jack, and Max knows you and Mr Chase had a... moment, so no punches are being swung. I thought it might be a distraction to have the two of you cooing over each other while I asked him about an old school friend.'

'Cooing?'

More likely to be squawking, or staring in stilted silence. They hadn't parted on bad terms, they had just parted, and where Jack had thought something would be forthcoming from the relationship, and where he'd thought Larkin offered love which he was, at the time, willing to consider, there had been no word.

'He may say it's alright for you to come,' Will prattled on. 'In which case, you can coo and ah as much as you want, as long as we make sure we extract any information he may have about Simon Stape and his possible whereabouts. How did you get on with the inquest report?'

That was another thing about his brother; once he started on something, he never let go until he reached the end, and he galloped there like a jockey desperate to win the Saint Leger.

'Yeah, I found it. It's on the desk.'

'Nothing about other family members or possible locations, I suppose?'

'No. Just says what Havegood already told us. What's the book?'

If anything could distract Will it was talk of books, and keen to eat, Jack threw him the chance to talk about something that didn't need answers.

'Ah, yes. From Mrs Norwood,' Will said. 'So I can understand.'

'Understand what?'

'Mr Wright's machine.'

'Explain.'

That was the magic word, and it set Will off on a lecture about how to read the coded strips that came from the telegraph, how easy it was to look up dot-dash combinations, because there were only limited letters in the alphabet, and how he'd know when one word was finished, and another started.

Jack enjoyed most of his main course without having to reply, and was heading for seconds when Will finally finished.

'It's practice,' Max said. 'If you want to read it like Jimmy does, you just have to practice. Sending it be another matter. I tried once, and fell down like a lame teg.'

The two chatted on until the meal was over, by which time Jack was full and his body was crying out for sleep.

It was only seven thirty, but all he wanted to do was bathe, rest, and give himself some time to weigh up the good and bad between a willing ex-renter and an educated man with his own house in Kingsland.

The coincidental fact that Larkin had been to school with their client, the missing man and the dead man of twelve years ago never entered his head as he stood at the window looking down over the yard. All he could think of were the temptations he'd encountered since coming to Delamere. Bax, freedom, wages, even Jimmy offered possibilities. After half an hour of the same irritating thoughts, and with the sun set, his eyes heavy, and his bed calling, he gave up and climbed in, only falling asleep after five minutes, during which the bedsprings creaked at an ever-increasing speed until reaching an abrupt but much-needed end.

* * *

The aloneness was overwhelming as he walked through the darkness of a forest where memories stirred alongside hedgehogs and badgers, and where leaves fell like paper torn from a book. That grove had once echoed to the shouts of young men, while the one beyond the ancient oak had played host to scheming and talk of flags and targets. Over the dead, fallen from trees and soft underfoot, to the near-dead Grange where there was nothing to do but wait and hide, and while waiting, reassure himself the truth would soon be known, and the ghost of a friend would finally be laid to rest.

Questions remained, and he tore at them with the determination of a faithful dog. Would that he had a dog with him for the long nights and the longer days of waiting. For the companionship he craved, and for protection against the threatening rustlings beyond the midnight hour as he settled into his temporary sanctuary. There was no such animal to devour the questioning, however, only himself and his imagination, and it invented one satisfying scenario after another. The truth in print, enquiring minds, and God looking down from above to see wrongs righted, and throw his forgiveness on a sinner repented. That was all he wanted, and if to achieve it, he had been forced to plot, to think, to act, then so be it.

'The plan,' he whispered to the lamp that threw more shadow than light.

It was simple. To be there at the hour so He could witness the contrition and the tears. To remember and regret, but most of all, to beg forgiveness. Then, more waiting while the truth took hold. Practical matters: newspapers, watching the story unfold to its conclusion, and then, only then, would he be free of the inaction of his past and the plague of his present. Only then would he be able to look to the future with a repented heart.

'Not long now,' he told the calendar as he turned the date to the next day. When he woke, he would be a little closer to God's forgiveness.

With that done, and beneath the protection of the night and the creatures that thrived in it, he lay down to sleep.

***

For Jack, the following day began no better than the previous one had ended.

'Nothing,' was Will's first word when Jack found him in the office after breakfast.

'Nothing about…?'

'Oh, sorry. Yes, the first post. Here, arranged for Jimmy, opened by Max, with only one letter for us, and it is not from Mr Chase.'

'Didn't expect it to be,' Jack said, taking his usual seat, and imitating Jimmy, took out his casebook and a pencil.

'Quite. What we have is from Mr Stape's work, and as with everything else so far, it is of no use. The man at the bank says he resigned under no particular circumstances, only stating he wanted to travel. Bless him, the manager enquired among colleagues for us, but none of them could offer any suggestions.'

'Same as the neighbours,' Jack noted. 'Same as the father-in-law. So, Mr Stape's gone abroad. Shouldn't we tell Havegood and be done with it?'

'We have no proof, only hearsay,' Will said, scratching on his chalkboard. 'I wonder how we could find out.'

Refreshed after a deep sleep that passed untroubled by dreams, and with his mind clear of yesterday's bawdy and confusing thoughts, Jack surprised himself by thinking logically.

'As far as I know, the ships keep lists of passengers,' he said.

'Oh yes!'

'But…'

'I could trawl through them.' Will leapt on the suggestion. 'We know it would have been a sailing within the last few weeks... I can check the most likely date... After he left work, after the neighbours last saw him... After the funeral for sure...'

'Hold on.'

'What?' Will turned, his face taught with annoyance. 'You're going to tell me it's not a good idea? You're going to tell me to slow down, hold a horse and count to ten? What?'

Jack whistled through his teeth. 'What's bitten you this morning?'

Will huffed, his shoulders slumped, and he took a breath.

'Frustration,' he said. 'We have no leads except what you just said, and I am keen to show Mr Wright we are capable of being good employees. So far, we are failing.'

'You have to fail so you can try again,' Jack said, pulling the phrase from a memory of Charlie Flex testing him on the knowledge.

'What a ridiculous thing to say,' Will tutted. 'We are already failing Mr Wright because he told us not to do anything, yet here we are, two complete amateurs trying to solve a case commissioned by a nobleman. Mr Havegood was in the newspaper today, did you see?'

'No.'

'It's downstairs. Apparently, the Honourable Mr Havegood was expected to attend a society event on behalf of his father, Viscount Beresford, but sent his apologies due to his health. I read between the lines, and I would say, he is still very worried. So much so, he is cancelling events listed in the Court Circular. His standing in society is in decline because of this case, and that puts more pressure on the agency for the matter to be resolved. Do you agree?'

Jack had to. They had decided to go behind Jimmy's back and solve the case to prove their worth, so they had to see it through to whatever conclusion they would have reached had Jimmy been with them.

'Good,' Will continued. 'So, I will see what I can discover about passenger lists.'

'Don't bother. It was a bad idea.'

'I disagree.'

'Surely it ain't possible to look at all the records of ships leaving the country, even if you knew the date.'

'Why not?'

'For a start, there's going to be hundreds of them from Liverpool to Southampton.'

'Logically, he'd have left from the south. London or Dover, Folkestone, maybe.'

'The eight docks in the East End alone get in over sixty thousand ships a year, Will.'

'He would have taken a passenger steamer.'

'Not necessarily. If he wanted to get away unnoticed, he could have taken a barque out of Millwall, or a cargo out of East India. Then there's Tilbury. That's still south.'

'No. A man like Mr Stape would have booked a passage on a steamer. Perhaps even with Thomas Cook. I could call in and ask.'

'Then there's the lists themselves,' Jack went on, not to frustrate his brother, but because he was enjoying considering the possibilities. It was as if, without being asked, his mind had woken up with the determination to be a good detective. 'How soon will they become public? If they ain't, then how do you get to see them? Who d'you ask? And do you spend the next month going between the south coast and the London docks trying to find them?'

'We don't have a month.'

'Exactly. Sorry, Will. If Stape's gone abroad, and if we need to prove it, we got to find another way.'

'Newspapers. Do they have passenger lists?'

'I don't know, but if they do, which ones. What section?'

Will scowled for a moment before his expression changed to a beaming smile.

'Good old Jack,' he said. 'It's about time you took the whip to the old horse which is your brain.'

Jack wasn't sure if that was an insult or what, and looked at the notes in his book. As Will had said, they had nothing. Will, however, had changed his mind.

'We should be ready,' he said, collecting items from his table. 'We have the case file, Mr Havegood's writing, the photograph you found in Clapham, and Mr Stape's strange diary entry... Ah!'

'What?' Jack heaved himself from his chair to stand next to his brother. 'What you found?'

'Not found, because it has been here all along. The diary.'

'What of it?'

'Only a few entries? Where's the rest?'

'It sounds like he wrote it just before he went off to top himself. Don't suppose he felt much like writing after that.'

'Not after, before. There was nothing at the house?'

'Not that we could find.'

'Odd.' Will paced to the window and looked onto the street. 'You looked in every room?'

'Yeah, but mainly his office and his bedroom. That was sad enough. There was a crib there, still made up and ready for a baby that didn't live.'

'No missing page obviously.'

'No. There was some kindling in the log bucket, torn paper and stuff, but Jimmy said it was blank.'

'But the neighbour, Mr Ashton, he has a free rein with the house?'

'He goes to water the plants, look after things, and put the letters on a table.'

'And he was a decent person?'

'He was, but his... the other one were a letch.'

'Excellent,' Will said, adding, 'Not the letch, but Mr Ashton's approachability.'

The sunlight silhouetted him against the sheer white nets, obscuring his face, but outlining his form. Mr Hoffman the tailor had found just the right cut to show off his narrow but proportioned shape, and even as nothing more than a black shadow, he radiated strength. It was as if Will had grown up overnight, and had become an assured man beyond his years. It must have been happening for some time, and seeing him there, thinking and directing, was like looking at a different person. Although Will was as precise and fussy as ever, he was no longer the boy of Jack's youth, but a man. His silhouette faded as he paced to the table, and he became real again. Jack couldn't help wondering what Grandad Reggie would have thought of it all. 'Will is special,' he'd said on his deathbed, but Jack hadn't appreciated how special.

'Another message, I think,' Will said, and scribbled on a piece of paper. 'Speed is of the essence.'

'Message to who?'

'Mr Ashton. I'll ask him to take another look for any other books that look like this diary. Where did you find it?'

'Jimmy found it in the office. Near the fireplace.'

'Then I will make him aware of the loose page, ask him to look in the area, and if he finds anything odd, to send it.'

Jack wasn't too sure that would help. 'We already asked him,' he said. 'I suppose a reminder won't hurt, but Stape wouldn't have written down where he planned to do himself in, would he?'

'All and any information, Jack. That's what we need. Do you think Mrs Norwood would send this as a telegram? I have not yet practiced, and she knows how to use the machine.'

'You can ask. While you're doing that, what am I doing?'

'I don't know. You are in charge.'

Jack laughed. 'Yeah, right,' he said, and snatched Stape's diary. 'I'll have another go at this.'

Will left to send his telegram, and Jack sat to read the brief journal entries. While doing so, he did something else he'd never done before, and looked for a dictionary. Finding one on Jimmy's shelves, he embarked on a second new endeavour, and looked up a word to discover its meaning. A third came when he caught himself silently thanking his grandparents for making him go to school, and as a reward for his gratitude, found what he was looking for.

Casemate. n. *historical*. **1** *a small room in the thickness of the wall of a fortress, with embrasures from which guns or missiles can be fired*. **2** *an armoured enclosure for guns on a warship*.

The turn of several pages later, and he found the meaning of *embrasure*, and realised that when Stape and one of his friends held their secret discussions, they 'fired' a barrage of complaints against the world as if they were shooting cannons from an opening in a castle wall.

Little different to Jack's complaints against the world when he was that age. How he had to wake early for work, how he'd been carting and mucking out since he was twelve. How the docks stank of deliveries, and the ships' chains stank of the worst of the sea, and how he had to pay to go to the boxing club.

Nothing unusual there.

In the journal, Stape made his complaints with a man he only called 'He.'

Caesar, Jack assumed, Mr Havegood, his lover. Both locked away talking about what wasn't fair, and in a place *among the dank and dripping walls, with the gurgle of the dying well a way beneath our feet.*

'The cellar?' Jack made a note. 'Stape and his mate used to meet in the cellars and share secrets. So?'

Stape was writing down what he'd dreamt about, and it was vague, so definitely no help in finding him. More interesting was what came in the next entry, the last one before the missing page.

Stape talked about the truth, but what was that truth? Was it one of his shared secrets? If it was, *the man of superstition and reasonableness, like the rest,* would know it.

When? was another question to note, alongside how? How would Stape let his truth be known if he had killed himself? Jimmy had seen the diary as the ramblings of a man in mourning, and Stape even described his mind as fevered, so that made sense, but he was also writing rationally.

I must plan this and make notes... For whom do I leave my next page?

Stape was planning not only his death, but also where to leave his suicide note, and, as far as Jack could see, that was the closest thing to a clue to his intended location.

'Would he leave a suicide note at home a couple of weeks before he went to do himself in somewhere else?' he asked himself, as he left his chair and stretched his legs. 'Someone might find it and try and stop him... Which is exactly what Havegood wants to do.'

Thinking, he stood at the window and watched the street. Maids and telegram boys came and went from the houses opposite, and a hansom trundled past, its driver tilted backwards, his long whip poised, but not in use. The horse trotted with delicate steps, thinking itself regal, and the passengers inside were laughing. A milkman delivering from a cart, while crossing-sweepers attended the junction, and dung collectors loaded their wagons before driving off to the laystalls over Hackney way. Everyday things, and far removed from an investigator's mission.

'Find me... Where?' Back at the diary, he finished the sentence. '*In the dried-up chasm of the past.* What the hell does that mean?'

Will had had the same thoughts, because on the chalkboard, he'd written:

The truth will be known—After suicide?
Missing page—Plan for own death?
Paper streets and rational black lines—Ravings?
Dried-up chasm—What is this?

'Paper streets,' Jack mused, and remembered a dream.

The night before the court case, when Will was missing, he'd dreamt of walking the streets of London with Jimmy, and they'd ducked under a railway bridge built of cardboard. The image was one of those twisted, impossible dream-pictures that sometimes stayed long after waking, and reading Stape's words again, it was easy see the comparison. Jack had been fretting, and his mind conjured up some very strange pictures. Stape had been suffering in the same way. Worse, because he'd lost his wife and child. No wonder, then, that when he wrote the diary, the man hadn't been himself.

'That's an understatement. He was barking. Well, you got to be to do yourself in.'

'I believe that be the case.' Max was at the door. 'Sorry, I were about to knock when I heard you talking. Alone, are ye?'

'Just me and me thoughts, Max. What is it?'

'The second post. There be a letter for your brother.'

'He went next door to send a message.'

'Ah. I'll leave it here fur him. Anything else I can be bringing you?'

'No thanks.'

'Right, then. I have another message, and it be from Baxter. Came up for a tea, and asked me to ask you if you were thinking of calling on your horse today? I get the impression the lad's lonely down there, and I can't blame him. He's still supping in the hall downstairs if you want me to pass a message.'

Jack had been studying the envelope addressed to *Master William R Merrit Esq*, and turned it over to see if there was a return address.

'Er... No,' he said, as his heart skipped.

The twinge of excitement didn't come from the thought of being invited to spend time alone with the angelic and available Ben Baxter. It was caused by the name printed on the back of the envelope. *Larkin Chase, Kingsland.*

'Hold on, Max.' Jack prevented him from leaving. 'Tell him we might need driving over to Hackney. That'd give him something to do. I'll let you know as soon as Will's opened this.'

'Your Mr Chase, is it?'

'Yeah.'

Max twitched a dark eyebrow, and gave a wry smile.

'We are to ask him for information,' Jack said. 'That's all.'

'Aye.' Max managed to make the word sound like an accusation as he left, to be replaced a second later by Will.

'Message sent to Clapham,' he announced, breezing in. 'Oh. For me?'

'From Larkin.'

'Perhaps we can start to get somewhere.' Will took it, snapped the wax seal with both hands, and pulled out a letter. His lips moved as he read in silence, and when he reached the end, he said, 'Excellent. We are invited at seven for an early dinner at eight.'

'Oh, well, that'll be...'

'More than acceptable,' Will interrupted, heading out the way he'd come. 'I will have Mrs Norwood reply with a yes. She is quite a marvel...'

Jack was going to say, 'That'll be complicated,' because every time he'd been to Larkin's house had been complicated. It would be even more so with Bax waiting in the stable to drive them home.

That was, if Larkin didn't invite him to stay the night.

SEVENTEEN

'I suppose you'd better come in.'

Jack had forgotten about Larkin's housekeeper whose manner teetered on the cliff edge of rude, and often fell over.

'You can hang your own hat, young man. I can't be doing with all that nonsense,' she told Will, and leaving them to their own devices, plodded into the sitting room. 'They're here.'

Larkin's handsome and welcoming presence replaced the permanently unhappy Mrs Grose, and he seemed as pleased to greet them as they were to see him. As pleased as Will was, at least. Jack was a torment of nervousness.

'Gentlemen,' Larkin enthused, grabbing Will's hand first. 'What more pleasure could a man require than to entertain the Merrit brothers? Come in, come in, I am intrigued. More, I am tantalised by your message as much as I am glowing with ebullience at the success of your new-found endeavours, and I will hear all the news.'

Jack might have forgotten about Mrs Grose, but he'd not forgotten how wordy Larkin could be, and when he replied, 'Hello,' he was reminded how ineffectual his language skills were compared to the writer's.

Writing, however, was the last thing on Larkin's mind as he took Jack's hand, and fixed him with a stare of intense joy.

'So good to see you,' he said. 'It has been too long.'

Yeah, and who's fault is that?

Jack kept his thoughts to himself. They were there to learn what they could about the case, and rather than clutter his head with images of what might have been had Larkin written, he did his best to focus on what needed to be asked.

'It has, Mr Chase,' Will said, before Jack could think of what to say. 'But we are here on official business. Not that it is not a pleasure to see you, of course. I wonder, we came in the trap, and our driver is outside, would it be possible...?'

'For him to park in the stable and take supper below decks? Yes, of course,' Larkin cut in before bellowing, 'Grose!'

'I'm right here.' The housekeeper grimaced as she emerged from behind the drawing room door. 'I suppose you want me to see to all that.'

'It is rather what I pay you for,' Larkin beamed. 'To the street, woman, thence, to the stable with their man, and from there, to your duties in the kitchen, and, with the joy of service which lights your otherwise etiolated heart, to the dining...'

She'd gone.

'Over here, Mr Chase? Shall I take the chaise...?'

Will set about rearranging the cushions, while Larkin swanned to the sideboard to clatter among his array of glittering glass decanters.

'Make yourselves quite at home,' he said, glancing over his shoulder at Jack. 'As I think I said before, my home is yours while you are here. Sherry? Dry for Jack, sweet for William. Ha! Sweet William, the flower of gallantry, and I believe, if I have read correctly between the limited lines of your letter, that you are both involved in the gallant act of investigation. Sit, sit,' he chirped, bringing over the glasses.

'How have you been, Mr Chase?' Will asked, satisfied with his seating arrangements, but distracted by the small table where Larkin placed his glass. 'Sorry, do you have a...?'

'A coaster? Of course, foolish me.'

In his haste to please, Larkin spun to the sideboard and flew back with a mat which, after some negotiation, he placed to Will's satisfaction. That done, and pleasantries out of the way, he took up his own chair, swung one leg over the other, and continued to grin at Jack.

The sight of him so enthused melted some of Jack's apprehension, and on seeing him clean cut, well shaven, and with his hair perfectly oiled and combed as always, trepidation was replaced by a warm glow. Admiration, most likely, but also something more fundamental. There was no denying the attraction both ways.

'It is very kind of you to see us,' Will said, unpacking his casebook, and reminding Jack they were there on business.

'Not at all. I was waiting for a suitable period of time to pass before I invited you back,' Larkin said. 'I thought it best to give you time to adjust to your new surroundings before ripping you from them to a place which, I thought, would hold unhappy memories for you, what with the kidnapping and everything.'

It held both unhappy and erotic memories for Jack, but he refused to wander there, and fished out his own book from his new satchel.

'I say, men of business indeed. I see you are keen to be at work, so let's to it. That will leave us free to talk of other matters over dinner. What can I do for you?'

On the journey, they'd agreed Will would do the questioning, and Jack would listen and take notes. His book held a list of things they wanted to ask, and it was his job to make sure Will didn't forget anything, not that it was likely. With that in mind, he gave Will a gentle nod, and held his pencil over the page.

'My message alluded to us needing a discussion concerning Sinford's school in Kent,' Will began. 'You must wonder how I knew you were once a pupil.'

'I did indeed.'

'I discovered some of the school's attendance and other records at the London School Board library. Your headmaster, Mr Marsden took them with him when the school closed, you see, and left them there when he died.'

'Yes, I heard this from the old school network some time ago,' Larkin said, sipping from his glass as he listened intently. 'Are you working on a case that involves my alma mater? Or did Mr Marsden transgress in some way?'

'The case doesn't involve anyone called Alma, Sir, and no, it is not about the headmaster.'

'I see.'

Larkin had been studying Will, but gave Jack a quick look, a smile, and a twitch of his eyebrows that took Jack back to their first meeting. The strange facial spasm was his secret way of showing admiration, but by the way he had been behaving so far, his admiration was anything but secret.

'I must ask you to treat this information in confidence,' Will said, sounding like one of the barristers Jack had encountered in court. 'We are about to discuss a client's case, and although part of our new job is to interview people, I don't think Mr Havegood would like us discussing too much of his private life. However...'

'Caesar?' Larkin jolted. 'This concerns Marcus?'

'The Honourable Marcus Havegood,' Will said. 'Yes. It is he who has asked us to investigate.'

'Really? The only thing I can think that needs investigating there is his health. From what I read in the newspapers, it is failing, and he has been missing important functions. Is the man unwell? Have you been tasked with finding a cure?'

'In a way,' Will said, and looked at Jack for reassurance.

Will and Larkin could trade words and barter elegant conversation for hours if Jack let them. 'Havegood's friend has gone missing,' he said. 'We have to find him before the end of the month, or he's going to top himself.'

'Marcus Havegood?'

'No. Simon Stape.'

Larkin's mouth fell open, and his moustache frowned. At the same time, his dark eyebrows came together in the middle, and he became a static impersonation of someone who had just learnt a horrible truth, which was, Jack thought, exactly what had happened.

'Apologies for my brother's bluntness, Mr Chase,' Will said, throwing daggers. 'I wanted to tell you in a more subtle way, because we believe the three of you were close.'

'Yes, twelve years ago,' Larkin stammered. 'We all rather lost touch after school, even though we attended the same university. Different colleges, you see. Different subjects... Diggs is going to kill himself?'

'On the thirty-first.'

'If we can't find him,' Jack added. 'Havegood thinks he can stop him if he can get to him in time.'

'Probably the very early morning of that date,' Will said. 'Most likely between two and three o'clock.'

Still gawping like a fish, Larkin said, 'How can you be so precise?'

'Because it will be the twelfth anniversary of the death of Jacques Verdier.'

Will explained Havegood's concerns, and how they had led to his declining health, but didn't mention the doctor had said the man had been concerned since before Stape went missing.

Jack enjoyed a welcome shiver of pride as he listened, but it was replaced by one of shock as Will finished the story.

'Mr Havegood's time and friendships at the school are interesting background,' he said. 'He went to a lot of trouble to explain why he is so desperate to find his old friend, but it doesn't help us with the current whereabouts of Mr Stape. It only explains how long Mr Havegood and Mr Stape have been lovers.'

Jack expected Larkin to object, because statements like that weren't the kind of thing men spoke about, not even among friends, but as he had done on other occasions, Larkin came up with a surprise.

'Why do you say that?' he asked, as if the accusation was nothing.

'I didn't. Mr Havegood did.'

'Marcus told you he and Diggs were lovers?' Larkin frowned.

'He wrote it,' Will said. 'Being too tired to talk at length, when he came to see us, he brought a written account of his years at Sinford's, and told us about his infatuation with Jacques Verdier, and later, his affair with Mr Stape. You look confused, Mr Chase, but I should explain that Mr Havegood came to us because he had heard of the agency's discretion when dealing with men of a similar inclination. I think you understand me.'

'I do,' Larkin said, slowly. 'But... Diggs and Caesar?'

'It was why they came to share a room. A-one, it was called.'

'Yes, I know.'

'You and Mr Verdier were in the one next door, A-two.'

'We were.'

'Then there we are. Now then...'

'But...' Larkin stared at Jack as if he was the cause of his confusion. 'I didn't know.'

'Didn't know what?'

'That the pair were a pair. They were good friends, yes. All three were, and I knew Marcus had long held feelings for Jacques. Many of the boys did because he was handsome, admired, and his father was the French Ambassador, but then, most grew out of it. Two hundred young men closeted together day and night as they traversed the wild experimentations of youth, sharing changing rooms and baths, looks and a great deal more... Yes, it happened, and I am sure it still does. I admired Verdier as I did anyone, but I don't think I was ever as infatuated with him as some. But Diggs?'

'Yes, Diggs, if we are to call him that,' Will said. 'He and Mr Havegood shared a room so they could be together. You and Mr Verdier arranged that.'

'We did not.' For the first time, Larkin was affronted, and put down his glass. 'That is, we did, but not for that reason. I initially roomed with Diggs, but we managed to change the arrangement in our last year in order to keep Marcus and Verdier apart.'

'Apart? But they were great friends.'

'Try telling Jacques that,' Larkin scoffed, but his confusion returned. 'Havegood told you he and Diggs were having an affair, and that was why they shared the study?'

'That is correct.'

'Mr Hogg would never have allowed that. Not if he had suspected, and he was acutely observant. No, our excuse for swapping rooms was so that I could help Jacques more with his languages, and Diggs could help Havegood with science. The real reason was because Jacques had tired of Havegood's endless attentions.'

'Is that why he might have jumped?' Jack threw in as he searched inside his satchel, and the question caused Larkin another jolt.

'Jumped? No. That theory was soon quashed. It was an accident.

Besides, after we changed rooms, everything settled down between them, and they returned to being friends, as were we all. Those three were closer than I, of course. I was more interested in the writings of the great novelists than conversations about sports and science. I was never part of the Triumvirate. How could I be? By definition, it can only accommodate three.'

'This is you, yeah?' Jack pulled out the photograph he had found in Clapham and passed it across.

'Yes,' Larkin said, and his confusion vanished as he smiled. 'I have a copy of it upstairs. Jacques was on his way back from a swimming competition held at the lake, and we ambushed him. I can't remember why or what was said, but it made us all laugh, me quite uncontrollably, as you can see.'

'Who took the picture?' Will asked, and Jack wondered why that was important.

'Mr Hogg, our housemaster. Always fascinated by technical advances, and one of the first to have a camera, if I recall.'

'You got along with Mr Hogg, did you?'

'As well as any pupil,' Larkin said, handing back the picture. 'It was easier to like him after the others had left, and we stayed for the two weeks of Praemisit. More informal.'

'Do you think Mr Stape kept in touch with him after the school closed?'

Jack began to understand where Will was driving with his questions.

'I don't think so,' Larkin said. 'I believe Mr Hogg has died; he was quite elderly even back then.'

'I know,' Jack said.' Jimmy... Mr Wright and I went to find him, and met his wife.'

Larkin chuckled. 'I'll wager you didn't go hungry,' he said, and when Jack shrugged, clarified. 'We used to sit behind her in church so we could help ourselves to the contents of her hat. 'It was extravagant with wild abundance at Harvest Festival, and Stape was certain he once saw a mouse among the produce.'

'Funny,' Will said as if it was the least funny thing he'd heard. 'But you don't think Mr Hogg would have known where Mr Stape might choose to die?'

That brought the conversation back to ground level.

'Mr Hogg is dead.'

'But he might have told someone else. I mean, Mr Stape might have talked about a favourite place to go, a place he was always happy being. We know he is not at home, and everyone we ask tells us he has gone overseas. Do you remember if he mentioned a favourite place abroad? I wondered about France, as it is the anniversary of Mr Verdier's accident. Would that make sense or be fitting?'

Will's questioning continued and intensified as he persuaded Larkin to dredge his mind of anything that might suggest a location for the man, but by the time Mrs Grose barged in and announced, 'Dinner. Now.' Larkin had been unable to help.

The dining room table was laid as Jack had seen it before, with gleaming glasses and silver candlesticks, a bunch of flowers in the middle, and small cloths for the lap. At Delamere, they ate in the servants' hall, and that was grand enough, but whereas before, eating with Larkin had been a case of watching how he did things and copying, Jack was now more accustomed to the finery and manners. Delamere House had made him used to living among luxuries, and he took his seat as though he ate in style every day. What was awkward was conversation, and he was grateful for Will's natural ability to adapt, and listened as he and Larkin discussed the china and what Larkin had been writing. Jack sat back when the maid put down the dishes, and muttered thanks which brought him crushing looks from the housekeeper, and Will kept his eyes on their host, avoiding those of Emily as she held his with the same look of awe she had employed on their last visit.

When Mrs Grose and her daughter had left, the conversation turned from polite discussions of the weather and Delamere, and returned to the case. As arranged, Will led the questioning.

'I see it like this, Mr Chase,' he began. 'Mr Stape appears to have been abandoned by his family and work colleagues, because none of them appear interested in helping us find him. Only Mr Havegood, and now us, have cause for concern, and that is because of a letter Mr

Stape sent to his lover. I should say previous and alleged lover, because their meetings had only been annual of late, and all but ended when Mr Stape married.'

'I should think so,' Larkin said, offering a basket of bread.

'The end, however, did not happen immediately. Mr Stape wrote to Mr Havegood in January to tell him he was to be a father and he might name the boy, if it was a boy, after Mr Verdier or Mr Havegood, who appears to have taken the news well.'

'Yes, I can imagine. For all his faults, Caesar was a loyal man, and I assume, still is. Why else would he be so concerned?'

'Quite,' Will said, cutting his bread roll into three equal pieces. 'Then, at the start of this month, Mr Stape wrote again. His letter told Mr Havegood that their yearly meeting was not to happen. This was understandable. The man had just lost his wife and child. However, it was in this letter that he said he wouldn't see anyone again, and would go, leaving behind only the truth.'

'I see.' Larkin offered the butter. 'But clearly he didn't say where he was to go.'

'No, and no-one can think where he might be, apart from abroad.'

'Abroad is a very big place.'

'Agreed. Something tells me, though, that he has somewhere closer to home in mind. I can't tell you why I think this, it is only a feeling I have in my stomach. Once again, I must ask if you can remember if he mentioned a special place.'

Larkin pursed his lips, and shook his head.

'I must disappoint you,' he said, and looked directly at Jack. 'I am sorry your visit has been in vain.'

The visit may not have proved helpful to the case, but it was serving another purpose; that of reminding Jack how much he was drawn to the man two steps above his station, fifty times richer, and three times as handsome. Random numbers, but the point was the same. Each time their eyes met, something stirred inside, and it was more than memories of the moment at the mirror and a private half an hour spent behind a locked door.

Cutlery chinked against china, glass against silver coasters, and through the sounds came a word.

Private.

It was followed by a couple more.

Locked door.

Which, in turn, were chased by the image of a dictionary, a scribbled diary and a cannon. That last image had a mind of its own and turned itself into the sight of Larkin naked, his lob firing off round after round over Jack's chest.

A hot flush of embarrassment, because Larkin was still smiling at him, and a quick clearing of the throat, and Jack knew where his memory had led him.

'Casemate,' he said, causing Larkin to widen his eyes, and Will to look up from where he'd been examining a strange vegetable. 'Sorry. Just came to me. D'you remember a casemate?'

Larkin pulled the expression men make when they are taken by surprise, yet know the answer to the question; a mix of shock and delight.

'From Sinford's? Yes.'

'What is it, Jack?' Will questioned from under his inquisitive eyebrows.

'Something Stape wrote in his diary,' Jack said, trying to recall the words. 'He used to meet one of his mates in this hiding place, and he talked about it like it was a place where you shoot from. He wrote it just before the part that mentioned what he was intending to do.' The more he spoke his thoughts aloud, the more cluttered they became, and he was about to lose the thread, when the word persisted, and he said it again.

'Casemate is a very old word,' Larkin said. 'Sinford's encouraged the speaking of out-of-fashion words such as discipline, respect, and tradition. All things which are falling from our daily lives these days, particularly among the young.'

'It was a thing.' Jack put his cutlery aside. 'A room where Stape and a friend met to put the world to rights.'

'It was hardly a room,' Larkin said. 'More like a cupboard with an arrow slit in the wall. Parts of the tower dated back to just after the Normans, you see. In fact, it was originally built as a water tower.'

'Yeah. There was a well under it which dried up. Is that right?'

'One of the reasons the school closed.'

'The other being its reputation after the tragedy of Jacques Verdier,' Will said. 'Jack, why is this important?'

Jack wasn't sure. 'Something about diaries.'

'I am pleased to see Mrs Grose's cooking is helping your process,' Larkin said. 'Don't let your asparagus go cold.'

'Oh, that's what it is.' Will held the strange green string on the end of his fork, examined it, and put it in his mouth. 'Most entertaining.'

'Diaries,' Jack repeated, to himself rather than to anyone else, and formed an image of Stape's handwriting. 'Leave my next page.'

'I'm sorry?'

'He wrote, "For whom do I leave my next page?" It was just about the last thing in his book. He'd been remembering this thing called a casemate, and dank and dripping walls... A place where... Yeah, the dying well was beneath his feet... A safe place. Will, d'you think...?'

'That is place he will return to for his suicide?' Will was with him. 'It might make sense.'

'I wouldn't have thought so,' Larkin said. 'If it is the place I am thinking of, it is in the cellars of Grace Tower. Years ago, when it was built, it would have been on the first or second floor. There are other chambers beneath, including the well and all the pumps that were put in to draw the water. The place where Stape used to retreat to is now one floor underground, assuming the tower hasn't crumbled in the twelve years it has been abandoned. Not a place he would choose to die.'

'Yeah, but...' Jack was still putting pieces together and making a mess. 'If he's going to do it the same time as his old mate did, why not do it in the same place?'

'There is a five-storey difference between the roof and the cellar, Jack.'

'Yeah, Larkin, but you know what I mean?'

'I still say it is unlikely,' Larkin countered.

Convinced Larkin was building barriers on purpose, Jack growled. Maybe he was upset that Jack hadn't been in contact. If that was the reason, it was childish and annoying.

'How deep is the well?' Will asked.

'The well?'

'Is it possible that a man intent on self-harm might leap into a dried-up well on purpose, knowing its depth would bring about his end?'

That wasn't what Jack was thinking, but it made sense. What made more sense, though, was that Stape should copy Verdier exactly, and jump from the tower roof.

'No, Will,' Larkin said, calmly cutting his fish. 'The well did run dry, I hear, and not long after we left. Yes, it was deep because the water table in the area is so far below ground, or so we learnt in endless and very tiresome lessons of geography. However, as all Golds did, we investigated the thing during our first week in the tower, only to discover it was impassable. Pipes, you see. At some time, they forced in pipes to draw up the water, and they cluttered the shaft leaving only the narrowest of gaps. Very disappointing for young men intent on throwing pennies for wishes. Besides, it had a grille welded over the top.'

That left Will's theory squashed beneath the wheels, but Jack's idea about a jump from the roof was still possible. He was about to say so with a certain amount of triumph, when Larkin spoke again.

'Diary,' he said, and dropped his cutlery with a clatter. 'Oh, my word.'

'You have thought of something, Mr Chase.' Will also left his meal alone and leant forward. 'What?'

'I have thought of a vague... I have a book. A collection.'

'You have many books,' Will smiled. 'Will they help us?'

'One might. If I can find it.'

'What is it?'

'A collection of memorabilia complied by Mr Hogg and the secretary of the Old Boys Association after the school closed. A private publication which has a section stating where some old Sinfordian's had gone. We featured in particular.'

'We?'

'The Triumvirate and I, being the last Golds to live on the top floor. Also, Stape helped put it together, and arranged to have it printed by the Pall Mall Gazette, financed by my brother's company.'

'Your brother?' Jack couldn't see where he was heading with this, but the idea that the book might contain another contact or address was one he couldn't ignore.

'Yes. Simon Stape and my brother were friends, vaguely. Stape's older brother was in the same year as Myles, who, when the school closed, was already well ensconced at the Gazette. But that's not the important matter. The book, slim though it is, may hold some information which might be of use to you, if I could only remember where it is.'

'Is it called, "The Last Gold of Sinford's"?'

Larkin clicked his fingers. 'That's it, Will.'

'Unless you have moved it—and if you don't remember its name, I suggest you haven't looked at it for a while—it is in your study on the second shelf down on the north bookcase beside a copy of "Bleak House." With your permission, I will fetch it.'

'No need, dear boy. I can go.'

'No, Mr Chase. You stay here and talk to Jack.'

Will left no room for debate, but he did leave a stilted atmosphere. The clock made its usual noises, Will's footsteps faded on the stairs, and a horse clopped by outside, but otherwise, the silence was as thick as the sauce congealing around Jack's dinner.

'I think we have been left alone on purpose,' Larkin said after their shared look had gone on long enough. 'Set up, as they say.'

'I know what that feels like.'

'Ah, yes. How have you been since the incident? No trouble from the Flay family, I hope.'

'No. I've been alright.'

'Adjusting to your new way of life?'

'Yeah.'

'Jack...'

'No, don't say nothing. It's all right.'

Larkin was not to be dissuaded, and took Jack's hand. 'I've missed you,' he said, and Jack's insides leapt.

'You didn't write me.'

'You didn't write to me.'

'Was that one of your corrections, or a statement?'

'A fact.'

'I didn't think you wanted to hear from me.'

'I came looking for you after the court hearing, but you had vanished with Mr Wright. I thought, by sending on your clothes, you might at least reply with a thank you.'

'Yeah.' There was no answer to that. Larkin was right, and Grandma Ida would have been upset at Jack's lack of manners. 'Sorry.'

'No need for sorry,' Larkin said, and his blue eyes smiled in the candle flicker. 'I am so happy to see you again.'

All Jack had to do was say the same thing, but he hoped a vague twitch of his lips would carry the meaning.

'You're still holding my hand,' he said, when Larkin said no more.

'Do you want me to let it go?'

Jack's eyes had pricked at the touch, and his heart had bounded to a canter, but as the warmth of Larkin's voice and fingers transferred, so his eyes dried, and his heart slowed to where it was meant to be, a gentle trot.

'No,' he said. 'Not until we have to.'

'Sadly, that moment is on us.' Larkin withdrew his hand.

'Oh, don't get all manly on my account.' Mrs Grose was in the room bearing a tray. 'You done with that fish? Only, your chops are ready.'

EIGHTEEN

The second course arrived at the same time as Will, who said it would be impolite to read the book while they were dining, and put it aside for afterwards.

'Grandma Ida always said it was rude to read while eating,' he said. 'Not that we could. It was a balancing act to arrange two dinner plates on our kitchen table, let alone anything else. 'It would be more polite if we left talk of the case for now, and discussed other things,' he added, and thanked Mrs Grose for his dinner, saying it was the best meal he had eaten since last time he had dined in her house.

Taken by surprise, the housekeeper made no comment, but left with a faint smile and her greying head held higher than usual, leaving the three men with a stilted pause in conversation until Will asked Larkin what he had been writing.

'Oh, this and that,' Larkin replied. 'I started a piece about the outcome of the recent general election, and the rise of the Liberal movement. They won eighty more seats than last time, and there is hope that the returning Conservatives may somehow be ousted in the near future. After a page, I realised that my interests do not lie in politics, but in welfare, and I began writing about the Shoreditch Workhouse. I was a guardian for a while, but did not stand for re-election. It has always interested me how...' Breaking off, he looked at Jack and grimaced. 'My apologies. I can see this is not a subject that interests you.'

'Oh, no, it's alright. Go on,' Jack replied, hoping he sounded sincere. 'I don't understand half of what you say anyway.'

'Jack!' Will chided. 'I am sure my brother didn't mean that.'

'No, he does,' Larkin smiled. 'We discussed this before. I use too many words.'

Wasn't that what Jack said to him the last time they were alone? Jack had been leaving for Delamere, Larkin had said something about him being in his dreams and wanting a kiss, and all Jack could do was say how he used too many words and walk away. It had been a worrying and confusing time, and he'd never been very good at expressing what he thought, not with matters of the heart. Not with anything emotional, come to that.

Will prompted him to say something, and Jack spoke without thinking.

'Tell us about the workhouse. I like when you talk about how you help people.'

Larkin's face glowed. 'I am touched,' he said. 'I will, if you are genuinely interested.'

'I am,' Jack said, and he meant it. 'Go on.'

As Larkin talked of good works for charity, how he brought issues to the public's attention through his brother's publication, and how he thought it his duty to help those less fortunate, Jack found his already-swollen heart swelling further. There was more to Larkin Chase than his good looks, mild manner and availability; he cared about strangers in a way that Jack hadn't seen in anyone else. The troubles of a neighbourhood's poor meant little to most people, yet Larkin saw it as his duty to do what he could, and when he spoke about it, he wasn't looking down on people, he was standing up for them. His language wasn't patronising, it was caring. Wordy, of course, but Jack listened, entranced, until the housekeeper and maid presented the last course, and the conversation ended.

'What about your spare time?' Will persisted in his questioning.

'Again, this and that,' Larkin said. 'I spend much time at home reading, I take walks along the canal to Islington, and I sometimes venture further north to Highbury Fields. Then, there are the theatres, when there is something worthwhile to see. The music halls if I can bear the crush, galleries, societies... There is much to do in our great city, but I would be the first to admit, I don't take as much advantage of the sights as I should.'

'Alone?'

'I'm sorry, Will. Alone?'

'Yes. It seems to me you do quite enough to keep yourself occupied, but I wonder who you make your visits with? Is it not lonely?'

'Now who's being rude?' Jack pointed his spoon, concerned about his brother's motives.

'I take no offence, Jack, because Will is correct. I spend much time on my own. I have been happy to do so since... well, since even before Sinford's. My father says it is because I have not found the right woman, and when he says it, I agree with him, because it is simpler. Luckily, Myles has children, so the weight of expectation has been taken off me somewhat, and I am happy to be the bachelor uncle. I also have Mrs Grose, so my mother doesn't worry that I am not fed and laundered. This leaves me free from family expectations.'

'Yes, but friends?' Although he was speaking, Will was concentrating on his plate of lemon tart, tidying fragments of pastry into small piles, and keeping his eyes well away from Jack.

'I am sorry if I am not sociable, Will,' Larkin said. 'I have a few friends, but none who are close. I have acquaintances rather than associates. I am not much of one for sharing intimacies with others. Rather, I seek the one person with whom I can be both intellectually and personally intimate.' A glance at Jack. 'By which I mean, I would rather spend my time with one than many—my charitable interests, meetings, committees and so on aside. Does that answer your curiosity? If so, I think we are ready to move to the drawing room.'

When Will did catch his eye, Jack scowled, but his brother gave a wink in reply, making it unnecessarily obvious he'd been directing Larkin's conversation for Jack's benefit. Touching hands, whispers about missing each other, and being forgiven for not writing added to

Larkin's admission that although he was content, he also looked for something more. Some*one* more, and clearly, that was Jack.

The drawing room came as a relief, because the conversation reverted to the case, and Larkin's book, about which he said, 'As you can see, it is only a small work, and rather a self-indulgent one.'

Will was huddled over it in an armchair, turning pages with one hand while the fingers of the other flicked over each other beside his ear. When he was intent like this, Jack knew to say nothing, and wasn't worried about his taut face and frown. Larkin, on the other hand, was.

'Is he happy?' he whispered, sitting beside Jack on the settee and passing him a glass.

'Yeah. Don't worry about it. It's how he reads sometimes.'

Larkin sat as close as Jimmy had the other day, and their knees touched. The effects of Baxter's bare torso, backside and offer were still strong behind Jack's outward appearance of calm, and the waft of Larkin's scent did nothing to quell the tightening in his stomach and the unrest in his crotch.

'A proposition.' Larkin's whisper was as soft as the badger hair shaving brush the barber used to trail over Jack's chin, and his shoulder pressed closer.

Jack's mind flashed to the bedroom opposite Larkin's, the time at the mirror, and the half an hour behind the locked door, and hoping for the same, he questioned, 'Yeah?'

'Tomorrow. A walk in a park. Lunch. Just you and I.'

Not what Jack's crotch was hoping for, but what else did he expect? There was no need for him and Will to stay the night, and there was no way they could slip away for another half an hour. Besides, Jack didn't want half an hour, he wanted more.

'Park?' he said. 'Rhododendrons?'

It was a reference to Larkin's misdemeanour of two years ago, and Jack regretted it as soon as they words were out.

He had no need to worry. 'No,' Larkin chuckled. 'A simple act of courting a man for whom I hold a great and deep desire to spend more time in the company of.'

Will looked up from the book. 'Mr Chase, you might like to rephrase your last sentence. It was not worthy of you.'

'Quite right.' Larkin cleared his throat, and bolder, turned to Jack and took his hand. 'Jack, would you like to accompany me on an outing tomorrow? A walk in a park, lunch or afternoon tea. Your choice, my treat.'

'But we got work.' Jack's mouth was as dry as a dusty axle, and the words more cracked than Grandma Ida's crockery.

'Just a few hours,' Larkin beamed. 'Not as much time as I would like, but time all the same.'

'Go,' Will grunted from within his pages.

'But if...'

'Go.'

'Alright.'

'Good. Now maybe we can get back to business.' Will closed the book with a finger inserted to keep his place. 'If that is acceptable to Apollo and Hyacinth?'

'Yes, of course.' Larkin shuffled away a couple of inches. His knee, however, remained touching. 'Is it of any use to your investigation?'

'No,' was Will's blunt reply, followed by, '...and maybe. There is only one section in this disappointingly thin volume which mentions the man we are interested in, but there is something at the back which might be useful. Shall I read to you?'

'Yeah, go on.' Jack reached into his inside pocket for his pocketbook, and found a chewed pencil.

'Most of this book is about sports records, achievements of previous pupils, and how many each year progressed to Oxford or Cambridge,' Will began. 'All very interesting to future generations of those mentioned, no doubt, but of no use to us. However, there is a small section about the silvers and golds Mr Havegood wrote about.'

'Ah, yes. The reinforcement of the British class system at its worst,' Larkin said. 'The brow-beaten and mistreated lead piping of the lower classes, the word *class* being a play on words, because the boys were from the upper classes of society and yet, took classes. As in, lessons,' he explained when Jack and Will didn't respond. 'Then, the rebellious coppers and bronze boys striving to be forged into better metals who, when they moved up, only turned out to be as base as their namesakes. Silver with no lustre who were certainly not chaste—

another play on words, Will—and, ultimately, the golds of the lodge and tower.'

That appeared to be the end of the pointless interjection, and to his credit, Will didn't say anything blunt.

'Thank you. The end section talks about the *Last Golds of Sinford's*, their title, not mine, and it mentions the man we are interested in, but little else. It says...'

As for reminiscences and jottings from the time, there are few. Sinford's had a great tradition of preserving its history, to wit, students were encouraged to write their daily lives in private diaries. It would have been of much interest to the reader and the old Sinfordian to have found the work of these diarists. Sadly, many of the works have been lost. However, a few have been preserved. The writings of Mitchell and Stanwick, who left the school in 1872, were published in India, and the memories of Mr Appleby-Snide, an alumnus of earlier years, often appear in Punch. Both gentlemen were golds of Grace Tower, and Appleby-Snide is the SOBA secretary.

There was no better place to live than the top floor of Grace, where, in 1880, four of the school's most academic students shared the two studies. Three of the four progressed to Cambridge, and after, sought worthy employment. Mr Chase, a most academic student is an author, Mr Stape is at the Bank of England, and The Hon. Marcus Havegood with the Board of Trade. Of the three, Mr Chase remains a supporter of the Sinford's Old Boys Association.

'And that's it,' Will said, turning to another page. 'Apart from this at the back which gives the address of the Association. I thought someone there might still know Mr Stape.'

'You are giving me a strange look, Jack,' Larkin said. 'A wry smile plays on the edge of your mouth, and I wonder why.'

'Most academic student and author,' Jack said. 'I'm impressed.'

'And also misled. I was no more or less academic than my compatriots, and I am not an author. I am a merely journalist and investigator of social malpractice. As such, I am willing and able to investigate the Association if you wish. I no longer attend their dreary annual meetings, nor the even more dreary cricket match, but I can call on the secretary on my way to you tomorrow morning, if that would be of use.'

'Yes please,' Will enthused. 'Will they know where he might be?'

'Unlikely. They hold addresses of members so they can, with alarming persistence, send them their impotent news sheet twice every year, and beg for more money than the subscriptions deserve. It is possible Diggs remained in touch with someone, and the secretary might know, because he is as nosey as a bloodhound. The news sheets are nothing more than tittle-tattle on which he thrives. Leave that line of investigation with me. You said you had enquired at the Bank of England?'

'Yes, and the family, the family by marriage, and Oxford University.'

That was news to Jack. 'When?'

'I sent a letter, but they couldn't help. It was one of the first things I did after I cracked Mr Wright's safe.'

Larkin's eyes widened, but Jack reassured him Jimmy hadn't minded.

'Glad to hear it,' he said. 'Well, gentlemen, it appears the case is in fine hands, tragic though it is.'

'Tragic?' Will put aside the book.

'Tragic if the man is not found.' Larkin gazed towards the fireplace and its embroidered guard. 'Poor Diggs,' he sighed. 'He was such a lovely man. Always calm, always loyal to his friends, particularly Jacques and me, and a gentleman to the younger boys. The path of his life has not been as smooth as he deserves, losing his wife and child, and now, driven to...'

A tear escaped the corner of his eye as his voice trailed away, and Jack took his hand.

'Don't get upset,' he said. 'We're going to sort this out.'

'I am sure.' Larkin composed himself, and gripped tighter. 'Thank you. I will do all I can to help. Just say the word.'

'The word is ten o'clock.' Mrs Grose was at the door. 'Wondered what you wanted me to do with the child labour in the scullery. It's past my finish time, and he's still lounging around as if he owned the place.'

'Mr Baxter is nineteen, Mrs Grose,' Will said as if he was her boss. 'And he is paid well and housed. However, it is late, and we have taken up too much of Mr Chase's evening already.'

'I don't mind at all,' Larkin protested.

'I do,' the housekeeper mumbled, and louder, said, 'If you don't want me, I'll go up, but you'll have to lock the back when the boy leaves. If you can get him out.'

'We will go,' Will decided and stood. 'At least, I will. Jack may want to stay longer.'

Jack wanted to stay all night, but that wasn't possible, not without a good excuse like having his house burnt down, and as he had no house...

'Must you?' Larkin also stood. 'You are welcome to stay. I am quite capable of locking my own back door.'

'You'd think so, wouldn't you?' Grose said.

It would be too obvious to remain, and even though Jack could think of little else than the room opposite Larkin's and the adventure it would hold, he agreed with Will.

'Lots to do tomorrow,' he said, not knowing what. 'Best get back. Shadow will want her stall.'

'Right. I'll send him round the front.' The housekeeper was gone.

The goodbyes were not as hard as Jack imagined, because he knew he would be meeting Larkin again the next day, and even though Will left them alone to wait at the front door, the parting was not awkward.

'I am already looking forward to tomorrow,' Larkin said, handing Jack his satchel. 'I shall call at midday.'

'That'd be nice, but if we're having lunch, I'll pay for myself.'

'We can negotiate.'

Larkin offered the exit with a swing of his hand, but made no other move. Jack didn't want to leave in the blunt manner he had last time they parted, and the hunger in his loins cried out to be fed, even if it was only a crumb.

'Tomorrow,' he said, and kissed Larkin briefly on the lips before spinning to the door.

* * *

The oil lamp lit the table in the window's alcove, throwing at him the reflection of a man determined but pale against the night beyond the glass. Silence comforted him because nothing else could, and it wrapped itself about his body and infiltrated his mind, there to hold back any other thoughts but those of his purpose.

There was time to change his mind, but he would not.

All the thinking was done, and the path ahead was set. No wavering, no doubts. No-one to tell but the world, and no-one to care but the dead.

The others would care after. Not for him and not about him, but about those who mattered, both the living and the departed, and perhaps, once the truth was known, the terrible story would be brought to its just conclusion by those who would know, and in knowing, understand.

It was a case of waiting. Lonely days on the Downs seeing no-one, lonely nights in the hide, but lonely no longer mattered.

What mattered was the story.

How many times had he written it, read it, torn it up and thrown it to the flames? How many pages had gone the same way while he planned, decided, planned again and recalculated? It had to make sense, it had to be perfect, the right place and the right time, and where no-one would know or care but one, and by then, it would be too late.

Someone else might discover his error, but he couldn't go back for what he had left behind. Important things he had been stupid enough to forget; distressed enough to overlook. Couldn't be helped.

Maybe he had done it on purpose? Maybe he wanted the one to find it, to work out the obvious, and to come. To come and do what?

To plead too late. To suffer his retribution as he himself had suffered His. He had lost a wife and child because the loyalties of his youth had angered a vengeful God; it was nothing for another to know the bitter taste.

The time had come for words on paper. There was to be no more indecision. The days were running away, and the time was drawing in as inescapable as the night.

A glance into the obsidian black through reflected eyes that, once young, showed age and behind them, learning. It wasn't so far to the place, and it was still there, the massive shadow of granite and pain. A place of memories and allegiances he had carried for too long. Of secrets—one secret—that must be known, for what had he left to protect? Not himself, not the Triumvirate, only the truth.

Questions filled the silence. Unheard, they mouthed and probed, shrugged, and waited for his answers equally mouthed to the man already dead in the glass, whose only companions were the necessities of a last act. The matches to light the candle that heated the bowl that carried numbing relief through the pipe to his lungs and his turmoil. A photograph, a book, paper, ink, and the pen he had used back then, still working, still faithful, like he had been since his foolishness of the past. His *devotion,* as he had corrected with the erasing knife when writing to Caesar and realising, as he wrote, that he had been foolish to be so devoted.

No more. What was there left to stay loyal for? They had to know, and he knew of only one certain way to ensure the truth was out.

Prepare it now, and it is done. Send it later. Trust in the old school network.

Quid faciendum est. Do what must be done.

His reflection was no longer watching. It was bowed towards the page, the pen and ink, and beneath the soft glow of the oil lamp, he began his last confession.

My dear Mr Chase...

NINETEEN

Larkin left his house in plenty of time for his two visits. The first was to Guildford Street in Bloomsbury and the home of Mr Appleby-Snide, the secretary of the Old Boys Association and editor of Old Sinfordians, the tiresome pamphlet the postman forced through the letter box twice a year.

Mr Appleby-Snide's housebound condition had been much publicised in the publication along with the information that he was always at home and welcomed callers *At any time between the hours of ten of the morning and six of the evening; other times by appointment; I am always ready for a chat about the balmy days of our Sinfordian youth, to reminisce, glean new information and...* a diatribe of other excesses designed to give the man some company.

Sure enough, he was at home, and ensconced in his front-room window as Larkin stepped from the cab, paid his driver and asked him to wait. Although he had never met Appleby-Snide, his columns in the pamphlet made it clear he liked to talk, and as Larkin was due in Knightsbridge at midday, he had to ensure it was a brief meeting.

'A word with your master, if I may,' he told the manservant as he handed him his hat. 'I shall not keep him long.'

'He doesn't have long anyway,' the man replied, leaving Larkin uncertain if he meant at that moment, or life in general. 'The drawing room. This way. He saw you arrive.'

Larkin would have called it a parlour, and a suburban one at that. The room was populated by potted palms and other foliage in the manner of a Kew Gardens glasshouse, and was just as humid, the window being closed and the fire alight, despite the raging summer. With the clammy air came the smell of damp soil and illness; a heady concoction of, earth, antiseptic and soap, and through a mist, the sight of a man as ancient as the hallowed walls of Sinford's itself. White hair protruded at all angles from beneath a tasselled nightcap, which sat atop of a face Mrs Grose would have had problems levelling with the hottest of flat irons. Among the folds, two black dots stood out from a shrubbery of white beard, and the rest of the man was lost in the folds of an immense dressing gown which reached to the front wheels of the bathchair in which the creature sat.

'A Mr Larkin Chase to see you, Sir,' the manservant announced, standing just beyond the door as if afraid to enter. 'A fellow Old Sinfordian.'

Not that old. Larkin kept the words to himself. They were pointless in any case. No-one could have been as old as Appleby-Snide.

The man beckoned him in with a finger reminiscent of a twig snapped from a hazel tree in winter, and it was the same action Mr Hogg had employed when inviting a student to his whipping. Approaching tentatively, Larkin waited by the chair and allowed himself to be examined by the two jet beads, expecting Mr Appleby-Snide to croak a gruff interrogation.

What the man actually said was, 'I admire your work in the Pall Mall Gazette, Sir,' and he said it with such a clear, deep voice, Larkin almost looked behind an aspidistra to see who had spoken.

'How kind. I apologise for calling unannounced, and I am unable to stay long, but I was hoping you wouldn't take offence if I asked for some advice.'

'Kippers,' the old crone said, giving Larkin another surprise. 'Always have kippers for breakfast. That what you came to learn?'

'Er... No, not exactly.'

'Can't beat a kipper.'

'I am certain of it, Sir, but I have come to enquire about an old boy.'

'Sorry. I am all out. Will a young one do you?'

'I beg your pardon?'

'I can send Pike to the shop.'

For a boy or a kipper? Larkin was quick to wonder if Mr Appleby-Snide was quite the full catch.

'Just a little information, if you have it,' he said, glancing at the room to see if he could spy anything that might suggest his host kept records. There was nothing but the jungle. 'About an old Sinfordian.'

'Now you're talking, man.' Appleby-Snide slapped the side of his bathchair with glee, and the dots became three-dimensional marbles, still black, but set in a background of yellow. 'Who? When? What's he done? Year? Gold? Prefect? Fire away, young fella, and I'll show you what it means to be a Sinfordian.'

'Good Lord, how confident you are, Sir.'

'No point bloody being anything else. Is he still at the door?'

'Your man?' A quick look. 'Yes. He hovers without while carrying the air of a man bored with life and keen to get on with something better.'

Which was exactly how Larkin felt at that moment.

'Pike. Something for my guest.'

'Oh, no thank you,' Larkin said. 'I have an appointment shortly in Knightsbridge.'

'It's been there since before Edward the Third. It will wait. Who d'you want to find?'

'Oh.' A third surprise in as many minutes. 'You know I want to find someone?'

'They only come here to find others,' Appleby-Snide replied, and wheeled himself away from the window, narrowly missing Larkin's toes. 'Same story every time. Had an affection for Tompkins Pri in the fourth year, were best of friends, did everything together, including buggery, and went their separate ways when they grew into men. Ten years later, a man realises he's getting on, and wants to relive his youth. I blame marriage. I also blame the chastity of women. And herrings.

Same thing. Who was your sodomite? Or was it a two-way street? Hurry, man. Pike tells me I shall be dead within the month.'

From the look the servant was giving, Larkin imagined the time and date had already been decided.

'I am enquiring for a third-party,' he said, but was interrupted.

'They all say that. No need to be ashamed, lad. Sinford's was an English public school. Sodomy came right after Latin and just before Classics. Unless it was a Wednesday, in which case it came after rugby or cricket. Honestly. What did they expect? Grappling in mud or swaggering with a strap and box padding out what was otherwise a disappointment to all and bumery... What d'you say your name was?'

'Larkin Chase, Sir. I am enquiring if you know the whereabouts of a Mr Simon Stape. Like me, he was one of the last to leave Sinford's before it closed. He has friends who are anxious to know...'

'Pike!'

'Here, Sir.'

'Last on the right. Top drawer. Stape.'

'Immediately, Sir.'

'Kippers.'

There was no answer to the last randomly thrown statement, except to ask if that was what the servant had been dispatched to bring, but Larkin thought it best not to enquire.

'You wonder how I know, Mr Chase?' Appleby-Snide turned his chair to face Larkin with a self-satisfied look of smuggery. 'I may have the body of a weak and feeble woman, but I have the heart and stomach of a king. Bloody woman, stealing my best lines. I also have entrails and organs, Chase, and one of them is my mind. Within it lives my memory, and within that, a list of all names pertinent to Sinford's. My life's work since the stock market crash of twenty-five. Does he subscribe?'

'I know not.'

'Well, if there's anything on him, I will have it. Up in court is he? Been fiddling with the wife's sister. Are there details?'

'Nothing like that, Sir.'

'Nephew then? Stable boys are so prosaic. Embezzlement? Perjury?

Run away from an unwanted bastard, most likely. Shocking how many do that. I bet he's involved in crime, eh? Tell me I am correct.'

The man's ramblings were becoming tiresome, and to keep himself amused, Larkin said, 'Selling counterfeit haddocks.'

'Quite right. Kippers!' the old man barked again for no reason.

Unless it was to summon the servant who, at that moment, returned with a cardboard folder, and placed it in his master's lap, enquiring, 'Spectacles, Sir?'

'Testicles, wallet and watch. No.'

The servant retired, and Appleby-Snide handed Larkin the folder, whispering, 'He thinks I am Catholic.' Touching the side of his nose to share a great secret, he added, 'Puritan.'

That was the most unlikely thing Larkin had heard since breakfast, and he replied, 'Oh,' before opening the folder to find two pieces of paper.

'Looks like the man doesn't subscribe,' Appleby-Snide said. 'What you got?'

'A family address, which I believe is already known, his employment, ditto, and a newspaper article.'

'Oh? Told you. Up in court?'

'No, Sir. How sad. He recently lost his wife and child.'

'Probably left them on the omnibus. They do that.'

'This would be all you have on the man?'

'Aye. If he's not a member, I only keep public knowledge.'

At least Larkin had tried.

'Sir, I thank you for your time, but I must leave.'

'Wife left me once. Only once but that was enough. She went to post an advertisement in the Lady. Never came back. Haddock, you see.'

'I really must be going. Thank you for your time, Sir.'

The man was insane, or bordering on it, and the names of various fish followed Larkin into the hall where he dared ask the servant if there might be any other information about an Old Sinfordian named Stape.

'No, Sir. I looked.'

'Well, thank you anyway, Pike.'

'My name's not Pike,' the servant said as he handed Larkin his hat. 'It's Salmon, but I daren't remind him. Thank you for your visit.'

It was a rare day in London that offered clean air, but that was what Larkin gulped before he hurried into his cab and ordered his driver onwards. With the promised enquiry out of the way, he was free to consider the day ahead, and most importantly, the time he would spend with Jack.

Freedoms. That was what being a single man of means was all about. Being free to come and go from his home as he pleased, free to escape the examinations of Mrs Grose and the never-ending pining of the lovelorn Emily. Free to write his pieces, investigate his causes, and take dinner when he fancied. To stay in bed until whatever hour, and to retire to it when he pleased. To have no-one to answer to if he was late home, and no-one to sit in his favourite armchair, or crease his newspaper before he'd read it. If he had responsibilities, they were to his readers and the unfortunates his articles aimed to help, occasionally to the family, and always to the staff on wages day, but otherwise, Larkin Chase was his own man. A bachelor of the first order, and more than happy to live that way until the end.

Yet, he wasn't.

Free? Yes. Happy being alone? No.

A cab driver from Limehouse was not the kind of match Larkin had ever imagined making. A man from four miles away and yet a whole world apart? His father would suffer apoplexy if he knew Larkin was cavorting with a man from a lower class. Then again, his father would drop down dead at the thought of his youngest son being 'a bloody Uranian like that nancy Gladstone,' as he had once rather surprisingly described the Fifth Earl of Rosebury. Larkin didn't point out that the word Uranian was so outdated as to be redundant, because furthering the discussion of his proclivities would have only heaped fuel on an already raging fire.

Free from the father, too. Another one to add to his list of the joys of being single. Joys that came without the ultimate happiness; someone to share them with.

That, he hoped, would be Jack Merrit. If anyone had asked him to explain why, he wouldn't have been able to tell them, not for all the words in his vocabulary nor those of Roget's Thesaurus. It simply felt right.

As did drawing up in the highly fashionable Bucks Avenue, paying his driver, donating a reasonable tip, and staring up at an edifice Knightsbridge was no doubt proud to host. Two, in fact, because where Delamere House on the left displayed its name carved in stone above the door, its mirror image on the right stated it was Clearwater House, and Larkin would have been hard pushed to find two grander-looking homes in the city.

Less than a month ago Jack was living cheek by jowl with the worthy unwashed of Limehouse in two rooms divided by a curtain, and now...

'Mr Chase. You are expected,' the butler said when he answered Larkin's ring. 'May I take your hat?'

'Good morning, Mr Pascoe. Good to see you out of disguise.'

Larkin had first met the butler in the guise of a grimy Cornish sailor, but he was now an upright and dashing man in a tailored uniform.

'Aye, well I do my job, Sir, and it's just Pascoe when I be in the tails. Mr Merrit be at work in the library, and asked me to show you in dreckly. It's been a bit of a broil here this morning. This way.'

Larkin was torn between admiring the stately young butler and the even more stately surroundings as he passed an elegant drawing room on his right and a glittering dining room to his left.

'What a lovely home,' he said. 'Not how one would imagine a detective agency.'

'All be left to the family by Lady Marshall,' Pascoe replied. 'Mr Wright had some changes made, but kept the trappings. Of course, the clients only see the office and the drawing room. Down there be the old breakfast room where Mr Blaze has his studio. Beside it be Mr Tanner's study, and here be where young Mr Merrit does his... whatever young Mr Merrit does.'

The guided tour over, they arrived at a pair of double doors, open to reveal a long, book-lined chamber of delights. With French windows on one side, an imposing fireplace on the other, and the middle of the room occupied by tables, cabinets, astrolabes, globes and other museum-worthy pieces, the only thing missing was the man he had come to see. It wasn't until Pascoe announced the visitor that a shape in the centre of the library moved, and Larkin realised he was looking at Jack in his shirtsleeves.

Will turned beside him, and both had been bending over a table. Will approached first, but he did so at the speed of a man wading through mud. Jack followed him, also with the gait of someone walking under water, and it wasn't until they were away from the table that they broke their silence and speed. Both rushed to greet Larkin, Jack beaming with more delight than Larkin could have hoped for, but it was Will who spoke first; or rather, raved.

'So much has happened, and we've not been able to wait to tell you, but I must tell you in order, because it's all very fascinating, and Jack thinks he has the answer, and I think he's correct, and it all comes down to puzzles, but you must not move.'

'Alright, Will,' Jack said, calmer and with a hand around his brother's shoulder. 'Morning, Larkin. Nice to see you.'

'A sentiment I reciprocate. What is all the excitement? Surely, it cannot be on account of my arrival.'

He was only a little disappointed when Jack said, 'No, it ain't, but I'll let Will tell you.'

Will wasted no time. 'We came home last night to find a message from Mr Wright. Mr Payne has turned a corner, and the doctor says he will make a full recovery, but it will take time. Mr Wright will be staying a few more days in Cornwall, though, and won't be back until after Mr Havegood's desired time for information. This leaves us free to continue the case Mr Wright told us to stop, and that is what we are doing. Continuing, I mean, not stopping. Then...'

'Slow down, Will,' Jack chuckled, and continued to smile at Larkin as the story continued at a more sedate pace.

'Sorry. Then, this morning, we received a letter from Mr Ashton, the neighbour of Mr Stape at number twenty. This was in reply to my request that he, when next in Mr Stape's home, looked for anything Jack and Mr Wright may have missed. Jack had told me Mr Wright found Mr Stape's journal near the fireplace in his study, and as it has a missing page, I asked him to look in the grate to see if the page had been burnt. It hadn't, but it had been torn up, and he found pieces in the log basket. I deduce from this that Mr Stape, having come to his wit's end, decided to rip up whatever he had written, but was too distraught to think logically, and threw the pieces to the wind. Assuming there was a wind in the room. Probably not, but the metaphor works. In a way. Maybe it doesn't, because had there been a wind, they would have blown all over the place and Jack would have seen them.'

'Will, take a breath, mate. Sorry, about this, Larkin.'

'Not at all. I am wrapped with intrigue. A journal? A puzzle? It sounds like you have been having a merry time. You are clearly quite enthusiastic about your work.'

'We are, Mr Chase. With less than three days before we must either succeed or fail, the puzzle has come at an opportune time. All we have to do is solve it.'

'And this puzzle is…?'

'Vital,' Will said. 'I am sure of it. The journal, you see… It is over there, but we cannot approach just yet…'

'It's delicate,' Jack put in, but that was all Will allowed before he rattled on.

'Mr Stape's last journal entry ends with a strange question. I quote, "For whom do I leave my next page?" The page is missing, and we know this from its torn edge. The journal was found near the fireplace, as were hundreds of pieces of the same paper, buried among the wood in the basket. Those are what Mr Ashton gathered and posted, and that's what came this morning. Mr Stape's unfinished work. Jack is convinced it is a clue.'

'Because his rambling suggests he's leaving something for anyone who wants to find his body,' Jack said. 'Also, his letter to Havegood said… What was it, Will?'

'Caesar, you must consider me nothing but wasted paper in the basket, the kindling of our old study that flamed for a moment, and then became ash.'

If those were the exact words of the letter, Larkin was impressed Will had remembered them, but his skin chilled.

'I can hear Diggs saying exactly that,' he said. 'We had log baskets in our studies and when we had finished with our classroom notes, or torn a page from a book full of scribbles, we would use the paper to light the fire.'

'So Havegood would have understood that thing about being wasted paper in a basket?'

'In what way?'

'Say, if Stape was leaving him a clue.'

Larkin couldn't see the connection. 'Clue?'

'It is a theory Jack has,' Will explained. 'That Mr Stape wants Mr Havegood to find him, but not too soon. Jack thinks he laid a trail to draw Mr Havegood to his location in time for him to witness the suicide.'

'Why?'

'I dunno,' Jack said. 'It's just an idea.'

'But if you can't work out his location, how will Havegood?'

'That,' Jack said, pointing down the room to the table. 'In his journal, Stape told himself he had to plan. What if he wrote that plan, then once he'd worked it out, ripped it up. What if that's what's on that page? It might tell us where he's going to top himself, and if we can prove he's there...'

'Before the thirtieth...'

'We can send a message to Mr Havegood...'

'Who can rush to save him, and our first case will be successfully completed...'

'Before Jimmy gets back and knocks ten bells out of us for not doing as we're told.'

'He wouldn't do that, Jack.'

'I was using one of your metaphones.'

'Metaphors.'

'Stop showing off.'

'You started it.'

A loud cough brought the brothers back from the edge of a squabble.

'You be wanting anything, Sirs?' It was Pascoe, waiting impatiently at the doors. 'Only there be plenty better I could be doing.'

'No, Max, thanks,' Jack said, his wide and excited eyes still fixed on Larkin as the butler left.

'I must admit, I feel quite exhausted,' Larkin said, hoping the brothers would understand his mirth.

They didn't. Will was retracing his steps to the central table, and Jack was grinning like a loon.

'I take it this puzzle-solving is urgent,' Larkin said.

'Yeah. Will's dead keen to sort it out, but there's loads of tiny pieces of paper. Some's got things written on them, but we ain't sure if the writing's on both sides or just one, so we can't glue them down. We got the left edge done, but then I sneezed, and it were like snowflakes.' A charming, almost comic, grimace followed, and he thumbed towards Will, whispering, 'He weren't happy.'

'Ah, hence the slow movements and closed windows. How long have you been at it?'

'Since early.'

'May I help?'

Jack looked at the table, and frowned. 'You wanted us to go out.'

'There will be time for that.'

Larkin braced himself for disappointment. Half of him hoped Jack would say time together was more important than the case, but the other half knew he would be keen to prove his usefulness.

'Maybe later this afternoon?' Jack said, using apologetic eyes as his weapon.

'Of course. Unlike you, I am not employed in anything so fascinating. Besides, if you allow me to assist, we will still be together.'

'As long as you don't cough, sneeze or throw your hands about. I tell you, it's delicate work is this.'

It was indeed. Some of the pieces were no larger than the petal of a daisy. Diggs hadn't just torn up his page, he had decimated it, and Larkin could only think he had run it through a threshing machine or some other contraption capable of shredding a folio into so many pieces. Each one was different in shape, which meant he hadn't folded and torn, but gone about his task with, as Will had suggested, wild abandon.

Will, on the other hand, worked in a calmer and more organised way, and had already identified and placed the pieces that fitted the lefthand tear of the page. There was a collection of all those with a straight edge, including the two remaining corners, and he was trying to make a frame. Jack had the parts that contained writing, a stroke here, half a letter there, and had set them to one side face up. Another part of the table housed blank fragments, which, although part of the puzzle, were not vital. What mattered was putting together the words, a fact that had escaped Will, who seemed intent on fixing the whole page back together, but then, that was indicative of his preciseness.

Following Jack's silently signed instructions, Larkin stood beside him to examine upstrokes and downstrokes, curves and punctuation, his eyes darting from one shard to another as he delicately turned a piece to fit its most likely position. After only five minutes of this, he was forced to remove his jacket and roll his sleeves, which he did having reversed from the table at the speed of a tortoise.

When he returned, Jack was pointing at three pieces which he had placed together. They fitted, and made a word. *Where...*

Larkin beckoned him away from the table, and when at a safe distance, whispered, 'It suggests a question, so we should look for a question mark.'

'I'm really sorry.'

'What for?'

'You wanted to go out.'

'I told you; it doesn't matter. Much as I was looking forward to spending time alone with you, it can wait. It must, for this is the most pressing task, and pleasure must come later.'

'Pleasure?'

The salaciousness of Jack's grin said it all, and nudged Larkin's excitement to a higher level. His cheeks warmed.

'Mind on the job, Mr Merrit. We have time enough for that in due course.'

Maybe they did, but the thought hampered his concentration, and more than once, he moved a fragment with haste, causing others to shift out of place. Some pieces stuck to his fingers, a complaint from which Will also suffered, and others simply refused to lie flat. The paper was lined, which helped with alignment, but it was a still a painstaking and uncomfortable task. Now and then, the men stood upright from their bent positions, clutched their backs, and groaned, and if they weren't careful, breathed a sigh of relief which affected the tabletop like a hurricane.

It was Pascoe who came up with a solution. Delivering sandwiches, he called the team to the far end of the room, and sat with them to eat and share two pots of coffee. During the break, Will told him how careful they had to be, and explained why.

'I know what you be needing,' Pascoe said in his rolling Cornish accent. 'You be needing a lantern glass, white vinegar and some Nelson's. As I don't have no Nelson's I'd have to be making me own, but I can do that on the stove.'

Will gave him a questioning look and said more or less the same words Larkin was thinking. 'Max, you may make a very nice sandwich, and your coffee is perfect, but your communication needs work.'

'Yeah,' Jack agreed. 'What you talking about?'

'You told me you got bits of paper flying all over, but you can't stick them down because there might be writing on both sides. I be right?'

'Yes, although I am coming to think there is writing only on one side,' Will replied.

'Just in case, I can make you a paste that stays clear when it dries. So, when you find bits that go a-gether, you can stick them onto glass, so you can see both sides if you need to. Be right, Mr Chase, wouldn't you say?'

'You can do that?' Jack asked before Larkin could express his own praise.

'Aye. Nelson's photographic gelatine would do it. It's what me fader used on the farm. Still does, I 'spect, but I don't have none here, so I'll have to make it. I got gelatine, flour, vinegar... Aye, be all I need.'

'That's impressive,' Will said.

'That be Cornish farming, Mr Will. Give me half hour while you finish your lunch, and I'll be back.'

The butler didn't disappoint, and when he returned with a jar of warm liquid and the three returned to their task, solving the puzzle became much easier. It still took time to identify possible matches, and having given up all hope of taking Jack to lunch or courting him over tea, Larkin contented himself with simply being by his side as the puzzle solving continued.

It was a while later, when Larkin was taking another break to stretch his back, that Jack crept over. 'I got four words and some strange numbers. I reckon I'm close to getting the rest,' he said with a heart-stirring expression of excitement.

Despite the discomfort and heat, Larkin was already drawn into what he saw as another cabman's adventure, and with equal enthusiasm, asked, 'What words do you have?'

'*Where? When? Why?* And the last one in bolder letters, *Truth*.'

'His diary speaks of the truth being made known.' Will had joined them. 'What else?'

'Numbers,' Jack said, mopping his brow. 'And they're really strange.'

Taking a notebook from the back pocket of his trousers, he wrote what lay in shreds on the table ready to be pasted.

NL-SOMoL+S

9 & 4

TWENTY

It wasn't until the sunlight was fading that Larkin and Jack finished their section. With Will intent on connecting the pointless, blank pieces, Larkin watched as Jack copied Stape's madness into his own book. The man had left behind a series of words and numbers, one street name, and not much else.

'The ravings of a madman,' was Jack's verdict as Larkin sat with him in the office, waiting for Will to finish and join them.

'It may not be madness,' Larkin said, leaning into his shoulder to read, and enjoying the scent of his damp shirt. 'Diggs was never one to do anything emotional. By which I mean, it is very against his character to rip up anything in that way. The Diggs I remember was methodical. Always. Life, to him, was a science, as was friendship, and thus, it follows, love. Not that I knew him to be in love.'

'With Havegood,' Jack said, and despite Larkin's proximity, did not move away.

'Havegood and Diggs were never in love.'

'Not what Havegood says.'

'Marcus was far too enraptured by Jacques Verdier to have eyes for anyone else. I am sure of it.'

'Well, it ain't what's written on Havegood's statement.'

'But there are different kinds of love, Jack. Those for a friend, those for a brother such as you have for Will, and those which involve the complicated emotions that come with things more carnal.'

'You talking about sex?'

Larkin's heart thrilled at the word, especially coming from Jack's lips, but he kept his composure.

'Indeed. As far as I know, Marcus held platonic love for Diggs, harboured erotic love for Verdier but demonstrated it as platonic, and played at the fringe of friendship love for me and a few others. Only in terms of caring for a friend, just as you might for, say, Mr Wright.'

'But Havegood wrote he and Stape shared the bedroom.'

'A study. Yes, they did.'

'But not as lovers?'

'Separate beds.'

Larkin took a moment to picture his past. The cold, damp walls of the narrow stone staircase, twisting and worn leading to the wider, panelled walls of the tower's top floor where a few lanterns cast weak light still supplemented by candles even in eighteen eighty. His imagination took him along the rear corridor where no-one came but the golds who lived there, and he couldn't resist popping his head into A-two as he passed.

His bed to one side, Verdier's to the other, the desk under the window, and the second against the passage wall, beneath the noticeboard that refused to hang straight. The lockers, the veneer flaking away on the cupboards and chests, the tuck boxes and the books, all chattels of a past life but not an unhappy one. There was also the silence broken only by the sounds of night creatures from outside, and the creak of the wire frame when Verdier turned over in his bed. No sounds from the study next door; they would have had to have been violently loud to penetrate the stonework and heavy oak doors, although, strangely, it was possible to hear if someone was on the roof.

The vision came with memories; games of chess with Verdier talking about nothing, and serious evenings when they sat by their fire, and Larkin explained the classics, as Verdier helped him with his French. Conversations in English, French and faltering Latin into the night, when Jacques didn't have an athletics meet the next day, always about nothing and yet everything, and most of the discussions long forgotten, leaving only footprints of a happy time.

Time enough spent in reminiscing. Moving on, he came to Diggs' and Havegood's room next door, and saw two gentlemen in their last year, one to be a viscount, the other to become a banker. Already placed at Cambridge, there was never anything remarkable to see in their rooms. Two similar beds, both apart, desks with one man at each, Havegood's books neatly stacked, Stape's in disarray. Scarves and ties hanging wherever was convenient, and Stape's sports clothes wherever they fell. A quietly ticking clock, the same furniture as next door, the same silence from without, and, in daylight, the same view of the grounds, forest and hills. No signs of love, no signs of disputes, only those of friendly badinage and prank playing when one had won a match or scored well in an examination.

The memory faded with the room as he left it, closed the door, and, at the far end of the corridor, opened the one to the steep wooden stairs that led to the roof. Happy memories waited up there too.

In the present, however, Jack waited at his side, still pressing against him, and now, growing restless.

'No,' Larkin finally answered the question. 'I have thought as much as I can, and I would not say Diggs and Caesar were lovers, simply the best of friends. I was not privy to what went on behind their closed door. However, a love affair between two golds would have been the ultimate disgrace if exposed. They never spoke of it to me, and Marcus only spoke of his great affection for Verdier, affection which Verdier had made quite clear would not be reciprocated physically.'

'Then Jimmy was right,' Jack said, and cast his notes aside. 'There's something strange about this.'

'What?'

'That's the thing. We don't know, and the idea came from Jimmy. Without him here, I can't tell you, but it's odd that Havegood said things to us that you remember different.'

'What I can remember comes from twelve years ago, and may not be accurate,' Larkin conceded, having resisted the pedantic urge to correct Jack's language. It would have been wrong to do so. Besides, he enjoyed hearing it. 'What is more recent is what Diggs wrote on his missing page. Do you think, while we wait, we should see if it means anything?'

'I've looked, and it don't,' Jack said. 'But, yeah, have a gander if you like, and again, I'm sorry.'

'What for?'

'For not giving you the afternoon you wanted. Only...'

'Time and tide are not of the waiting variety,' Larkin said. 'I understand, and please, stop apologising. Your time and presence are all I want. We can take lunch or go to tea once you have solved the case.'

'You think we will?'

A smile grew on Jack's slightly protuberant top lip, causing Larkin to shudder with pleasure, even though Jack moved away to slump in the opposite armchair. There, with his legs splayed, he rested his head on a balled fist, a man at ease in his new surroundings and with his company. A delight to witness.

'I think you will,' Larkin said. 'You and Will both in equal measures. I see you have chalkboards with what I assume are notes and information. Shall we add this enigmatic page to the list?'

'Yeah. Will you do it? My writing's rubbish enough without trying to put stuff up there.'

More than happy to be involved, Larkin took the book in one hand and chalk in the other, and added to the ordered lists and words already on the boards. When he finished, he stood beside Jack's chair, aware his crotch was only inches from his face, and together, they stared at the meaningless words.

NL-SOMoL+S

9 + 4

Where? 53.W.24
When? LCDRW Dickens Street
Why? 58.G.28
To: Cannock. 15.N.19 (Before and in time)
At: 16.M.24

'Dickens Street,' Jack said. 'If it's London, that's north of Wandsworth Road in Battersea. Mean anything to you?'

'No, but it must mean something to Diggs.'

'It's not far from Clapham Park where his house is.'

'What is LCDRW, do you think?'

'Hang on.'

Jack stood, and did something that reminded Larkin of Will. He paced to the window, paused there, returned, and passed his chair to the far wall, all the time blinking rapidly with his face taut with concentration.

'It's the map in my head,' he said by way of explanation. 'If it's a street I've not been to in a while, I have to picture it. It also helps to remember fares.'

'Imagine you are driving me there.'

'Oh, right then.' The taut face melted into cheerfulness. 'From here south to the Chelsea Bridge and across. Battersea Park on me right and into Battersea Park Road, straight on to Queens Road railway station. One and six so far, Sir. After, under the arches, Queen's Park Crescent, not as grand as it sounds on account of the shunting, and south onto Silverstone. Then... Dickens Road is first left. Railway worker's cottages down one side, past St Andrew's Road and you switch back into Robertson, which saves turning the cab in the street.'

'Impressive,' Larkin said, his eyes on the chalkboard. 'LCDR.'

'Yeah, and the W on the end.'

'Railway worker's cottages, arches...?'

'Shunting yards and works.' Jack finished for him, and grinning, announced. 'London and Chatham District Railway Works. It's bloody got it on a wooden arch over the way in.' With cheek twinkling in his eyes, he held out his hand, and chirped, 'Two shillings, please, Sir. A tip would be most welcome.'

There was no denying the look of joy on his face, and it continued when Larkin took his hand, and said, 'A big tip, cabbie. I will thrust it upon you with my insistence.'

Jack's face fell, and with it, Larkin's humour and hopes.

'But it don't mean nothing,' Jack said, pulling away and spinning to the boards. 'Not unless you got something?'

The case was too much on his mind, and again Larkin had to tell himself not to be disappointed. Jack was about his new work.

'Nothing, I'm afraid,' he said. 'I can think of no connection between Simon Stape and the London and Chatham District Railway. Nor why it should relate to his question, *When?*'

'Yeah,' Jack agreed. 'If it were next to the *Where*, that might make sense. Anyway, we know when. The early hours of the thirty-first. How d'you get to that from a bloody railway works?'

'I'd go by cab, Mr Merrit.' Like the genie from the magic lamp, Pascoe appeared in the doorway and only knocked after he had made his statement. 'Just to say, Sir, dinner will be on the table come one hour. I made enough fur Mr Chase, case he be staying.'

'I don't want to be a burden...'

'Yeah, Mr Chase is staying,' Jack said, with a look that warmed Larkin's heart to simmering. 'If you want to.'

'I would enjoy and appreciate it,' Larkin replied. 'Dinner with the Delamere gentlemen—and I include you, Mr Pascoe—will be a delight. Thank you.'

'Right y'are.'

Pascoe left, and Jack made a suggestion which took Larkin from simmer to a near boil.

'I want to change and wash. I could show you the room Jimmy's given me, if you'd like to see?'

'I would be fascinated.'

Fascinated, thrilled and hopeful were all words Larkin might have used to describe himself as he followed Jack through the drawing room to the hall. As they climbed the imperial staircase and bore left where the flight became two, Jack was keen to tell him all the details of his new circumstances.

'Dalston and Joe have a suite down there at the back,' he said. 'Same as the one me and Will got on this side of the house. Jimmy's opposite them at the front, and there's still a spare. Don't ask me what all these paintings and chattels are about. Here's Will's room. Won't go in in case I put something out of place, but he's got what was the sitting room, and we got a door connecting, and share a bathroom between us smart as you like, and this great a big cupboard. You'll see.

I ain't tidied nor nothing. We even got a maid who does that, but not today.'

It was a pleasure to witness Jack's enthusiasm. It lent him yet another endearing quality, and by the time he threw open the door to reveal a bedroom larger than Larkin's, and with far better furniture, they were both beaming.

'You really have fallen on your feet, haven't you, Jack?'

'Fall on the bed an'all if you want.'

The door closed with a thump, and Jack's hands were on Larkin's face before he knew what was happening.

'Kiss you too if you like,' Jack said, hope displayed like a billboard across his face.

'I would like very much, Mr...'

There were no more words, just passionate tongues, and an embrace from Jack as hard as that of a drowning man. It wasn't a struggling embrace of released desperation, played to the underscore of carnal grunts and groans, it was a clutch of a man who didn't want to let go a thing he held dear. Larkin returned it in the same way, his ardour growing uncontrollably when Jack's pressed against him.

The embrace continued until passion took over and they grappled with each other's clothing, all the time moving along the wall towards the massive, unmade bed. They reached a wardrobe, and Jack had Larkin trapped, their shirts open, vests pulled from undone trousers, hands delving deeper, with no need to ask permission.

Knowing what he wanted to do, Larkin turned them both so Jack was against the wall, and releasing his lips, took a moment to stare deep into his eyes and relish his wonder. With a telling raise of an eyebrow, he slowly sank to his knees, taking in the manly bittersweet tang of Jack's bare flesh when he lifted his vest and kissed his chest. Lower, his firm kisses brought small gasps of pleasure to Jack's throat, that became gasps, when he took his rigid manhood in his fist, and among the musky aroma of his crotch, sank it into his mouth. First the salty tang of the tip, and soon, half the length, his mouth widening, his throat adjusting as Jack filled him, until his nose was pressed into the forest above. Jack pushed hard and fast, but Larkin held him back, forcing him to move slowly, guiding him by his hips as his lips tightened around his prize, and his tongue played.

'Oh, heavens. I should have knocked.'

Jack's knee swiped Larkin in the face, and he fell backwards as the bigger man leapt over him, swearing. A moment of confusion was followed by the burning skin of panic and a heartrate double that of a second before.

'Bloody hell, Will!'

'I'm not looking.'

'What you playing at, you fuckin idiot. Get out.'

'No need for language. I didn't see anything.'

Still on the floor, Larkin pretended to be searching for something, and, buttoning his trousers at the same time, stumbled about on all fours until he was semi-presentable.

'Mr Chase, your shirt has become undone.'

'Will, get out!'

'I have it, Jack.' Will was apparently oblivious to the scramble. 'The heading. I have it.'

'Will…'

'No, shush and listen, the pair of you. I have noted it here. You won't believe it, Jack.'

Reasonably presentable, Larkin staggered to his feet, his flesh cooling along with his ardour, and found Jack sitting cross-legged on the edge of the bed, red in the face, fuming, and fiddling with his collar.

Will had helped himself to an armchair and was studying his notebook. 'Tell me when you are suitable,' he said, without looking up.

A look of annoyed apology from Jack came with a shrug, and Larkin returned it with one of helplessness and a smile he hoped would suggest it didn't matter, although it did. It was designed to calm Jack, and it succeeded.

'Later,' Jack mouthed, and Larkin nodded an affirmative reply. 'What did you find, Will?'

'Perfect sense,' Will said. 'Once I'd cracked the title, the rest was easy. Or will be easy, because I have yet to locate the book in question.

Really, Jack, I am surprised you didn't see it straight away. Can I look up yet?'

'Yeah, and you can say what you've got to say, and bugger off.'

Will raised his head, but kept his eyes away from the couple. 'When I tell you this, you will want to race to the resource and translate the rest of the message,' he said. 'I thought we could do that before dinner.'

'Get on with it.'

'Yes, indeed. The title reads, N L, hyphen, S O M, a lowercase O…'

'I remember. So?'

'So what do you think they stand for?'

'No idea. What?'

Will looked away from the windows, his eyes danced from one man to the other as if he was making sure what he saw was suitable viewing, and when he decided it was, continued.

'This arrangement of letters came to me as I thought about Dickens Street,' he said. 'And what I have discovered leads me to believe Mr Stape, at first, did not, in fact, want to kill himself. Rather, as you suggested, I believe he might have wanted to be found, and more, he wanted to be found by Mr Havegood. Who else would come looking for him? Admittedly, it appears as though he then changed his mind, because his clues are… well, not exactly easy to find, but…'

'Will…' Jack was calmer, but threat remained in his voice.

'Yes, yes, I know. One thing at a time. First, then, the title. These letters are initials, and there is only one thing they can stand for.'

'Really?' Larkin thought it time he said something. 'They looked like a chemical formula to me, and coming from Diggs, that would not have been surprising.'

'Maybe, but they are not,' Will said. 'They refer to a book, and Max tells me there is one in the house somewhere, and he is finding it.'

'What book?'

'Honestly, Jack, and you a cabbie. We know that Mr Stape had an interest in cartography, and you yourself said he had books on the subject in his home. Maps, too. These letters stand for *New Large-Scale Ordnance Map of London and Suburbs*. The numbers relate to the nine-inch and twelve-inch maps the book contains. It is the same book of maps with which I helped you learn the cabman's knowledge, and if I am correct, the rest of the torn-up paper gives us page numbers and grid references. Now, unless you two intend to continue rutting, I suggest we reconvene in the office and use this book as a cypher. Mr Chase?'

'Yes?' Larkin was still flustered.

'Your shirt tails are sticking through your trouser fly in an unseemly manner. Just thought you should know. Come along.'

TWENTY-ONE

There were times when Jack could quite easily throttle his brother, but the opportunity passed as Will hurried out, leaving Jack and Larkin staring at each other, panting, but no longer with passion.

'Don't be angry with him,' Larkin said, adjusting his trousers. 'It's our fault for not taking enough care.'

'Couldn't help meself.'

'I am glad.'

'Sorry.'

Larkin took his hands, and pulled him close. 'Nothing to be sorry about. There will be time. What matters is that you know my strength of feeling for you.'

Jack knew the strength of his erect lob; he still sensed it pressing against his own even though it wasn't, but he wasn't sure how a quick grapple proved anything other than their need to 'rut.'

'I mean for us to be more together than simply what almost happened,' Larkin said. 'Attraction begins from the outside and works its way in, and mine to you has burrowed deeply and fast. Beyond the external, I stir within my loins, but more within my heart.'

What the hell did that mean?

'Too many words, Mr Chase,' Jack said, reminding them both of the time before, but on this occasion, he was grinning. 'Save them for when we can get to be alone proper. We better get downstairs.'

'Leave me a kiss within the cup, and I'll not ask for wine.'

'You what?'

By way of an answer, Larkin kissed him, long and hard. Jack reciprocated, trying not to let his hands travel lower than the small of his back. The memory of Baxter climbing the stairs infiltrated the moment, but it didn't belong there, and he kicked it out, knowing that although he might lust after other men, he could never know such shared happiness with anyone but the man now making his head spin; Larkin bloody Chase.

'We must go,' Larkin whispered when they broke apart, their lips glistening. 'Your new career awaits.'

It waited in the shape of Will bent over the table in the office, and turning the pages of a large book.

'I think you two should look at this, and give me the answers to write on the board,' he said as soon as they entered. 'This atlas contains both nine and twelve-inch maps of the city, and as nine plus twelve are on the torn page, I can only think we are on the right lines. Or, the right road, I suppose.'

'Yeah, alright,' Jack sighed, crossing the room and nudging Will out of the way. 'Where's the torn-up paper?'

'Here.'

'Can you imagine Mr Stape doing this?' Will asked Larkin who was examining the remade page.

'He *did* have an interest in maps,' Larkin said. 'And it would be in his nature to prepare a theorem before setting out to prove it. If you are correct in your assumption, Will, I am interested to see what parts of this map he has highlighted, and why. However, it is not that easy to read.'

'His journal mentions paper streets and black lines as being beside him when he asked for whom he left his notes,' Will said, resting the lantern glass against two candlesticks with a table lamp glowing behind.

'Oh, yeah,' Jack said. 'And there was a book missing... I bet this is what Jimmy saw in his desk.'

'But you didn't think to connect the two?'

'We hadn't read the journal by then, Will. No reason to assume the maps had anything to do with anything. We'd not found the scraps neither.'

'Yes, alright,' Will tutted. 'There, now we can see what we are about.'

Even though the paper had hairline cracks running all over the place like of one of Grandma Ida's ancient jars, the writing showed through well enough against the lamp. With the book of maps between them, Jack and Larkin drew up chairs, while Will cleaned a section of already clean chalkboard, and announced he was ready.

'Starting with the *Where*,' Jack said. 'The numbers read fifty-three, then W and twenty-four.'

'Logic suggests map number first,' Larkin said, and his moustache twitched as he flickered his eyebrows. 'This is exciting.'

Jack turned to map fifty-three and found himself looking at an area from Lower Tooting to Upper Norwood. The streets were lodged in his memory, and as he took in the random spread of roads and fields, railways lines and boundaries, he wondered how he'd ever managed to learn the routes on this page, let alone the rest of the atlas.

Larkin must have been thinking the same, because he whispered, 'Good heavens. How on earth do cabmen...?' but Will interrupted.

'Grid square W twenty-four?'

'Yeah... hang on...' Jack trailed his fingers to meet on the square towards the top right. 'Dulwich Common.'

'Is that written within the bounds of the square?'

'It's only half a square, because it's on the edge of the page.'

'Within the grid, then,' Will leant over his shoulder. 'Ah.'

'What?'

'Only two whole words are complete enough to be clues. *Grove* and *The Grange*.'

'What's that? One of your fancy poems or something?'

'It is a location,' Larkin said, and sat back in his chair. 'Well I never.'

'Yes, Mr Chase?'

'This message definitely came from Diggs?' Larkin queried, and when Will told him it did and asked to explain what he had seen, he sat forward again and placed his finger on the map. 'We must always remember the possibility of coincidence,' he said, speaking as if he was thinking aloud. 'But, at Sinford's, within the grounds, but away from the main school, there was a hide. It was rarely used, but some masters would take pupils there to watch for woodland wildlife, and some boys would be allowed to do the same unaccompanied. It was known colloquially as The Grange. Schoolboy satire, because it was little more than a dishevelled hovel.'

'A hide?'

'More of a small cottage, Jack. Apparently once a hunting lodge or similar, it was in pretty awful repair in my day, but didn't stop boys using it for all manner of things. Illegal smoking was popular with the silvers, while those maniacs into military drills used it as HQ for exercises and games of war.'

'Was Mr Stape one of them?' Will was again hovering behind.

'No more than we had to be,' Larkin said. 'The Triumvirate used it in our last year, mainly to get away from the world and our studies, all very innocent and noble. I went once or twice, but with those three out of the way, I had the tower floor to myself and could revise without a long trek while remaining near the conveniences and comforts. It makes no sense, though.'

'What doesn't?'

'If I follow you correctly, this is where Diggs plans to take his life, yes?'

'Well, the paper says *Where?*' Jack pointed out. 'So, yeah, I suppose.'

'Why would a man like Simon Stape choose to end his life in a ramshackle old hide in the middle of a forest?'

'One might as well ask why any man would want to take his own life at all,' Will said. 'But men do, and women, and who are we to understand the why and where? In this case, we suspect his state of mind is unbalanced due to tragedy, although I have yet to explain why I believe that not to be the case.'

'What?'

'Not now, Jack. First, we should translate all of these references, note possibilities and coincidences, and see what we have. Then we can debate. What is next?'

Beneath the first set of numbers was another line in what Jack called brackets, and Will called parentheses.

'Whatever, you got the word *Near*, then thirty-nine, H-eighteen.'

Larkin was already turning to the page, and when he found it, revealed half of Islington on one side, Highgate and part of Parliament Hill on the other. The square they needed contained a jumble of small roads and streets joined in random order as they were in most of the city, with a railway line running straight through.

'Near?' Will queried. 'Near what?'

Jack scanned the street names, but they could have referred to anything from Mr Stape's life. Larkin pressed closer to look, and Jack slipped his hand onto his knee. It was just a quick squeeze, and Larkin responded with a longer one, but whispered, 'Concentrate, Mr Merrit.'

'It's hard,' Jack replied at no volume.

'I suffer the same condition.'

'No, it's hard to concentrate when you're so close.'

'Then unhand my knee, and focus.'

'Yes, do.' Will slapped Jack on the back of the head like a schoolmaster, and he pulled himself together.

'Kentish Town,' he said, causing the others to ask why. 'Look, right in the middle, Kentish Town station. Your old school's in Kent, ain't it? So, the Grange is near a Kentish town. Yeah?'

'Your brother is brilliant, Will,' Larkin enthused. 'The hide is indeed not far from Biddenden.'

'Then we can safely assume what we have here are Mr Stape's plans for his own death, and nothing is a coincidence, Mr Chase. Well done, brother. What's next?'

'*When?* LCDRW Dickens Street.'

'When?' Will mused, seemingly as confused as Jack. 'When... railways... Dickens? Do you think it is a reference to one of his works, Mr Chase? Is there a Dickens title that includes a time or date?'

'Hard Times,' Jack said. 'Even I've heard of that one.'

'Christmas Carol?' Will paced to the window. 'We know the *When* has nothing to do with Christmas....' And back again... 'Old Curiosity... No. Twist?'

'When is the assumed when?' Larkin asked, searching for something towards the back of the atlas.

'Three nights from now.' Will said. 'Fifty-five hours at the most.'

'Of course. Then this clue is irrelevant to us.'

'Why do you say that?'

Larkin turned to a map muttering, 'Dickens...' and landed his finger in a square. 'Dickens Street.'

'Yeah, I know where it is,' Jack said. 'What of it?'

'Map number?'

'Thirty-one.'

'Date of projected suicide?'

'Thirty-fir... Ah, I get you.'

'This is confirmation of the client's concern. We know where and when for sure,' Will scribbled on the board. 'We can tell Mr Havegood, and fulfil Jimmy's case for him.'

'Hang on, Will...'

When Will was excited about something, his usual sense and logic became lost in his enthusiasm. Jack saw it coming, and needed to calm him before he fixed his mind on telling Havegood the news and became unable to think of anything else.

'Slow down, mate,' he said. 'There's still stuff to work out, and besides, we don't know Stape is at that shack in the woods.'

'He plans to be.'

'We can't say that for sure. Maybe he wrote this stuff as a test, then decided against it and threw it away. Changed his mind, like you said.'

'Indeed, it could be one of many theorems,' Larkin agreed.

'No. I am adamant. He did this in the hope that Mr Havegood would come looking for him, find the pieces, knit them together, and translate the clues...' Will began to slow under Jack's incredulous gaze. 'Hoping Mr Havegood would realise where Mr Stape was to be, and... Yes, well, I see it sounds rather farfetched.'

'And rather destroyed,' Larkin said, pointing to the lantern glass. 'I fear the heat is melting Mr Pascoe's home glue.'

Some of the fragments were sliding down the glass, and Jack lay the page flat.

'I can see it well enough,' he said. 'Why are you so sure he left all this for Havegood to find?'

Will weaved his fingers together as he paced back to the window, saying, 'It was one of my feelings combined with Mr Wright's assertion that something wasn't right about the case, but I can't explain it. Now I have told you what I thought, and heard my thoughts aloud, I can see my theory is unlikely. Perhaps this was only the first draft of a plan. That would explain its condition.'

'Possibly,' Larkin said. 'In my investigations into the lives of the wretched, I have learnt the sad truth that people take their lives in one of two ways. The means to the final end are, like eternity, endless, but the act itself is carried out either on the spur of the moment, or after some planning, such as this might be.'

'Spur of the moment?'

'Indeed, Jack. You would be surprised at the number of people who, while admiring the view from atop the Monument to the great fire, suddenly have the urge to throw themselves and caution to the wind. If a man is contemplating the act, and has been for some time, it is sometimes easier to act impetuously, before he has time to change his mind.'

'And after some planning?' Will enquired.

'That is less common, I admit, but a determined man may well decide on a date and place and convince himself it is a foregone conclusion. Imagine: "I am at work on my dockside crane tomorrow, and it is my wife's birthday. I shall teach her the ultimate lesson at midday." This sounds more like our quarry, like Diggs, I mean. However, there are dangers associated with this afore-planned suicide.'

'Sorry to interrupt, Mr Chase, but what exactly do you investigate?'

Larkin gave a weak smile. 'I know, it is not always a savoury occupation, but nevertheless, a fascinating one.'

'Right, but the danger?' Jack was keen to return to the map before Larkin wandered off into a forest of words.

'One danger is that by setting an advanced date, a person leaves himself open to reason, indecision, and a change of mind. In these cases, doctors say, the person does not really want to kill themselves, and is, in a way, asking for help. I have said that Diggs was never a likely candidate for any kind of self-harm, but he is being driven by his recent suffering. On the other side of his internal debate would be his instinct to survive, and perhaps, by leaving clues to his intentions, and knowing Havegood would be concerned, this is exactly what he has done.'

Jack found himself holding his breath, but letting it go, said, 'And that's your way of saying he wants to be found, is it?'

'We should acknowledge the possibility.'

'But why leave such obstreperous clues?' Will said.

'In order that they were not found too soon? I cannot say,' Larkin smiled. 'Perhaps there is another possibility.'

'Which is?'

'Perhaps Diggs left this jumble for Havegood in the hope he would find it and head in the wrong direction. This could be a false path.'

'Whatever it is, it's all we got,' Jack said, tiring of the debate. 'Max'll be up soon telling us it's dinner time. So... Will, to the board. Larkin, to the *Why?*'

'Of course,' Larkin said. 'I see this reference has been crossed out. Should we still consider it?'

'Yes,' was Will's verdict, and Larkin read the note, while Jack found the page.

'Nothing in this square but the village name of Addington,' he said, his eyes flicking over a place he didn't recognise. 'That's out in bloody Surrey. I never learned this far from town.'

'Why?'

'No point. If a fare wanted to go that far, they'd be better off getting a train. If they insisted, I'd get as far as I could, then ask someone local for directions. I mean, it's...'

'I wasn't asking.' Larkin interrupted him by placing a finger on his lips. 'I was thinking aloud.'

'An idea, Mr Chase?'

'Not as such, Will, more a vague memory.'

'To do with school?'

'No.'

It was Larkin's turn to pace to the window, and from there to the bookcase where he bent his head to read some spines.

Jack and Will had just exchanged blank looks, when he dragged a book from a shelf, and muttering to himself, returned.

'Post Office London Directory, last year...'

'Surrey, Mr Chase, is not in London.'

'Indeed, but neither is the truth. Or should I say, just Truth.'

Another exchange of shrugs didn't help, but when Larkin put down the directory open to a page and pointed, his meaning became clearer.

'Truth Magazine has its main offices in Great Queen Street, but their sub-editors work from Addington Square,' Larkin said. 'I notice your board mentions the word Truth.'

'Yes. It comes from Mr Stape's journal where he mentions it several times as though it was playing on his mind. At one point, he says... One moment...' Will found and read from his casebook. '"Jacques will at last bear witness on his day, and the man of superstition and reasonableness, like the rest, will know the truth."'

'Good Lord.'

'What is it?' Jack touched Larkin's arm as he lowered himself into his chair, staring at nothing, and presumably thinking.

'The man of superstition and reasonableness is Caesar,' he said. 'It was how Shakespeare described him. Not in the text, as far as I remember, but there was a debate about it one year.' The chalkboard drew his attention. 'The lodge on the morning of the thirty-first, so Caesar will know the truth?'

'That is about it, Mr Chase. Does this mean anything to you other than the obvious?'

A long pause followed during which Jack was happy to watch Larkin as he thought, and Will took the time to correct a misspelling, dust his fingers, and reset the chalk in its tray.

'No,' Larkin said at length. 'I can think of nothing else but what you have already found. Is there more?'

'There is,' Jack told him, and read from the lantern glass. 'After the crossed-out numbers, it says, *Cannock, fifteen, N-nineteen, in time*, and if you can make head or tail of that, I'm a monkey's brother.'

'Oi! D'you mind?'

Jack sniggered, Will threw him a sneer, and Larkin reminded them that time was moving on.

'Map fifteen, square... Oh. This is easy,' Jack said, peering at half a section at the bottom of the map. 'There's only three streets here. Waterloo Place, Carlton House Terrace, and Pall Mall.'

'Meaning this clue reads, Cannock Waterloo Place in Time?' Will's sneer remained. 'Or Cannock Pall Mall in time? Nonsense.'

'Well, I dunno,' Jack protested. 'You're the clever one, you work it out. Pall Mall sticks out the most, it's in bold.'

'Mr Chase, you have gone quite pale,' Will said.

'You have a bit. You alright?'

'Hmm? Oh, yes, perfectly, thank you. Yet, not.'

'This means something to you don't it?'

'Pall Mall does, yes. And Cannock.'

'Would you like to explain, Sir? There is this and one more clue to unlock, and you have been so helpful up until now.'

Will's words sounded like a put down, but if they were, Larkin didn't seem to mind.

'I am glad to be helping,' he said. 'The mention of truth led to the thought that Diggs might be referring to Truth magazine, or the address thereof. It's crossing out might suggest he thought of something more pertinent and more obvious. To draw attention to Cannock and Pall Mall... It is as if he changed his mind from one periodical to another. Like his, my mind remains with publications, and in particular, my own. That is, my brother's publication, the Pall Mall Gazette.'

When it looked like Larkin would say no more, Jack prompted him with a gentle nudge, and he woke from his daydreaming.

'Apologies. It begins to make sense,' he said. 'At least, it might make sense to me if I could understand what is behind it all. You see, there is a place in the Midlands called Cannock Chase, a place, like the area surrounding Sinford's, noted for its forests and scenery. That, however, is possibly by the by. My brother, Myles, was at Sinford's before me, so there is a connection. In the school tradition, Myles was given a nickname. Where I was Hunter, because of an eighteenth-century publication on fox hunting titled "The Hunter and the Chase", so

Myles was known as Cannock after the place in Staffordshire. He is the editor of the Pall Mall Gazette. Cannock, Pall Mall...? What *In time* may mean, however, I cannot say.'

'All worth writing down,' Will said, scratching on the chalkboard. 'And the last one, Jack?'

'Sixteen, M, twenty-four... Blimey, there's a load here. Aldgate Street, Fenchurch Street Railway, Trinity Square, Tower of London, St Olave's church, Trinity House. Take your pick.'

'Mr Chase?'

'Sorry, Will, nothing that relates to Sinford's in the way the Grange being near a Kentish town might relate to the case. Like my thoughts on Truth Magazine and the Pall Mall Gazette, which are but hairline coincidences, I could relate Trinity Square to the school chapel, dedicated to the Holy Trinity, or indeed, to the Triumvirate, it also involving three. A square has four sides, and we were a fellowship of four. I could equate the Tower of London to Grace Tower simply by the word tower. They are of a similar age, but of no other resemblance. Trinity House? Again, Sinford's chapel or the triumvirate, but there is no lighthouse within the school grounds, nor anywhere nearby.'

'Well then,' Will said. 'What do we do, Jack?'

'Me?'

'You are Mr Wright's assistant. What we do from now on is entirely up to you.'

In one way, that was gratifying to hear, because it reinforced Jack's authority and reminded him he had a respectable job. In another, it was terrifying because a man's life was in his hands, and if he made a wrong decision, Stape might kill himself, and Havegood wouldn't pay his bill.

'Jack?'

'Yeah, right...' Rising to look at Will's notes, he considered his options and came to a decision. 'We write to Havegood to tell him we have a lead and will investigate it tomorrow. It's about time we told him what was going on. Then, tomorrow, I'll go down to Kent and snoop about, see if I can find this hide, and see if Mr Stape is inside. If he is, I can message Havegood, and we're done.'

'How will you recognise Mr Stape?' Will asked, adding notes to his lists.

'How many blokes are going to be hiding in a shack?'

'I could come with you,' Larkin volunteered. 'In fact, I should. If Diggs is there, perhaps I can persuade him against his course of action.'

'A good idea for you to go so you can identify him,' Will said. 'But we are not to intervene. Mr Havegood was adamant on that, wasn't he, Jack?'

'Yeah, he was. It was his only condition.'

'But Diggs knew me as well as he knew Havegood,' Larkin protested. 'He was also a friend of mine, and I'd be loath to see him succeed in his enterprise knowing there was something I could have done to prevent it.'

'No.' Jack was apologetic but firm. 'We ain't under contract for that, and we can't mess up the agreement made between Mr Wright and his client. We'll go, and if he's there, you can see if it's him, and we'll tell Mr Havegood. Agreed?'

'Yes,' Will said. 'Perfect.'

'Then that be that, and we be done.'

Jack leapt with shock at the voice which came from behind where Max had slunk into the room.

'Be getting cold, gentlemen,' he said. 'Ye be ready?'

Before he followed the others out, Jack took a last look at the boards to see what Will had written, and stopped to consider how on earth they were to succeed in Jimmy's case.

Where? The Grange, Sinford's woods, near Biddenden.
When? After midnight, July 30th.
Why? Truth, possibly magazine. (Crossed out.)
To: Cannock Pall Mall in time. (Myles Chase?)
At: Trinity, Church, Lighthouse, (?)

The only conclusion he could reach was that with a little over two days in which to solve the puzzle, he could do nothing more than try.

TWENTY-TWO

There was much discussion over dinner, which was elegantly served by Max in the servants' hall, but it fell to Jack to decide the course of action. It was simple, and if all went well, the case would be concluded the next day.

Jack was feeling good about it until Larkin said it was late and he should be at home. Jack had hoped he would stay longer, but he wanted to change, take a good night's rest, and come armed the next day in suitable clothing and with a spyglass and a map, because it had been several years since he was last in the area. When Jack offered to drive him to Kingsland, Max pointed out Baxter had little to do as it was, and Jack was a lead investigator, not a driver. On reflection, he thought it a good idea. Had he driven Larkin, he might have been invited in, and that might have led to who knew what, which, in turn, might have taken his mind away from the case.

There was no might about it, and he waved him off from the front of the house, with young Master Baxter confident behind the reins.

As soon as he closed the door, he missed the man more than he thought possible. Not only his presence, but everything else. The way he spoke, his calm voice, the way his eyes flashed when he smiled, and the twitch of his moustache that moved so little, but said so much.

Then, there was the way he liked to sit so close, as if reassuring Jack of his feelings. Touching even a hand to a knee sent Jack into wild imaginings, and that was without the memory of what had been happening when Will interrupted.

The thoughts, longing, and sadness at Larkin's departure stayed with him into the late evening, and hung above his bed as he tried to sleep. It came eventually, but only because he let his imagination wander among what possibilities the future might hold, and how they would soon be alone together in the countryside.

The next day arrived with a nondescript sky of grey cloud which dulled the sun, but none of Jack's enthusiasm, and armed with his new satchel, his casebook and some money, he set off early to Charing Cross.

'Did Mr Chase get home safe?' he asked Baxter as he stroked Shadow's nose before climbing into the trap.

'That he did, Mr Merrit. Fine gentleman.'

'You look tired.'

'Bit of a late one, is all. Took a walk through the park after Shadow was abed.'

Jack didn't want to ask for what reason. In fact, he didn't need to. When he said, 'I hope you were careful,' Baxter said he always was, and jangled some coins in his pocket.

Jack said no more, but couldn't help thinking of the times Grandad Reggie had said, "Old habits die hard," when failing to give up tobacco. Baxter's business wasn't his. His was to find a man who didn't want to be found, and having found Larkin waiting for him by the lost and found, they set off to find the nine o'clock Folkestone train.

'Only you,' Jack said, as they walked to the platform.

'Only me?'

'Only you could suggest I find you by the lost and found.'

It hadn't been so much a suggestion, more a riddle. When departing the previous evening, Larkin had said, 'I will be discovered where others are reunited with the unexpectedly absent.' Jack wasn't going to admit that it had been Will who came up with the solution.

'Seemed appropriate,' Larkin said. 'For I can't help feeling I was somewhat lost when I found you that lonely night in Kennington.'

'Yeah, alright. Don't get all fancy on me.'

It was said and received in jest, and the pair nudged each other like schoolboys sharing a bawdy secret.

Their compartment was full, giving them no opportunity for private chat, and they passed the journey with Larkin reading the newspaper, and Jack reading his case notes, with the book turned away from prying eyes. Few of the passengers left them on the way, and by the time they reached Headcorn, they had still not discussed what they were to do. It was only when they were through the ticket hall and into the grey morning, that conversation could begin, and when it did, it wasn't what Jack was expecting.

'It was madness,' Larkin said, standing on the step and taking in the empty station forecourt.

'What was?'

'This place on the first day of term. The London charter teemed with the swarm of a hundred boys fighting, playing pranks, being told to sit down and refusing to do so. It all changed once we touched the platform, of course, as if the holiday only ended when we breathed the Kentish air. Then, it was a battleground of trunks and porters, stewards and drivers. The younger boys had charabancs and carts, the senior men had carriages. Some were private, like the one Havegood had waiting for us. The Triumvirate and I travelled in style in our last two years.'

'Yeah, nice,' Jack yawned. 'You ready?'

'I see no carriage.'

'That's 'cos there ain't one. There weren't last time, so we walked, and then got a lift in a dray.'

'Good Lord. I am wearing Mr Hoffman's finest tweed.'

'Yeah, and you're looking like you're sweating in it. I could go into town and see if I can find a livery, if you like.'

Larkin pulled a map from his pocket, already folded at the appropriate place, and turned to face the road.

'Sinford's is ten miles that way,' he said. 'Through Biddenden and East End. However, we could take this narrower lane through Three Chimneys and cut across the fields to Hemsted Forest. That might take off a mile or two.'

'East End? Chimneys? What you on about?'

'It is a long way, Jack, and we need transport. When arriving for school, it was arranged in advance, but now...? I shall enquire within.'

Larkin skipped into the ticket hall leaving Jack thinking, and when he returned, announced it was unlikely they would find a cab in the town, and the ticket man knew of no nearby livery stables.

Jack had expected that to be the news, but had thought of a solution.

'How well did you know Mrs Hogg?'

'As well as anyone with an interest in fruit baskets. Why?'

'She's down that lane a few miles and she's got a buggy. More of a gig, really, but a fine horse. Think she'd do a favour for an old boy?'

'Less of the old,' Larkin said, passing Jack and giving him wink. 'Onwards to the hoggary.'

'You ain't taking this seriously, are you?'

'I am. Of course, I am. An old school friend is in dire need, and I have a chance to help. This fills me with both concern and joy, for I worry about Diggs, and yet, am happy because I can help. If I appear facetious or trivial, it is simply because humour is my natural cover for apprehension.'

'Blimey,' Jack sighed. 'A simple yes or no would have done. Come on old man, keep the pace.'

* * *

I am away for a few days.
Burgle if you must, but please don't break the glassware.
The key is under the mat.

'She always was odd,' Larkin said, after reading aloud the note pinned to the front door of Rose Cottage. 'I fear we must continue on foot.'

Jack wasn't concerned at finding Mrs Hogg absent, because something caught his nose as they arrived at the cottage, and it was more worrying than the absence of a dotty old lady who spoke to graves.

'Can you smell that?' he said, lifting his nose to the air.

'Jasmine. I am surprised it is noticeable at this time of day.'

'Not that. Dung.'

'This is the countryside, Jack. Home to sheep and cows.'

'Horse dung.'

'You can tell the difference?'

When he'd visited with Jimmy, Mrs Hogg had driven from the side of the house, and telling Larkin to follow, Jack took the same path. The closer they came to the back garden, the stronger the smell became, until, approaching a small stable, his suspicion was proved correct.

'Bloody stupid woman,' he grumbled, opening the lower door, and stepping into the gloom.

'I believe we may be trespassing,' Larkin said remaining outside with his handkerchief to his nose.

'And I believe she invited us to burgle her,' Jack replied.

His heart sank when he saw what Mrs Hogg had left behind: Her horse, its head hung low, its water and feed troughs empty, and its stall awash with at least two days of manure.

'Hello, girl,' he greeted the horse gently, aware it would be nervous after being abandoned. 'No-one come in to feed you?'

'What is it?' Larkin called.

'Can you give me a hand?'

Jack's eyes adjusted to the weak light, enabling him to locate bags of feed and a bucket, and when Larkin dared a pace inside, pointed to a shovel.

'I'll sort her feeding, if you can start shovelling that,' Jack said, looking for a tap.

'I beg your pardon?'

'Shovel shit, shift it over there. I'll barrow it out once she's watered.'

'In Mr Hoffman's Saxony tweed?'

'Take the bloody lot off if you want. Unless we get his animal sorted, she'll be dead within a week.'

Jack found a tap, filled the bucket, and put the horse to water while he loaded her trough with feed, all the time reassuring her and checking her over to see if she was up for work. She was, he concluded, having examined all of her including her shoes, and when he asked her in a whisper if she would like a walk, he was convinced she nodded her head.

By the time he was satisfied with the animal, Larkin had shifted what looked like two spoonfuls of manure. Jack took over, and dumping the waste by the door, emptied the stall in minutes.

'I'll put down fresh when we get back,' he said, and turned his attention to the tack.

'You mean we are to snaffle the lady's horse?'

'Snaffle? Don't know about that, but we're going to borrow her.'

'It all sounds rather illegal to me.'

'Yeah, well, to me, we'll be doing the old girl a favour.'

'By which you mean the horse or Mrs Hogg?'

'Both.' The horse was skittish when Jack fitted her bridle, but he calmed her with a pat and comforting words. 'You wait here,' he told Larkin. 'I'll ready the gig and lead her to it. She'll go. She already thinks I'm her new owner.'

'She thinks? You can lead a horse to water, Mr Merrit, but you can't make it think.' Larkin chuckled.

'What?'

'In the same way a university Don told me when I once suggested donating classic literature to ladies of the night, "One can lead a whore to culture, but one cannot make her think." Witty, eh?'

Jack rolled his eyes, and passed him the leading rein. 'Hold this and try not to be funny,' he said, and stomped into the sunlight to locate the vehicle.

That found, and having greased its axle and checked its wheels, he hitched it to the horse, and prepared to drive.

'Perhaps we should leave a note,' Larkin said, and before Jack could tell him not to bother, hurried to the front of the house.

Jack met him on the lane, with the horse keen to be moving, and Larkin keen to share what he'd written.

'I wrote, "Dear Mrs Hogg. Thank you for the invitation to help ourselves to the trinkets of your life. Tempting though I am sure they are, we have temporarily borrowed your transport instead." I signed it from a grateful traveller. I think she will approve.'

'Bloody hell,' Jack sighed.

Much as he relished being alone in Larkin's company, and much though he usually enjoyed his banter, they were closing in on their target, and the time left to tell Havegood what he wanted to know was fast running out. Investigating a missing man was another thing on his ever-increasing list of new experiences, and it would have been a more daunting task without Larkin. His confidence was catching, even though Jack was taking his duty one step at a time with little thought for the one that came next.

'Now,' Larkin began once he had settled with the map. 'We take this lane to the end. I suggest a slow walk so we can remain aware of...'

Jack jerked the reins, the horse set off at a trot, and Larkin fell backwards in his seat with a yelp.

'I'm the driver,' Jack said. 'You just admire the scenery.'

The scenery consisted of flat fields with crops, and pastures with cows grazing, and farmhouses placed as randomly as the clumps of trees. Unlike London, the air was fresh and scented with the same smells Jack had enjoyed on his last visit. Flowering and berry bushes lined the lane, with single trees here and there, and birds chirped and called above the repetitive clop of the horse's hooves, and the turning of the wheels. Although there was little time left to find Havegood's answer, his previous mood of anxious impatience withered, and among the folded fields and tranquillity, he realised there was no rush. Stape would either be there or not, and if he was, all he needed to do was telegram Will to pass forward the message. Besides, Jimmy had told him not to bother with the case, so if they didn't find the man, he wouldn't be in trouble. Jack was involved in a game devised by and for rich boys from a private school, what did it matter to him what they'd done or intended to do? What mattered to him was he was spending time alone with Larkin.

They stopped to buy bread and cheese from a shop in Biddenden, and sat to eat in companiable silence while the horse took water, and the clouds darkened further.

'Not quite the lunch and walk in the park you was hoping for yesterday,' Jack said, once they'd set off again and after nothing had been said for too long.

'Far better,' Larkin replied, and placed his hand on Jack's knee. 'May I?'

'You may, but best not go no higher. You never know what's round the next corner.'

'Indeed.'

There was more silence between them as Jack enjoyed the feel of Larkin's warm palm on his leg, and tried to understand what he had done to deserve such an unlikely, but welcome, day.

It lasted until Larkin said, 'Actually, I do know what is around the next corner. This slight incline is deceptive, and in a moment, we shall reach a high ridge. That will give us a view down to the forest and the school. Assuming it still stands. But...' He broke off as if unsure what to say.

'But?'

'I am concerned.'

'About Stape? I ain't surprised.'

'Yes, about Diggs, but also about my part in this.'

'How d'you mean?'

Larkin shifted in his seat, and sighed. 'If he is there, surely we should do something? I knew the man well. We spent our childhoods and formative years together. We shared much that young people share, and whether we are still in touch or not, those years form a bond that is hard to break, and impossible to forget. If Diggs really is planning to end his life tomorrow night, and he is there while I am here... I am compelled to do something. To speak with him, at least.'

Jack was irked he'd mentioned the subject again.

'He was clear,' he said. 'Havegood said we weren't to contact Stape, only find out where he is.'

'You said, but he didn't know that I would become involved. How could he?'

'Not important.'

'But it is, Jack. Diggs was a friend, and he is in need. I must do something.'

'You are. You're going to identify him, so I can finish Jimmy's case.'

'I am going to witness him from a distance and walk away. The next time I see the man, he might be in his coffin.'

'That's the job,' Jack said. 'Can't do nothing about it.'

'You can.' Larkin spoke sharply, and he moved his hand from Jack's knee. 'You can decide what is best to do, and I think it is best for me to intervene.'

'Well, I don't. Me orders are simple. See to them, and Jimmy gets paid, I get paid, and I prove I can do this bloody job what I didn't want in the first place.'

'You didn't?'

'I dunno. I might have done.' Jack was more intent on his driving, and more concerned about the gathering clouds and passing time, than arguing. 'Anyways, I'm doing it now, and I'm in charge.'

'Yes.' Larkin gave a sigh. 'You are in charge.'

'That's right.' Jack clicked his tongue to encourage the horse up the last of the incline, and decided that was the end of the discussion.

It wasn't.

'And as you are in charge, you can decide to come with me to speak to Diggs and talk him out of his intentions.'

'Bloody hell, mate. Ain't you listening? No. We do that, and he'll run off and do it somewhere else. Then what do I tell Havegood? We had him, but lost him?'

'The man might be dead if we...'

'If he's going to do it, he's going to do it. My job's to find him and report. If you don't like it, you can get off and wait for me here.'

Not even the hooves and birdsong could fill the awkward silence that fell on the gig as they crested the hill, and not even the sight below could calm Jack's annoyance, as he pulled the horse to a halt.

They were looking down on a carpet of green formed by the tops of trees in a wide-reaching forest that spread from left to right and ahead to a distant horizon. Darker lines that looked like tracks crisscrossed the woods, some leading to clearings, others to junctions, and over to the south stood a massive, black building which could only have been the school. The central tower was clear to see, and around it, other, smaller buildings and open fields marked Sinford's boundaries. An impressive view, perhaps, but not of much help to Jack, who even though he squinted, couldn't make out a hut or hide, nor even a cottage.

'Of course, you are correct,' Larkin said, and his hand returned to Jack's knee.

Jack gave it a squeeze, hoping that would be the end of the awkwardness, and said, 'That's the school, is it?'

'It certainly is. Would we have time to visit?'

Not wanting to deny Larkin another request, Jack said, 'It ain't being used no more, so I suppose it'll be boarded up.'

'Again, you are correct, and we would be trespassing.'

'Where next?'

'Down the hill a little way, and to the left. We should find a road bordering the edge of the wood. The hide is, or was, not far inside in the bowl of a glade, and we will need to be close enough for me to see clearly. I have a spyglass.'

'Let's hope we see something before it gets dark, otherwise, we're in for a long night in the open, and a wet one too, by the looks.'

'It wouldn't be my first time,' Larkin said, and set Jack's mind wondering.

'Right,' he said, and jerked the reins. 'Let's go have a look.'

* * *

A man's appearance changes in twelve years, Stape thought, and although he was confident no-one would recognise him, shuffled into the village with his head bowed, and his shoulders hunched. The disguise was designed to deter any enquiries that locals might address to a vagrant, and the smell he had acquired from living rough in the forest for nearly four weeks added to the deterrent. Beneath the stink of sweat and unwashed clothing, however, walked a man confident in his purpose. After much deliberation, drafting and rewriting, he had finalised the letter. It was in his pocket as innocently waiting to be posted as any he had sent, and the stamp was already attached. His research had included the hour of the last local posting, and the time it would take to travel from the town to the recipient's desk. Thus, its delivery was assured. Also a certainty was its arrival first thing in the morning, setting in motion the desired chain of events that, no matter what he did, would bring satisfaction.

What he'd not been so certain of was whether his intended victim would have read between the lines, and was looking for him. The possibility had played on his mind over the past many nights, but he had reassured himself that any trail he might have left, would not have been left in vain. No matter what happened, once his confession was out of his hands, his victim would fall from grace as quickly as Jacques Verdier had fallen from the tower, and whether Stape had his say or not, the end result would be the same.

It would, as the house captain used to say, be *lights out*.

A quiet laugh accompanied him to the post box, where he checked the collection times and found them as accurately displayed as they had been reported, compared them to the church clock, nodded to himself, and dropped another man's fate into the gaping mouth of the pillar box.

It was done. There was no turning back—not that he had seriously thought of changing his mind—and having purchased a few more supplies from the grocer on the corner, he began his walk homewards.

Home? The old hide where masters took their favourite boys for private wildlife watching. A very dubious excuse he had always thought. Where he and Caesar, Jacques, and sometimes Hunter had gathered to be raucous with a snaffled bottle of wine or brandy. The place where Jacques had run to that time when his admirer's persistence became too much, and where Stape had comforted him, talking him away from thoughts of escape, of leaving school and worse. It was a safe place, for them at least, and although the memories of twelve years ago still hung in the damp air, it was scented with pine needles just as much now as then.

The walk there wasn't bad either. Through the fallen school gates with their rusting ironwork, and the unguarded grounds. Around the wide lawn now alive with wild flowers, keeping to the treeline just in case, and past the unforgiving walls of the 'workhouse', as the boys called the main building. A pause to consider the broken windows, the doors hanging from hinges and the crumbling mortar. To stare up at the tower and reflect on the why and how, and to remind himself that what he was doing was right. Then, onwards, past the gymnasium and the science building to what had been the cricket pitch and into the great *beyond the boundary* of his youth; the forest.

He would step beyond another boundary the following night, but for now, it was a case of returning to the hide, lighting the fire before the afternoon died, and preparing his supper. There was the day's newspaper to read, and several books he had always meant to get to, the oil lamp to read by, a little opium for his resolve, and enough peace and quiet to calm even the most troubled of hearts.

Simon Stape was so intent on the idyllic evening ahead, and the even more idyllic time to come, he failed to see two dark shadows above him on the hillside. Both were lying on their fronts, and one had a spyglass pressed to his eye, its barrel tracking him as he stepped over fallen boughs, wove through saplings and ferns, and stopped to pick wild mushrooms.

By the time he reached his hide and settled in for the evening, his watchers had returned to their vehicle, as certain as Stape that their plan was coming to fruition, and success was guaranteed within the next thirty-six hours.

TWENTY-THREE

'I am unhappy about this.'

'Yeah, you keep saying.'

'Is there nothing we can do?'

'I'm doing it.'

They were driving towards Biddenden through a light drizzle which, if it didn't stop, would soon soak their overcoats and hats, but which wasn't yet heavy enough to force them to find shelter.

'We are turning our backs on a man in need of help.'

'He'll get help. As soon as I tell Will and he tells Havegood, he'll come down and find his mate.'

'I could go to him...'

'How many more times?'

Relief was the first thing Jack felt on hearing the man in the forest was the one he'd been searching for, soon followed by elation that he'd finished his first assignment. However, Larkin hadn't stopped bleating since they'd returned to the gig, and with that and the rain, his patience was wearing thin.

'I can't stop you jumping down and running back there,' he said. 'But if you do, you'll mess everything up. I'm just doing me job. What you do is up to you.'

Larkin said nothing for a while, and when he did speak, it was with resignation.

'I have upset you.'

'No, you ain't.'

Another stilted silence followed, filled only by the trundle of the wheels and the steady rhythm of the horse's shoes, and Jack was obliged to say something.

'Look. Havegood and him were lovers, right? Stape's going to listen to him more than he would you. You weren't one of the three, were you?'

It had sounded kinder in his head.

'I still find that hard to accept,' Larkin said. He'd spent the first mile looking back over his shoulder as if he expected Stape to come running after them, but he'd stopped when the hill blocked the view. When Jack glanced, he was staring ahead, his eyes half-closed against the misty rain which found a route from his brow to the tips of his moustache before dripping. 'Just because they shared a study, didn't mean they were lovers any more than Jacques and I were. Every study in the tower bar one was a two-man arrangement.'

'It carried on after they left. Havegood didn't say much about university, but they'd been seeing each other for at least one night every year since. If anyone can put Stape back on the right track, it's Havegood. D'you think you could be happy for me?'

Another pause, shorter this time, and Larkin repeated, 'I *have* upset you.'

'Leave it out.'

'I shall, Jack. Much as I wrestle with my ineptitude and conscience, you are correct. This is your job, and I know you are keen to make it a success. I cannot say with certainty that Marcus and Simon formed such a bond, it seems unlikely that I would not have known, but I will take your word for it.'

'It's his word.'

'Then I must accept that too. I am sorry. I will be happy for you.'

'Yeah, well, there's no need to go too far,' Jack said, and again, it sounded different in his head. Spoken, it sounded like sarcasm. 'I mean, I ain't happy we've got to let the bloke get on with it, but it's what I got to do. If we'd done as Jimmy told us, we wouldn't even be here. At least I done what the client's paying for.'

'Then we shall say no more, and I shall trust your judgement.' In the same breath, Larkin added, 'Do you think this drizzle will stop?'

'Yeah. Maybe not this afternoon, but it's got to stop some time, ain't it?'

'Your logic, Jack, is as always, frank.'

'Thanks. Two miles and I'll send the message.'

The message he sent was as simple as his logic, but it didn't only concern the case.

Stape found where we thought. At hide now. Maybe tower later. Inform client. Home tomorrow PM. Jack.

Jack was pleased Larkin had accepted his decision to leave Stape to his fate, but where it had taken him some time, it took him no time to accept Jack's suggestion they stay in the country for the night, even though he gave the worst excuse he'd ever given for anything.

'Too wet to travel by train.'

'I agree, but first, we must return Mrs Hoggs's belongings.'

'Yeah. I got an idea about that.'

In the fading light and increasing rain, he pulled up outside her stable, and as Larkin went to retrieve his note from the front door, unharnessed the gig and led the horse back to the lane.

'I thought you intended to clean her stable as a thank you,' Larkin said, joining him with his coat wrapped tighter and water dripping from the brim of his hat.

'Who knows when she'll be back.' Jack pointed to the line of tall trees bordering the next field. 'There's a churchyard behind that lot, and it's a mess. She can feed as much as she wants on the old grass, and this rain'll give her water.'

'Mrs Hogg?'

'The horse,' Jack laughed.

The graveyard was as overgrown as he remembered, and having led the animal through the gates, he took her to the far side where the trees would give her shelter, and where the rain was already gathering in puddles.

'Won't it run away?'

'Might do, but she's a horse. She'll look after herself. I expect someone'll come by in the morning and see to her. If not, she'll be happy here. Most of all, she'll be free.'

As soon as he'd removed her bridle, the horse shook her mane in agreement, skipped, and trotted to a patch of dead grass. Jack hung the bridle from a nearby tree, and the last he saw of the horse, she was tucking into a feast, unbothered by the weather, and with her tail swinging with contentment.

'Two good deeds done,' Larkin said as they rejoined the empty lane. 'Let us hope someone passes and does us one by taking us on to Headcorn. With all this walking, I shall have a chest by supper time.'

From what Jack remembered, Larkin's chest was covered with dark hair, shaped like a statue, and solid, and he looked forward to examining it later, when, if he was lucky, he would find himself in the same position as he had been with Jimmy that night. Only, this time, there would be no misunderstanding.

In the meantime, there was to be no favour and no lift in a dray, but the walk back to Headcorn caused him no physical effort. Nor did it affect Larkin, who chatted about the weather, the countryside and what the Station Hotel might have on its menu. Jack listened, his contentment growing along with his anticipation, and he didn't even mind the aggravation caused by the rain when it slid in beneath his shirt. The dusk darkened to night, leaving them blind and being careful so as not to stumble, and although it made for slow going, it allowed them the chance to hold hands.

'For safety, you understand,' Larkin said, to which Jack replied, 'Yeah, right,' and they laughed their way towards the increasing glow of the town.

The guests of the Station Hotel paid them the minimum of heed when they entered, dripping, sweating and still chatting, and on seeing their condition, the landlord sent his wife to prepare a room, and insisted he light the fire.

'There is no need,' Larkin protested as he signed the register. 'You will only turn your bar into a Swedish sauna. The air is close despite the precipitation. Our clothes will dry in our room.'

'Then I'll have the girl light you a fire there, Sir,' the man said, doffing a cap he wasn't wearing. 'Such an honour to have an esteemed guest.'

'More steaming than esteemed,' Larkin replied. 'You are very kind, Landlord, but a little misguided in your praise. You should aim it at my friend here, the much-lauded detective, Jack Merrit.'

'Give over.'

'I can find you separate rooms, Mr Chase,' the landlord offered. 'Molly won't mind being turned out.'

'I shouldn't dream of turning poor Molly from her manger,' Larkin said, flashing Jack one of his cheekier looks to show he was, at last, having fun. 'Let the girl alone, for I assume you refer to a girl and not a horse. Thank you, but we are gentlemen of the road and accustomed to sharing facilities. However, a little supper...'

'A lot of supper, actually.'

'My companion requires a lot of supper. Therefore, please inundate us with the best you have on offer. We shall salvage what we can that is dry about our person and return in a short while. An extra towel or two wouldn't go amiss if you run to such luxury.'

Jack smiled at Larkin's words. It was more the way he spoke than what he said that appealed to him. Some would call him affected, but he found it charming, and the flouncier Larkin was, the cleverer he sounded, and the more Jack was proud to be in his company.

The landlord's wife took them to the same room Jack and Jimmy had used before, and fussed at the fireplace. By the time a girl arrived with towels, flames were flicking in the grate, and coats were steaming on the backs of chairs. Jack opened the window to let the humidity escape, and looked out at the sheer blackness of what, on his previous visit, had been countryside. The runoff from the roof gathered at the eaves and dropped into the night, and the steady rainfall provided a background hiss to match that of the gas lamps, and contrasted with the homely crackle of logs. With the bed turned down, the lights giving just enough of a glow to see by, and having checked the door came with a key, Larkin said, 'The scene is set for later,' and Jack knew what he meant.

Having wrung their socks, and put them back on damp, but no longer squelching, they returned downstairs as dry as they could be, and found the feast Jack craved.

There was nothing uncomfortable about dining in a restaurant, and taking a glass of brandy in the lounge afterwards, and there was no awkwardness to their conversation. It was as if each knew what was to happen, and as if it had happened before. Jack suffered no nervousness, and had no qualms. They didn't need to use hidden meanings as they talked about life at Delamere, what Larkin was planning to write next, and how Jack was, after his misgivings, enjoying his new work and way of life. There was laughter when Larkin suggested they send Mrs Hogg a gift for the loan of her horse, and Jack said she might like a basket of fruit, and they enjoyed more when Larkin told him stories from his schooldays, how the boys had tricked the matrons, pretending to be ill so they could miss examinations, and how Larkin often came in for mild rebukes because of his classroom cheek.

They didn't once mention Stape nor Havegood, and sitting high in the saddle of success, Jack was able to enjoy the company and speak about his own past, his limited schooling, and life working at the docks before Granddad Reggie died and he took to cabbing.

The evening became night, the bar began to empty, and when it closed, Larkin said it was time they took to their bed.

'I am dry, at last,' he announced to anyone within earshot as he stood on unsteady feet. 'I could sleep the sleep of the dead.'

'Not until I've finished with you,' Jack whispered as they attempted to climb the stairs with dignity, and wove their way to the landing.

'We shall celebrate your success in whatever way you wish,' Larkin said. 'And tomorrow, sleep late, breakfast late, and, if the weather gods are with us, perhaps enjoy a country stroll before a slow train home.'

'You and your plans.' Jack threw open the door to let him enter first.

'To plan is to be prepared, and to be forewarned is to be forearmed.'

'Well, don't know about you, but I only got two arms,' Jack said, already unbuttoning his shirt.

'Two will be enough,' Larkin grinned, and opened his in welcome.

* * *

It had been a long game, but it was, at last, coming to an end.

As soon as Stape's letter had arrived, Havegood had read between the lines and understood his intentions. The past kicked him in the gut, and he knew his years of freedom would come to an end unless he acted.

'This will not go away,' was the first thing he'd said to himself, as if accepting the horror of the inevitable would lessen the blow of reality.

It didn't, but it did force him into action, and he spent weeks in subtle enquiry, trying to cover his dread with normality. The mother, the brother, the distant family, work, even enquiries with the old school network made under a pseudonym brought no results. When his mind allowed, he thought without fear and employed reason. He visited Clapham and watched the house; no-one. He spent time in Threadneedle Street and watched the bank; nothing. A day and night in Kent, observing the deserted grounds and then walking through the early dormitories of his youth, the tower with its cellars, and even the old studies brought no results. There had been no sign of Simon Stape, and every day, the crushing panic of discovery pressed harder, until he remembered Clearwater's agency and the rumours it attracted. Men of a similar inclination, they said behind the wings of wingback chairs in Whites and other clubs. Professional work, and no questions asked, because it was connected to the great and the good. Even the Met called on the services available from Delamere House, and if they were discreet enough for Scotland Yard, they would do for him. They had to, because he had run out of options, but so far, even the agency had come up with no results.

Since his visit to Mr Wright, Marcus Havegood had spent the time pacing his house. Every time the letter box clacked, or the bell rang, panic stabbed his heart, and he hurried to examine the post or receive a telegram with trepidation. A committee he had failed to attend, invitations to dine, well-wishers and secretaries, newspaper men requesting an interview, outraged diatribes from his father about duty and appearance, all had been skimmed and discarded. Nothing else concerned him except news from Wright and his men, and none had been forthcoming apart from a vague letter from the assistant which he ignored for its dreadful grammar, and two telegrams, both of which did little to calm his apprehension.

*We continue to follow leads and are hopeful of success.
William Merrit. Assistant to Detective Wright.*

Hopeful was not good enough, and he had contacted Lord Clearwater for assistance. His Lordship's reply, however, had been adamant.

Let them do their job. I have absolute faith. All will be well.

If all was to be well, they had little more than twenty-four hours, and during that time, all Havegood could do was wait and reassure himself the plans he had prepared were right and foolproof.

Whether the news was forthcoming and to his advantage, or whether it was not, his preparations involved a journey, and he had gathered the necessary belongings. A suitcase stood waiting in the hall, railway and steamer tickets wedged beneath its handle. That was there in case the news was bad. If it was good, his other, drastic options lay on the hall table. Over the days, he had opened, unpacked and repacked his case several times. Letters to friends and family were also prepared, ready to be left behind or burnt, depending on the outcome of the investigation, and all his other affairs were in order.

The housekeeper was away enjoying a holiday he had gifted her as a surprise, his caretaker too. The delivery boys continued to come when called, but he had brought in his own groceries only once they had left the yard, so as not to arouse suspicion. In the same way, he had opened and closed curtains, turned on and off the lamps, and given the house its usual everyday appearance. When callers came, he spied them from the upper rooms, refusing to answer the door but noting who they were and, later, dispatching a message or letter with a delivery man to explain he was unwell and what he had might be contagious. He'd been careful to reassure the concerned he would be in the best of health before long. So far, the ploy had worked, and despite time running out as fast as his apprehension mounted, he had done what he could to enjoy his solitary, secret life while he waited.

The years had taken their toll on his body, but once he had decided to act, his appetite had returned, although not publicly, and since contacting Wright, he had regained his strength. It had been a job to only pick at the dinner the detective offered, and to deflect the doctor Wright no doubt invited to assess his condition, but he had kept up the charade as well as ever, and no suspicion had come his way.

Whatever was to happen, it was to happen soon. He would hear if Wright had been successful, or not, and know which path his future was to take.

The clock struck eight and he poured himself a drink. Turning the desk calendar, he stared at its announcement with hope fading. Thursday, July, and the number twenty-nine. They said Jacques died between midnight on the thirtieth and two in the morning of the thirty-first. The anniversary was between twenty-eight and thirty hours hence, but there were only four left until he knew which plan he was to take. If Clearwater's faith was well founded, and if Mr Wright was as good as his word, the answer would come before midnight. If, however...

The clatter of the bell, and a peek from behind the curtains revealed a messenger waiting on the step.

Havegood was there within seconds.

'Shall I wait for a reply, Sir?'

Havegood told him no, slammed the door, and stood between the suitcase and the table with the envelope trembling in his hands. Using a paperknife, he slit the paper with trepidation, and turned the message to the light.

Be advised Mr Stape located this evening at the Grange. If not the hide then probably the tower. Sinford's School grounds. Hemsted Forest.

The relief was momentary, the joy lasted longer, and he read and reread the message as he descended to the kitchen, there to eat a hearty meal before taking himself to bed. All trepidation gone, all concern vanished, the Honourable Marcus Havegood enjoyed a deep and nightmare-free sleep for the first time since Simon Stape had written to say, *I shall see no-one, and far later than I should, I will face the truth and accept the consequences.*

TWENTY-FOUR

Last night, before falling asleep wrapped in Larkin's embrace, Jack had thought there could be no better new experience. Waking in a comfortable bed to the sound of birds singing, and with the solid form of a man now wrapped in *his* arms, proved him wrong. Naked, remembering what they had done, yet suffering no shame or awkwardness, he opened his eyes to soft sunlight and listened to Larkin's softer breathing. The time wasn't important, because he'd finished his first case, and satisfied his curiosity about his attraction to men. Or had it been confusion? Whatever it was, he was fulfilled, and it wasn't a temporary feeling. This was where he always wanted to be, and better, he was safe in the knowledge that Larkin thought the same way. He'd whispered so, as they'd touched, not fumbled, explored, not plundered, and loved, not rutted.

Love?

It was journey's end, but a journey was nothing without distance, and as contented as he was, they'd only known each other a few weeks, and Jack had only known himself for certain for a few hours. A nighttime's length, in fact, with not much sleep, but enough rest to dispel the effects of the brandy and leave his mind refreshed, clear of the clutter of clues and cases, and free to look forward.

Washed, dressed and sitting by the ashes of the fire in no hurry, he watched Larkin until he woke. The first thing he did was search Jack's side of the bed, only to find it empty, at which point, he sat up, concerned, until their eyes met, and he uttered a coy, 'Good morning.'

'Morning? It's nearly noon.'

'Is it?' The concern returned. 'Mrs Grose will put me in detention.'

'Well, ain't you the romantic one?'

'Oh, to hell with her. She has a good wage. Must we get up?'

'I dunno what time they kick us out, but it's getting late.'

'This isn't the workhouse, Jack, we can probably stay as long as we like.'

'Yeah, but I didn't tell Will what time I'd be back, and he'll worry.'

Larkin rested against the headboard, and pulled the sheets to his chest.

'Why you doing that? I've seen it all.'

'Hm?' Realising, he let the sheet drop to his waist. 'It's a habit. A precaution against Mrs Grose's morning appearance.'

'You're more than safe,' Jack smiled. 'And I'm more than hungry.'

'Then I shall rise like a phoenix from the ashes of passion, take my life in my hands to explore the bathroom, and return as fresh as a spring flower, ready to adorn this bright day with my much-invigorated presence.'

'You mean you'll get dressed?'

'I shall.'

Jack waited patiently while he did, and enjoyed every detail. The order in which he put on his clothes, how he buttoned his shirt, the way he tucked it in, and the effort he put into tidying his moustache at the mirror. It was like seeing someone familiar in a new light, a discovery of sorts, maybe even an investigation, and thinking so, reinforced his realisation that he had enjoyed the case. Everything that had happened in the past week in no way compared to the routine of cabbing.

Nor did the rest of the morning compare to any other day he'd known. With the landlord paid, they strolled into the sunlight to find the air fresh from the rain. The town offered a mismatch of houses, some with weatherboarding or black timber beams, others with steep roofs, and a wide unmade street played host to children at their games. A flock of geese wandered through, protesting about something, and a farmer drove his sheep, forcing Larkin and Jack to the side where a pub sign announced, 'The White Horse.' According to Larkin, it was where 'Luncheon calls us like a siren,' to which Jack replied, 'Oh,' because he wasn't sure what he meant. The word lunch was involved, though, and a decent meal it was too. They ate beside a fireplace made by someone called Inglenook, or at least that was what Jack thought Larkin said. It was the size of the old kitchen in Limehouse, and he was grateful it wasn't lit.

The conversation continued from where it had left off the evening before, with no talk of Stape or Havegood, but talk of Will and how he had found his perfect job. Larkin asked many questions until Jack told him he should keep his nosiness for his newspaper.

'It is a periodical,' Larkin said. 'Your point, however, is taken. I simply want to know more about you. We have had so little time.'

'That's because you put fifty words in one sentence when five will do,' Jack said. 'That's where all the time goes.'

'Then I shall say no more until spoken to. Ask what you will.'

Nothing was said for a few minutes while Jack tried to think of something, but he gave up.

'I'll learn as we go,' he said, and continued to sip his beer.

'By which I dare infer our current status is ongoing, and the adventures of last night will be repeated?'

'If you want.'

'If *you* want.'

'Yeah, but only if you're sure.'

'Why should I not be?'

'I dunno.'

'There is no reason. Yes, Jack...' Larkin glanced around the bar, as he reached for Jack's hand, but he withdrew it, and whispered, 'Later, we may discuss what we will. There is no expectation of anything other than for you to do what you think is right, what you feel comfortable doing, and when ready, telling me how you want us to proceed. Assuming you are happy for there to be an *us*.'

Jack blinked as he waded through the words.

'Yeah,' he said. 'That last thing you said, but give me time to get used to the idea.'

'All the time you wish,' Larkin beamed, happier than Jack had seen him. 'Meanwhile, and talking of time, we should think about returning to the greatest city in the world. I for one, could do with a change of clothing.'

'You're right,' Jack sighed. 'I need to make sure Will sent on the message, and I ain't spoken to Shadow for over a day. You going straight home, or what?'

'What,' Larkin smiled. 'I feel as much as part of this case as you. I too would like to know that Havegood received the message, so I am satisfied Diggs won't be left on his own to carry out his intentions. Besides, a gentleman should always see his beau home, and it will lengthen the time I have with you.'

Larkin used far too many words, but they were all the right ones.

Few were said on the train to London, however, because they weren't alone in the compartment. Jack had to make do with stolen glances as he browsed through his casebook, and Larkin read a newspaper. Jimmy had said something about writing a report, and the only reports Jack knew of were the ones cab yard masters provided to licensing inspectors and the magistrate court. A report, he assumed, had something to do with noting what he'd done and why, and if he read his casebook from the beginning, he could use the two-hour journey to make notes in the back. It would save him time later. Time he could spend with Larkin, and when he had to go home, with Will and Shadow.

The first few pages consisted of jottings he'd made when reading Havegood's story about his time at school, and he'd forgotten he'd written half of them. They started with a note about Havegood and Verdier becoming friends, and there were odd words and half sentences such as *Leads, Coppers, The tower and its mysteries... Sex talk... Dirty buggers.*

The second page was headed *1879 Silvers to 1880 Golds*, and contained another list of random phrases; *Pet names, Diggs is Mr Stape, Hunter is Mr who? (Mr means older boys, 18. Posh.) Still fancies Verdier but*

Stape as well. 17th birthday in same bed. Havegood: Bloody sex mad. They called it "love."

Things became more interesting on page three which he had titled *The Disappearance*, but the scribblings beneath it were just as random.

July 30th, last day at school. Why is this important to the disapp.?

More sex. Havegood and Stape 'dallied long' in his bed. Slept there. Accident discovered on 31st early morning. Havegood heard it first from his bed. Stape still asleep in his own. Verdier dead.

All that told Jack was that Havegood fell asleep in one bed and woke up in another, and it had no bearing on Stape's disappearance, yet he must have thought it interesting enough to note. It was Havegood's way of telling Jimmy how important Stape was to him, and that was his way of justifying his concern. Fair enough and difficult to do, Jack thought as he looked from the window to rest his eyes. The client was admitting to a love affair with another man, and all kinds of trouble got heaped down on men who did that.

The thought made him shiver, and he returned to work.

Inquest. Accidental death. Havegood not sure. Crennela... Krena...? High walls. Can't fall over unless sitting. Against chimney to smoke pipe. (Another suicide?)

What did that mean?

His gaze again wandered from the page to fields and farms, and over to Larkin's hat, which was all he could see of him above his newspaper. Caution was to be their way forward too. Jack had been in two gaol cells in his life, and although not for long, he had no desire to go back, or spend two years in a prison treading the mill or sewing the sack while the world outside talked about him with unkind words.

Back to the notebook.

1880 to 1892. Havegood and Diggs still friends, but not so much contact. (Still lovers?) Both wanted Verdier at some point. (These men are worse than rabbits.) Two-handed reunions.

There was no need to wonder what that was all about.

Last year. Stape married. Not sure how Havegood felt about that. So what?

This year. Wife and boy dead. (Reason for suicide.) Stape not at house, not at work, not with family. Missing since early July.

There was then a break in his notes until he'd copied parts of the letter from Stape to Havegood.

The vengeance of a greater power. The evil deeds of my life. Other memories and knowledge... (Leading him towards suicide.) Inactions. Fail to do. Face the truth.

There were no notes about Havegood's appearance, because there was no need. The sight of a man worrying himself to starvation wasn't hard to forget, and at the time, Jack thought Havegood was lucky. There were hundreds, thousands, starving in Limehouse and the East End; at least the wealthy and to-be-titled Havegood had the luxury of worrying about nothing more than a missing friend. People went missing by the river all the time, leaving their families not knowing where they were, and those families didn't starve through worry. They didn't need to because they starved every day through lack of bread to put on the table.

From then on, his notes concerned instructions from Jimmy, the jottings he'd made about the school which included another question, *Why is the school important?* And later, *Something doesn't smell right.*

It smelt fine to Jack now he'd located Stape, yet something still nagged. It was like the background stench of the Thames, the Limehouse reek, Granddad Reggie called it. Jack grew up with it, so never noticed unless someone mentioned it, usually, an outsider. Even then it was only the stink of the gutting factories, stagnant mud, and dead fish blown this way and that according to the wind. It was so common, he'd only miss it if it wasn't there.

There was something behind his notes that had the same stubbornness and refused to blow away; something that didn't quite fit, but a thing he couldn't detect.

It could have been one of many things, he reasoned. Havegood's rambling lecture about his schooldays was the first Jack heard of such a life. Privilege beyond imagination. Cricket matches and teas. In Limehouse, they played cricket with three stumps of rotting driftwood from the shore, the bat was the same, and they were lucky if someone owned a ball, otherwise it was down to imagination. Tea? Scrapings stolen from a warehouse floor half the time, or a much saved-for packet from McGregor's, often paid for week by week, and with one measure of tea a day to go around four people. Forget sugar, unless there was a crafty thief in the household who happened to work for one of the German sugar bakers, or someone who brought in more coins than went out in rent.

Reggie and then Jack had managed to provide that, so they hadn't been as badly off as many, but still, there had been no open playing fields, no servants, and no tower to live in, not for the poor of 'The world's wealthiest city.' If it was the world's wealthiest, where was the money? In the hands and pockets of parents who could send their brats to schools in country houses set among forests and hills, where the air was clean and didn't smell of fish.

Maybe that was the stink behind the case; not the fish, but learning how the wealthy lived and grew up. Perhaps it was jealousy getting up his nose.

Another glance at Larkin as he lowered his newspaper to fold it, and they shared a smile that said so much. There was no need to be jealous. Jack was wealthier than Havegood in ways that mattered more than money, and he put away his casebook to savour the sight of the man opposite until the locomotive wheezed and sighed to a halt.

Where the train rocked and clattered its way to the city, the hansom they took rocked and plodded its way from Charing Cross, and despite Jack having told the driver his preferred route via The Mall and Constitution Hill, the cabbie took them through Westminster and Belgravia, no doubt aiming for a larger fare.

Jack didn't pay it. 'Should have been two miles. One shilling,' he said, flicking a coin up to the disgruntled driver. 'I know the tricks mate. I was a cabman meself.'

'Yeah? And what are you now? Bleeding toff?'

The cab drove away leaving Jack to consider his own hypocrisy. Hadn't he just been thinking about those he'd left behind in Limehouse and cursing the wealthy? Johnny Clarke was probably still injuring himself at the wharf; if mad Mrs Mushkin wasn't yet dead, she only had her neighbours to care for her; and the woman in the rooms above those he'd escaped was probably homeless thanks to the fire. Eighty pounds a year was more than the cabbie would take back to his family, and look at what Jack now called home. A massive house with eight bedrooms, electricity, its own telegraph machine, and marble steps he took to the painted door with a knocker polished by maids that opened into the hall where the butler rushed to greet him.

'About time,' Max said, forgetting all formality, and grabbing Jack by the arm to hurry him through the drawing room towards the office. 'You best come in here. Evening, Mr Chase. You too. I don't know what be going on. Started this morning when I came down to tidy up before the maids came in, and I found your Will still awake from yesterday. He'd been at his chalkboards all night. I got him fed and persuaded him back to bed a while, so least he slept a bit.'

'Slow down, Max, what's going on?'

'You'll see.'

Jack stumbled into the office, but couldn't see what was wrong.

'Where's me brother?'

'In a moment, Jack. It be this he were working on.'

Max indicated the chalkboard, and again, Jack couldn't see what might cause such a flap. The two boards were covered in his immaculate handwriting as before, although there was something different about the writing on one of them.

'He wouldn't tell me what it was,' Max continued. 'Not that it were none of my business, but through the afternoon, he got himself more in a state. Kept saying something wasn't right.'

'Did he get my telegram?'

'Aye, last night. Happy as a sandboy he were. Said you'd all three solved the case, and ran next door to get Mrs Norwood to send the news on to your client. Came back all triumphant, then went to tidy up in here because he were jittery agin. You'd said you wouldn't be home, see, and I reckon he didn't like that. I left him not long afore midnight, by when he'd rearranged Jimmy's bookcase, stitched a tear in one of the cushions, and rearranged all the whatnots.'

'Sounds about right.'

'Aye, but it ain't right, see. Not this morning when there were a thing he couldn't put his finger on. Not until middle of the afternoon when a caller came. He were looking for you, Mr Chase.'

'Me?'

'Aye. Said he'd been to your home and a rude woman sent him here.

He brought something for ye. Didn't want to leave it at first, and asked what your business was at Delamere. Told him we're detectives, and you were helping Mr Merrit down at a school in Kent, and he said, "Ah, then this may be what he needs."'

'This what?'

'Can't tell you, Sir. It's there on the desk still in its envelope.'

Larkin threw Jack a bemused look which Jack threw straight back.

'Where's Will?'

'Bain't sure to tell honest,' Max replied. 'Left not one hour ago.'

'Did Baxter drive him somewhere?'

'No. He took a cab.'

'Where?'

'Last thing he said, were to tell you to look at the boards and you'd understand. Then he said, you were a be quick about it, as he didn't want to do it on his own, but he would if he must.'

'Do what?'

Jack looked to Larkin for suggestions, but he was reading papers he'd taken from the envelope.

'Something about maps.' Max knocked his knuckles against the chalkboard. 'It all be on here.'

Jack stared at the writing, and through the mist of names and question marks, and alongside the tables, and lines joining one idea to another, began to see a list of words Will had written over twice. They didn't stand out much from the rest, but they stood out enough, and as he read them, not only did his imagined smell of fish grow stronger, but so did his fear.

Apart from the highlighted words, Will had left a message: *You missed 16, M-24.*

'The book of maps?'

'Here.' Max handed him the atlas. 'He left it open.'

Map sixteen, grid M-twenty-four, one third of a square that continued on the next page.

'Aldgate Street,' he read, running his finger downwards to every possible reference. 'Fenchurch Street, Jewry, John, Blackwall Railway, Trinty House, Trinity Square, Great...'

It hit him like the train he'd just come in on. The pieces fell into order, and he gawped over at Larkin to find him gawping back.

'The caller was my brother,' Larkin said, waving the paper. 'Stape sent a confession to the Pall Mall Gazette.'

'What were it Will said? Cannock Pall Mall in time?'

'Yes, as in, my brother "Cannock" Chase at the Pall Mall Gazette, but in time?'

Everything made blood-chilling sense. 'In time to be published before the anniversary,' Jack said. 'Will's gone to save him.'

'To save whom?'

'Simon Stape.'

'Ah. From himself. Good.'

'No, mate. From Havegood. He didn't want Stape's whereabouts so he could talk him out of suicide. He's going to murder him, and we've told him exactly where to find his victim.'

TWENTY-FIVE

Think like Will. Think like Jimmy. Look at the chalkboard.
Verdier's accident happened between midnight and two in the morning twelve years ago that night. Work backwards. Calculate.

The railway station to the forest. Ten miles, two and a half hours on foot. At least. It would be dark. Three hours. Walking? Not an option.

Train to Headcorn, just under two hours. Jack had been twice and neither time had he found onward transport.

Walk to Mrs Hogg's, borrow the gig, find the horse. Better than walking all the way.

'Jack?' Larkin pale-faced at the desk.

'Hold on.'

It was half-past seven. Where did that day go?

Concentrate.

The why could wait. What was important was reaching Stape. No, what was vital was making sure Will didn't put himself in danger.

'Jack?'

'Max?' Jack began collecting everything he could about the case and stuffing his satchel. 'Get Baxter to hitch up the trap to Shadow. We'll leave from the back yard in ten minutes. I'm driving. When's the last train from Charing Cross?'

'I couldn't tell you. Soon, probably.'

'Then make it five minutes. Have you got lanterns?'

'I'll fetch you a pair on my way.'

'Make sure they're filled.'

'You be better off taking the oil in its can and lighting them when you get there to save spillage...'

Max's voice vanished with him into the drawing room.

'You should read this, Jack.'

'On the train.'

'How did Will get there ahead of us?'

'We probably crossed on the river.'

'I mean how did he work this out? I see nothing on those boards.'

'It's all there, Larkin, and it's all in here.' Jack slapped his satchel and hoisted it over his shoulder. 'You can read it on the way.'

Shadow was ready, and Max had the lanterns. Apart from money which Jack had, he couldn't think what else they would need, and he pulled himself onto the driving bench as Larkin scrambled into the back with the stable lad.

'Max, do your best to get us a ride from Headcorn station, will you? They said there's no livery, but do what you can. Don't know what time we'll get there.'

'Aye, will do, if the telegraph office still be open.'

'Jimmy would have found a way.'

'That be true enough. I'll do what I...'

They were off. A short trot to the gate, and from the mews up to Bucks Avenue, where Jack set Shadow to a canter.

Seven forty-five. Piccadilly to Haymarket? Too busy. Theatre traffic all the way to Coventry Street.

Hyde Park Corner, Constitution Hill. A free run.

He'd just turned Shadow into the wider road and had taken her to a gallop when Larkin scrambled on to the bench, and Baxter grappled his way on Jack's other side.

'What you playing at?'

'You've not lit the lamps,' Larkin shouted over the rushing wind and clatter of hooves. 'You will be stopped.'

The two men leant out to open the lantern glass, and struggled to light the wicks while clinging onto the front bar, but Jack wasn't prepared to slow down.

'Sit,' he ordered when they'd succeeded. The shifting weight affected his balance, and the last thing he wanted was for Shadow to stumble.

They did as instructed with Larkin clutching his hat to his head, and Baxter hollering with the thrill. His voice petered out when he, like Jack, saw what waited at the end of the Mall.

'Trafalgar Square's chocka, Mr Merrit.'

'I can see that. Fuck!'

'Jack, please! We are within sight of the Palace,' Larkin complained as Jack had no option but to slow the horse.

'We can also see the bloody pile up,' he shot back, standing to squint over the tops of carriages and carts. 'All the way from West Strand to Northumberland Avenue.'

'I believe there is an entertainment opening this evening at the Gaiety Theatre,' Larkin said. 'Likely a throng desperate to witness *Uncle Dick's Darling.*'

They'd never get through. Jack closed his eyes, pictured page thirty-two, bottom left, opened them, and saw the map in real life. Cockspur Street, P & O Office, next right, Spring Gardens all the way to the Admiralty... Wide enough? Just.

He was already turning into the narrow street. It narrowed further before a sharp left corner brought him onto Whitehall, which he crossed, ignoring the shouts and whistles of protest as he wove through two lines of traffic.

'It's a good job we lit the lanterns,' Larkin shouted, as they raced into Scotland Yard, past the police offices and out onto Northumberland Avenue. Right to the Embankment, and he drew Shadow to a stop beneath the railway arch.

'We'll walk from here. Bax. Take her home and no messing about in that park, right?'

'As if I would.'

Jack took him by the collar, not in anger, but out of concern. 'I'm serious. Straight home.'

Baxter cowered before he toughened his expression and said, 'Will if I like.' It changed to agreement when Jack growled, and he was at the reins by the time Jack and Larkin started running towards the railway station's side entrance.

Larkin saw to the tickets while Jack scanned the platform in the hope Will had been delayed, but there was no sign of him. There was no sign of a train either, and when Larkin joined him ten minutes later, he didn't bring good news.

'The next one is at eight-thirty,' he said. 'It's a slow service arriving at a little before eleven. The faster one is the last one of the day. It leaves later and arrives only five minutes after ours, and I thought you would rather be moving than standing here. I bought us a lunch basket in the hope its contents have, by some miracle, remained fresh.'

'What's this?' Larkin hadn't told Jack he had booked first class. 'How much?'

'As Havegood is paying expenses...'

'He won't pay anything if he's inside for murder.'

'In which case, I will treat us,' Larkin said. 'As this is to be my third excursion on this line in two days, I asked for a discount because of my loyalty, but the man laughed. Never mind, first class is more likely to allow us privacy, and if we are to talk about the dubious shenanigans of men in a state of passion, I thought it a good idea.'

It was. Their compartment was empty and remained so when the train pulled from the station and crossed the river, allowing a brief glimpse of lantern-lit boats weaving below, and the lights of the breweries and wharfs reflected on the water wherever the mass of river traffic allowed.

'And to think I thought I might have a change of clothing,' Larkin said as Jack unpacked his satchel. 'Ah well, we have more important matters to attend to.'

'We certainly do,' Jack muttered, arranging his papers in the same order in which he had first read them.

'Perhaps we should be about our business before others join us. Unless you would rather eat first.'

'Like Havegood, I'm too worried to eat,' Jack said. 'Though I can now see that was all playacting.'

'Caesar has duped you,' Larkin said. 'You won't have been the first, but despite my brother's delivery, I am still confused as to how Will, and you, conclude that Caesar is on his way to murder Diggs. It seems extreme.'

'Passion, Larkin. It does strange things to a man.'

'Clearly. But passion? Even now?'

'Looks like it.'

'From my youth do my passions war against me,' Larkin mused, and shook his head with a sigh.

'What?'

'Saint Gregory Palamas. Eastern Orthodox saint. A Byzantine-born Greek monk, prayer of the heart, blah-di-blah, apparently died declaring, *To the heights!*'

'Which is where we're going.'

'Oh? But the forest hide lies in a valley.'

'Yeah, but Stape's not going to be at the hide.'

'Surely...?'

'He's going to be on page sixteen in square M-twenty-four.'

'Which, if I remember correctly, had something to do with Aldgate. In that case, we should be travelling north.'

'Aldgate Street is at the top of the grid square, yeah, but down the bottom is the most obvious bloody clue of the lot.'

'Fenchurch Street station?'

Once again on the move, and with nothing else to be done except explain and understand, Jack had to laugh. Larkin was keeping his tone light to distract him, and it was working.

'No,' he chuckled. 'The Tower of London.'

'Ravens?' Maybe Larkin hadn't understood. 'Oh! Midnight dreary, once upon a?'

Jack grinned as he tutted. 'I don't know what you're on about half the time, but it makes me laugh. No, not that tower. Grace Tower.'

'At Sinford's?'

'No, in bloody India. Where d'you think? Yes, at Sinford's. This is all about your school and what happened there twelve years ago, and why it had to close.'

'Water? The Tower of London is beside the river. Is that it?'

Larkin might have gone to a posh school and university, and he might have been amusing, but he was either dim or playing the fool.

'Stape's going to be at Grace Tower. I said it before, and I'll say it again; it's bloody obvious.'

'It is?'

'Yeah. It's the anniversary, ain't it? I'll lay you a wager that when we get to the hide, we'll find it empty and him at the school.'

'But why do you think Havegood is on his way there to kill him? He could stay at home with his feet up and let Stape take care of it himself.'

'I don't reckon Stape is going to top himself. If you ask me, Havegood made that up to make us work harder. Stape's in hiding while he gets his blessed truth out there. Where he'll be is so bleedin' obvious, you have to wonder why Havegood involved us at all. Lazy oik.'

'Obvious?'

'Don't that thing you got from your brother tell you nothing?'

'It tells me you are incredibly blessed with foresight, both of you.' Larkin patted the envelope beside him on the seat. 'But I am fascinated to know how you deduced Stape's intentions from the writing on the chalkboard.'

Jack passed him his sheets of paper. 'Read this lot,' he said. 'It's what Havegood came to us with, and there's also what we found at Stape's house, the inquest report, news cuttings and stuff. It'll take you most of the journey, but I won't get in your way.'

Larkin took it in exchange for his envelope. 'And while I am doing that, you can read his confession, although it seems you have no need. You know, Jack, you are remarkable.'

Jack flushed with embarrassment. 'No,' he said, emptying the envelope. 'It's Will what's remarkable, I'm just the driver. So, put your muzzle on, and let me read.'

JACKSON MARSH

To: Mr Myles Chase, Editor, The Pall Mall Gazette

My dear Mr Chase,
I write in the hope that you remember me and are willing to help.
Should the name seem familiar, it is because we are both Old Sinfordians. You attended the school with my older brother, Stephen, and I, with your younger, Larkin. It is as a fellow alumnus that I write to you.
What is enclosed is for publication. If, however, you feel unable, I would be grateful if you would direct it to the appropriate authorities.
Yours

Simon D. Stape

The Events of July 30th and 31st 1880. Sinford's School, Kent.

It is in the nature of young men, when educated in gated surroundings according to ancient regimes and traditions, with little shared interest beyond the bounds of education, mental, physical, spiritual and temporal, to form energetic bonds of friendship.

Such was the attachment I made with three fellow Sinford's pupils in particular; the Honourable Marcus Havegood, Jacques Verdier, and Larkin Chase. Within our coterie of four, the strongest ties were between Havegood, Verdier and myself, Mr Chase being something of an outsider, though still a valued friend.

Without wishing to disturb your readers or cause your publication embarrassment with direct language, it may be inferred that the *energetic bonds* of youth, in some cases, extended beyond the platonic.

For this to happen was a wish held by one of our three, our 'Triumvirate', as we presumptuous youths titled our group.

For many years, one of our three held a fascination for another, and during that time, made his feelings known within our group, though never outside it. His infatuation grew as we did until it matured into something more threatening, to the extent that between us, we arranged for the pair—one might say the infatuated and the object of his desire—to live as separately as was possible.

However, the man's fascination grew beyond his control and flourished in the summer of 1880, our last term at the school.

Most men, when denied a thing, are able to accept rejection like gentlemen, but in this case, there was to be no self-denial. The infatuated became the obsessed, and on realising his defeat, became maddened. Unknown to the other three of the four, he formed a plan of retribution, and, I assume, frustration became resentment. This, I have only come to understand during the intervening years.

Here, I state my case with the facts I knew then, and those I came to realise later.

July 30th was our last full day at Sinford's. Having stayed for the fortnight of Praemisit, and attended the last-night dinner with other students, we four returned to our two studies atop Grace Tower, there to finish our final packing. Not too late of the evening, we retired to our beds in the usual fashion.

I woke during the night with the impression that someone was about on the roof overhead. On lighting the candles, I discovered my study companion's bed empty and saw the time was approaching one of the morning. Concern for Mr Havegood leapt to my mind, for it was he who had developed an unhealthy fascination with our neighbour, Jacques Verdier, and I imagined he (Havegood) was above, wrought with agony that the two would soon be parted. Thinking my friend was in need of reassurance, I climbed to the roof to ensure all was well.

On arriving, I found Mr Havegood looking over the parapet and in possession of Verdier's pipe. He was distraught to the extent of incoherence, and it took me a little time to persuade him to drop the pipe he clutched, and calm him enough to bring him below. It was the right thing to do. No sooner was he abed than he was asleep, and soon, I was able to return to the same state.

On the morning of the 31st, Jacques Verdier was discovered to have fallen by accident from the same roof. A tragedy for all who knew and loved him.

I am not here to express sentiment, however, but to record the facts, some of which did not return to me until much later. At the time, I could not see anything beyond my own grief and that of my closest friends, all of whom mourned Verdier's passing in the extreme. Havegood included.

I can't say if it was weeks or months that passed before I thought again of that night, nor can I say why the realisation came to me, I can only assume it was because the cloud of grief took so long to pass. What I must say in my defence is this: By the time I realised what had happened that night, there was nothing I could do. To make public my suspicions would have led to more sorrow for others, and I buried the truth deep within to protect my friends, the memory of the Triumvirate, the families, and the reputation of the school.

How I regret my foolishness of the time. Foolishness? Perhaps it was devotion.

Now, however, a tragedy even closer to my heart has dug those memories from their frozen grave and laid them bare for me to see plain. It is only now I have suffered God's punishment for my silence, that I accept the time is right for the truth to be known, and the truth is this:

The Honourable Marcus Havegood killed Jacques Verdier in a fit of desperate frustration. Unwilling to return Havegood's unnatural affections, Verdier refused him his deviancy even on the last night. Equally unable to accept the refusal, Havegood's wits gave like the proverbial bough, and broke. In a fit, he threw Verdier from the roof moments before I appeared there, keeping his victim's pipe as a souvenir to remind him of the man he could not possess.

My evidence? From the obvious to the later remembered, Sir, is this:

The crenelations of Grace Tower are of a thickness and height that makes it impossible for someone to fall by accident. The embrasures reached to our chests, the merlons beyond our heads.

Verdier was averse to heights, thus, would not have stood or sat upon the battlements to smoke his pipe. Instead, on nights when we four visited the roof to gaze at the stars, he invariably sat against the chimney for security. Chase and I can attest to this.

The smell of his tobacco was strong in the air when I arrived on the roof that night, but I paid it no heed at the time, because it was not unusual. I expected to see him in his usual place, but Havegood's distraught condition was more of a concern than wondering where Verdier might have been.

I draw attention to Havegood's state of near hysteria witnessed upon my arrival, a state which calmed the instant he returned to his bed, and his ability to sleep only minutes later. Not, I suggest, the behaviour of a man genuinely distressed.

How he and Verdier came to be on the roof together at a late hour is no cause for consideration. It was Verdier's habit to be there late at night to smoke, and he had no intention to meet Havegood.

How may I be certain? Because, as was the tradition at Sinford's, the men were encouraged to keep journals. We all did. Most went the way of all things and did not survive. Verdier's, however, did. On the morning his body was discovered, I retrieved his journals from the casemate where we often met; him to unburden himself of Havegood's persistence to my willing ear, me to offer him comfort and hope, reassurance that as soon as school ended, so would his torment. His journal, he wrote in his study but while his roommate slept, returned to the lower-floor chamber, and hid it behind one of the many loose stones. This, he did to keep them from Havegood. These diaries I later sent on to his father, the then Ambassador to France, keeping only one. His last one in which he wrote of his fears for Havegood's behaviour, his dilemma at protecting our Triumvirate and close friends, the school's reputation and more. This, I enclose, so the full truth may be known from the pen of Jacques Verdier himself. It includes his last entry, here quoted.

Tonight, I take my last pipe atop the tower of my youth. It will mark the end of my time here, and the point of my greatest achievement: To have survived Sinford's with my life, sanity and virtue intact. This is assuming Havegood does not come for me, for of late, he has become maniacal to the extent I fear for my safety. Only two days past did he threaten me with harm should I not give in to his desires.

Tomorrow, however, I shall be a free man.

Havegood did come for him. I suspect to plead, and on finding a refusal, and having no more opportunity, 'broke.'

Our statements to the police mentioned none of this because it was unknown at the time, and unthought of by me until later. However, I believe there was evidence found at the scene to corroborate what I have written. This evidence was concealed for the good of the school, but when the news of the murder spread along the tight-knit vine that exists between Old Sinfordians, fathers and old boys alike withdrew their patronage out of shame for their alma mater. (This can only be confirmed through them; I cannot state this with certainty.)

The issue of the water supply was the perfect excuse for the school to close, and the perfect way to cover the scandal that would have otherwise touched the lives of so many.

All of the above may be investigated, but it is my intention to save the authorities the time and trouble by drawing Havegood towards a confession. The man is of two minds. He was, and still is, suffering from what Heinrich Schüle called 'dementia praecox.' Havegood has the ability to see his fantasies as real, and it was his fantasy that he also loved me in an unnatural way.

I state categorically I did not reciprocate. In retaliation, he saw Jacques Verdier as the recipient of my deflected love, and Jacques also refused to succumb.

Had I been able to accept Havegood's intentions, perhaps Jacques would still be living. That is the final burden I must bear, and no matter the outcome, I intend to end this matter with Havegood at one of the morning on the thirty-first; the hour of the murder. If my communication to him does not cause him enough concern to act, if he thinks he is beyond reproach and fails to take what some would call my bait, then this document will, I trust, be cause for his arrest.

At the least, it should be enough to instigate a re-examination of the death of my friend, Jacques Verdier.

History judges us not by what we do, but by what we fail to do, and I have failed the truth for twelve years. The time is right for that truth to be known, and I care not what happens to me because of my telling it.

This is it, Mr Chase. Do with it what you will.

Simon D Stape

* * *

It was a lot to take in, and there were many questions left unanswered, but it confirmed Jack's suspicions. While he took a moment to stare at the passing night and rest his mind, Larkin continued reading Havegood's papers, with his jaw somewhere near his chest, and uttered the occasional, 'Lies. Not true! This is a madman's fantasy.'

They were both madmen as far as Jack was concerned, and he wasn't sure who was the victim and which the criminal.

The man who had pushed another from the roof and was on his way to kill the only witness? Or the one waiting for him who intended to kill his reputation. They were out there in the darkness somewhere, and so was Will, heading towards both.

The thought caused him to shiver, but there was nothing he could do until he was off the train, and he set about rereading the confession before turning his attention to the journal.

TWENTY-SIX

Jack didn't care how, but Max had arranged for a carriage and a horse to meet them at the station. The darkness would have been complete were it not for the moon, waning among the broken cloud, the carriage lamps, and an ineffective streetlight at the station exit which did their best to illuminate a shadowed figure holding the horse.

'Mr Merrit?'

'That's me.'

'A Mr Pascoe sent me,' the figure said. 'I've come a fair way from Staplehurst, and he weren't able to say how long you'd need her. I'm instructed to stay at the hotel until you come back. When will that be?'

'Morning, most likely.'

'Then I must charge you the full rate. Three pounds six shillings including the hotel. Mr Pascoe said you'd pay in advance.'

Jack gave him four pounds, and when the thankful livery man offered to show him how to drive, told him not to bother. Instead, he asked about the horse, her temperament, and when she had been last fed and watered. He also asked when she'd been shod, and made sure the carriage wheels turned freely, while telling the man he was a decent bloke for providing a Barouche. While he was doing that, and the livery man was scratching his head in wonder, Larkin took his place on the bench to fill and light Max's lanterns.

'I can see you know what you be about, Sir. I'll leave you to it and wish you well.'

Jack was in his seat, and they were moving before the man could doff his hat.

As if he understood Jack needed time to adjust to the horse and vehicle, Larkin didn't speak until there was nothing ahead but the tree-lined road lit in the limited light of the carriage lamps.

'I never knew,' he said, as close to Jack as he could be without affecting his driving. 'I'd never have put Havegood down for insane. He had a ridiculous crush on Verdier which was never reciprocated, and I assumed he was of my persuasion, but... All that in his writing? I cannot believe it.'

'It's what we have,' Jack said. 'Like all we got from Stape is his letter to your brother. Why didn't he go to the police?'

'That is a question for him. I can only assume his loyalty to the old school runs deep.'

'There are too many bloody questions,' Jack said. 'What's the time?'

A fumble, the rattle of the lantern handle, and Larkin told him it was eleven thirty. Jack took the horse to a canter, watching the half-lit verge to keep him on course. As it began to curve, so he followed it, watching for junctions, potholes and wildlife, while his mind fixed on what might lie ahead.

The forest of tall, narrow trees, static in a breathless night. Still, but not silent. The hoot of an owl, the rustle of a snouting badger, and the crack of twigs underfoot as a man picked his way towards a memory that lived in the world beyond the boundary.

The hide was empty, but Diggs had been there, and there was only one other place he would be.

Havegood's father had sent him to the school to be among men he came to know as friends but saw as desirable objects. First, the shimmering angel that was Jacques with his soft voice, his blue eyes, and gentle, pale skin. His presence. The way others paid attention when he entered a room, and how he commanded their gaze, but never let adoration taint his modesty. His glittering form when he waded from the lake, the summer sun beaded on his back, and jewelled droplets tumbling from his carved chest, strong arms, buttocks. The swing of his head and the waterfall of sparkles that flew from his hair as he wiped it from his marble face with long fingers Havegood ached to feel clasped among his own.

Then the darker, more serious, but powerful form of Diggs, with his darkly-covered legs, and his firm, stubbled chin. They coy way he undressed each night behind the bookcase edge, where his clothes flew from hiding to the chair and lay there, releasing their scent of exercise and the outdoors. The way he drew the curtain when bathing, as though tempting Havegood to take the lead and peek, and the distance he maintained so no-one else would suspect his real attraction to the man across the room.

It was fantasy. He'd always known that and fought the knowing, but he saw it now more clearly than the leaf-strewn path through the saplings and ferns. The darkness drew its forces closer. The faint cloud threatened the moon and dimmed the forest in the way his hopes had dimmed the moment he'd read the letter from Diggs, complete with its excuses and threats.

Other memories and knowledge, however, do not lodge so tenderly... They were never tender. Had they been, they would have been an outlet for his repressed passion. *Reflect on my inactions.* Yes! He should have come to the bed when invited. Should have shared the joy of a friendship extended beyond the platonic. Could have given himself to love. *My devotion of that time.* His devotion had been to all of them, but more to Jacques, whom he protected from Havegood's love like Cerberus transported to the gates of heaven. Instead, he threw the denied man to hell, confining Havegood in a state of perpetual longing. Tantalus among the perfections of youth, and the unsullied waters of first experience, surrounded by the possibilities, yet unable to touch or taste, parched of their potential and desperate for it, because it was so right and so needed. To deny physical intimacy, to withhold his perfection, to guard the faultlessness of Jacques, and to deny Havegood all he craved in the name of right and proper. That was no friendship.

Havegood speared the ground with his cane as he climbed an incline.

I will face the truth and accept the consequences.

The truth.

What did he expect? If Jacques would not bend, if he would not give Havegood what he needed, then he was no friend, and he had no purpose. If Diggs had appeared seconds earlier, he would have understood, he would have sympathised. To have perfection present for five years, to see it mature and have it become closer and trusted, to have the friendship reciprocated, offering everything he longed for, only to have the path blocked by refusal.

That was no friendship, and *that* was the truth.

In Havegood's mind, Diggs had already joined Jacques beyond Cerberus at the gates. It happened the moment he made it clear he intended to tell what he knew. *I will face the truth.* Diggs planned to make it known once the anniversary had passed, and it didn't matter whether his suspicions were provable, or if anyone believed him; Simon Stape intended to break the oath and betray the last member of the Triumvirate. That, Havegood could not allow.

So what was this? A call to a night of passion so long denied to Havegood in his youth? A chance to apologise for not loving him? A meeting to beg forgiveness for cancelling the anniversary, or an opportunity to say, 'Yes! The next time we meet I will stay for the night, we *will* share a room, a bed, for I let my chances slip by when we were eighteen, and I am not going to let them go now.' Stape's voice rang through the dank and dripping forest as Havegood speared and trod. 'Forgive me, Caesar. Let me finally agree to *us*, to give you what you have always imagined but never lived, and let me do it in the name of Jacques. We can have him with us, happy for us, for you, because he did love you, and were he here, were the Triumvirate complete again, he would love you still as I do, as I always did...'

Havegood scowled, and wiped tears of frustration from his eyes.

'Yes, you will join Jacques,' he whispered, and the night around him trembled.

If not at the hide then at the obvious and fitting tower.

Havegood could have worked it out for himself. Had he not been so addled with fear, and unable to fight through the horror of what would happen if the truth came out, he could have seen the obvious. Had he been able to think for himself since the letter crashed into his life, stopping his heart with realisation, he would have seen it sooner. If Stape had not brought back the past in one great flash of veiled threats, Havegood would have had no need for Wright and his men. Stape had emasculated him with his decision to tell, but thanks to the Delamere men finding his location, the truth could remain a secret.

It was the only way, and atop the tower was the most fitting place. The phallic symbol of burgeoning youth where they became men, and where, as men, the memories and falsehoods of the past would soon rest like Jacques, beneath the earth.

The memory rose from beyond the hill blacker than the night behind it, sturdier, more constant than the moon-lustred sky that watched as it had that night, impassive to the desolation of a soul crying for love.

Havegood stopped on the ridge, the expanse of the school grounds laid out before him like the chessboard of his life. Moves to be made. Moves already played. Games of hunting and tracking already won and lost, with only one more step to take. It would soon be done, and the secret would remain unknown.

The thought brought a rush of practicality. No-one would suspect, but if suspicion fell his way, his bags and tickets were ready. The train would deliver him to the port and the steamer to the continent. His father would rant and rave and fear for the title, but Father would never hear from the dishonourable honourable again. The title, like his hope of ever being loved by Jacques or Diggs or any man, could go to hell with the rest of them.

The memory beckoned from its hollow, but there was time to wait, and the place to do that was in the cellar where Stape could not hear him rehearse both words and actions. There, he would bide his time until the significant hour among the dried-up well of his past. Beneath the place of horror and pain to which his father had sent him, and to which he'd vowed never to return.

'God forgive us the Sinford's of our fathers,' he sighed, and continued towards the inevitable.

There had been no-one at the hide. No Stape, no Havegood come to silence his victim, and no Will. Someone had lived there, though, the charred remains of a fire, and the empty bags and bottles had attested to that.

'Why didn't he just hide in the tower?' Jack whispered as they stalked the woodland path, the fragments of lantern light swaying either side.

'Too many bad memories, I expect,' Larkin replied.

'What's the time?'

'Past twelve thirty. Not far now, but Jack, what do you intend to do?'

'Stop a murder.'

'How?'

Jack held a brass tube in the lantern glow, and Larkin said, 'Oh dear.'

Until he'd tethered the horse by the lane beyond the hide, his mind had been too focused on finding Will to think of the details. It wasn't until stepping down that the realisation of what he was doing began to trouble him, and it was only when they were ready to enter the forest that he considered what he would be up against. When he unscrewed the piece of dash rail from the front of the carriage, Larkin had said something about paying for repairs, but the reassuring metal pipe in his hand would be worth any extra payment.

How he was to stop Havegood, what they would find at the tower, if they were to be in time, and what he would do if he found a man dead, were questions he was unable to answer. There was no point planning without first seeing what needed to be done, but he'd known he needed protection, and the dash rail had been the only weapon to hand.

They said no more as they walked. The soft rustle of leaves underfoot, occasional scurries in the darkness beyond the path, and his heart beating in his ears were the only sounds. Shadows and a few feet ahead were the only sights, until the cloud released the moon and trees appeared from the gloom like static spectators lining the road to a funeral. The ground rose beneath them, and the path became steeper, until they crested a rise, and saw below in a valley of silvered trees and black spaces, a wide block of stone with a tower at its centre.

'Look.' Larkin hid the lantern behind his back, and when Jack did the same, it became easier to make out the details as his eyes adjusted.

The windows were rows of hollow rectangles spaced with enough precision to satisfy even Will. The doors stood as uninviting gateways to who-knew-what dangers, and the roof glistened above like Thames-bank slime. He was looking at a monster from childhood tales invented to scare the misbehaving into their beds, there to quiver beneath the covers expecting pain and punishment for the slightest offence. How many boys had felt that in this place, and for how many years?

'A light.'

A drop of yellow among the scene of black and grey; a light at the top of the tower.

'Stay behind me. I will lead you there.'

Jack followed. Down the incline and back among trees until they emerged into a meadow which may have once been a lawn. The school loomed closer, shadowless because everything was shadow, but ahead, a gaping, mouth-like arch darker than the rest.

'Don't see no-one.'

'Me neither, but that doesn't mean we aren't being watched.' Larkin pulled him to a halt by the arch. 'Are you sure you know what you are doing?'

"Course I bleedin' don't, but I got to do something. Keep going.'

Larkin took his hand to guide him into the void, and it struck Jack that at the same time the night before, they'd clasped their hands in the same way but tighter, and their palms had pressed against soft sheets, and found their way over warm flesh. Now, he touched only unforgiving, cold stone.

Not the time to think about that. It was the time to be alert, to listen for voices, to grip the bar tighter and hope they weren't too late.

'Careful.'

They'd reached a staircase without Jack realising. Careful indeed.

The dusty air was clammy and weighted with anticipation. The worn stone steps were curving and narrow, and they rose to a series of landings and passages which, with his head tipped to look above, Larkin ignored. Windows were slits or arcs, some had glass, while others were blinded by decay, and still there were no voices, only the faint sound of their laboured breathing, until there were no more steps.

Larkin stopped. A finger rested on his lips a second before he pointed into a passage half lit by the struggling moon.

'A-one and A-two. Home of the golds.' His words were little more than escaping air. 'If they are here, they are above us. To the end and up.'

Jack followed into the hostile corridor of Larkin's past until they reached a doorless opening, where Larkin hung his lantern on a candle sconce, turned to Jack, and with a dull cry of surprise disappeared into the darkness.

A disembodied hand appeared in the glow searching until it met Jack's lapels, and before he could utter a similar cry, dragged him into a room.

Will, beckoning, led them to a window recess, his candle-lit face reflected in leaded glass, white and ghostly.

'One of them has gone up,' he whispered, as if Jack had been with him the whole time. 'I have not yet seen anyone else pass.'

Jack's instinct was to shout his brother out for vanishing and taking things into his own hands, but that had to wait.

'Which one?' he said.

'Not Mr Havegood. I imagine he is waiting until one o'clock. Ten minutes. If we are to dissuade Mr Stape from his actions, now is the time to do so.'

'Or we could jump on Havegood when he gets here, and take him back to the carriage.'

'And leave Mr Stape to throw himself from the battlements?' Will was aghast. 'You are thinking like a man who doesn't care.'

That was true enough, but still a slap in the face, and one that forced Jack to focus.

'I don't think he's going to top himself.'

'Why?'

'Can't say. Just don't feel right.'

'Can you risk it?'

'It ain't my life these idiots are playing with. Larkin, will Havegood have to pass here to get...?'

Larkin wasn't beside him. He was a way off, a shape in the darkness staring at a broken bed frame.

'Mine,' he said, with regret in his voice. 'It is still here.'

'Yeah, and so are we. Havegood will have to pass us to get to the roof, yeah?'

'Yes. Is he not here?'

'If he were, we should see the victim fall by this window at any second,' Will whispered. 'Here is what I think we should do. Mr Chase, because you know Mr Stape of old, you should go up and talk to him. Jack, being the sturdiest of us, should wait here and accost Mr Havegood when he appears. I will speak to him, as I am sure we can bring this unsavoury matter to a conclusion with words and reason.'

'Blood hell, Will,' Jack tutted. 'That ain't going to work.'

'No, I think Will is correct,' Larkin said. 'If Diggs is alone, and if he intends suicide, maybe I can dissuade him from his action.'

'Will he listen to you?'

'I can but try.'

'Let him go, Jack. While we have time.'

Let him go? Jack had only just found him, and to send him to a roof with two madmen...?

'I will be fine, Jack,' Larkin said. 'I will do what I can while you two prevent Caesar's advance. You have your pipe.'

'This is no time for tobacco.'

Jack showed Will his brass tube.

'Oh. Good idea. Go, Mr Chase, and good luck.'

Jack resisted the urge to kiss him because it seemed wrong considering the circumstances, but what also seemed wrong, as Larkin slipped from the room, was Havegood's absence.

'Why ain't he here?'

'He will be. It's nearly the hour of the anniversary.'

'You sure you ain't seen no-one else?'

'I arrived just after eleven and saw no signs of anyone. No lights, I mean, which would have shown clearly in the night. Mr Stape came past the door a little before twelve.'

'How did you know to come here?'

'The clues were all there. They just needed some lateral thinking.'

'I mean, how did you know how to find this place, get in, and get up here?'

Will held up a hand for silence, and with his ear cocked, lifted the window latch. It scraped metal on metal as he pushed the window open, and he waited, listening with his other hand still raised.

Muffled voices drifted down. One was Larkin's but Jack couldn't make out the words. The calm tone, however, was discernible.

'I looked at a map,' Will said, stepping back from the recess. 'I didn't know where the hide might be, but I knew Mr Stape, after biding his time there, would come to sixteen-M-twenty-four. The tower. You found my reference?'

'Yeah. Obvious.'

'Quite. And the building is easy to see from the road even at night. The cabman brought me to the school gates.'

'No questions?'

'Not at all.'

'Where did you get a cab from? We had to have Max pull some trickery to hire a carriage, and it's a bleedin' Barouche.'

'That would be because you took the standard service to Headcorn. I, on the other hand, enquired about the new line to Goudhurst. It is not due to open for another two months, but I reasoned there would be a workmen's service, and there was. It's only four miles away, where your journey was nearer ten.'

Flushed with admiration, Jack ruffled his brother's hair.

'Please, don't do that. You know how... Shush!'

'What?'

Jack spun to the doorway, but heard only the fading click of a cane.

Will pushed him forward, and no longer whispering, hissed, 'Havegood. Quick, Jack. This is it.'

TWENTY-SEVEN

Blundering in the gloom, the pipe in one fist, keeping Will back with the other, Jack reached a set of steps as Havegood's cane clicked out of sight at the top. With no time to think of anything other than Larkin in danger above, and Will following him into the same, Jack scrambled upwards until he broke free into the breeze. The uneven battlements were the hue of pewter, the stone floor a carpet of grey, and a silver beam caught a dark figure dashing out of sight behind a central chimneystack.

'Marcus, stop!' Larkin's voice.

'What the hell are you doing here?'

'I knew you'd come, Havegood.' A third voice. Stape, but where? They could only be behind the monument of clay pipes.

'Hold this, and stay here.' Jack thrust his satchel at Will.

Will took it, whispering, 'Words and reason, Jack.'

'A bloody crack on the head'll do the job.'

The brass raised, he inched to the chimney as the voices continued on the other side.

'You came to plead, I assume.'

'If that's what it takes.'

'It won't do you any good. The world will know what you did.'

'They will know I tried to save him.'

A mocking laugh interrupted by Larkin.

'Listen, the pair of you. We can settle this as gentlemen.'

'And Hunter Chase. The outsider.' Stape's voice again, bitter and sarcastic. 'What do you think you can do here? Jacques was as much your friend as mine. You did nothing to stop this murderer then. How are you going to stop him now?'

'Think, Diggs. Think of your family.'

'I am, Larkin, for how can I serve my family if I do not speak the truth?'

'What is your intent?' That was Havegood's voice. 'To tell him what you thought you saw, and hope the swat will testify to it? Chase isn't brave enough for that. He's a man who hides behind evidence, and there is none. What are you doing here, Chase?'

'Preventing my old friends from killing themselves. Diggs, you have your mother, your brother, they need you. Please, turn your thoughts away from self-destruction, and find an amicable...'

'Self-destruction?' Havegood derided. 'Stape's another coward. He's no more going to throw himself to the ground than I am.'

'At last, Caesar sees the truth,' Stape said. 'I am glad you came, Havegood, for like you, I was in two minds. Should I simply invite you to the moment, or drive you mad with suspicion? The latter seemed the most rewarding for me, and I see, my vagueness has worked.'

'The moment?' Havegood was just as derisive. 'How, pray, do you intend to tell the world of Jacques' death in a moment? Will you shout it from this rooftop and hope the birds flock to the newspapers?'

'I refer to the moment the story is published, and your deeds are made known. That moment has come, Havegood, for as we debate, my story is being set in steel and rolled with ink ready for tomorrow's readers. Even a whiff of a scandal, and your house will fall.'

'Even if something were to be published, I shall be gone.' Havegood was doing a good job of keeping his nerve. 'Even if you are telling the truth, they won't hang me for it. I am prepared. By the time they find you both dead, I shall be lost abroad.'

Find you both dead? Jack's arms tensed, and he stole a peek beyond the chimney. His position only allowed him a glimpse of Larkin, a hand at his side signalling for Jack to stay back.

'Justice will find you wherever you go. If not the justice of the law, then that of God who has made me see the foolishness of my youth.'

'I am tiring of this,' Havegood said. 'If I cannot dissuade you from betraying me by breaking your oath to the Triumvirate, and if even Hunter Chase cannot turn you from sullying the fine name of Jacques Verdier by accusing me of his murder, then there is only one option remaining.'

'The option is to accept the consequences of your past,' Larkin said. 'You are too late, Havegood. I have read the confession he sent to the Gazette.'

'An interesting lie.' Havegood's voice was eerily calm. 'He is too much of a weakling to do such a thing, for the world would have to know of his infatuation for me, our meetings at the hotels, our passions played out in the study rooms below, his lust for Verdier...'

'Keep your foul mouth to yourself, Havegood,' Stape threatened. 'And keep your filthy imaginings within it. I had no infatuation for you, nor for Jacques. I met with you all these years out of loyalty not lust, and there has never been any passion. There was nothing but platonic friendship. Larkin believes me, why can't you?'

'He lies, Chase.'

'It is not a lie! Just as you throwing Verdier from the roof is not a lie.'

'If that were the truth, and if you could prove it, you would have exposed me years ago.'

'I stayed silent to protect you, to protect all of us.'

'You see? Because you loved me.'

'No. To protect the brotherhood of the Triumvirate and the good name of our school,' Stape shot back. 'Nobody could love you.'

Probably not the best thing to say, Jack thought, his eyes fixed on Larkin's hand, and ready to make his move.

'I can believe Stape has acted to protect all of us.' Larkin was assured, and Jack held back. Perhaps words and reason would end this after all. 'We swore to be loyal to each other, and the bond is as strong now as it was then. There is nothing we can do for Jacques but remember him and mourn. Diggs, honour his memory by accepting the fact. Withdraw your request to publish, and let the past remain buried.'

'No more, Chase, no more.'

'And you, Caesar. Put down your cane and accept the foolishness of your youth.'

'I did nothing.'

'You killed him because he would not give in to your unnatural desire,' Stape wasn't listening to anything but his own voice. 'You were mad with lust, and you still are.'

'I rushed to save him, but he was gone.'

'You threw him. You killed my friend because he wouldn't give in to your perverted demands. He even predicted it in his diary.'

'I came up here for a last look at the night sky...'

'And found him as he always was, at his pipe against the chimney. You persuaded him to the edge to view the stars, safe from his fear of heights because you were by his side. There, after pressing yourself on him, and after he refused and tried to struggle free, you lifted him as easily as if he were a rugby ball, and...'

'That is not how it happened. He wasn't smoking his pipe...'

'The air was thick with it.'

'Alright, he was, but he was already standing on the ledge.'

'Impossible.'

'He meant to jump. I rushed to save him...'

'If he was there, it was to flee from you.'

'No. I meant to say, he was calm, and smoking in his usual place...' Havegood struggled; a man desperate to deny his own lies. 'Diggs, Chase is right. Whatever happened, the past is done. Let it alone.'

'Only when you're dead.' Stape roared.

'No!'

Larkin's cry brought Jack further from behind the chimneystack in time to witness Stape rushing forward but staggering to a halt as Havegood whipped a narrow, glinting blade from his cane.

'Oh, really?' Unperturbed, Stape was almost laughing.

'If Sinford's taught me anything it was *Quid faciendum est*,' Havegood gloated, once again worryingly controlled. 'Do what must be done.'

'I have,' Stape sniggered. 'I have corrected the inactions of my past and done what I failed to do. Run me through if you must. I will welcome the end knowing the truth is even now being printed.'

'I don't believe that for one second. Towards the battlements, if you will. I may look withered and weak, but my mind is as strong as my resolve.'

'Put down your sword, Havegood,' Larkin said. 'Stape has indeed written his side of the story as evidence, and submitted it to my magazine.'

'Why should I believe you?'

It was the first time Havegood sounded uncertain.

Jack waited. Pressed against the wall, drawing no-one's attention, he was intrigued. The confession was in his satchel, and he wasn't sure what Larkin had planned. No doubt he was hoping his reasoning would win the day. Jack, on the other hand, wasn't waiting for reason to prevail; he was waiting for a time he could attack Havegood from behind and knock the sword from his hand.

'Hunter speaks the truth,' Stape said. 'Hunter has never been able to do anything but. My confession is with his brother. Did you think I was naïve enough to come here knowing you might follow without first arranging insurance?'

'You are lying. Both of you.'

'They most certainly are not, Sir. I have the document right here.'

Jack's stomach lurched, and his knees almost gave way as Will stepped into the scene waving a paper.

'Who the hell...?'

'William Reginald Merrit, an investigator hired by Mr Havegood,' Will said as if he'd just walked into a party. 'Is this the document you mean, Mr Stape?'

'What is this charade?' Havegood's blade wavered between Stape and Will. 'What are you doing here?'

'How did you get that?' Stape held his lantern towards the paper. 'Is this your doing, Chase?'

'I suppose so,' Larkin said. Although he too sounded puzzled, he continued to signal for Jack to be patient. 'My brother sent it on to me.'

'But why? They must know how Jacques died,' Stape wailed. 'Hunter, you've ruined everything.'

'Not at all,' Will said, as assured as Jack had ever seen him. 'Mr Havegood. I am prepared to set the lantern flame to this confession once you have thrown down your weapon.'

Havegood laughed. 'That could be anything.'

'Then take a look.' Will shoved it into Stape's face. 'Is this not your handwriting, Mr Stape?'

'Give it to me.'

'It is, isn't it?' Will snatched the paper away and held it as close to Havegood as he could reach. 'You see? *My Dear Mr Chase...* A covering note for what is written below. Mr Stape's evidence, what he saw, how he was too shocked to realise what had just happened, but later came to understand how the man's death could not have been an accident.'

'What are you talking about? Where is your proof?'

'A pipe,' Will said. 'You were holding Mr Verdier's pipe. Were you going to keep it as a memento of your triumph over him, I wonder?'

'His pipe...?'

'And the way, when you were taken to your bed, you fell instantly asleep. Is that the action of a man who just saw a beloved friend jump to his death? Did you have no thought to raise an alarm, or to rush to him to see if he might still live?'

Will has been reading far too many detective stories, Jack thought, as he inched closer.

'Your infatuations as described in the diaries of other students,' Will continued with his list. 'Your disturbed condition that night, and the way you confessed to the murder as Mr Stape led you back to bed.'

That wasn't in the confession.

'I professed no such thing,' Havegood spat. 'I am not so stupid as to put in writing that I killed the man.'

'But, apparently, you are stupid enough to announce it now,' Will said. 'And before witnesses. Thank you. All the same, I am willing to burn this if you hand me the blade and walk away. You, Mr Stape, may then be free to join your old chum by dropping yourself from the crenelations, if that is, after all, your intent. If not, you could make yourself available to give your evidence to the authorities. I suggest that would be a more practical course of action.'

'Who the hell are you?' Stape clutched his head, his panicked eyes flitting between the paper, the flame and Havegood.

'Well, Mr Havegood?' Will continued, unaffected by neither Stape's confusion nor the blade pointed at his chest. 'It was you who hired us, and I am only giving the client what he wants. Drop your stick, and walk away. Please.'

Jack's gripped tightened as he waited for Havegood's decision, but he didn't know how much longer he could hold himself back.

'Burn it first.'

'No!' Stape protested.

'The knife.'

'The flame.'

The lantern was already dancing in Havegood's wild eyes.

'Together,' Will said, and opened the glass. 'You are an Old Sinfordian, Sir. Do what must be done.'

'Very well. If it will bring all this to an end.'

There was something in his tone that unnerved Jack. It was too calm, and he'd agreed too readily. Havegood lowered his sword to the ground, and at the same time, Will set fire to the corner of the document. Stape wailed louder, and rushed to grab the confession, but righting himself and stepping away, Havegood drew a pistol.

'Stay!' He clicked back the hammer and no-one moved.

'Wait.' Except for Will, who held aloft the flaming paper. 'See it burn,' he teased, floating it in Havegood's line of sight like a mesmerist with a fob watch. 'The sins of your past are turning to ash.'

'What have you done?'

Stape scrambled to save the document, but Havegood was quicker, and snatched the lantern. His pistol lost its aim as he took the paper, and laughing, forced it into the flame. With him distracted, Jack leapt, and slammed the bar down on his arm. The gun fired, and the bullet ricocheted from the stone floor to the wall. Jack raised his bar a second time, but Stape robbed him of his target by shouldering into Havegood's waist. With his arms wrapped around his middle, he rushed him towards the battlements, pushed himself upright, and with a yell, slammed his victim onto the ledge. Screaming, Havegood swung the lamp and lashed out with the gun, but lost his grip on both, and they fell into the night as Stape heaved him towards the edge.

A blow to the head sent Stape to the floor, and the brass bar followed, as Jack grabbed for Havegood's arm. His hand connected, and he clamped the man's wrist as the body spun outwards. Havegood went over, and a heavy tug pulled Jack against the ledge, knocking the breath from his lungs.

'Give me your other hand,' he gasped over the man's panicked sobs, but it made no difference. As Havegood dangled, he kicked and struggled, pulling Jack further up the wall and closer to the drop.

There was a weight on his back as Stape grappled to prise his grip from Havegood's wrist, all the time shouting in his ear, 'Let him fall.' Then he was gone, leaving Jack staring into the void, and Havegood writhing above the drop. There were the sounds of a struggle behind, and he heard Larkin's voice. With Havegood's struggling pulling him ever closer to the fall, his feet scrambled for purchase, but found none.

'Let me go. Let him die.'

Stape was hysterical, but through the man's madness came sense. If Jack didn't let Havegood go, he would be going with him. Let him drop; the man was a killer. Or was he? Who could he believe? Stape might have invented everything, or Havegood might have forced the boy over the edge. Maybe Verdier jumped. The letters, the diaries, confessions and accusations. What was real?

Real was a man about to fall to his death, and Jack having the chance to save him. It wasn't his job to decide if a man lived or died. It was his job to see justice done, and death was no justice for anyone.

'Give me your other hand.'

The moonlight caught Havegood's face in a moment of tranquil clarity, and he said, 'I shall live in eternity with my love.'

Hands pulled on Jack's shoulders. Will's voice was in his ear. 'Don't let him fall.'

Larkin on the other side. 'We can't hold both of you.'

'Your other hand,' Jack screamed, as they pulled, and Havegood, woken from his state of madness as if he had just realised his peril, struggled harder.

His arm flew up, Jack grabbed it, and slid forward another inch.

'Hold me,' he grunted, as the rough stone tore through his shirt, and pain seared across his skin.

Will and Larkin anchored him with their bodies, and pulled. With a scream to match Havegood's, Jack braced his knees and wrenched upwards. His determined howl continued, driven by pain and desperation, as Will and Larkin dragged him back until he was balanced and could haul Havegood from the battlements, to let him drop in a heap.

Jack slid down the wall, and turned his back to it, his chest burning inside and out. There before him was Stape, dead or unconscious, and beside him, Havegood, a crumpled heap of pathetic sobs.

'Bloody hell,' Jack panted, the shock rippling through his body and threatening to release itself as vomit.

Someone clutched him in their arms, increasing the pain, and unsure who it was, he pushed them away to discover it was Larkin.

'This is something of a mess,' Will said, as if nothing had taken place. 'Made worse by the fallen lantern which appears to have set light to the shrubbery.'

'Don't let him get away.' Jack forced himself to his feet. Whatever this mess was, it was not yet over. 'What you done to him?'

'Took a leaf out of your book,' Larkin said. 'Clubbed him on the head. I can't say how long he will remain thus or what we do, but they will both need more restraint than I just exhibited. Ah! Inspiration. Stay here.'

'Where else am I going to go?'

Larkin scurried towards the stairs, leaving Jack to retrieve the swordstick, and examine his scrapes by the undisturbed moonlight.

'The flames,' Will said leaning over the edge. 'The paraffin must have exploded from the lantern. It doesn't look like it's going to put itself out. We should hurry.'

Where to? Was Jack's first question to himself, quickly followed by, how? Havegood and Stape wouldn't go without a fight.

Will provided the answer to the second question by holding Havegood's arms behind his back, removing his tie and wrapping it around the madman's wrists. Tying off a secure knot, he told him, 'This matter, Sir, is one for the authorities. We shall present them with both of you and all the evidence we have. The police can decide innocence or guilt. That is, after all, their job.'

'Blimey, Will. Where d'you get them words from?'

'Some Penny Dreadful,' Will said, and took the swordstick from Jack's trembling hand. 'I will hold onto this, Mr Havegood, and turn it over to the police at Goudhurst along with Mr Stape's confession, Mr Verdier's diary and everything else.' To Jack, he said, 'We are expected at any time of night. Can you drive?'

"Course I can bloody drive. What d'you mean we're expected?'

'I called at the station on my way. Told them who I was, showed them one of Mr Wright's letters of authority, and ordered them to stand by. They, of course, thought I was a crazed loon and laughed me out through their front door. So, if they have taken to their beds, and I have to wake them, that is their lookout. Ah, Mr Chase. Just in time. It looks like Mr Stape is about to rejoin the fray.'

Larkin returned with his lamp and clutching something in his other hand which he said were wires he had pulled from his old bed.

'As they held me then, so they can now hold these lunatics,' he said, as he wrapped them around Stape's wrists. 'What a strange thing to be doing to an old fellow.'

'Unhand me, you...'

Larkin gagged him with his handkerchief, reassuring his old schoolmate that it was quite clean, and reinforced Havegood's bonds with more lengths of wire.

'The smoke is rising,' Will warned, as he hauled Havegood to his feet. 'I don't think we can be blamed for the fire, as it was this man who threw the flame.'

'The flame that burnt Stape's confession,' Jack said, wincing as he collected the brass rod.

'Not at all,' Will replied. 'The original is here in your satchel. I showed him a copy I made before I set off from home.'

'You opened my correspondence?'

'Certainly not, Mr Chase. I am not a man to do such a thing. I paid Max to do it. Amazing what a butler has up his sleeves.'

'But Stape recognised his own handwriting,' Jack said, puzzled.

'Of course he did. It's a common cursive script as taught to every boy who paid attention in school which, unlike you, I did. A uniform hand and easy to emulate. I think we have everything.'

Jack wasn't sure if he should be angry with his brother, or impressed by his composure, but congratulations and explanations could wait until later. They still had to get the two men to the police, and as soon as they realised what they were in for, they were bound to struggle.

The brass bar ready in one hand, and Stape in the other, he followed Larkin and Will, holding the blabbering, incoherent Havegood between them, and began a careful descent. Smoke met them on the stairs, and they hurried through with their heads down, their way lit by an ever-strengthening red and orange glow.

It wasn't until they reached the fresh air that Stape began his protests, but with no-one to hear him or witness their escape, Jack let him struggle and shout, but never let him go. Even when they reached the carriage with the burning building a distant blaze, he continued to writhe, wedged against Havegood, with Will pointing the blade between them both as though he'd handled a sword all his life.

Twenty minutes into the drive they passed a racing fire truck, and reached the Goudhurst police station half an hour later. Two officers transformed from sleepy, to angry, to intrigued, and finally apologetic policemen as Larkin spoke, dropped his brother's name and publication as though they were threats, and Will introduced Jack as, 'One of Lord Clearwater's finest detectives,' as if he had an army of them.

With statements made, criminals handed over, and contact addresses given, the three stepped back into the night to find it had changed.

'It will soon be dawn,' Will said. 'In fact, by the time we return the carriage, the sun will be up. We should be in time for the early train.'

'Yeah, and on the way, I got questions for you,' Jack yawned as he untethered the horse.

'I think we all have questions,' Larkin said. 'We also have plenty of time in which to answer them. Meanwhile, may I suggest we enjoy the dawn ride together on the driving bench. Seated thus, I can ensure you don't nod off at the reins, Jack, while Will ensures I remain awake, and you keep an eye on your illustrious brother. Will you do that?'

'I would if I knew what illustrious meant.'

'It means Mr Chase considerers me in some way eminent,' Will said. 'Very kind of him, but as the word can also mean lofty which, itself, could be taken to mean arrogant, I am not sure it is the compliment he intended.'

'Bloody hell,' Jack sighed. 'Too many bleedin' words. The pair of you, get in before I leave you behind.'

TWENTY-EIGHT

'I still don't see how you solved it before reading the confession,' Jimmy said with an expression that suggested he was too astonished to be displeased. 'Care to explain, Jack?'

'Yeah, but I'll let Will start.'

They had rehearsed how they would justify their actions while waiting for Jimmy to return from Cornwall. When he did, he came with the news that his man was back at work, and the outbreak of Russian flu was over. Maybe it was that news which prevented Jimmy from outrage when he learnt they had continued the investigation against his orders, or perhaps he was pleased that they'd brought such a high-profile case to a successful conclusion. Either way, they still had some explaining to do.

'It was a mixture of things,' Will began, standing by Jack at the chalkboard. 'Firstly, what I call Mr Havegood's memoirs. All that business about his school days and intense friendships, platonic love for Mr Verdier, and later, physical love for Mr Stape. That played on my mind from the moment I broke it free of your safe and read the papers.'

'Yes, well, least said about that...'

'I have found a fascinating thesis on codes, Mr Wright,' Will said, seeing where he was looking. 'I'll distil it for you and give you some tips. Meanwhile, Mr Havegood's writing. Why, I asked myself, would a man be so open in his descriptions of his feelings for another man? I admit, he came to you knowing that he would find a sympathetic ear, you being...' A glance at Jack and Larkin. 'The three of you being of a similar, um, *understanding*. Still, to commit such things to paper is unsafe, particularly for a respectable man of business and society, let alone one destined for a title. Yes, he wanted it burnt, Jack told me, and was reticent for you to keep it, but that also made me wonder why. He let you keep it because it was designed to dupe you, and he thought there was no chance that someone from his past would see it and know it to be untrue. However, that is what happened when Mr Chase became involved.'

'Having read it, I can attest to its falsehood,' Larkin put in, reclining in the corner of the sofa. Although less weather beaten, he looked as much at home in the office as Jimmy's satchel. 'Havegood had fancies in his schooldays, but not fantasy fancies such as those. His condition appears to have worsened with age.'

'And how could you tell his memoirs were false?' Jimmy asked, jotting notes in his usual fashion. 'Mr Chase didn't see them until later, by which time, you were on your way to the school. Correct?'

'Correct,' Will nodded and addressed the list he had made on the board. 'Thanks to you alerting us to something being not quite right, and then vanishing to the West Country, we had to pick up where you left off. Thus, Jack came to the case with more scepticism than before, and I with a determination to do a good job and examine every detail.'

'Always a good idea,' Jimmy said.

'We didn't want to let you down. Jack was on about the smell of fish, and once I had translated his meaning, a few elements of Havegood's story set me to wondering. His emphasis on the sexual. All those memories of him and Verdier discussing the subject. Who shares that information with strangers? How he so easily moved on from a mad infatuation with the Frenchman to a reciprocated one with Stape, and how Verdier approved. Really? I thought. Is it that easy to fall for another man, and with the blessing of your friends?'

Jack couldn't help but throw a smile at Larkin. Jimmy noticed, and said, 'It can be.'

'Very well. Even if that part were true, there were factual elements to his story that made me doubt its authenticity.' Will underlined a line of writing. 'The night of July the thirtieth. Their last night at Sinford's. Havegood tells us he and Stape were alone in A-one by ten thirty, and Verdier was next door in A-two. In the next sentence, he contradicts himself and says Verdier was with Stape in A-one. Maybe it was just bad storytelling, but it jarred enough to make me reread the section several times, and I couldn't help but think about one sentence in particular. *Although we dallied long in his bed, we were asleep in it before the chapel clock struck midnight.* Dallied is a euphemism, of course, but the important part there is, *we were asleep in it.*'

'If we are to believe Havegood's ramblings, he and Stape enjoyed many a night in the same bed,' Larkin said. 'I was never aware of that, and although I can understand Stape keeping it a secret, if it were true, Havegood wouldn't have been able to keep it to himself.'

'He told Verdier,' Jack put in.

'But only according to this.' Will waved the memoir. 'And Mr Verdier is not here to object. Anyway, he contradicts himself again by saying he rose from his own bed, and then, *Diggs dragged himself from his bed.* This is the following morning when Havegood wakes up and says, *Someone's had an accident* before he knows why there's an ambulance in the grounds.'

'Yes, alright, but wait,' Jimmy interrupted. Sitting back and playing with his pen, he pursed his lips in thought before laying down challenges. 'Havegood simply returned to his own bed during the night. Maybe Stape snored or moved around too much.'

'Possible, Mr Wright, but the point is, he got out of bed at some point, and if he was so infatuated with the man, he'd have put up with anything to stay beside him, especially on their last night together.'

'Alright...' Jimmy's face tightened. 'How about this: The ambulance could have been called for any number of reasons. On seeing one, it's logical to assume someone's had an accident.'

'I see how you are presenting a counter argument,' Will said, smiling at the boss. 'I expect this kind of debate is what the police detectives are currently holding. Maybe they will find a way to prove what is, as yet, only circumstantial evidence. Feel free to ask more questions and raise more obstructions as we go.'

'I will, seeing how this is my agency and you work for me.'

'However...' The rebuke flew straight over Will's head and landed somewhere beyond the chalkboard. 'On seeing a body below his window, Havegood then writes, and again, I quote, *it was as if I instinctively knew who it was four storeys down and dead.* How did he know the person was dead? It could have been a gardener having a reaction to a wasp sting, or a parent having the vapours after receiving the end of term bill.'

Larkin snorted a chuckle.

'Havegood also wrote that they left the school as hurriedly as possible,' Will went on. 'Suspicious? Maybe not to you, but suspicious enough for me to question the man's motives for hiring an investigator to find a missing friend. Particularly if it was a friend who had seen him a second after the murder, and may have seen more.'

'You didn't know that at the time.' Jimmy still didn't look convinced, and Jack had to agree, Will's reasoning was more about opinion than evidence.

Will, however, ignored Jimmy's expression of doubt. 'No, but there was nothing to prevent me from thinking what if? Then, there is the phrase, *Not knowing is the worst of all punishments.* Did he mean, not knowing what had happened to the man who fell from the roof? No. Mr Havegood's punishment of recent years was guilt. Not knowing if Mr Stape knew the truth and if or when he would release the secret. When things were running well between them, he could pretend he had done nothing wrong, but when Mr Stape wrote following his tragedy, Mr Havegood's long-held concern that he would be found out, worsened. That brings me to Doctor Markland.'

'Mr Havegood's emaciated condition?'

'Quite. Jack?'

'Yeah.' Jack clutched his lapels, and stole a peek at the report beside him on the table. 'The dinner, and before that, when Havegood bleated about being too worried to eat. Like Will says, he weren't worried about Stape wanting to do himself in, because he don't actually say in his letter that's what he's going to do. No, he was worried because Stape's letter suggests he was going to tip over the beer barrel and slosh out the ale. Going to gut the fish on the path, as they say down Limehouse docks. Alright, we now know Stape's suicide was Havegood's invention, but when I saw what Will had written up there...' Pointing to the board, he read aloud. *'Doctor's diagnosis: He is worried about much more than the fate of an old school friend.* It was that what set me to ask myself what he weren't telling us. What if the Frenchman's death weren't an accident? Once I'd thought that, I couldn't think of nothing else, except what you said about not trusting even your client.'

'So, you acted on instinct?'

'I suppose.'

'You both did.'

'In a way, Mr Wright,' Will said. 'My instinct is to notice details and I have no option but to be precise, but it is instinctive for Jack to be untrusting. That has something to do with being brought up in Limehouse, I imagine. Call it scepticism if you will.'

'I'd call it having what you need to be decent detectives,' Jimmy said, displaying good humour for the first time since the meeting began. 'Go on.'

'The rest is about Stape,' Jack said. 'For a start, why vanish? If he wanted to kill himself he'd have done it straight away, like Copper Tom did a couple of years back, you remember, Will?'

'I am unable to forget.'

'This docker what lived down the end of our street. Decent bloke. Used to make Palm Sunday crosses out of newspaper and give one to each of the street's kids with a penny wrapped in the middle. Anyways, lost all his money on some gamble and couldn't face the workhouse. Told Elsie Clarke he was going to look for work at the slip basin, but carried on walking. Straight into the river. If you're going to go around saying you're going to top yourself, you ain't really going to top yourself. I reckon, you just want someone to pay attention, but why you can't just dance a jig on Ratcliffe corner in your unders, or eat a live eel in one swallow... I mean, that'd get you noticed better than going round with all this woe is me shit...'

'Yeah, I get the point, Jack.'
'Right. Well, that's the way I saw it.'
'And I can agree,' Jimmy said.

'I got to asking meself, what was Stape up to? So, I read his letter to Havegood again, and there it was. Will's second list what I saw when Larkin and me got back from Kent. He talked about his memories and *knowledge*. What did he know? *My inactions*, he wrote. What didn't he do? *My devotion of that time*. Devoted? Who to? Like he said up on the roof, he kept quiet to protect his old school chums, but then, when his wife and boy died... Well, maybe he did see it as God's punishment or some hogwash, and thought he'd try and put it right. Who knows? But it's what happened.'

A knock at the door interrupted Jack's derailing train of thought, and he was glad of the time to pause and remind himself of his report. It was the first such thing he'd ever written, and he was pleased he'd remembered so much. Larkin and Will had helped write it, of course, but Jimmy didn't need to know that.

'How be?' Max said, taking long strides into the room and dropping a newspaper on Jimmy's desk. 'Sorry to disturb, but the afternoon edition might be of interest. Dinner be at seven thirty. I catered for Mr Chase, in case he be staying.'

'Ah.' Larkin pulled an apologetic face. 'Jack and I have a table at Simpsons. I should have said.'

'Aye, would be helpful, Mr Chase.' The butler rolled his eyes. 'Unlike the rest of you, I bain't be no detective.'

'Who's in next door?' Jimmy asked.

'Mrs Norwood and His Lordship's new footman, be all.'

'Then why not invite them? Baxter too.'

'Right y'are.'

The butler left, and Jimmy nodded for Jack to continue.

'That's it. Except to say, Will and I think Stape knew what Havegood would do.'

'In that he would go to any lengths to find him,' Will clarified. 'The letter, written in terms only Havegood would understand, stated Stape was going to tell the truth about the murder. He knew Havegood would come looking for him, and where more fitting than at the school on the anniversary of their annual meetings, and at the place and time of Verdier's death? It's the stuff of romantic novels.'

'Stape wanted a final say before he watched Havegood's reputation fall apart when he got done,' Jack put in. 'Like he said, he was in two minds about making it obvious, so he dithered about leaving clues, and in the end, hid his book and tore up some of his notes. It was them what made me think he weren't going to top himself.'

'You're referring to the journal and the ripped-out page, yes?'

'Yeah, Jimmy. Made more sense when I remembered he wittered on about... What was it?' Jack referred to his report. '*The paper streets and black lines of rationality.* A map's nothing more black lines set out on paper, and who leaves a map to their suicide?'

'Havegood was doomed either way,' Jimmy said, his attention straying to the newspaper. When he realised the others were waiting for him to explain, he said, 'I mean, whether he found Stape for their showdown or not, Stape had already released his side of the story to the Gazette. Either they'd have killed each other at the school, or Havegood would have died under the glare of the public, which is what's unmetaphorically happening as we speak. The police have the confession?'

'They do,' Larkin said. 'And the other evidence.'

Jimmy nodded to himself, and put the paper aside.

'Well, gentlemen,' he said, his smile still apparent. 'I am impressed. What can I say but well done? Your part in this is also noted, Mr Chase. Should you want a job, I'm still short of staff, and can always do with more intelligent minds like Jack's.'

'Intelligent mind, me?' Jack laughed. 'I'm just the driver.'

'You are so much more than that,' Larkin said, causing Jack to blush. 'Thank you for the flattery, Mr Wright, but I investigate society in a different way. However, I am always willing to assist, particularly if Jack is involved.'

'Yeah, I think I've detected that,' Jimmy smirked. 'Right then. You can expect to be called as trial witnesses, but I'll go through all that with you when it happens. Nothing to worry about, so... that's that, and...'

'Apologies, Mr Wright.' Will spoke up. 'There is one outstanding matter which concerns me.'

'And that is?'

'Payment.'

'Will!' Jack admonished. 'Not now.'

'Not ours,' Will clucked. 'The agency's. With Mr Havegood incarcerated at Her Majesty's good pleasure, how will the agency receive what is owing?'

'Don't you worry about it,' Jimmy said, and held up the case file. 'It's in here, and I will send it on to Creswell in the morning.'

'Send what on?'

'Havegood signed the contract as most desperate clients do, without reading the detail. Creswell drew it up to include a clause whereby, should the client die or... *In any other way find himself in a predicament which excludes the possibility of direct payment of said fees arising from contracted agreement...* And so on. In other words, whether he's hanged or not, we can claim what's owing from his estate.'

'Quite right,' Larkin agreed. 'Quid faciendum est. Do what must be done.'

'You have done what had to be done,' Jimmy said.

'Which would be, Quid faciendum *sit*,' Larkin said.

'Whatever.' Rising, and approaching the safe, Jimmy said, 'Which means, we can put this file away, and turn our attention to what comes next. After the publicity of the Havegood case, I predict we will soon be busy.'

With the file in the safe, he closed the door and spun the dial. On his way back to his seat, he stopped to give Will a look through narrowed eyes.

'I reset the combination as soon as I got home.'

'I imagine you did,' Will replied. 'However, it will only be one of three permutations, involving the numbers two, five, nine and eleven, in that order.'

Jimmy's jaw dropped. 'How do you know these things? Did you see me do it?'

'No. It's just a guess based on that book I mentioned. I'll find it for you. It tells us to know the man whose safe it is, and then offers ways in which the human brain makes its connections. In this case, I assumed the distance between Larkspur Hall and London, which is advertised as two hundred and fifty-nine miles by the Great Western Railway, and you were away eleven days. As you travelled west to east, it stands to reason you would have started the combination by first turning the dial clockwise.'

Overflowing with admiration, Jack reached to ruffle Will's hair, but thought better of it. This wasn't the brother he knew from the East End. Will was no longer the strange young man who walked the Millwall loop, counted his steps, and moved objects until they were just so. Well, he was, but not so much, because he had other things to occupy his mind; a wealth of books to read, lists to make, puzzles to consider, and a new way of life that made him as happy as he was when everything was in its right place.

'Thank you, gentlemen,' Jimmy said, and with the meeting over, reached for his newspaper. 'We'll gather in the morning, promptly at nine, Jack, and see what's next. Meanwhile, have a pleasant evening and enjoy whatever you're doing.'

Jack and Larkin's eyes met across the room. If Will was happy, Jack was more so, because everything was fitting into its right place for him, too. That included Larkin, and he couldn't imagine how he'd ever been without the man.

'I should get changed before dinner,' he said, and Larkin's moustache twitched.

Delamare House assured acceptance and privacy, but even so, Jack would remember to lock the door.

Hoxton, East London

Etch watched from a safe distance as his mother spun the afternoon edition across the table, spat on the floor, and bit the cork from the gin bottle.

'You read it?' she carped, after she'd taken a swig, grimacing at both the taste and the newspaper.

'Yes, Ma.'

'Same Jack Merrit, ain't it?'

'Yes, Ma.'

'Same bloody Wright, only this time, it ain't your brothers they've put inside, but some rich toffs. One to drop for murder, the other gets a straight waistcoat down the bedlam. Don't give a tinker's cuss about them, but thanks to Merrit, we still got the rozzers snouting around our business. You got to ask, what they going to do to us next?'

'The question should be, Ma, what are we going to do to them?'

Violet Flay's painted eyebrows rose, and a smile bothered her thin mouth.

'Go on.'

Unlike his brothers, who solved every problem with fists, knives and iron bars, Etch was of the opinion that a man's greatest weapons were cunning and patience. Although not yet thirty, he had waited a lifetime to usurp his older siblings and reach the top of Mother Flay's chain of command. With the two eldest serving time, and Crank and Dodge hiding out in Essex to avoid the grubby hands of the law, his chance had come. The in-laws didn't count. Husbands of daughters were as pointless to Violet Flay as the daughters themselves. It was direct male blood that mattered, and not only was Etch that, but he was also the only son she had to call on. His youth and good looks were of no use to him, it was his skill with a knife, his quick wits and deviancy that the woman appreciated, albeit grudgingly.

She'd not always been so motherly.

Since she discovered his proclivity when he was sixteen, and tried to drown him in the bath, he'd learnt to employ a ruse that had eventually won her over. Self-preservation was the watchword in Hoxton, and within the family, deception was everything.

Etch had no love for his mother, and she had not much for him, so he added caution to cunning and patience, and chose his words with care.

'Griffin Music Hall,' he said, knowing that to say the name Samson Merrit would send her into a rage.

'Yeah?'

'Same family.'

Violet spat again, this time rubbing the glob into the carpet with her foot before taking another swig. Dragging her flabby fist across her mouth, she slammed the table.

'So?'

'A way in, Ma. A way to dig out the rot that's plagued the family these past years. Once and for all.'

'Nah, we can let that die along with me old man.' She rattled her rings at the newspaper. 'These Merrit boys ain't got a clue about that stuff. It's Wright and that rozzer Adelaide what keeps sticking their noses in. Them's the ones we got to be rid of.'

'You're right, Ma,' Etch said, and employed his most devious tactics. 'And we will, but you don't need to worry your head about it. You worry about Arty and Badger's appeal, and while me brothers are away, I'll cut the grass at Delamere House. It's going to take time, but like I said, Merrit's the way in. Give us a bit of time, and we'll be done with the lot of them.'

Continued in Book Three
Follow the Van

AUTHOR NOTES

I don't have too much to tell you about the background of this story. Although some details are accurate, others are fiction based on fact.

Sinford's School

What might be confusing for some is that the English *public* school system actually refers to *private* schools. A clearer definition would be fee-paying schools as opposed to state schools funded by the public through taxation. Many such schools still exist in the UK, and are usually boarding schools catering for two age groups. Preparatory schools, aka, prep schools as mentioned in Havegood's memoirs, cater for children aged eight to 13 years, with some also having a pre-prep for children from the age of three. After prep school, men like Stape and Havegood would have gone on to a school like Sinford's, known simply as public or boarding school, but more often, known by their name. One doesn't say, 'I went to public school' if one went to Eton. One simply went to Eton. The name is enough. These are what we might call senior schools, or secondary schools, and cater for young people from 13 to 18 years of age.

Public schools have something of a mixed literary reputation. *Tom Brown's Schooldays* (Thomas Hughes, 1857) is set at Rugby School (a real school) and describes some of the harsher conditions and bullying. It also involves a character called Diggs. *The Loom of Youth* (Alex Waugh, 1917) is another. There are also several films set at British public schools, including *If* (1968). Although it is part fantasy and modern, much of the traditions and conditions depicted in it were rife in 19th century boarding schools, and many still exist today.

Sinford's is imagined, and is not based on any particular school. It is located near to a couple of well-known public schools in Kent, but that is where the similarity ends. Some of the finer details come from my experiences at a British prep school, which gave me a thorough grounding in education and if nothing else, taught me how to enjoy learning. The hierarchy outlined by the characters, from 'leads' to 'golds' is peculiar to Sinford's, although such things exist under different titles.

NL-SOMoL+S

The books of maps referred to exists, and the map references that make up the clues are accurate. Or, as accurate as I can make them from my 1987 publication of 'The A to Z of Victorian London' (Ralph Hyde) which presents a reprinting of the original 1888 London street maps in their original order and page/map numbering.

If you had a copy, and looked up, for example, the *15.N.19* clue, you would find, at page/map 15, the grid reference N-19 is only part of a full square, because on this, the nine-inch map of central London, the square N-19, continues on page/map 23. However, in the page 15 part, you would find Pall Mall as the prominent typeface just below the bottom of Saint James's Square (sic).

This is the book of maps from which Jack Merrit learnt his cabman's 'knowledge', and his route decisions when driving, are accurately based on the publication.

Places, People and Publications

There are passing references to other places and publication which are also factual.

Truth was a British publication founded by the Liberal politician Henry Labouchère, he of the ominous 'gross indecency' clause fame mentioned by Jimmy Wright. It was a periodical in print between 1877 and 1957.

The Pall Mall Gazette was an evening newspaper begun in 1865, and it's first editor was Frederick Greenwood, brother of James Greenwood, on whom Larkin Chase's investigative journalism is based. *The Pall Mall Gazette* has found its way into many novels, including *Dracula, The Time Machine, The War of the Worlds*, and some Sherlock Holmes stories.

When Larkin mentions the Gaiety Theatre and *Uncle Dick's Darling*, he is talking about a real theatre at Aldwych, in Strand (*The* Strand as it's incorrectly known). Here, I took a liberty. Unable to resist having Larkin say *Uncle Dick's Darling*, I shifted the production from 1870 to the night Jack was racing to Kent. The original play starred Henry Irving (who appears in one of two of my Clearwater books), and was the last play seen by Charles Dickens before he died. By 1892, the Gaiety was known for its 'girls' musicals featuring the Gaiety Girls, and later, its 'boys' musicals with a similar lineup of respectable young men as the chorus.

The theatre moved up the road a little way in the early 20th century, and needing extensive restoration and alterations to conform to the, then, modern standards, finally closed in 1939. Its second site is now occupied by offices and shops.

When Jack and Jimmy are visiting Phineas Ashton, Jack reads the wording on a theatrical poster: 'A work of deep resonance by Raffalovich and Gray. The Dean Street Theatre Club is *Not* for Women!'

Raffalovich and Gray were a couple, and friends of Oscar Wilde. They were also the authors of an 1894 play, *The Blackmailers* which contains a 'suspect' relationship between a blackmailer and his younger protégée. The Dean Street Theatre Club is slightly made up, in that the Royalty Theatre used to stand in Dean Street, Soho, and was where the still-performed farce, *Charley's Aunt* was first shown (in 1892). The "*Not* for Women!" is taken from an advertisement for another theatre of 'dubious patronage' existing in London at the time.

AUTHOR NOTES

One last thing to mention will offer clarity to anyone who has followed the Clearwater, Larkspur and now Delamere series.

When I began with Deviant Desire, I imagined a parallel London, and, for a reason I now forget, decided to rename some areas but not others. This is why the previous two series mention South and North Riverside (Kensington and Chelsea), Greychurch (Whitechapel), and Limedock (Limehouse), yet employ the real placenames of Hampstead, Soho, and elsewhere. Starting on the Delamere Files, I decided to finally do away with that, and rather than go back and edit the previous novels, have hoped the reader doesn't mind that Delamere House is now in Knightsbridge, and not North Riverside, and Limehouse is Limehouse, not Limedock, etc. From book five of the Clearwater novels, I have used the real names of places, other than those that were already alternatively named in the early Clearwater books.

You can find all of my books on my [Amazon Author page](.).

Please leave a review if you can. Thanks again for reading. If you keep reading, I'll keep writing.

Jackson

Printed in Great Britain
by Amazon